THE ESCAPE

Ruth Kelly is a journalist who has ghosted a string of *Sunday Times* top ten bestsellers – most recently *The Prison Doctor*, which sold over 250,000 copies, and *The Governor*, which went straight in at number one on the Amazon charts and number five in the *Sunday Times* bestseller list.

The Escape is Ruth's follow-up to *The Villa*, and features a dream home in a holiday destination that turns deadly. It's also a cautionary tale exploring the darker side of social media. Having spent most of her life travelling and exploring the world, holiday destinations feature heavily in Ruth's thriller writing. Her family relocated to Papua New Guinea when she was seven years old and the travel bug hasn't let up since.

The simmering threat of what lies beneath the surface and the dichotomy of how paradise can also be hell fascinates Ruth. Making a destination a character in its own right – both a friend and an enemy, not someone to be trusted – is a thread explored throughout her writing.

By Ruth Kelly

The Villa

RUTH KELLY
THE ESCAPE

PAN BOOKS

First published 2023 by Pan Books
an imprint of Pan Macmillan
The Smithson, 6 Briset Street, London EC1M 5NR
EU representative: Macmillan Publishers Ireland Ltd, 1st Floor,
The Liffey Trust Centre, 117–126 Sheriff Street Upper,
Dublin 1, D01 YC43
Associated companies throughout the world
www.panmacmillan.com

ISBN 978-1-0350-2536-7

1 3 5 7 9 8 6 4 2

A CIP catalogue record for this book is available from the British Library.

Typeset by Palimpsest Book Production, Falkirk, Stirlingshire
Printed and bound by CPI Group (UK) Ltd, Croydon, CR0 4YY

Visit **www.panmacmillan.com** to read more about all our books
and to buy them. You will also find features, author interviews and
news of any author events, and you can sign up for e-newsletters
so that you're always first to hear about our new releases.

RICHARD AND JUDY TELL US WHY THEY LOVE *THE ESCAPE* BY RUTH KELLY

Richard writes:

There's a touch of Dickens's *Great Expectations* at the start of this story: mysterious, impossibly wealthy benefactor; smooth-talking lawyer; baffled but grateful recipient.

But the similarities end there. Ruth Kelly has written a spine-tingler of a tale, full of haunting twists and turns. It has the feel of something of a classic as you turn the pages, although it starts off in a very modern, contemporary way. Adele, a struggling online influencer in a struggling marriage, gets tipsy late one night and has 'a lightbulb moment'. She appeals to her few thousand followers to crowdfund her 'dream' of buying a romantic French chateau.

The response by the next morning is overwhelming. In the worst possible way. Adele is roundly reviled by hundreds of trolls. 'Entitled whore!', 'Scrounger!', 'Bitch, you're almost 30 – try growing up!'

Her 'lightbulb' has been comprehensively blown.

Richard

Judy writes:

Or has it?

In the midst of Adele's despair and bitter self-recrimination comes a glimmer of hope. A lawyer's email informs her that a wealthy philanthropist was touched by her appeal and wishes to buy the chateau as a gift for her and her husband. Intrigued, Adele and Jack meet the lawyer and are assured the offer, even if eccentric, is genuine.

And so, they move to rural southern France. At first, all is well. The villa is beautiful – nine bedrooms, gorgeous gardens, luxurious swimming pool – and Adele's fickle followers multiply as they follow Adele and Jack's progress in Provence.

And then, just as their first winter sets in, the couple vanish. Into thin air. Adele's desperately worried sister Erin drives direct from England to investigate. She finds an empty chateau and a secretive, openly hostile local community. What has happened to Adele and Jack? Who is their shadowy benefactor?

An electrifying winter read. We promise you'll love it.

THE ESCAPE

PROLOGUE

ADELE

ONE WEEK BEFORE NYE

YouTube
1.2M subscribers

Hey, lovelies. (**wipes tears away**) I don't know why I'm filming this; I won't end up putting it on YouTube because it's so stupid recording yourself crying. (**wipes away more tears**) Especially when I can't explain why I'm upset and as far as YouTube, TikTok and influencing goes, it couldn't be better but my life away from that feels like it's falling apart. I've never felt so lonely.

Anyone who knows me, knows I rarely get upset. This isn't *me* but I can't stop crying and I can't shake this anxiety and I feel like there's nobody I can talk to about it, not even Jack. There's so much I need to say that I've been bottling up because I've been too afraid to . . .

(**looks nervously over shoulder**)

Can you hear that?

(**strains to listen**)

I think someone's there.

'Hello?'

(**waits, listens**)

'Who's there?'

(**shakes head**) Christ, I'm going mad. I'm hearing noises, look at the state of me. I'm all worked up again over nothing. This place – it's making me lose my mind.

(**breathes out heavily**) I thought moving to the French countryside would help us, a fresh start, that it would be calm and peaceful – it's anything but.

Coming here was a huge mistake.

(**starts crying again**)

I know from the outside my life must look perfect and you must be thinking: what has she got to be upset about? But trust me, guys, when I say – it's not.

I guess sharing this shows the real side of influencing. It's important for those watching to know that the people they follow get upset too.

What am I trying to say? That's the thing, it's almost impossible to put into words because it's more a feeling. Something about the house *feels* wrong.

I don't usually believe in ghosts or paranormal stuff like that, but it's these old rooms, this creaky dark building, the way it moans, it's like there's someone here with me.

Even Jack's been behaving strangely. I think he's keeping secrets. There's something he won't tell me.

You're all going to say I've lost it when I tell you the next bit, but I have to get it off my chest, it's eating me up not being able to tell anyone.

(**looks behind again, lowers voice**)

I think I'm being followed. I keep getting this ick sensation that someone's watching me and it's really creeping me out.

(breaks down in tears)

I don't know what's happening to me. **(rakes hands through hair)** It's frightening.

(looks camera dead on)

I'm scared, I'm afraid something really bad is about to happen.

CHAPTER ONE

ERIN

SEVEN DAYS AFTER NYE

The snow is flawless. Linen white and crisp. It doesn't register at first how there's no fresh tyre tracks.

I'm too busy studying the road for black ice. My foot tensed over the brake pedal; I feel the pinch of nerves as I slow into another hairpin bend.

It's never-ending, the driveway to their house. Narrow and twisty, carving up the woodland.

I open the window letting the cold flood in, rinsing away the air of my long journey. The scent of sunshine, frost and pine sweeps through the car.

The radio is interrupted by the weather report. More snow on the way, treacherous driving conditions, there's threats of road and public transport closures. My stomach tightens at the thought of being trapped out here. *It's fine, I'll be gone before it turns.* I switch it off, sponging up the silence instead.

Besides, it doesn't feel like the reports will come true.

4

It snowed all of last night but now – everything is still. Nature has taken a breath and you can almost hear her hold it. Nothing is quieter than freshly fallen snow.

The forest either side is a tight knot of fir trees and tall skinny birch. Frosted branches glisten in the fading light. Beneath the canopy, an uninterrupted expanse of white. A duvet that's been shaken out until it's thick and fluffy.

Concealing what lies beneath.

Something about winter frightens me – it's how suddenly the darkness moves in. By 5 p.m. it's pitch-black outside and that's when my sense of being trapped awakens. An emotion I've struggled with since I was little. I've always been untrusting of the night.

Mum complains I tiptoe through life – I'm too hesitant, too uncertain. I must try to be more like my younger sister, Adele, who strides confidently wherever she goes.

Adele. The thought of her and why I've made this twelve-hour drive to Eastern France now fills me with anger.

My self-absorbed baby sister.

The words swell like a storm and soon I'm so consumed with resentment I don't notice how everything around me has changed. The trees have parted. The sky has expanded into a blaze of sunset.

It appears like a mirage in the clearing, shimmering with the frosting of snow – the chateau.

Adele's videos haven't done it justice.

Puncturing the sky with its tower and turret, it's far bigger and more impressive in real life.

I slow to a crawl, my breath catching as I drink in the view.

Perfectly proportioned – as tall as it's wide. Built from limestone the colour of butter with granite rimming the windows like smoky eyeliner. There are sage-green shutters, a Juliet balcony wrapping around the upstairs room. The roof is spiked with hooded windows, pointy like witches' hats.

The courtyard circles around a fountain. A statue of a woman cradling a child, the pale folds of her robe falling loosely around her waist. I imagine what it must be like when it's switched on in summer with the patter of water drifting through the estate.

Dazzling in the low winter light, the building commands attention. It speaks to you with an air of arrogance – *I've survived hundreds of years. I've weathered storms fiercer than you'll ever know. Look at me.*

Adele's been calling it 'small' in her videos compared to other chateaus in the region because it only has nine bedrooms. *Only nine!* There's no doubt in my mind – this is the grandest home I've ever seen. I feel a stab of jealousy as I can't help but compare her life to mine. How far I've been left behind.

My eyes are stuck on the view as I slow to a stop and it takes me a moment to notice – I'm the only car here.

They'll be parked around the back. She'll have had the stables converted to garages; I scoff at the extravagance of her new life.

Turning off the engine, I sink back and take a moment. Pulling my emotions together, building up courage.

How will I break the news to her? I'm still trying to process it myself. It's all been so sudden, the doctors promised Mum was getting better. I steal one last breath and then open the door, stepping out into the fray.

The powdery snow reaches past my ankles and within seconds the cold's worked its way in, seeping through the fabric of my trainers. I'm not dressed for this weather. It was sunny when I left home in England. I hunch into my coat and tighten the belt.

Slipping into the shadow of the building, my senses become alert. Instinctively, I look up, eyes scanning the facade, taking in the weather vane, the gargoyles clinging to the corners. The slits in the tower where the archers would have hidden. It's a hotchpotch, the styles of centuries soldered together.

I feel another surge of emotion coming on but this time I catch myself – a skill I've learned from years working as an ICU nurse: mastering the art of keeping calm. I've learned how to understand feelings so as not to be overwhelmed by the emotional intensity of my job.

I have no doubt as to what's driving this new wave.

Envy.

I envy how Adele and Jack's life has turned out. Escaping abroad. Starting over. Isn't that what we all long for?

While I worked long night shifts with no energy left to keep my eyes open. While I was caring for Mum, Adele slid into a new life fit for a princess.

I've lived on a hand-to-mouth salary for years, always saving, always having to hold back on the things I really want to do. Adele – she's now throwing money around like it doesn't matter.

My sister's always had admirers, people bending over

backwards, giving her things for free – because she's pretty, because she's mastered being the damsel in distress. But *this*? My eyes narrow at the magnificent view; this is another level. How did she afford to buy a chateau?

None of it makes sense.

There's one thing about her new life I wouldn't swap for anything – Jack.

Jack's the reason Adele and I aren't close. He drove a wedge between us soon after they started dating, determined to be her number one. He filled her head with poison. That said, she could have fought for us. Perhaps it's what she wanted? Adele used him as the excuse to sever our bond? I often find myself thinking this.

It's been fraught for years, but communication finally broke down with her move to France last spring – not long after we found out Mum has breast cancer. Instead of putting her plans on hold, Adele disappeared on her big adventure with the expectation I would be the one to deal with it.

Of course, that's what I did, I brought Mum home to my flat in Bournemouth where I cooked and I cleaned and washed her. It was me who held her hand through those three gruelling months of chemo. I alone patched her up and got her back on her feet.

For her entire life, Adele has run from responsibility and anything that might cause her pain. I'm the protector cushioning her from the blows of life. Well, not any more. Death has caught up with us both. The cancer has returned and the oncologist has given Mum just a month.

Fighting off the tears, I begin the mantra. *STOP. Don't*

let your emotions control you. Because who will be there to pick me up if I do?

I look ahead to the grand entrance. A columned porch, white stone banisters rising up to it.

Adele's always been self-centred, but her behaviour worsened when she started filming a diary of her French life for her YouTube channel. The constant documenting of every bloody thing she does, revealing intimate details to imaginary friends in exchange for likes. I swear her obsessive fans mean more to her than our family. Vlogging has brought out the very worst in her.

I tuned into the first few, but I couldn't bring myself to watch after that. Her fake life and who she's pretending to be. She's not being honest – about any of it.

We haven't spoken properly for months but things have now reached new levels of rudeness. She's not answered calls or messages for over a week now, not since New Year's Eve. I don't know if she's ignoring me, or still mad at me. But if this is what it's come to, it speaks volumes about how far our relationship has deteriorated.

Adele takes no interest in me and what's going on in my life. She has no idea of the trouble waiting for me back home.

I feel a swell of panic. I push it aside, focusing on what I've come here to do.

Her ghosting me is the reason I've driven all this way. She's forced me to hunt her down and I'd go as far as to say I hate her for it.

But I can't afford to get into an argument with her because time is something we don't have. I'm not here to build bridges; I've come to collect my sister and bring her home.

I swallow down my hurt, anger, envy and start up the wide stone steps to the grand entrance.

The thick oak door has a bright gold knocker in the shape of a lion's head.

Jack's doing. I grimace at the tasteless feature. Then I role-play how the next few minutes will go: Adele will pretend she didn't get my messages; Jack will act like I don't exist.

But there's no fake welcome. Only silence as the sound of the knock drifts. I try again, smacking it so hard the vibration travels up my arm.

Calm down. You'll only make things worse.

It never crossed my mind she wouldn't be here. Have they gone away for the weekend?

I head into the grounds to look around. Shoes squeaking as I power through the snow. My angry breath misting.

The first window I come to offers a glimpse into their new life – a house full of heirlooms and inheritances. Nose pressed up against glass, I catch the last of the light pouring into a high-ceilinged room.

Walnut-panelled walls and biscuit-coloured parquet floor. There's a long oval dining table in the centre and a piano to one side, beneath a solid gold-framed painting of a hunting scene. Opposite is a large open fireplace – white marble veined with black. The lemon-yellow curtains tied back with silk tassels add a homely feel. It really is spectacular in an old-fashioned gentry way.

I move around to the side of the building where the

entire wall is hidden with ivy and the snow is piled up against the windows. A dimly lit room. A library, an actual library with floor-to-ceiling shelves full of leather-bound books. A tapestry hangs across the length of one wall. A battle scene with horses rearing, spears flying, it's violent and gruesome.

Impressive, but it's not very Adele is all I can now think as I search for some evidence of my sister. Despite our differences, I'm quietly relieved when I find a piece of her on the polished wood side table. The gaudy pineapple candlesticks she'd always bring out, back when we used to have dinners together. Even the bright gold looks tarnished in the muted light.

A partially open door at the other end reveals an entrance hall with a vast chandelier and a sweeping staircase.

Amid the grandness, something else strikes me as odd. The rooms, they're spotlessly clean. Uncharacteristically so for my typically messy sister. There's no clutter, it's eerily precise – they seem unlived in.

I don't realize I'm frowning until I catch my reflection in the window. As I make my way back to the front of the chateau, my thoughts shift to Adele's vlog and how she's amassed a cult following almost overnight. More than a million subscribers, thousands of views per video, but what's really bothering me is how she's made no secret of where they live and any weirdo could turn up on her doorstep.

I make a slow full turn, taking in the isolation. The thought of how vulnerable Adele is out here suddenly makes me shudder.

Should I take a look inside?

As I search near the front door for somewhere you might hide a key, something else catches my eye. Glinting in my footprint.

I crouch down, plucking the sharp object from the snow. It's much bigger than I first thought. Holding it up to the light, the stones sparkle as I roll it between my thumb and finger. I breathe in sharply.

Diamonds, they're *real* diamonds.

Adele might be living the high life, but she couldn't afford earrings like this. Also, the fussy drop design isn't her style. So, who does it belong to?

Indistinctively, I turn to face the woods, as if the answer will be waiting for me there. But now the sun has dropped, the scene I'm met with is a black impenetrable mass. The air is completely still and quiet except for the distant hooting of an owl.

My throat tightens. On my next inhale I call out: 'ADELE!'

Casting around, my eyes rake through the darkness for signs of life.

Erin, relax! They'll be visiting friends or have gone away for the weekend, because *that's what couples do.*

I overreact, I'm easily triggered – I've come to understand this.

Yet, despite my self-awareness, I know something is off. I can sense it.

'ADELE!' I yell again. 'JAAAAACK.'

My voice sounds small and weak, suffocated by the snow's insulation.

Then, powdery flakes start to fall. Fine-milled, gentle

like butterfly kisses, that is until the cold spreads. I blow into my hands; my fingertips are numb and white.

What should I do? Wait here until they come home? The satnav is showing me some houses five miles away but there's unlikely to be a B & B, not somewhere this remote. And if I leave, I might miss her.

The chateau is eerily quiet but the forest is coming alive. There's a faint rustling, the snapping of twigs, the sound of night animals moving through the trees.

I hate it when the darkness arrives.

I force myself to take a long deep breath but my self-soothing does nothing to calm my nerves. That *thing* that's planted itself in my thoughts is taking root.

And that's when I sense it, the stirring of winter. A current of something unfriendly and hostile has drifted in. Nature is trying to tell me something and her words are fierce enough to make me shiver.

I feel a sudden tug of dread, but what I'm afraid of, I'm not sure.

CHAPTER TWO

ADELE

NINE MONTHS BEFORE NYE

YouTube

5,300 subscribers

Revealing Our Secret Plans

Hi lovelies, happy Monday, welcome back to my channel. I know you like to hear about my week but today I want to do something special. I have some UBER important news I need to share. You know how I try to tell you everything that's going on in my life. Well, this is probably the biggest decision Jack and I have *ever* made and because your support means *so* much to us, we want you to be the first to know.

For those of you who are new to my channel, Jack and I have been together eight years and we're still *stupidly* in love. Quick recap on how we met – randomly, house hunting. I'd finished college and was searching for a place and Jack was advertising his spare room. I went to take a look around but it was him that caught my eye. He didn't waste any time asking me out and that same night we went for our first date. I probably shouldn't tell you this (**giggles nervously**) but we slept together. I was panicking he wouldn't want to see me again – I'm probably oversharing right now (**laughs again**) but the next day a massive bunch of roses arrived with a note from Jack asking if I'd like to move in – but not into his spare room. Yah, talk about a fast mover! But here we are, still together, all these years later. (**jazz hands**) Anyone wanting to hear our full love story can catch up on my previous vlog, HOW I KNEW JACK WAS THE ONE. I'll leave the link below.

Slight tangent there, lovelies. Back to what I've jumped on here for, and this isn't easy – I was in two minds whether to share, but I feel it's important to be honest, especially with all of you who've been on this journey with me from the start and hopefully what I'm about to say will raise awareness and help those going through similar hard times.

(**breathes in deeply**)

Three months ago we received the devastating news that Mum has cancer. (**fights back tears**) A routine breast scan revealed a lump and the tests came back as positive. She's been having chemotherapy and various treatments, and although she's weak she's doing OK – the doctors are optimistic as they caught it pretty early on – but we're all worried sick and it's been such a shock because Mum . . . since Dad walked out on us, she's been the glue holding our family together. Always happy, always positive and kind, and I don't know what we would do without her . . .

(**clears throat**)

But— I can't bear to even think about that now.

(**clears throat again**)

15

If that's not bad enough, last month Jack was made redundant from his job at the council where he's been working for the past seven years, so (**pauses, wipes tear from eye**) to say life is a liiiitle bit rubbish right now doesn't even come close.

(**pushes out a smile**) Oh, by the way, Jack says hi. He's sorry he can't be on the vlog tonight – you know he loves you guys, but he's helping a friend move house. That's my Jack, always putting others first, even when he's going through a rough time himself, but that's why I love him.

So, with everything that's happened, we've decided to do something completely spontaneously crazy and insane but if we can pull it off . . . it will be life-changing.

Which is where YOU, my lovelies, come in. As always, we want to include you in our plans.

Our big reveal, which I've been *dying* to share, is that we're going to be moving to France. We've found our dream home.

In the cutaway (**points finger above**) you'll see why we've fallen in love.

Chateau Bellay is a seventeenth-century manor house in southern Burgundy, in the heart of the Côte Chalonnaise wine region. I hope I've said that right? Dreamy, huh?

It has everything you'd imagine a chateau to have – a tower and turret, boiserie wall panels, a ballroom, a huge dining room, a really pretty library and there's nine bedrooms. And don't even get me started on the vineyards! It's on the Route des Grands Crus, THE world-famous wine route through Burgundy.

The chateau has belonged to the Du Bellay family for

more than three hundred years, which is why it's kept so much of the original beauty. It needs renovating, but nothing too major. Luckily the offer to buy comes with the furniture included, but I'm planning on a massive refurb. I've a whole bunch of ideas on how we can redesign the rooms. (**claps hands excitedly**)

We want to give Chateau Bellay our own spin while preserving its historic features. We plan to grow our own vegetables and use sustainable materials for the renovations, and the place will be powered by renewable energy, everything will be eco-friendly.

Isn't it something out of a fairy tale?

I am *obsessed*. Honestly, guys, I cannot deal with how stunning this place is. Above all, it'll be somewhere peaceful, tucked out of the way, where Mum can recuperate after the chemo.

There's just one teeny little problem. (**pinches fingers together**) It's a tad out of our budget at 1.2 million euros. (**giggles**) I'm laughing because I know I sound absolutely INSANE saying this, but hear me out . . .

(**pressing hands into a prayer**) We need you to make our dreams come true.

From today we are setting up a GoFundMe crowd-funding account to buy Chateau Bellay.

Help us restore Chateau Bellay to its former glory. We'll run it as a B & B so all you lovely, wonderful people will eventually be able to stay with us.

I plan to regularly upload videos on my channel so you can follow our renovation project, keep up to date with everything we're doing and stay connected. And hopefully feel part of our journey to the finishing line. Those signed up to our Patreon account will be granted exclusive VIP access to extra content as well as discount member rates on rooms when we open.

Just think, you'll be able to stay in a chateau for massively subsidized prices and drink world-renowned Burgundy wines, eat French cheese while hanging out with me and Jack and . . . (**prayer hands**) we need you. This has been the most unbelievably tough year for us, God, it's hard me even saying this, but please, *please* help make our dream come true.

I'll leave a link to our GoFundMe below. We're grateful for anything you have to spare. And as always, if you could click the like and subscribe button that would be ah-mazing. Big love and kisses from me and Jack.

(**blows a kiss**)

I love you all so SO much.

CHAPTER THREE

ADELE

NINE MONTHS BEFORE NYE

There's a throaty rumble from outside and the violent slam of a door. The noise pulls me out of bed; I throw off the duvet and cross to the window that looks out on our street. A man in a Barbour jacket staggers out of a taxi but it's not Jack.

The knot tightens in my stomach.

I check my phone: 3.24 a.m. and still no message. He knows I'll be panicking and all it would take to ease my anxiety is a message. He's doing it on purpose.

Grabbing my dressing gown from the door, I slip out of our deathly quiet bedroom. From the landing I hear the faint meow of the neighbour's cat coming from our back door. I let him in one night when I was feeling especially lonely and now he won't leave me alone.

Secretly, I'd glad he's become my friend, comforting me in those eerily quiet hours when I can't sleep.

It's the third night this week that Jack's been out drinking.

I've lost count of how many evenings I've spent alone since he was made redundant.

It's as if he's trying hard not to be around me. He's never home and when he is, he's not there, not really. He's either watching TV or on the computer with his earphones in, blocking out the world. Blocking out – me. But if I say anything, if I even broach the subject or, God help me, attempt to be positive about the future, he'll snap or, worse, shut down. More recently there's an edge to Jack's tone.

It's as if there are ten different people living inside him. Every morning I wake up not knowing which Jack I'm going to get.

If I'm honest, it's terrifying.

A natural born 'fixer', I've been searching the internet for answers. Googling symptoms, the diagnosis always taking me back to the same place: depression.

He's ticking all the boxes – retreating into his shell, lack of sex drive, lack of drive in general. Then there's stress rash across his scalp and knuckles. And the most obvious tell – he's stopped taking care of himself. Jack's always paid attention to how he looks, but he's stopped bothering to shave, he leaves his bed-flattened hair until the afternoon, and he won't stop wearing that ugly jumper with the hole.

Part of what attracted me to Jack was the pride he took. We were the well-turned-out couple at dinner parties. The most attractive couple in the room. I enjoyed that label and I want it back.

I will bring him back.

I won't lie, there are days when I want to give up – especially when I'm dealing with all my own stress over Mum not being well. Which I know I'm not dealing with.

But then I remind myself relationships need continuous work, perfection doesn't exist and giving up is easy.

Jack wasn't always like this. He was confident and assertive and didn't need me propping him up.

Gentle. Thoughtful. Like making sure the fridge is stocked with my favourite snacks or bringing me coffee in the morning. He'd surprise me with tickets to a show in London. Or he'd treat me to an expensive meal at a restaurant that had just opened. This temper, this short fuse he's developed – it's not him.

We *will* find a way out of this.

My new obsession with optimism, manifesting goals and drawing up vision boards is what's carrying me through. If you believe the cancer will go away, it will. If you behave as if you already have what you want in life, if you let yourself feel those emotions, the universe will listen, respond and make it happen. The Law of Attraction – I practise it every day, much to Jack's amusement and ridicule.

Manifesting a better life abroad is how I came up with the idea of crowdfunding – a solution to affording my very own fairy-tale chateau.

As a child I dreamed of being a princess in a castle. I'd dress up in Mum's going-out clothes. I'd sit behind her dressing table swamped in fabric, trying on her lipsticks and splashing my wrists with her most expensive perfumes. I'd twirl around the house wearing a plastic pink tiara.

Mum would have to wait until I was asleep to take it from me or I'd have a meltdown.

I'll own up, I was spoilt and my parents indulged my fantasy, buying me princess gowns and even curtseying for me. I'd force my sister into playing castles – poor Erin, she was always stuck with the boy part. The court jester or the knight who had to rescue me from the tower. I'd boss her around, but she'd always go along with it.

I feel a pang of guilt and quickly push the feeling aside.

As I cross to the bathroom, something catches my eye. The light from my screensaver, spilling onto the landing. Calling me to attention.

I wasn't going to post it, not until I'd talked it over with Jack and Mum. But the video I recorded earlier today is now burning a hole in my thoughts. I'm drawn to the light, towards my laptop on the desk inside the study.

I say study but it's more a dumping ground for Jack's things. Boxes piled high crowd the tiny room. Golf clubs, old trainers, sports gear that hasn't been used since we started renting here four years ago. Stacks of magazines Jack will never read. Shelves sagging under the weight of pointless stuff.

As I study the chaos our lives have become, I can't help feeling disappointed. Like I've been short-changed somehow.

Some days I struggle to breathe. As if the walls are moving inwards, crushing the life out of me. My parents promised me a fairy tale. I dreamed of more, is that so wrong?

My imaginary castle was my happy place back then, so it made sense to return there for sanctuary.

While Jack's been at the pub, I've been soothing my anxiety scrolling through French property websites. Fantasizing about which chateau we'll buy. I've been losing myself in the grand architecture, the ballrooms, libraries, outdoor pools, orangeries and sweeping estates.

Then there's shows like *Chateau Rescue DIY*. A look at how other couples have made it work. If they can do it with zero experience, then so can we.

Twenty-six and still dreaming of playing castles. Immature, I know, but everyone has a dream that keeps them going. Perhaps the only difference is, I won't stop at the fantasy.

The thought of becoming a châtelaine has become lodged and every day the roots grow deeper.

Most of the chateaus I found were either insanely expensive or ridiculously cheap but needed huge amounts spent on renovation. Others didn't quite have that fairy-tale vibe. But then there was Chateau Bellay, who only needed a moderate amount of TLC to bring her back to her former glory. With her wood-panelled, high-ceiling rooms, four-poster beds and a real princess tower, I only had to see the photos on the website, and I knew.

She's the one.

The GoFundMe idea came from watching my favourite YouTubers and TikTokers – learning about the *new* way to afford your dreams.

Renovation projects have become the hottest new charity, springing up all over the world.

You wouldn't believe how many influencers are turning to the platform to ask the public to help fund projects, whether it be building and structural work, restoration or interior decoration. GoFundMe is now the world's largest crowdfunding platform, raising $9 billion since it was launched in 2010, and there seems to be no limit to what you can ask viewers and subscribers to invest in.

Once you've secured funding you can begin earning money creating content documenting your journey. The average influencer earns £3,000 a month – that's £36,000 a year doing what they love. Talking about their passion projects. Then there's all the add-ons like advertising, brand sponsorship and, with so many new formats, like YouTube shorts and live streaming, members-only content, the possibilities to make money are endless.

Makes you think, why bother with school and university and all the debt that goes with it when you can just film and document your own life. If they're doing it, why can't I?

I'm part way there. I started YouTubing several months ago and I have a small following, a few thousand subscribers. It's not much, but it's something. Mostly I chat about random crap like my morning routine or what I do at the gym, sometimes a GRWM – that's short for get ready with me. I guess I don't have a fixed identity, a USP. But a chateau will change all of that.

In the meantime, I do have a *real* job: assistant manager for a hotel chain near the motorway flyover. It was only meant to be a stopgap, a stepping stone to greater things. I can see that now.

Erin doesn't approve of my vlogging, but then she's never thought much of my life choices. With six years between us, Erin took on the role of the responsible older sister. And she never lets me forget it.

I've been there for her too. When we were growing up and she was afraid of the dark, it was me who comforted her in the night. It was *me* who'd cuddle her until she fell asleep. But that's all conveniently forgotten so Erin can play the martyr.

It wasn't always like this between us. After Erin qualified as a nurse, she changed, behaving as if she was above her own problems, and turned to fixing me instead. *Project Adele*. Studying me as if I were her patient. And don't even get me started on Jack.

The problem is, she won't let it drop, that thing he did. I almost wish I never told her. I know she wants to protect me, but doesn't she realize it makes it impossible for us to spend time together when she's dripping poison in my ear?

I want to pick up the phone and tell her everything that's been going on since Jack lost his job. When I'm frightened and feeling helpless, when I'm scared about what will happen to Mum – because I'm terrified – I want my big sister back.

Instead of reaching out, I take myself off somewhere quiet and go over old ground. Was what Jack did my fault? I worry I'm not sexually adventurous enough for him. I bore him in bed. There's so much pressure on women to be perfect. To be sexy *and* capable. Sometimes I think I see disappointment in his eyes and it breaks me. But then I pick myself up and promise I'll fix that too. I won't quit on our relationship. Not now, not after everything. Adele Davenport does not give up.

Erin's upset because she's desperate to settle down and takes that out on me. It's her choice to sacrifice her life to her job instead of seeking out what she wants most – a husband, a family.

I swallow down the lump that's jammed in my throat. *It's OK,* there's still plenty of time for Jack and me to have children.

It's then the file on my desktop shows itself, swimming into view.

The window in our study overlooks Granville Close. I widen the gap in the curtains and stare out onto our street where every house looks the same. A two-up two-down with a rectangular fenced-in garden, a driveway and garage. The faint sound of the ring road rumbles in the distance. Cars circling the roundabout. A constant reminder of how we're stuck in purgatory. A nowhere place between urban and rural.

The heating went off hours ago because we're trying to save money. I wrap the gown around me more tightly to keep out the cold and I glare at the house opposite with its Christmas lights still up. What the hell? It's almost spring! Santa's still pissing on the roof while his reindeers graze near the porch. Outlined with flashing LED lights, blinking into the night.

Strangers. All of them. After all this time I barely know my neighbours. The most interaction we've had was a disagreement over parking. A French rural community won't be like this. Nitpicking over the small things – not a chance. All of a sudden I'm imagining a rosy-cheeked woman with plaited hair cycling up our drive with a basketful of local meats and cheeses to welcome us into the community.

I won't miss this place, not one bit.

Mum will come stay as soon as she's had the chemotherapy, and she'll love it. What could be more healing than the French countryside?

My girlfriends – yeah, I'll be sad to say goodbye, but they'll come visit. I can see the garden parties now – with lanterns and hammocks strung up between fruit trees. Wine glasses brimming with rosé. Ice cubes clinking.

Manifesting. I can feel it, the sweet sharpness of the wine slipping down.

I need a drink now. It might be gone three in the morning but sod it. It's not something I'd normally do alone but sometimes you have to take the edge off and I know just the thing.

In one of the boxes is a bottle of Chevas Regal whisky. A present from Jack's Scottish uncle Glen which he's been saving for a special occasion. I reach in, rummaging for something I can drink from.

World's best girlfriend. Blowing hard on the mug, a small cloud of dust mushrooms into the room. Illuminated by the glare from the street, the motes dance around like fireflies.

Just as they will in France. Swarming around the lanterns in our palatial garden.

I fill it halfway and then slug it back, my throat working hard to get it down. The alcohol scalds but the warmth spreads, moving across my entire body. My face flushes with heat and I immediately top it up, this time to the brim.

Yes, I'm stubborn, but that's because I know what's best for us. It's those friends of his, they're to blame for leading him astray. I've got to get Jack away from them. Call it an intervention if you will.

Another swig from the mug and my body takes over, forcing me to sit down behind the desk. I strike a key, waking up my laptop. The bluish light splintering the gloom.

There you are. I smile lazily at the file on my desktop, at the GoFundMe vlog I filmed earlier. Edited and waiting to be set free into cyberspace.

I falter.

Hang on, I should talk to Jack first; he has no idea what I'm planning. And I need to tell Mum, my friends.

I frown.

But they'll only talk you out of it. They won't understand. They don't get how the world is changing, that it's possible to make a living through social media.

The cursor blinks at me impatiently.

Then, an even more terrifying thought sweeps in. *What if nobody helps us?* The possibility of having my dream snuffed out is scarier than any thought I've had.

I snap the screen shut.

Returning to the gloom of our little study, the empty feeling quickly returns. My mind starts to race. My fingers move to attack the desk, drumming the Formica. I've dared to let myself dream of a better life; I can't box it away now.

Adele, listen, you don't need his permission. People will want to buy into your dream, they'd be mad not to. You have as much right to be happy as the next person. Everyone's doing it; it's time you took the plunge too.

I reach for the whisky, forcing more down.

Lying awake in bed imagining my partner of almost a decade is cheating is not what I call fun. It's Jack's fault for breaking my trust.

Wow, the alcohol is doing a terrific job of dredging up the past.

I can do better than this. *I deserve better.*

Closing my eyes, I imagine I'm sweeping away the mess. I'm pushing against the walls until the bricks fall away revealing a picture-perfect meadow in the heart of rural France.

Now I'm in the countryside, striding through the field to Bellay. The long grass brushing my knees. There's buttercups and cows grazing and the sweet smell of honeysuckle, the bright yellow mimosa lighting up my path. Ahead is the driveway that curls around, leading me to our future.

I *will* do better.

I reopen my laptop, blood surging through my veins.

This is the only way.

The neighbour's cat is still crying, trying to claw me back to reality. I fight back, taking him with me to France. He's now weaving between my legs in our kitchen with its marble stone floor. The dogs are outside on the terrace and there'll also be chickens who'll lay fresh eggs for breakfast. And finally, I dare to let myself dream about our children playing on the emerald-green lawn. Raising my glass, I make a toast: 'Jack, you'll thank me later.'

Without pausing this time, I press <UPLOAD>

CHAPTER FOUR

ADELE

My head throbs from the whisky and my neck aches from where I cricked it sleeping at a funny angle but I'm happy because I can hear him breathing. The relief of knowing Jack came home outweighs all those anxious thoughts.

Now the storm has cleared I feel calm again. I'm back in control and there's no need to rake up the past.

Pushing myself upright, I tie my hair back with the band I keep around my wrist. It's then that I notice the trail of clothes. A trainer by the door. Black socks next to the bed. His jeans flung over the chair.

My gaze swings back to Jack, his face planted in the fabric, cheek pushed up to his nose. I can tell his mouth is dry from the way he's breathing. Red sticky sauce crusted in the corner of his lips, a tell-tale of last night's fridge raid. His hand twitches, he must be dreaming.

Beneath his crumpled appearance a charm still burns brightly. He'll never lose that. Jack's always been weak when it comes to women, he can't resist a flirt, but I know that's where it ends. There's no one else. Anxiety drops a surprise ball into my stomach and I have to look the other way to chase off the thoughts.

Across the room, the winter light forcing itself around the curtains warns me it's late morning, my shift at the hotel will be starting soon. I reach for my mobile to check the time, my breath catches when I see what's on my screen.

One long stream of notifications.

Alerting me that people have been commenting. Responding.

The vlog! *Shit*. I forgot all about uploading it.

I turn back to Jack, flushed with adrenaline.

'Hey, wake up.'

He groans and rolls over, dragging the duvet with him.

'Jack.' I nudge him.

He wraps both arms around the pillow, hugging it into his face.

'Sleeping,' he tells me.

'Come on, you've got to see this.' I can hear the tremble of excitement in my voice. I return to the phone, to the dozens of new alerts that have appeared. I swipe right, Google taking me to my YouTube homepage where I can read what they have to say.

152,000 views. *What?*

This is insane. I've never had more than 2,000 for any of my videos. I only uploaded the vlog – I check the time – seven hours ago.

'Jack, hey, come on, you want to hear this. No exaggeration – our lives are about to change!'

He reaches a hand out for me. 'Come back to bed.'

'Listen, I may have done something without asking you,

BUT – don't be mad, I wanted it to be a surprise. I didn't actually think it would work.' I pause, letting air in. 'Last night while you were out, I uploaded a vlog.'

He peels open one eye.

'Yeah, so erm, the vlog may have been asking viewers to help buy us a place in France.'

He squints. 'You what?'

'I found us a chateau and it's perfect. Just the right size and it doesn't need much renovation. It even has a pool. So I've set up a crowdfunding account to help buy it,' I say too quickly.

He stares at me, blinking. His unwashed black hair is lying flat to his scalp. His face is lined from the bedding. 'Sorry, repeat that last bit again.'

'Look, it's easier if I show you.' I turn back to my screen.

Jack props up his back with pillows and looks at me closely with the same incredulous expression.

'Show me then.'

A sickness swells as I study the screen.

'Come on, let's see,' he says. 'Adele?'

Noises become muffled and Jack's voice has slowed to something stretched out and distorted. His words, unrecognizable.

'A . . . d . . . e . . . l . . . e?'

My heart is thundering, beating so hard I can hear the pulse in my ears. A deep, rhythmical thud, thud, as I read through the comments. The vile, abusive, hateful words.

Entitled whore.

Hundreds of them, attacking us for 'begging'.

I'd like a chateau too – wouldn't we all, love. You
need to EARN your way in life. Stop begging for
handouts, you scrounger.

And:

In our dreams we'd all like to be paid to do exactly
what we want when we want, but, Adele, your level of
entitlement is astounding.

And if not horrible, they're weird and obsessive:

Two hours ago I didn't know who Adele Davenport was
but now I think I'll die for you.

I search for something supportive, *anything*. The best I
can find is an 'It's a nice idea', but even that sentiment ends
with a schoolmistress-style telling-off. A reminder how many
people in the world are struggling and we shouldn't be
taking money away from charities and worthy causes that
actually need funding.

I drink in air before the next attack launches:

Bitch, you're almost 30, try growing up.

But it's the final comment that cuts the deepest.

Milking your mum's cancer to get attention and
people to pay for your life. U 2 should be ashamed of
yourselves.

I look up at Jack. He's still talking and I study the way
his mouth is moving, opening, closing, but I can't take in

what he's saying. My eyes step from the screen, to him, back to my phone, which continues to light up with fresh abuse. My thoughts veer into a dark place as the reality of what I've done takes hold.

This can't be happening. I don't understand – what went wrong? I didn't mean for it to come across like we were begging. Those tears I shed for Mum were real. How could they think I'd fake something like that? So what if the Adele in my vlogs isn't 100 per cent representative of the truth? Nobody wants to watch the *real* Adele in her average boring life. I was being genuine. My life *is* rubbish, and, it's just got a whole lot worse.

Fuck.

What should I do?

Destroy the vlog, that's what. Delete it, right now.

Paralyzed by indecision, I'm gazing at my phone screen when the call comes in.

'Are you going to answer that?' I catch the sour smell of beer on his breath. Turning my head away to take the call I can still feel the intensity of his gaze. The weight of expectation.

'Hello?' My voice, small and brittle.

'Adele, it's Cara.'

'Hi, yeah sorry, I'm on my way now.'

'About that,' my boss pauses, for a beat too long. 'Before you come in, I think it's best you know we've seen the video.'

'I can explain.'

'We're hoping you will, Adele. We're all still in shock over here. Disappointed we had to find out your plans to leave via the internet. When were you going to tell us?

'It's not what you think.'

'We assume this is your resignation letter?'

'What, no—' *Christl* What have I done? I didn't think anyone would watch it, not really. It was a pipe dream. I was drunk when I posted it. My heart skips a beat as the seriousness of the situation sinks in. If I lose my job, who's going to pay our bills?

'It was just a stupid prank. Really, Cara, I have no plans to resign.' I feel myself cringe. If I can hear the uncertainty in my voice, so must she.

'Clearly you're not as committed to the job and the brand as we first thought. With summer, our busiest season ahead of us, we need someone who's fully invested in the business.'

'I'm one hundred per cent committed—'

Cara cuts me off. 'Let's have a chat when you get here, hey. Best if we leave it for now. See you shortly.' Her voice disappears and her number vanishes, only to be replaced with more alerts. I don't realize I'm shaking until I look down at my hand.

Jack catches me with his eyes. Speaking more softly but with the same intensity, he says: 'You need to start explaining what the fuck's going on.'

I slide off the bed, phone clutched in one hand as I make a quick retreat to the bathroom. Out of the corner of my eye I catch Jack turning to his mobile. He'll see for himself soon enough.

A sickness is building. What have I done? I need time

to process the damage. Work a way out of this. *Think, Adele.* Maybe I don't delete the vlog but issue an apology instead. As I cross the landing, I'm rehearsing the lines. *Hey lovelies, there's been a bit of a misunderstanding.* If I could just persuade Jack to be in the vlog this time, that will add sincerity to my apology. The viewers will like that.

I feel the thud of his footsteps close behind.

'We're a laughing stock.' Jack's tone has sharpened. He's reading the comments.

'It'll be fine, I'll take it down,' I say, quickening my step.

'Too late for that. Everyone's seen it now. What am I going to tell my family? What will the boys think? They're calling us scroungers. *Scroungers,* Adele! Me! I'd never accept handouts.'

I bite my tongue as I slip inside the bathroom, closing the door just in time.

'Adele.' He smacks the wood.

'I'll be out in a minute.'

'ADELE!'

'I'll fix it!' More quietly, I say, 'Just give me a sec. Please.'

The hallway falls eerily quiet and I take the chance to breathe. Gripping onto the sides of the sink, I bow over the basin. Last night's whisky is threatening to make a reappearance.

I know Cara and her tone was unmistakable. She's going to fire me. That bitch never liked me anyway, always dismissing my interior design ideas. She disapproved of my vlogging. Cara's been waiting for this day. I draw a long breath in, hold and release. *Shit.*

I lift my head and take a moment to study my reflection in the mirror. All colour has drained from my face and, despite my fake tan, I appear sickly grey. My blue eyes look dull and my dark auburn hair has lost its healthy sheen. Jack's not the only one to let things slip. I hate myself for putting a less than perfect foot forward.

And there's something else hiding behind my eyes. I know it's there but I'm not willing to confront it.

The knock startles me.

'Adele?' Jack sounds calmer but his voice is still thick with irritation. 'Can you come out here and explain what you've got us into.'

I hold my breath. Still clutching the sink, the cold of the porcelain feeding into my hands.

It was about starting a new life. It was about dreaming of something different.

'Were you even going to tell me?' He laughs through his nose. 'Fuck's sake, we can't even speak French.'

We would have learned. We would have adapted to living abroad. Our lives would have fallen into place.

'Adele, seriously, what's going on with you?'

With me? I feel like screaming. Tears prick my eyes.

'You've lost the plot. A chateau, seriously?' He laughs again. 'I blame your parents, spoiling you. Filling your head with rubbish.'

I close my eyes. Shutting down my reflection.

'They're right. What they're saying about us. What were you thinking? What makes you entitled to more than anyone else?'

The bitterness from his redundancy, *other Jack* is really coming out now.

'You know what?' he says, then stops.

I stiffen. Bracing.

'The thing is, Adele,' he says more softly, 'you should have married a rich bloke; you'd have been much happier.'

I swallow down his words. Eight years together and he still refuses to get married. 'We don't need a piece of paper to prove our love,' he says. Jack believes marriage is a form of control and for couples who don't trust each other. I used to think that was some crappy excuse to justify his fear of commitment but now, I don't know. So many years have passed it's become confusing. Maybe he's right? We're still together after eight years, and that's longer than most marriages, so it must be love, surely?

My energy drains just thinking about it. I don't want another row, I want to fix things, I want the old us back. We're a good team, and I know he loves me. If I tell him I'm sorry, he'll cool down. And I'll let him know I'm there for him. I'm always there, supporting.

Like a drug addiction, my eyes find their way back to my phone. This time I skip over the messages and click on emails, half expecting Clara to have already sent me my P45.

Buried between the spring sales promotions and junk mail, a new message has arrived in my inbox with the subject line *The Gift*.

Hang on, I didn't give out my email address.

My finger pauses, stuck between whether to open or delete. But what drew me to the flame before is whispering in my ear again. *Open it.*

I click on the tab and the email expands, filling up my screen. Only a few lines long but my breath catches as I read over them.

CHAPTER FIVE

NOW

Sky News

A special report coming in from France, our reporter, Kate Lovell, is outside where the couple were last seen. Kate, what can you tell us?

Hi Justine, as you can see, we are in the very cold, snowy wine region of Burgundy outside this magnificent historic Chateau Bellay.

All we know at the moment is that a British couple who moved to this rural community to begin a new life abroad have vanished. The alarm was raised by the sister.

The missing female is twenty-six-year-old YouTube star Adele Davenport, famous for her video diary *Chateau Life*.

Adele moved to the remote Côte Chalonnaise wine region last August and has since amassed a massive 1.2 million subscribers through her weekly vlog. Her through-the-keyhole look at her life with her partner Jack Reed has grabbed the imagination of thousands wanting to start over abroad, and piggybacks on the success of TV shows and renovation projects like *Chateau Rescue DIY*.

Part of Adele's meteoric success could be that she doesn't look like the typical curated influencer. She wears sun dresses and trainers and appears like the girl next door. Happy and bubbly, inviting viewers into her home – she's the girl you want to be friends with.

Her fan base appears to be a mix of ages, both male and female, all wanting a slice of the ambitious journey she's on.

Could there be anything linking her channel to the disappearance?

We're looking into that now.

It's unclear when exactly the couple were last seen, but it could even be as far back as ten days ago, around New Year.

The weather conditions are slowing down the investigation. Police are doing all they can for now.

Thanks, Kate. We'll have more on the chateau disappearance soon, but now over to our main studio where we'll be looking at France's political unrest in the build-up to the election.

CHAPTER SIX

ERIN

SEVEN DAYS AFTER NYE

It's evening and the snow's falling heavily. Fat flakes tumbling and twirling, their gymnastics caught in my headlights. I've had the engine running and the lights on to stave off the night, but I can't keep wasting fuel like this.

I try Adele's mobile again but it goes straight to answerphone. Messages sent to her WhatsApp aren't arriving. There's no time stamp to know when she was last online, but two blue ticks show my New Year's Eve message was the last one she read.

I study her last reply. A single heart emoji sent a quarter of an hour before midnight. No Happy New Year, no *I'm sorry*. That's the last I heard from her.

Searching for Jack in my contacts is pointless. I don't have his number saved; that's how bad things have got.

I turn back to the chateau. Despite the vastness, there's a sense of claustrophobia about this place. I feel like I can't breathe.

The question always boomeranging: how could Adele and Jack afford to buy a chateau? It wasn't crowdfunded – there were no updates, no more vlogs appealing for contributions after the first. Her friends who tune into her channel say it's weird how Adele's plans to renovate vanished. She never mentioned the B & B idea again to me, and questions over how they've been affording to live out here – dodged.

Adele has become increasingly secretive these past months.

Yes, she's earning money from filming her life in France but that doesn't explain how she could afford a chateau in the first instance.

Something about this is really fishy. And it wouldn't surprise me if Jack's involved.

Adele's always been good at dodging questions. When we were children she'd nick my toys, deflecting by bursting into song or some tap-dance routine and if Mum or Dad got involved, she'd ramp up her performance. A *look at me* moment. That's Adele all over, always stealing the spotlight.

God, I sound bitter, and I am as I think about Mum in those tense final moments before I left for France, when she made me promise.

Rake-thin, fragile, tubes feeding into her nose, more wires trailing from her arms. Her body is wasting away and I pray that's not how I'll remember her.

'Promise me you'll bring her home,' she whispered as I held her hand in the hospice. Mum's last dregs of energy spent worrying about *her*. After everything I did and sacrificed to try save her, the daughter she wants most by her bedside is still my sister.

Mum's words, *Why can't you be more like Adele,* play on a loop in my head.

I often wonder if Adele being an IVF baby is why Mum and Dad love her more. The fact they had to fight so hard to bring her into the world. After their divorce, Adele became Mum's everything.

I feel myself start to cry and bite the inside of my cheek. *I'm not doing this to myself, not again.*

Usually, I put Mum's insensitivity down to the cancer talking. Not today; I'm exhausted by the lies. And I have enough problems of my own. I feel a twinge of panic and I push the fear aside.

Where *the hell is* she? I glare into the blizzard. I'll be out of petrol soon and then I'll really be stuck. Sleeping in the car isn't an option, I'll freeze to death out here.

I need to find a way in.

On the passenger seat there's a small rucksack with essentials I packed just in case. Washbag, phone charger with European adapter and pyjamas. I grab what I have but nothing can prepare me for outside. The cold shocks my system and now there's a biting chill. The wind whips the snow sideways, pummelling my face.

I hunch into the wind, fighting my way around the side of the building in search of a way in. It's so cold I'm getting a headache. An icy fist squeezing my temples.

The path is narrow and overgrown, marked with bronzed urns and sinister-looking sculptures. There's a hare dancing on its hind legs; it feels like it might come alive and jump out at me.

In the distance is the outline of a barn. Up ahead, a

stretched-out building with wood beams, exposed rafters and high, wide windows. It takes a moment to register: the orangery.

In summer it would be glorious with light streaming through the glass ceiling, turning its insides golden. A more unfriendly sight greets me now: folded-up sun loungers and collapsed parasols parked against the wall. A deflated pool toy in the shape of a unicorn shrivelled into the corner.

The unicorn triggers a memory of Adele in a bikini, oversized sunglasses with a cocktail in one hand. Her long thin legs stretched out as she glides across the pool in her blow-up toy. I remember the flush of jealousy watching her Instagram story. I unfollowed her after that.

If it weren't for the glint of the silver ladder, I'd have fallen right through the tarpaulin covering the pool. The surface is hidden beneath a thick sheet of snow. A continuous mass of white blurring into the rest of the estate.

I skirt the edge, arriving at a back entrance. I try the handle, but it won't budge. There's a window but it's too high up. I search for a key under nearby plant pots but there's nothing except mud and worms.

There's another window a little further along but that's also locked. I cast around, feeling increasingly desperate. The wind picks up again, striking my cheek and a burn spreads.

I'll have to break in. Adele will understand.

Beside the door is a rusty old boot jack. I recognize what it is instantly because as kids, living in a house that led on to the marsh, Mum got so fed up of us dragging the mud inside that she sent Dad into town to fetch us wellies and he came home with a jack too. Some of my last happy memories as a family. Then I shiver, thinking about what lay beyond our garden. Where my fear of darkness began.

I squash out the past by lugging the jack into my arms. Solid cast iron, it weighs a ton and I cradle it into my chest as I return to the window.

I heave it through the air and it hits the glass with more force than I intended. The entire window shatters and a surprise fizz of adrenaline arrives. Christ – I'm getting a buzz from destroying something of theirs.

Reaching my hand inside I feel around for the catch. The lock releases and the window swings open. I lift myself up onto the windowsill and carefully crawl through into a small dark space.

The room is alive with the hum of electrics. With the moon to my back, I can make out some kind of utility area with a freezer, a washing machine and tumble dryer. There are metal shelving units along the wall crammed with paint pots and brushes. Glass crunches beneath me as I edge towards a door.

It's pitch-black inside and eerily silent.

'Adele?'

I reach around in the dark, feeling the wall until I make contact with an old-fashioned turn switch. The light snaps to life revealing a room with a black-and-white chequered floor and a domed ceiling. A kitchen, three times the size of my living room.

In the centre stands a modern-looking chrome fridge. My stomach growls in response – it's been hours since I last ate. With echoey steps I cross to the posh-looking thing that feeds ice from its door. But when I open it, there's a far less impressive sight. Empty shelves. Not even a carton of milk or a tub of butter.

That's weird. Even if they've gone away for the weekend, you'd expect there still be something, wouldn't you?

I run myself a glass of water. Ice-cold, it almost stuns my throat into not working. I stand still, picking up on something else.

There's a smell in the air. Something strong and chemical, but what, I can't quite place.

An uneasy feeling grows as I head towards the next room. Another high-ceilinged echo chamber.

Adele's chateau reminds me of a Russian doll, only in reverse. Each room opening up into something grander and more impressive. I arrive into the entrance hall, the one I saw through the window with its vast chandelier, marbled floor and a sweeping staircase lined with gold-framed portraits. Ancestors of the original owners, no doubt.

Someone is watching me, or that's how it feels as I pass under their eyes, holding on to the polished wood banister.

More rooms splinter off a long, dimly lit corridor. Too many to count.

It's here as well, that weird smell, only it's much stronger. Familiar, but out of reach. Could it be coming from one of the bedrooms?

I poke my head around several doors, glimpsing the luxury I'll never be a part of. Persian rugs, four-poster beds, a ruby-red velvet chaise longue. Ornate turn-of-the-century craftsmanship at every turn.

The deeper in I go, the more disorientated I become.

I'm swallowed up into a maze of corridors and rooms. The uneven walls and floor give a sense the building is moving, they shift and bend like a fairground ride. The eerie feeling is helped along by the noises. The creaking. Everything seems to lean and groan and there's a constant ticking. The sound of pipes cooling down, only it can't be that. I can't feel my hands it's so cold.

A lot about this place doesn't make sense. There are too many dark corners where things could lurk.

The thought of spending the night up here leaves me more chilled than I am already.

I reach the master bedroom. Despite the creepiness it's something to be marvelled at. A duck-egg blue parlour with fabric wallpaper made with gold embroidery. A crown hangs above the bed and heavy velvet curtains reach over the king-sized mattress.

It has to be her room – it's fit for a princess.

Pristine. Sheets ironed flat and the surfaces spotlessly clean. A show home. It's almost too perfect.

I look inside the wardrobes.

OK, that's weird. They're empty.

I check the en-suite bathroom and there's no sign of Adele there either. No face creams, no shower gel or even toothpaste.

Apart from the gold candlesticks, there's nothing to show Jack and Adele live here. It's as if they've vanished without a trace.

I laugh. That's ridiculous – this is their home.

Suddenly drained, I take a seat at her dressing table, a polished teak antique with a large oval mirror. Calling up the image of my sister, I imagine her where I am now, brushing through her glossy auburn hair, running a mascara wand over those long thick lashes. Adele never has to try to look beautiful.

It's impossible to avoid my own reflection. Cheeks blotchy from the cold, my features still pinched. I've always hated my hair, the unremarkable brown colour. It stops at my jaw, lies flat against my scalp and now I'm picking I can't stop. I notice how age is catching up with me, lines are creeping in around my eyes and my mouth and grey has found its way into my hairline. There's a resemblance to my sister, only I'm the much less pretty version.

I look away, pulling open the drawer, expecting to find a trillion lipsticks and foundations because if there's one thing Adele loves, it's her make-up.

Again, it's empty – except for a single hairpin wedged into the corner. I pull it free and place it in my palm. An extra chill attaches itself to the cold metal.

Chateau Bellay might belong to Adele, but it feels like I'm inside a stranger's house.

Maybe I should accept the fact that I don't know my sister any more?

Moving between the rooms, I grow increasingly uneasy with my snooping; it feels like an intrusion. I let the last of the heavy doors close behind me and return to the landing, making my way back downstairs.

Back in the heart of the chateau, I pick up on something else. There's a vibration about this place. A pulse, like the chateau is alive. Ghosts of centuries past are rubbing shoulders with each other. It would sound crazy saying it out loud, but it feels like the building wants to tell me something.

The light of the chandelier pulls my gaze up and slowly, I make a full spin, drinking in the spectacular mural across the ceiling. The air swirls along with me and I stop short.

That's it.

The chemical – the zingy ammonia pervading the entire chateau – it's the same smell as when I visit Mum at the hospice.

Disinfectant.

But not just any sort. An industrial-strength bleach.

CHAPTER SEVEN

ERIN

Why, WHY am I allowing my fear of the dark to take over? Adele and Jack will be home soon so I can stop catastrophizing.

I allow the chill to work its way through me, forcing myself not to react. All I need to do is sit tight until they are back. With the snow showing no sign of easing off, what choice do I have? The roads will be freezing over, it would be dangerous to risk it, and what if there's nowhere nearby to stay?

So, Erin, keep calm and try to get some rest.

Doing everything possible to avoid going upstairs again, I use the sink in the kitchen to clean my teeth and wash my face and then I quickly cross back to the far wing.

The drawing room, with its tall wide windows and a clear view of the courtyard feels the least sinister place to wait. I move around, turning on all the lights, then I take up post on the sofa. I shake out the throw folded over the armrest and, keeping my coat on, pull it right up to my chin. It's warm but my body won't stop trembling. The cold's worked its way in, right down to my bones.

It's almost impossible to switch off now my ears are tuning in to every creak and groan. The tick-ticking. I think I hear feet shuffling around above me. I calm my imagination with another deep breath.

I've always disliked old buildings. My apartment in Bournemouth is in a modern development overlooking the sea. The walls and floor are at perfect right angles, there are no draughts or unexpected noises. The sound of the boiler boosting up in the mornings is reassuring – a lulling hum that tells me it's time to get up for work.

I grip onto the blanket a little more tightly.

They won't be long. It'll be OK. But no matter how hard I try soothing myself, the words keep jarring.

The BANG shakes me awake. For a moment I have no idea where I am and then the *slam* hits like a punch.

I blink my way back to consciousness, only it's much darker now. I could have sworn I had kept the lights on. I search around, my eyes drawn to the brightness outside. The falling snow appears luminous in the moonlight. A wall of silver.

I must have drifted off, a miracle considering how anxious I felt. How long was I asleep? I reach for my phone, it's 4.17 a.m. and, there's still no message from Adele. I check the courtyard. *Empty*. They didn't come home. The knot in my stomach tightens.

BANG.

I startle. The noise is followed by a clanging, a metal scraping across metal, so loud the sound travels the length of the building.

I'll pretend it's not happening. If I hide under the blanket, whatever it is will soon stop.

BANG. BANG. This time, firing in quick succession. Drumming me into action. My pulse takes off at the thought I'm going to have to look.

I force myself onto my feet and wrap the blanket around like a protective shield. I cross the entrance hall where the wind is whistling past the windows, rattling the glass in their frames. The banging grows louder, deafening, like a gun going off.

I lift up the closest object to protect myself with: a thin-necked vase.

None of the lights are working, the storm must have cut the power. I use the torch on my phone to enter the library, sweeping the beam over the bookcases. The gold lettering along the spines glints in the light. They're old-fashioned, leather-bound classics, not the sort of thing I'd expect Adele and Jack to read. The room smells of old paper, wax and more detergent. Shapes lurk in the corners and I try not to look.

Get a grip, Erin. For someone who deals with accidents and emergencies, I'm doing a terrible job of staying calm.

The thud strikes again, shaking the bookshelves, and it seems to be coming from outside. I lift the vase above my head, tightening my grip. The muscles across my shoulders tense as I edge towards the window.

BAM. BAM. BAM.

My heart is thudding as hard and as loud as the noise as I peer into the night.

I let out a little laugh. *Shutters* – Christ, that's all. The hook that holds them flush with the wall has come loose. I place the vase on the ground and I'm still smiling with relief as I open the window, letting the cold rush in.

Wind wails through the trees and around the chimney stacks and it takes me in its grip, pulling me this way and that as I lean over.

Reaching into the night, my fingers grapple for the hook. I'm stretching much further forward than I'd like to be, my body dangling half out the window – it wouldn't take much to slip and fall – but I manage to fasten the shutter before the next blast of snow. I shut out the storm, bolting the window closed.

As I'm turning back to the room, a movement catches my eye. My gaze is pulled outside, to something dark and blurred moving quickly through the snow.

At first, I think it's a deer but as my eyes focus, I can tell it's not an animal.

My breath sticks in my throat.

It's the outline of a person.

Jack?

The shadowy figure is dressed in black. Tall, slim and wearing a padded bomber jacket with a fur-trimmed hood pulled up over their head. A pit of black where their face should be. I can't tell if it's a man or a woman, although something about their movements makes me think it's a he. And he's heading right for me.

Should I call out for Jack? Something is warning me I need to stay quiet.

His steps are confident, measured, like he knows the estate well. As he draws closer, I notice the oversized combat trousers and there's a glimmer of metal from his steel-capped boots.

He slows to a stop at the edge of the courtyard. Waiting. But for what? He lifts his hand and a tiny crimson dot appears where his face should be. It's the end of a cigarette.

Jack doesn't smoke.

I feel all my hairs stand on end.

He's watching me. I can't see his eyes but I can feel them, the intensity of his stare, and I'm too frightened to move.

What does he want?

He takes a moment more, as if enjoying the fear he's instilling. Then, he flicks the cigarette into the snow and turns, vanishing into the woods.

I'm shaking. My heart banging louder than any noise I've heard tonight.

CHAPTER EIGHT

ADELE

NINE MONTHS BEFORE NYE

Morning, loves. Actually, I don't know why I'm saying that (**huffs out a breath**) *when it's the afternoon – 3.17 p.m. to be precise – and YES, I'm still in bed, because my life, as I once knew it, has fallen to pieces and—*
    (**doorbell rings**)
    And, now the sound of the doorbell is in my vlog, which is just as well because I have absolutely no intention of posting a video about how I've managed to screw up my life on a pipe dream and how, unless I find a job within the next two weeks, Jack and I will be homeless.

I snap the recorder button to <OFF> and throw my phone onto the bed.

It's been two days since Cara fired me and I still can't bring myself to face the world. Even though I hated that job, now I feel lower than ever. So down, I can't pull myself out because the enormity of what I've done, of what we're facing, is paralyzing and then there's the worry of what's going to happen to Mum.

With no Erin, no Jack to lean on and no hope left of escaping to France – the sudden weight, the pressure of knowing that I alone will have to fix this, presses down like a lead weight. If only I could take it all back.

Ding dong.

'Jack? Can you get that?'

I feel my frown deepening. A flare of rage at Jack's uselessness. Can't he even answer the door? And when did I become such an angry, hateful person? When did gratitude and manifesting stop working?

I refuse to do it for him. Instead, I reach for my phone again so I can read the email, although it doesn't matter how many times I go over it, I still can't connect with the words.

Dear Adele and Jack

I represent a wealthy philanthropist who has instructed me to inform you of their intention to purchase Chateau Bellay. My client was deeply moved by your plight and wanted to stress that this should be considered a gift. They ask for nothing in return and wish you good fortune in your new life abroad.

I will be in touch shortly with all the necessary paperwork.

With warmest wishes,

Marissa White

Solicitor and partner at Gerald and Sons

45 New Bond Street

London W1

Somehow, it feels more malicious than all the online trolling and abuse that's gone before. A bogus lawyer, going to the lengths of tracking down my email! A Google search confirmed what I thought – there is no Marissa White or Gerald and Sons of Mayfair.

A gift? A GIFT? Someone's really getting a kick out of giving us false hope. Who could be so cruel? I know they say never to interact with trolls, but I had to reply with a piece of my mind, and I felt better, for all of three seconds.

Finally, I hear Jack turn down the TV and get up off the sofa, followed by the dull thuds of his feet crossing the hallway to the front door.

I can make out a woman's voice.

'Adele?' Jack yells. 'Can you come down here.'

Sighing heavily, I force myself out of bed, reaching for a blouse.

'Just a minute.' I button up my jeans.

I turn to face the mirror.

'Someone's here to see us,' Jack shouts more insistently.

More rushed than I'd like, I tidy my hair into a low bun. Then I sweep bronzer across my face, followed by blusher, setting powder, and finish with a nude lip gloss. It hurts not to be perfect, but it'll have to do. I rest a cardigan over my shoulders and head downstairs to where there's a strong smell of perfume filling up our hallway.

'Adele, this lady says she has something for us.' Jack gives me a look.

A tall woman in a smart coat with a shiny black helmet of hair turns to greet me. Our eyes meet and I instantly feel intimidated. But her face lights up on seeing me.

'Adele.' She holds out a hand. 'It's an absolute pleasure.'

Hesitantly, I take it, noticing the jewellery sliding out from under the cuff of her jacket. A fine gold chain wrapped around her wrist. Her fingers, decorated with several diamonds. In the other hand she carries a briefcase.

Sensing my apprehension, Jack comes to my side protectively.

'Who did you say you were?' I ask.

Jack moves to speak but the woman cuts him off.

'Marissa White.' There's an expectant pause.

I frown. 'I'm sorry, I . . .'

'I sent you and Jack an email?'

I blink quickly.

'About the gifting programme.'

Impossible. That was a joke. Wasn't it? I gaze warily at the stranger in my home.

'You?' I clear the frog in my throat. '*You* sent me the email about Bellay?'

'I thought it would be better that we speak in person. I knew you couldn't have meant your response, but don't worry, it's perfectly understandable you'd react that way under the circumstances.'

I blush, remembering my reply. The raft of insults. I glance at Jack, who's looking even more confused than me, then back at her. 'How did you find us?'

'Easily, you're in the directory.'

'We are?'

Jack shrugs.

'Sorry to turn up unannounced like this but I thought

it was the simplest and quickest way to show our sincerity. Unfortunately, time is against us.'

I frown, still trying to connect the dots.

'Hang on, when I looked you up, I couldn't find you.'

She smiles reassuringly. 'That's because we're not a practising law firm. I have only one client. I can explain, but first' – she ushers us towards our living room with her eyes – 'shall we sit down?'

I hesitate and somehow she's managed to slip past us.

'Who is she?' Jack whispers as we follow her into our home.

'Adorable neighbourhood.' She sweeps her eyes out the window. 'How long have you lived here?'

'Four years,' Jack says defensively.

'Must be difficult getting into the city from here?'

'It's not that bad.' He looks even more offended. 'We like it around here.' He turns to me and hisses. 'Who is she?'

'I'll tell you in a minute,' I whisper, still trying to figure out who could do all that. Find out your details so quickly.

Marissa White, who looks to be in her mid-forties, removes her coat and carefully places it over the back of a chair, then takes a seat at our dining table. Jack leaps into action, snatching away his plate from last night, and she flashes him a smile bordering on flirtatious.

Placing her soft leather briefcase on the table, she unfastens the gold clasp. Jack and I watch, transfixed, as she presents us with a stack of A4 white sheets, stapled into sections. She lays them flat and hands us a pen each.

'Please, have a seat.'

Jack and I swap looks and then do as we're told.

'I should begin by explaining a little more about my client, the offer and the contract.'

'Contract?' Jack quietly echoes.

'First of all,' she smiles, 'you should know my client was deeply moved by your GoFundMe appeal. It's not often you see such honesty on a public platform. To lay bare your soul like that takes courage. My client has respect and admiration for your project, and your candidness.'

'Right.' Jack laughs.

'As I mentioned in my email, my client is a philanthropist who regularly gives money to charity, and this seems a project worthy of investment.'

I feel Jack staring at me.

I'm busy studying our guest, conjuring up an image of her workplace: some glass-walled office with a panoramic view of London.

'My client also happens to be a lover of all things French.' She presses on. 'They own a vineyard in Provence and keep a yacht in Cannes. Securing a third home in the most famous wine region seems a natural step forward.'

Jack turns to me. 'OK, what's going on?' He pushes a hand through his hair anxiously.

'This lady knows someone who wants to buy us the chateau I showed you.' I recite the email by heart, as if everything's perfectly normal. Why am I so calm?

Jack laughs. 'Come off it.'

'No really, her client watched my vlog and wants to buy Chateau Bellay for us as . . .' I hesitate, looking to the lawyer for confirmation. She nods and I finish: '. . . as a gift.'

'This is too weird.' Jack leans back, hooking an arm over the chair. 'What sort of mugs do you take us for? Nobody gives away a chateau. What's the catch?'

'No catch,' the lawyer says flatly. 'As I said, my client is extremely wealthy and your appeal struck a chord, both with the mention of your misfortune and your dream of starting a new life abroad.' Smiling, she adds: 'Having recently overcome a difficult circumstance themselves, my client can identify. They derive great enjoyment from bringing happiness to the less fortunate.'

Less fortunate. I kick Jack's leg under the table before he can react. A sharp smack to his shin – because I won't have him ruin this. This could be the answer to all our problems. A way out.

He scowls at me. I ignore him.

'Shall we press on with the signing over?'

'Signing over?' says Jack.

'We've made arrangements for our donation to be deposited into your GoFundMe account for use as the down payment for the property.'

A new life abroad. A fresh start – this can't be happening. I take back what I said; this is a sign from the universe.

'My client is aware of the urgency to complete due to the fast-moving property market. To ensure your chateau won't be snapped up by someone else, we must finalize the transaction as soon as possible.'

I feel myself start to shake.

'You mean, it's ours? It will all be ours?'

'Once the paperwork is completed with the agents in Paris, the deeds for Chateau Bellay will be transferred into your names. All we need in return is for you to agree to the terms and conditions listed in our contract.'

My heart is racing, none of this seems real. I know I should be asking questions, looking for the catch. A mysterious woman claiming to be a lawyer has turned up on our doorstep giving away a free chateau – this is crazy. But I don't want to, *I won't*, because all I can see is a way out of our problems. And the thing I've wanted my entire life – my own fairy-tale castle.

The groove in Jack's brow loosens. He wants this too, I can tell. I know him, he's still smarting from me posting the vlog but once he calms down and sees how all of this makes perfect sense, he'll come around.

He's bored with his life here. France will be a chance to reinvent ourselves. Renovating, running a B & B – it will give us purpose.

Back in the day, we used to have fun, we'd make plans, he'd want to spend all his time with me. And we'll have that again. Jack is loving, he's caring. *This* – who he is today, who he's been for the past months – is not the real Jack.

And when he's happy and we're settled in France, we can talk about trying for a baby.

I call up the photos: the tower, the pool, the opulent rooms. Our future is sprinting ahead of me.

I reassure the lawyer: 'We'll pay you back, I promise. As soon as we've got the B & B up and running, we can charge a lot for rooms that size.' I see it now, the guests arriving, boasting on social media about their holiday at our chateau. Posting photos that feature my interior designs.

People will come from far and wide to see how we turned an old crumbling chateau around.

'That won't be necessary,' she says with a sharp nod.

'No, really, that was always the plan.' I glance at Jack. 'We'll pay you back.'

Her mouth lifts into a smile and I notice Jack's head turn.

'Please. As I said, it's my client's wish that the chateau is *a gift*,' she stresses.

'So, what, we can't run it as a B & B?' says Jack.

'A gift that should not be shared with anyone else.' She meets his eye, an edge creeping into her tone.

Jack laughs. 'If we can't make money from the B & B, how do you expect us to afford to live?'

'All running costs will be taken care of while you establish yourselves in France. It would be counterintuitive not to give you a helping hand.'

'And after that?'

'Shh, Jack, you can't expect them to pay for everything,' I say angrily. My bitterness of the last few months resurfacing. 'We can get jobs out there.'

We'll find a way to make ends meet. I have my vlog which, with enough viewers, can be monetized. And Jack – he'll find a job in the community.

'I can still vlog the chateau, though, can't I?' I check.

'Of course,' Marissa says, her warmth returning. 'In fact, we encourage you to film. The preservation and celebration of such a historic building needs to and must be celebrated.'

My brow knots. The contradictions do seem a little confusing.

'It's a security issue.' She clears her throat. 'Strangers coming and going, potentially damaging the building – that's my client's primary concern.'

Seems reasonable. I brush any doubts aside, focusing on what matters. Our future.

'See, Jack, we'll manage.' We always have. This is a turning point. And it's more than the chateau. I can feel it – call it woman's intuition – our lives are about to change forever.

The rush of adrenaline makes me heady and euphoric. I feel like springing out of my chair and yelling the house down.

'Our friends will lose their minds! Jack, think of the parties, it'll be epic. Your mates won't be taking the piss much longer.' I can hear the *told you so* tone in my voice, but I can't help it after how triumphantly he made his point earlier.

The lawyer clears her throat. 'I'm afraid a few of the terms of agreement might conflict with your celebration plans. To protect my client, you understand. In return for the chateau, there are some things we'll need you to give up . . .'

A silence tiptoes into the room, neither of us knowing quite how to respond.

'Such as?' Jack says eventually.

She returns to her stack of papers. 'Let's take a look at the contract, shall we. Won't take a minute to run through the points.'

She puts on a pair of wire-framed glasses and waits for us to catch up.

'Good idea,' I join in.

Jack snaps his head around. I try to ignore him and let myself be swept up in the fantasy, the worry of having lost my job washing out to sea. A calmness descends, and I give Jack a nod of encouragement.

The noise of crisp pages turning fills the silence. I've lost track of how much time has passed wading through the documents and my vision blurs from the mass of words. Jack and I are both hopeless when it comes to these sorts of things. And with the sense of urgency looming over us, it feels even more difficult to take in the small print.

I feel her eyes on me, studying our reaction. The pressure heightening under the scrutiny of her gaze.

'A final document to read over.' She places a single sheet of A4 in front of us. 'Mostly concerning the use and aesthetic of the building. A few dos and don'ts, that's all.' Jack sighs and I blink, trying to focus on the text.

> Those parties entering the agreement do so with the understanding of the conditions listed below:

1. The chateau must not be altered in any way. Building renovations or changes to the design will be decided by my client.

I look up and the lawyer smiles.

'But I wanted this to be our renovation project!'

Bellay is beautiful, but it's a diamond in the rough. Some of those rooms need more than a lick of paint.

'My client is involved in numerous heritage conservation projects and the preservation of the past is something they are particularly passionate about, you understand.'

'But, what about my interior designs and—'

'However,' Marissa cuts me off. 'My client is very understanding, and I'm sure minor adjustments will be considered, if put in writing.'

Jack laughs. 'What if we don't *like* what your client *likes*?'

She looks over her glasses. 'My client has impeccable taste.'

He falls silent and I feel myself nodding submissively. We both move on to the next clause.

2. You may only bring essential items with you.

'Same thing applies here,' she says quickly. Almost apologizing. 'Clothes, those sorts of things are all fine, it's more to avoid any larger pieces of furniture destroying the aesthetic. The heritage. A small sacrifice to make really.'

I hear Jack swallow. He'll be panicking at the thought of being separated from his things. It could be good for him though. I search for the silver lining. OK, so Marissa White's client does appear to have control issues or OCD or *something*. But the thought of leaving it all behind, starting afresh, feels instantly liberating. It's what I've been after – a clean slate. Maybe this is the push we needed?

3. My client shall have a bedroom reserved for
their sole use should they desire to visit.

Once again Marissa is ready for me, armed with a powerful smile.

'My client is unlikely to visit,' she says. 'Work commitments take up most of their time, but we need the option there in the improbable event . . .'

I look to Jack and he shrugs. He appears more shell-shocked than anything now.

4. No guests are permitted

What? No, hang on. 'Look, we've got to be allowed guests!' I hear the strain in my voice.

'As I said, my client is very particular about security.'

'But, what about Mum, she's family.'

Marissa won't meet my eye. That same apologetic look creeping in.

'She's not well—'

'One final thing, if you could sign this too.' She produces another wordy document.

'What is this?' Jack asks.

'An NDA.'

He frowns.

'A non-disclosure agreement. Under no circumstances must you talk about my client or this arrangement. If you do, the contract will be void. My client is a very private person.'

When she notices us falter, she adds: 'You can also appreciate my client is incredibly busy. This is a one-time offer and the option ends when I leave here today, I'm afraid.'

Jack shifts in his seat. 'Sounds like an ultimatum.' His tone matches hers.

'Jack, leave it,' I hiss, my eyes skating across the final clause.

> 5. Failure to adhere to the terms and conditions will lead to eviction from the property.

Jack turns to me. 'You're not thinking straight. This is weird. We don't know this woman. What are these *rules* we have to agree to? We don't even know who her client is. It could be an arms dealer, some cartel drug lord.' He laughs. 'Or, I don't know, a serial killer.'

'Or, a really nice person.'

'Seriously? You're being naive. What about your mum? You said the whole point of moving to the countryside was to give her somewhere to recover after the chemo. So now what? That doesn't matter? You going to leave her behind?'

The reminder of Mum being sick spears my insides. I look away. He's right, of course, but I can't bring myself to think of the alternative. *Staying here.* Watching Mum struggle through the treatment.

What if she doesn't recover? The memory of losing Dad is as raw today as the day he walked out on us. The feelings of loss and grief swallow me.

I can't. I'm not strong enough.

Searching for yet another dead-end job?

Forget it. I'm done with England.

How can I pass over a once-in-a-lifetime opportunity?

Clauses, rules, whatever this lawyer calls them – they're only guidelines, nothing more than that. I'll find a way to get Mum in. What's the worst that can happen?

'Adele, you're seriously considering this?'

'Have you got a better idea?' I snap back. 'It's not like you're doing anything to get a job.' I stop myself short of entering into a full-blown row.

Blushing, I look away, although I know the lawyer is watching, enthralled by our domestic. I suddenly feel acutely aware of the impression we must be leaving. *Stop screwing it up for us, Jack.* I shoot him angry eyes.

I'm thinking for both of us, and about Mum. He needs to trust me.

'A bad person wouldn't offer to do something like this,' I say more softly.

'Ms Davenport is right,' the lawyer steps in. 'Let me assure you, my client is an honourable member of society with a seat on the board of innumerable charities. They have your best interests at heart. Their desire for anonymity is largely a result of being a well-known public figure who wishes to avoid their philanthropy being scrutinized or publicized by the press. You know what journalists are like, always misinterpreting things. It's becoming almost impossible to do good these days. If there's anything I can do to put you at ease . . .' She touches Jack's arm. Her tone skating back to breezy.

He blushes, looking away.

There's a speed about all of this, a sense of urgency that's stopping me from thinking clearly. I should take a moment, read the contract more carefully, look into this woman's credentials. I should listen to Jack and research who her client could be – a well-known public figure – but that voice on my shoulder is back screaming JUST DO IT.

Stop overthinking, Adele. This *gift* is the result of all the work I've been doing on myself. I manifested it. I believed it would be possible, the universe listened and now it's happening.

'It's fine, Jack,' I tell him confidently, assured this is all happening for a reason.

This is how it so often plays out. I have the idea, which I push on Jack because I know it will be good for us; he puts up a small fight but eventually comes around to my way of thinking.

I can see Jack's mind working, he's coming around. His scowl is loosening and he's doing that gentle nodding as he reads over the paperwork – a good sign. Marissa's explanation of our sponsor's philanthropy must have helped.

I can't say I've warmed to Marissa, but I doubt we'll have anything to do with her after the contracts are signed.

'Hey, where's your head at?' I say more gently to Jack. 'Moving abroad will give space to think about what you want to do next with your life, and we could set up a workshop. Remember when we first met, you told me you wanted to try carpentry.'

I'm being manipulative now, but I can't stop. I want what's best for us.

'And if it doesn't work out, we can always leave. Come on, it's a free house!' I can't hide my smile this time because it's taken over my face. 'What's not to love about that?'

His shoulders lift as he lets out a laugh, eyebrows going up. 'What's not to love, hey?'

The next fifteen minutes is spent reassuring Jack over a few more minor points in the contract, but he doesn't take much persuading. He knows it would be madness to turn down an opportunity like this.

Jack and I lock eyes.

Something brushes my knee and I jump. It's Jack's hand, giving me a squeeze. I can't remember when he last did that.

Looking back to the lawyer I feel my eyes blazing. 'So, where do we sign?'

'Wonderful!' Her face brightens. 'Just here, and here and also here' – she brushes the paper with her mani-cure-tipped finger – 'and here, if you will. Obviously it will take time for the paperwork to be finalized and things seem to move much slower in Europe, but I can't see any reason why you won't be able to move in before the end of August.'

August. Summer in France. I feel my face flushing with the warmth.

Swirling through the letters of my signature, my thoughts swim off into the future. I'm planning our adventure; I'm smelling the French lavender and feeling the warm earth between my toes as I walk barefoot through the long grass. Lightness is returning to me already.

It's only after I pass the papers back that a thought occurs. From the way Marissa spoke, it's impossible to know whether her client is a man or a woman.

'Everything OK?' she says.

I nod. Shrugging it off. I can't see what difference it makes. And besides, by the sound of it, our paths are unlikely to ever cross.

CHAPTER NINE

NOW

Sky News

Back to Kate Lovell reporting from Chateau Bellay in France where Missing YouTube star Adele Davenport and her partner Jack Reed have been reported missing.
Kate, any update?

Nothing as yet. There's been an unprecedented amount of secrecy surrounding the investigation, the police aren't sharing much information and we have little more to go on at the moment. The police have explained they are doing the best they can but the weather is making it difficult for them to carry out as thorough a search as they would like.

Any indication how long the couple have been missing?

We're still looking for clarification on an exact date, but we can confirm it was Adele's older sister, Erin Davenport, who raised the alarm after growing increasingly concerned for Adele's whereabouts. Sources have informed us the sisters' mother is terminally ill and there's a sense of urgency for their return to England.

How tragic. What's the general feeling out there?

There's a lot of confusion over what's happened. Initially there was great excitement surrounding the couple's plans to renovate the chateau but when those plans never materialized there appears to have been a shift in the way they were received by the local community. There's a sense of hostility towards them.

Any indication why?

Nothing confirmed. We think it could have to do with the chateau's former owners.

Any more on that?

We're looking into it now.

Thanks, Kate. We'll have more from France and the disappearance soon.

CHAPTER TEN

ADELE

FOUR MONTHS BEFORE NYE

YouTube
70,000 subscribers

Tour of Our Chateau!

Guys – my first chateau vlog! Can we just take a moment to appreciate. (**closes eyes and smiles**)

(**snaps open eyes and waves**)

Hi lovelies, BONJOUR, salut and welcome to . . . Chateau Bellay! (**pans camera around**)

I'm beyond happy I can show it to you finally. We arrived late last night, and Jack's already gone into the village to pick us up some croissants. Real French buttery melt-in-your-mouth pastry. (**squeals**) He's such a hero.

So, while he's out, I'm taking you on a little tour. (**strides up driveway towards main entrance**)

Wow! It's the end of August but it's 28 degrees today! I'm roasting in my T-shirt and shorts. As you know, I'm a believer in everything happening for a reason and this weather (**looks up**) – it's a sign that good things are on the way. Does anyone else trust in the universe? Leave a comment in the box below, love to know.

Anyway, so here we have the main entrance, a seventeenth-century oak door. Come on in! (**heaves door open**)

Voila! The entrance hall or the grand salon, which all the rooms splinter off, I think of it as the beating heart of our chateau. It's a bit of a maze upstairs, so I'll take you there another time.

As you can see, the original beams have been preserved and on the ceiling is a stunning mural, all painted by hand. And check out our crystal chandelier. But do you want to know the first thing I fell in love with? Obviously, the sweeping staircase. Isn't it insane? (**camera pans around**) Italian marble, fit for a princess. I can envisage me in my ball gown and Jack in his tuxedo, looking SO FIT. We just love LOVE everything about this feature. And guess what? We've discovered the floor and the staircase are an exact copy of those in the Queen's house in Greenwich built by Lord Jeremy Jones in around 1740, so the architect must have travelled to England to take notes, then gone on to Italy to source the marble and then (**points**) this magic happened. How crazy? A little piece of England here with us. (**clutches heart**)

Back in the day, getting dressed up would have been the norm. We've learned the chateau was used as a retreat for royals and important people. They'd come here to hunt deer and wild boar (**grimaces**) but in the evenings they'd host these grand, decadent parties. According to Google, that's what Chateau Bellay became famous for. Apparently, this was THE PLACE to party. People would dress up and then (**pushes open another door**) they'd come dance in here.

(**spinning camera around**) Oh man, would you just look at the light streaming into this room! (**gasps**) Stunning!

The other thing I need to show you is this – the fireplace. As soon as I saw it, I was in luuurve. I mean seriously, guys, (**runs hand across marble top**) imagine the fires in winter, how cosy?

Now I want to take you somewhere *uber* special which I only discovered today . . . just passing through the games room first, check out the billiard table, it makes Jack *so* happy. And once we swing around this corner, we end up in the library. I don't know why I'm whispering but you just have to, right? Look at all these books (**runs finger across spines**) – I *cannot* wait to dive in. I can see myself getting lost in Jane Austen, and . . . erm . . . right . . . so over there (**points camera at plush leather sunken chair**) that's going to be my reading nook. And over there, that's Jack's corner. (**points to big oak leather-topped desk**)

Speaking of Jack, I think I can hear him in the drive, let's go outside and see.

(**camera jogs through rooms**)

Hey babe, what you got there? You're being filmed, say hi.

'Hiya.'

Jack got up early for me. Best boyfriend ever!

'Croissant for madame.'

Ahhh thanks, babe. You're so thoughtful. (**kisses Jack**) Wave to the fans!

(**Jack waves**) 'I'll see you inside.'

Laters, babe! (**opens bag with pastries**) OMG, this is THE MOST delicious croissant I've ever seen. I am obsessed. (**zooms in on croissant**) Would you just look at that buttery crust! I swear they make them different over here to Tesco's.

Ooh hang on, there's a man who's just turned up, our first official guest – how exciting is that, guys? Maybe I can introduce him to you—

(**starts walking**)

(**stops walking abruptly**)

OK, tad awkward, he's saying he doesn't want to be filmed. (**giggles nervously**) Oops. Anyway, I better go and find out why he's here, cos he looks a little agitated. Be right back, lovelies.

Oh, and I love you all so SO much. Big kisses from us, and au revoir. (**blows camera a kiss**)

CHAPTER ELEVEN

TheREALAdele003 Active five minutes ago

When I watch your videos I'm there with you. You make me feel like I'm one of your best friends. Jack's a lucky man. He should be careful or someone might steal you away.

CHAPTER TWELVE

ADELE

THREE MONTHS BEFORE NYE

None of this feels real.

I made it. *We* made it. We've left our old life behind.

This morning I woke up to more sunshine and stepped out onto my Juliet balcony and basked in light as I gazed across our estate. It's been another blazingly hot autumn day, a gift from our endless summer.

Our estate. Sounds like something from *Pride and Prejudice* and I sound like a tool for throwing pretentious words around, but, it's impossible not to feel like I'm on a film set. I've dreamed of this moment for so long.

What can I say about the rest of the day? It's slipped past in a haze. I caught up with admin, did some vlogging and chatting with subs – that's subscribers. Then, a bit of baking, I'm experimenting with French recipes and Jack's loving my glazed apple cake, I mean, *la tarte tatin* – I'm trying to learn French too – but mostly I've been relaxing, browsing through stalls at the *brocante* in town and tasting local cheeses. I've stopped caring so much about what I look like, I want to appear more natural in my vlogs. Life has slowed down and I couldn't be happier.

I close my eyes, letting the rose-gold light wash over my face as the heat of the day subsides. The water gently lapping as I float aimlessly across the pool in my unicorn inflatable. I've got nothing to do, I've got nowhere to be. *This is heaven.*

There's the faint gush of the fountain somewhere in the distance, hypnotic, lulling me into a meditative state.

Make this summer never end.

Things are finally moving in the right direction with Jack and he's finding himself, getting back into his DIY. He's always busy tinkering on something and his ideas are returning, like I knew they would. The countryside has done us good – having space has brought us back together. He seems to like being around me again. He wants to be intim-ate with me. I feel a quiver thinking about last night. Even if it wasn't quite what I like.

A small part of me is braced, waiting for the bubble to burst because fairy tales like this don't happen. Not to normal people like us. Especially with how quickly we signed those papers, the whole thing seems so unreal, a blur, when I think about it.

Out of curiosity I tried googling the account the deposit was made from, Eden Investments Limited, but the name didn't come up. Nothing you'd associate with a *'well-known public figure'* anyway. Jack told me to relax, that I was being weirdly suspicious. It's nice to see him happier with our arrangement. And I trust him; he knows more about these kinds of things than me.

It's not healthy to live with that sort of mindset anyway, so I'm working harder on replacing negative thoughts with goals and affirmations, and I have many of those planned for the months ahead.

Our new life.

Thoughts of Mum in hospital rush at me and I quickly push them aside. I rang her again last night; she seemed OK without us visiting, and Erin is there. Erin's always looking out for her. There's another wave of guilt and I swallow hard. My sister's getting suspicious, wondering why we haven't invited them to visit. I'll have to tell them something soon.

To escape my anxiety, I splash into the pool. The water is fresh, instantly cooling my sunburnt shoulders. I sink to the bottom and then tip my head back, lifting my gaze to the sky. The dappled skin of the pool brings the blues and whites together. It's peaceful down here in the hush of the water, where the summer colours swirl like a living modernist painting.

Coming up for air, I push my hair from my face and swim to the side. Lifting myself out, I cross the hot stones to the sun lounger, where I ring out the ends of my hair and wrap my oversized towel around me. My book lies open on its spine, the pages warmed by the heat. I take a sip of freshly made lemonade. Zesty and refreshing, it slips down my throat and I follow through with a smile.

Hashtag dreams come true. Hashtag make it happen. I'm reminded of the hundreds of new subscribers I'm getting each day, all of them wanting a slice of chateau life. They seem to have bought into my new YouTube identity and forgotten about the old one I had back in the UK – the former me. Not only do I get to live here for free but I'm now starting to earn a decent income from influencing, bringing in money with every 1,000 views I get for each video. And then there's the advertising revenue. More recently, I've been branching out into TikTok and even teenagers are following me. It's crazy, but nothing about this makes sense.

I turn to meet the setting sun, low slung but still powerful and blinding. A surprise streak of movement makes me jump.

'Jack?'

Lifting my hand to shade my eyes I realize he's much too tall to be Jack.

'I didn't see you there,' I say, squinting.

He continues to stare while rolling a cigarette.

I move into the shade to get a better look at our new gardener. He's been elusive since he turned up on our doorstep two weeks ago, always slipping off before I have a chance to ask him anything. Studying him now, I notice how strong and square his jawline is, although it's mostly hidden with stubble. His hair is bristly, shaved close to his scalp and he has stormy eyes. His expression, as usual, is unreadable. He would be good-looking if it weren't for his standoffishness.

His jeans hug his thighs and his boots look too hot for the weather. Sweat rings the armpits of his T-shirt. His eyes narrow when he notices me looking. He lifts his cigarette to meet his lips, lights it and inhales, all the while not breaking eye contact.

I feel a flash of anger. The arrogance. Leaving his fag butts all over the lawn and never doing any work. He doesn't behave like a gardener. What's the point of him?

An uneasy feeling lodges in my chest.

'*Pardon*,' he says eventually. But he's not sorry. In fact, I have a creeping sense he's been watching me for some time and, despite my bikini and a thick towel, I feel more exposed than if I'd been wearing nothing.

I reply with a tight nod. A tense smile.

Clutching my towel to my chest, I fold my arms and slide into my flip-flops.

I need to find Jack, right away.

The rooms beneath the chateau are a labyrinth of gloomy caves. Once used as garages, they now house the leftovers from the previous owners, who we still know barely anything about. Jack's working his way through it all, each day discovering new treasures. I find him hunched over a cardboard box, rifling through its contents.

'There's something really off about Pierre,' I announce.

'Jesus Christ.' Jack startles, clutching his heart. 'You scared me. Where did you spring from?'

The room is barely lit with a single bulb dangling from a wire. I move into the spill of light so he can see me better. He's wearing shorts, a crumpled shirt and flip-flops. His legs and arms are brown and freckled from the Indian summer.

He crosses to where I'm standing, taking hold of my waist, but I pull away.

'I don't trust him. There's something really off about the way he looks at me.'

Jack looks hurt but I can't breathe, not with the thought of how Pierre was leering.

'He's giving me the creeps.'

He sighs. 'What's he done now?'

'Watching me while I was taking a swim.'

'You sure you're not being overly sensitive? He could have been gardening and happened to be near the pool.'

'No – he was perving on me.' Anger breaks through my voice. 'I caught him staring.'

Jack walks over and takes my hand. A sudden excitement flashes in his eyes. 'Come check this out.'

I frown but my protest is lost in darkness as he leads me into the shadows where it smells of dust and earth, the musty spores making my lungs work hard.

'You need to see this.'

'I'm serious, I'm trying to tell you our gardener's a creep – and, I don't like it in here, take us back where I can see.'

'It'll be worth it, I promise.' He switches on his phone torch, shining it across a large lumpy mound hidden beneath a white sheet. 'Wait there, you need the full experience.'

'Jack—'

'One sec, it's coming . . .'

He grabs a corner and pulls off the sheet in one sweeping movement, whipping the dust into a tornado. I'm coughing while he exclaims:

'Isn't she a beauty!'

My gaze settles on what could only be a collector's item. I'm no car expert but it looks old. Really old. The tyres are flat, the paintwork is damaged and the leather seats are ripped to shreds.

'A 1931 Austin Seven. Only a million were ever made. Can you believe that? Four-cylinder side valve engine.' He turns back to the car, running his hand across the long sleek bonnet. 'Why would anyone want to leave you behind, hey?'

'Jack—'

'I'm going to make her beautiful again. I've checked online and there's a guy in Germany who sells parts—'

'Jack!'

'What? I thought you wanted me busy? Honestly, your moods, I can't keep up.' An edge now to his tone. 'You've got everything you wanted. Here we are in paradise and you're still not happy.'

'That's not true.'

'Look, I hear what you're saying about Pierre, and maybe you're right, on some level, but—'

'I am happy.'

'We can't manage this place alone. It's too big and he was thinking about us when he hired Pierre.'

'We don't know it's a *he*.'

'He, she, Marissa White's client, whoever. You've got to admit, we're struggling. We can't look after Bellay by ourselves.'

'They didn't even warn us. He just *turned* up. Isn't that weird? That wasn't part of the contract. I thought it was going to be just *us*.'

'I'm sure they had our best interests at heart when they brought him in. And yeah, Pierre might be a bit standoffish and he's not perfect, but he's lending a hand and it's not costing us a thing.'

Moving back into the light I watch as Jack picks up a tumbler of clear liquid. Ice clinks against the glass and I know it's a gin and tonic. I decide to leave it; last time I mentioned his drinking he ignored me for the entire day. I felt so lonely I almost called Erin. *Almost*.

But I couldn't face the interrogation. I wish Mum was here with us, I'm missing her more than Erin could ever know but we're locked into this agreement now and it doesn't feel as easy to break the rules as I first thought.

More recently I've been turning to Delphine for comfort.

She's a sweet girl from the local bakery – not someone I'd typically hang out with in England, but that's what's so nice about living abroad. You meet new people; you can reinvent yourself. She knows nothing about my past and she won't judge me for it.

I'm still getting to know her, and even though there's a jump in age between us, Delphine's a good listener and really seems to care. Weirdly, we chat like I used to with Erin. Back when Erin would listen and not judge.

I take a deep breath and plant my eyes on Jack's glass.

I wish he'd stop, it's the only hangover he's brought with him from England.

He takes another sip. 'Let's stop giving this guy such a hard time and' – he shrugs – 'try to be a bit more grateful for what he's doing.'

'I *am* grateful.' But my words sound brittle.

I feel a knot in my throat, I don't want us fighting. Not out here, where it's meant to be perfect.

'Come on, you.' He reaches for me again and this time I let his arms wrap around my waist. I feel a warmth spread as Jack takes me in, pulling me close to his chest. 'Relax, it'll all be fine. If he does it again, I'll have a word.'

His breath is acrid; stale, it's more than one drink. But I like the feeling of being held.

I nod slowly and smile. 'OK.'

'That's more like it.' He plants a kiss on my forehead. I can smell his suntan lotion now and I feel myself softening.

He holds me closer still, my Jack, the only person who really gets me. He's right, I sometimes feel overwhelmed and forget about the good stuff. I stop seeing the small things Jack does for me; the little shows of affection like hugging me as soon as he wakes up in the morning, keeping me warm like he is now.

'All right.' I kiss him. 'I just want everything to be . . . different from before.' Then I bury my face in his shoulder, packing away my mistrust.

Not wanting another run-in with Pierre just yet, I spend the next hour watching Jack loot cardboard boxes. Every time he pulls out an item, his eyes widen and excitement floods through him. He's like a kid at Christmas, and seeing him happy helps me forget my concerns.

Jack's a little envious when it's me who spots the treasure of the day – a long roll of parchment paper bound with ribbons at either end – pushed to the back of a metal cabinet. I pull it free and carry it underneath the light.

I slip off the ties and unroll it across a clear patch on the floor, pinning it down with pieces of broken brick.

It's hard to see in the low light but it looks like a map of some sort. Drawn in pencil, sketchy lines marked with measurements.

'What is it?'

'The original plan of the chateau,' Jack says over my shoulder.

'It doesn't look anything like it.'

'Look' – he crouches beside me, tracing his finger across the sun-worn paper – 'that's not there any more and a whole section's been added on here. *Incredible*,' he whispers.

'What's it doing down here?'

'Forgotten about, like everything else. Let's get this upstairs and take a better look. There might be parts we don't know about yet.'

'Like a secret room.'

'Exactly like that.' Jack grins.

CHAPTER THIRTEEN

ADELE

THREE MONTHS BEFORE NYE

YouTube
250,000 subscribers

Meet My New Best Friend

Hi my lovelies, I've nipped into town because it's market day and you need to see the community we've become part of.

(sweeps camera up and down the high street)

This place is ADORBS. It has everything you could possibly want: a butcher, pharmacy, bakery, a hairdresser – and there's a bar at the end of the town which Jack's already found. (little laugh – flips camera around and waves) Hiya, check out my beret. (points to head) I'm going to fit right in, aren't I?

So, Thursdays are farmers' market day, when all the locals crowd into the square and sell their produce. You can pick up cheeses and olives, merguez sausages – the skinny ones filled with herbs and spices – and, hey, have a look at this, there's an entire stall dedicated to sun-dried tomatoes. Ah, smell that (**points**) – there's a rotisserie van with whole roasted chickens and crispy potatoes, I think I've died and gone to heaven.

(**walks past fish stall**) Bonjour, monsieur!

(**he walks off camera**)

(**whispering**) They're all a bit shy around here.

And if we cross the square (**walks quickly – waves to several more stallholders**) we come to the butcher's. This is where I pick up Jack's steak. He says it's insanely tender, like nothing you'd buy in the supermarket in England.

(**pokes head around door**) Bonjour!

(**man in white overalls slips away**)

(**pulls face**) I guess vlogging is a tad unusual out here. They probably think, *Who's this lunatic?* Oh well, they'll get used to me soon enough. (**grin**) Let's try the boulangerie, (**walks next door**) because I know (**door jangles**) for a fact there is someone here who wants to say hi. Isn't that right. (**flips camera around**)

(**girl behind counter waves enthusiastically**) 'Salut!'

This lovely human is Delphine and isn't she the sweetest? (**puts arm around her**) You grew up here, in Rémy-Vienne, isn't that right?

'Oui! My whole life I've been here.'

THAT is adorable, I'm super close to my family too, it's the hardest thing about living out here. You're so lucky to live near everyone you care about . . . um . . . Anyway, I need to tell you guys a secret about Delphine. She's the master baker – isn't that right, girlfriend? She's responsible for those delicious-looking pastries I showed you in my last vlog.

'*Non!* (**blushes**) They are Madame Toussaint's.'
(**zooms in on Madame Toussaint, who smiles awkwardly**)
You're doing an epic job of feeding this town.
'*Merci.*' (**looks away shyly**)
(**Delphine hands over a bag of pastries**)
'What's this? You shouldn't have, babe! I'm going to balloon if I keep eating all these refined carbs, but thank you.'

(**waves**) Have a wonderful day, lovelies, and I'll see you tomorrow. (**leaves bakery**)

Guys, you can see why I've fallen in love with this place, can't you? There's something special about it: the people are kind, they're generous – it's everything I manifested. A close-knit community where your neighbour actually cares. I get the feeling the people here keep an eye out for each other. What's not to like about that?

(**roots around in paper bag, pulls out a mille-feuille and takes a bite**)

More from me next time. (**wipes vanilla cream from face**)

Love you all so SO much! Oh, and don't forget to like and subscribe!

CHAPTER FOURTEEN

TRIXYLADY99 Active one minute ago

You're no better than a prostitute sharing everything about yourself on the internet. Flaunting what you've got, thinking everyone cares. You're a whore, Adele Davenport. Your mum's so ashamed of you she wants to kill herself.

CHAPTER FIFTEEN

ERIN

EIGHT DAYS AFTER NYE

Leftover Christmas decorations waiting to be taken down blink lazily. Bleached-out buildings with broken shutters make up this easily forgotten street. In the cold light even the snow appears grey. The only flash of colour in Rémy-Vienne is the pharmacy sign, green lights chasing each other around a cross.

Last night's scare still rattles around inside me and the vision of the man in the snow won't leave my thoughts. Who was he? Why was he watching me? I didn't sleep after that. I spent the hours until sunrise securing the chateau, battening down the hatches. Nailing pieces of wood to the window I broke in through.

And now, I'm here, in the only town for miles around. Exhausted.

The high street's deserted. It's almost too quiet and there's a heaviness about it. I can't put my finger on it, but it feels like a town in mourning. I park in the square – a shabby arrangement of broken stones and trees pruned to look amputated. There's angry graffiti carved into the stumps and a laminated missing person's poster nailed into the bark. A black-and-white image of a teenage girl. Beautiful but ghostly looking, like she was crying when the photo was taken. I move away from her face and the sad feeling it's giving me.

I've come to Rémy-Vienne for answers. If there's one place someone would have seen Adele, it's here.

There's a queue spilling out of the boulangerie onto the pavement. The old man in front wearing a quilted jacket cradles a small wiry dog underneath his arm. He gives me an unfriendly look before heading inside. I catch the door before it closes in my face.

The jangle of the bell over the door is followed by a rush of heat and the smell of freshly baked bread, warm salty pastry and vanilla sugar. A woman tips a tray of croissants onto the counter. The heat mushrooms up to the glass, clouding it with heat.

'Bonjour,' she says cheerfully.

She's everything you'd expect from a village boulangerie – round, plaited greying hair and rosy cheeks with a light dusting of flour. She reminds me of the brioches in the window.

'*Que désirez-vous?*' Her voice has a sing-song way about it that instantly puts me at ease. Finally, a friendly face. Someone approachable in this vast cold landscape.

In my best French I ask for a croissant and then a baguette, and as she's dropping them into a paper bag I ask about my sister.

At first, I think she didn't hear over the hum of the ovens and the whirring of the kitchen, but when I repeat the words Adele, Jack and Chateau Bellay I notice her falter as she knots the bag. She hands it to me with a tense smile.

'Pardon, but, erm, do you know Adele? She lives in the chateau' – I turn and point into the distance, which is ridiculous, but something about her has made me uneasy and awkward.

Her smile tightens. Then she hands me my change.

'Adele Davenport?' I enunciate. Maybe she didn't understand.

She blinks. I try a final time in my bad French and she cuts me off.

'I can't help you.'

Wow – her English is perfect.

Another customer walks in and she moves her attention away. I clear my throat.

'Pardon, madame, if you know something—' I feel myself losing patience.

She's moving around more quickly, keeping busy. A teenager emerges from the back room, giggling at something on her phone. She slips it into her apron pocket and folds her long hair into a net, preparing for her shift.

'*Qu'est-ce qu'on vous sert?*' Her smile for me is wide and warm. Her French accent, soft. She's model pretty with hazel eyes outlined in thick grungy black liner. Her skin is flawless except for the slight flush of heat from standing near the ovens. In a small community like this, she certainly stands out.

'Maybe you can help me?' I say quickly.

I notice the older woman falter. She gives the girl a sharp look but it goes unnoticed.

'You're English?' The teenager's eyes flash.

'Yes, I was hoping you could answer some questions about—'

'Tell me, is London as beautiful as in the movies?' She sighs dramatically. 'I want to visit so badly. I plan to study music and theatre – my dream is to star in the West End.' She gives the older woman a look and lowers her voice. 'When I get out of this shithole, I'm going to be famous!' A grin lights her face, then she stops and frowns, studying me more closely. 'You look really familiar.'

'I do?'

'We don't get many tourists in Rémy-Vienne.' Her voice is heavily accented but girly. 'Are you on holidays?'

'I'm looking for Adele Davenport. Red hair, petite, sporty-looking – she moved into the chateau with her partner Jack just over four months ago.'

Her face lights up.

'*Mais oui*, they come every morning.'

Finally.

Then I notice how the older woman is tensing. Listening in while she serves.

'She's lovely and so pretty!' The girl's eyes sparkle. Adele has that effect on people, and I feel a pinch of jealousy.

'They all make fun of me around here for liking nineties rock music, but Adele reassured me it's OK to be different. And she listens to it too.'

'I didn't even know she listened to rock.' I feel a blunt pain in my chest. There's much about Adele I don't know. 'When did you last see her?'

The girl screws her face up as she searches her memory. 'Not sure. Before the party, I think.'

'The party?'

'Delphine!' the older woman hisses.

'New Year's Eve, at the chateau—'

The baker stands between us, severing our conversation. She whispers to the girl in French and they speak quickly. It sounds urgent and threatening.

I notice the red flush that's worked its way up the girl's neck.

'What New Year's party?' I say again.

The girl turns to the display, rearranging the cakes.

'My sister's missing, if you know something . . .' *Missing.* Saying the word out loud gives me a start.

Delphine turns and stares at me for a long moment. A look of shock crossing her features. Then she hurries into the back room.

'Hey!' I call after her.

'She's busy,' the older woman says coldly. 'You have what you need, now leave.'

The door jangles and an old lady tugging a trolley bag shuffles in. The baker recovers her cheery smile. 'Salut!'

My stomach tightens. Why are they being so cagey? What party? I think back to the last message I got from Adele. If my sister had had a NYE party, she'd have sent more than a heart emoji, surely? Or maybe not, if she felt bad for not inviting me.

I peer into the back room but the girl has disappeared. I cast the older woman an angry glare and then leave.

Returning to the empty street I've never felt so lonely. Everything about this place feels otherworldly. I've always done well travelling alone, I went interrailing around Europe when I finished university and I got by just fine, but here, nothing makes sense. It's as if the place has a language of its own.

It must be the tiredness kicking in, the long drive and the broken night's sleep.

The worry over Mum and how time is running out. That'll be it.

Although, I know that's not it. I'm not sure I've slept properly in weeks with the worry of everything I'm facing back home. I've been waking up in hot sweats. Fear finds you in the quiet of the night when it knows you can't escape.

I can hear the roar of the alarm. The panicked scream across the hospital ward. His skin turning blue. I bite down on my lip, jamming the memory back inside its box. I need to focus on finding Adele.

I look across, studying the facades, the forlorn row of shops, and it reminds me of a Western film: bleached-out, abandoned. I have no idea where to ask next and the thought of it exhausts me. I wrap my coat more tightly around me but the chill has already found its way inside.

'Psst, madame.'

It's so soft I don't hear it at first.

'Adele's sister, over here.'

There's an alley that passes between the bakery and a bar. Narrow and dark, it smells of bins and other things.

I notice the yellow stains where urine has melted into the snow.

The teenager from the boulangerie is waiting for me there, shivering despite her shearling coat. Under her apron she's wearing ripped black tights and biscuit-coloured Ugg boots. She holds a cigarette down by her side.

'I can't talk for long.' She looks over her shoulder. 'We must be quick.'

She moves closer, the smell of smoke filling the space between us.

'You didn't tell me you were Adele's sister.' She studies me closely. Her expression is different from earlier. 'Don't let Madame Toussaint upset you – they're all the same around here. Nobody likes it when you talk about the chateau. It has a bad reputation.'

'Reputation?'

She hesitates.

'The things that went on there.' The girl checks behind her again.

'I don't understand.'

'They say your sister brought back the curse.'

'The curse?' I laugh nervously.

'Don't worry, they're all stupid around here.'

This sounds absurd. 'What can you tell me about the party?' I say more sharply.

'Please, forget the party.'

'But there was a party at Adele's chateau?'

'I shouldn't have said anything.'

'On New Years' Eve?'

She looks nervous and shakes her head.

'And my sister was there? And Jack?'

She stares at me wide-eyed, her face becoming increasingly strained. I feel a flare of anger. Frustration.

'You called me over here, so . . . what did you have to say?'

I notice that she's not shivering but trembling. Visibly shaking like a frightened little girl. And there's something else – a vulnerability.

I know because I recognize it in myself. The burden I've carried with me to France. That *thing* that, when I'm not thinking about Mum or my sister, comes to get me. A constant heaviness in my chest.

I ease off.

'If there was a party, Adele would have vlogged it,' I say more gently.

'There's more to Adele than people think,' she says defensively.

'You seem to be close to her. Maybe there's something—'

Delphine glances behind again as if expecting someone to appear.

'Listen' – she looks at me with a sudden intensity – 'you must stop asking questions. It's not safe.'

'Not safe?' The words shoot out.

'Oui,' she whispers. 'I came here to warn you.'

'Warn me?'

'I like your sister, I want to be your friend,' she says. 'But you must go. These people, they don't like you asking questions.'

'Who?'

There's a slam from behind. The echo of a bin snapping shut. Someone making themselves heard.

'Who are *they*?' I feel my eyes flaring, my voice breaking. 'Is someone threatening you? Don't be frightened, I can help.'

Her boss appears and I watch the girl stiffen.

'Please, it's very important I speak with Adele, if there's anything you know—' I stop. 'What aren't you telling me?' I can pay you . . .'

Her eyes spark.

'OK, you need money? That's fine, you only needed to say.' I reach into my bag for my purse.

'Delphine!' the woman shouts.

'Who are *they*?'

'Adele would want you to leave.' Delphine touches my hand. 'I have to go.'

'*J'arrive*,' she tells her boss, tossing her cigarette to the snow. I can feel the old lady's eyes stalking me until she follows the girl back inside.

CHAPTER SIXTEEN

ADELE

TWO MONTHS BEFORE NYE

We've gone over the drawings so many times this past month but it's still impossible to make head or tail of the measurements. They date back to 1775 and the markings are sketchy, faded, the lines half rubbed out. Jack's given up and tells me to stop wasting precious time but I'm determined, I *will* find something I can vlog about.

I need fresh content for my subscribers, which is becoming increasingly difficult to come by since I can't film any renovation work. Who knew being an influencer would be so exhausting – it's become a full-time job. I love it though. Mostly because I'm struggling to make friends out here and it feels like my online community are the only people who give a damn.

There are still the trolls and the haters, but you get them everywhere. At first, I'd leave their comments up but recently I've been deleting them. They're becoming abusive. Really vicious. Saying I'm worthless, or even going as far as telling me I should kill myself.

I push away the panic. Scrunching up my eyes, opening them.

It's still there. That feeling. *I mustn't let them get to me.*

Questions about Mum are the hardest to ignore. Those who remember my GoFundMe vlog are still asking why she hasn't come to France. Jack told me to lie but some of these fans know more than they should about my life, and I worry they'll catch me out.

I'm also constantly panicking that Marissa White is checking I'm not breaking the rules, which is why I've become fearful of letting Mum visit. Jack says I'm paranoid, maybe I am, I'm more on edge than normal. I can't shake the feeling I'm being watched. Crazy, I know.

Jack's gone into Chalon-sur-Saône to speak to the bank, something about setting up a business account. There's been another donation from our mystery benefactor. I'm still trying to get my head around this cash flow. Neither of us can quite believe it, which is why Jack's checking there's not been some glitch.

He'll no doubt use the time away to drop in at the bar for a drink and a smoke. Jack gave up years ago, but I found a packet of cigarettes in his jeans pocket when I was searching for his phone. An old habit of mine that I can't shake – checking his messages.

It feels like he's changing but I daren't bring it up. I don't want to sound naggy or like I'm spying on him.

It's a half-hour drive to Chalon-sur-Saône, so while he's

gone, I've returned to the past. Poring over the plan which I've rolled across the kitchen table.

The drawing is split into top and ground floor, the height and width of the rooms are marked in old metric. *Pieds*, feet and *ponce*, inches. Some rooms have seen vast extension over the years, whereas others have shrunk – like the grand ballroom where the parties would have taken place, which is now a games room.

I trace my finger across the rough paper that's yellowed with age. Over the old lines, reaching into the past. The tower seems the obvious place to start, somewhere you'd expect a secret room or a hidden escape passage into the main house. But no, the only door leading in and out is the original seventeenth-century oak one that takes you into the courtyard.

Where then? My history is embarrassingly poor. My knowledge of my own chateau, abysmal. Some of my viewers have been sending in weird stories about the previous owners, but I ignore them. More trolling. Positive vibes only. And I like not knowing too much about the past; that way I can make Bellay my own. It's the small things that count now.

Hmm, where would I build a secret room? I return to the map of the ground floor, comparing past to present.

Not even the library, where you might expect a hidden door in the bookcase, has any promising areas on the plan. I sit back heavily. This is stupid, something you only see in the movies. Maybe there isn't a secret anything because, if there was, we would have found it by now.

My jaw clenches. I snatch up the plan under my arm and take it with me upstairs.

*

From the landing window I have a clear view over the west side of the chateau where the woods are advancing, the grass is long and wild and there's an abandoned chicken coop. Nearby are several old barns which we still can't find the keys to open. That's where I see Pierre. I feel prickle of heat when I notice he's on the phone, again.

He turns his head; his coarse features seem to have sharpened since I last saw him. His brow is furrowed and his mouth is moving quickly. He's locked in a heated conversation.

I'm reminded of how unnaturally he behaves. A simmering anger, as if he's irritated by being out in nature. Which makes me more suspicious of why he's here. Jack's fed up of hearing me complain, so I don't bring Pierre up any more, but I can't shake the feeling our so-called gardener isn't who or what he says he is.

I move from the spill of sunlight into the shadow of the corridor. The faces of the past observing me from their gilded frames. If I had a choice, those ugly Bellay family portraits would be the first to go. There's so much about this house I would change. It's the nonsensical rules, the controlling ones, that get to me the most about our arrangement. Cracks keep appearing in our new life here, or maybe I'm noticing them more now.

Only when I'm tired though. I breathe out heavily. Aside from that, everything is perfect. Jack's right, we're living the dream, I mustn't sweat the small things.

Opening the parchment wide in my arms, I try again. My eyes slip between the historic outlines and what I have to work with now.

I will not give up.

Reaching the room at the end of the corridor I turn the key, unlocking our mystery investor's room. I notice a veil of dust has collected on the surfaces. I should really give this place a clean, although, is there any point? It's sitting here unused like a museum piece. The thought makes me shiver and I cross into the small adjoining room, which, by the looks of the map, was once a nursery.

I swallow hard as another empty feeling creeps in. I quickly look around at what I'd hoped Jack and I would be decorating by now, and then close the door behind me, my heart feeling a little heavier.

I'm suddenly overcome by tiredness and my body pulls me back to our bedroom. I lower myself onto the bed, exhausted. Defeat washes over me, and there's something else too – that thing I'm fighting to block out.

Doubt – about whether I've done the right thing moving here.

I hate being alone in the chateau. There, I said it. I'll never admit it to Jack though. Can you imagine? I wouldn't hear the end of it. But I can't keep running from the feeling. There's something about the lofty rooms full of objects I can't connect with, and the echoes, the noises I don't quite understand. And then there's Pierre, always lurking. It's starting to get to me, this feeling that I'm a stranger in my own home.

And I don't know if I'm imagining it, but things keep going missing. I could have sworn I brought over my black silk shirt from England, but I can't find it anywhere. And then there's the Mickey Mouse nightie Dad got me on our holiday in Florida. One of my last happy memories of us as a family. Vanished.

Shaking my head, I try loosening the negativity. Hashtag *gratitude*, I remind myself. We were so rushed leaving England, I probably put it into storage by mistake.

According to the plan, I'm in one of the oldest rooms, the original beating heart of the chateau. Our en suite is much newer – renovated from a dressing room, perhaps.

I follow the lines with my finger and stop.

Hang on. Something doesn't add up. I run over them again, but the numbers still don't make any sense. According to the dimensions, our bathroom should be bigger. So, where's the missing space gone?

With a surge of renewed energy, I push off the bed to investigate.

Our bathroom is small in comparison to others in chateau (though at least three times the size of the one we had back in England). The decoration is in keeping with the refurbishment. Less cluttered, with only a mock Venetian mirror above the sink and a bath with copper feet. The walls are white and bare, and I run my hand across the one which, according to the map, shouldn't be there. I give it a knock, like they do in the movies. It doesn't sound different. There's no hollow noise to indicate anything lies behind it.

I laugh at myself.

Returning to my bed, I sit down heavily. *What a waste of an afternoon.*

I stare into the bedroom, my eyes fixing on the modern-looking wardrobe pressed up against the wall. Only now does it occur to me: why, in a room full of antiques and heirlooms, would anyone install a brown lacquered monstrosity from the 1960s?

Pulling open the doors, I reach through the wall of clothes until my hand makes contact with something hard. To my surprise, it's not the wooden backing of the wardrobe. It's the original fabric wallpaper, dating back to the eighteenth century.

I grab an armful of hangers, slinging Jack's shirts across the bed. Then another and another, until I've emptied out the entire contents.

I try knocking on the wall but there's nothing unusual about the sound.

I step back, running my hands through my hair. *I'm going mad. The isolation is turning me into a lunatic.*

Yet, something won't stop niggling. I turn on my phone's torch and go in for a final inspection.

The wallpaper is damaged. A brown water stain has bled up from the floor, which explains why the wardrobe has been placed there to hide it. But, what's this?

I aim the light a little lower.

There, where the gold thread meets the blue, is a hairline fracture. I follow the crack, tracing around the outline, feeling an opening of some kind. It's a door – a very small one.

Adrenaline fires into my veins. The viewers are going to LOVE this.

There's no handle or anything to grab hold of, so I try pushing instead. The door is heavy and stubborn and refuses to budge. I throw all my weight behind it, forcing my shoulder up against it until the sound of stone grinding against stone fills the space around me.

The door releases with a sigh, as if it's been holding its breath all this time. As the gap widens, the smell of musty air and damp rush towards me, flooding my senses. My heart is drumming as I peer into the hole. A pit of darkness.

This is a terrible idea.

It could be centuries old. What if the tunnel collapses?

Then I think about my vlog, about Jack. You want to impress them, don't you, Adele?

I drop to all fours, using my phone to guide me through the passage. The surface is uneven; hard abrasive edges graze my knees as I crawl through solid stone, emerging into a dome-shaped chamber. An airless, windowless pocket buried deep within the old walls.

A new smell fills up my lungs, something much more acrid, and I'm coughing as I arrive. It is so cold I can see my breath in the torchlight and the walls are icy to the touch. What is this place?

The ceiling is high enough for me to stand up, but still the room feels like a tomb. I read somewhere once about rich aristocrats having secret rooms to hide their lovers from their wives, but this doesn't look like the sort of place you'd want to have sex. Being in here would feel more like a punishment.

With walls this thick, at least a metre deep, nobody would hear if you were trapped inside. I cast a tense look around, my mouth suddenly turning dry.

As I slide the torchlight up the exposed bricks, it catches on two metal rings. Attached to the wall and evenly spaced apart. They're rusty and worn, and beneath are scratches, deep grooves caused by some sort of repetitive movement. My eyes move slowly down to meet the floor: thick slabs of stone, gently sloping into the centre where there's a drain.

My skin prickles.

Aiming the light to one side, it lands on a piece of old wood with three long rusty nails. I kick it away. Then I falter, sweeping the torch back over where I've just been. The weak arc of light catches on something else.

I kneel to get a better look, tilting my head to one side so my eyes line up with the ground. It had been concealed beneath the wood, too small to notice unless you were searching carefully.

All my hairs stand on end.

Carved into the old stone floor – the word HELP.

CHAPTER SEVENTEEN

ERIN

EIGHT DAYS AFTER NYE

Beer mats hang on the walls like medals of honour. It's the first thing I notice when I walk into Fredy Brasserie.

The tiny bar-cum-pub feels like it's collapsing under the weight of the collection of beer mats, the trinkets, the bad watercolour paintings. There are some black-and-white framed photos of a young farmers' club by the bar, next to a small TV with the football on mute.

The furniture looks like it's been picked up at the local market. I slide into a reclaimed church pew. The back is uncomfortably upright, the pitted seat strewn with circular cushions covered with fabric from the seventies.

It's one of two pubs in the town, the one I'm told all the locals frequent. I look around; if there was a party, someone here must know about it.

A couple of wall lamps with orange shades push out an amber glow. The air feels thick with the past. All sense of time is lost in here; it could be morning or night, the place is so gloomy you'd never know.

The clientele give off an equally depressing energy. Mostly crumpled-looking men, shoulder to shoulder at the bar. Talking in low conspiratorial whispers, throwing me looks.

The foreigner. An outsider. Is it that obvious I'm not from around here?

The landlady catches my eye and gives me a nod. She's wearing pillar-box-red lipstick, her hair a mess of tight ringlets that drop past her shoulders. Dark and mysterious looking.

She smiles. 'I'll be with you in just a sec.'

She's sexy, in an undone way, and her bold lipstick tells me she doesn't care what other people think. I wish I had her confidence.

She heads over and reaches across my table. Hair falls across her thick-framed glasses. Her tunic top hangs loose over her jeans. A simple chain and a locket around her neck. Bright gold against her peach freckled skin.

'What brings you out here?' she says, producing a stained rag.

'You're Scottish?'

She lifts the salt and pepper pots, wiping underneath. 'Aye, Glasgow born and raised. It's Iona, by the way.'

I look back to the eyes watching us from the bar: 'What made you move out here? This place feels a bit out the way.'

'I didn't come for the countryside.'

I look at her.

'A man.' She sighs and wipes the table down some more. 'Chasing after some guy, story of my life. If only I'd had my crystal ball back then, I could have read what an utter arse he'd turn out to be.' She meets my gaze and laughs. 'Don't worry, lovie, I'm not a white witch – if only!' More quietly, she echoes. '*If only.*'

'Sounds like there's a spell you'd like to cast?'

She laughs. 'Anyway, didn't work out so I found myself here.'

'It's your bar?'

'Manage it for a French couple who're never here.' She straightens, tucking the wet rag into her back pocket. It hangs like a workman's tool. What can I do you for?'

'Information—' I stop. Taken aback by my abruptness. 'Sorry, that sounded rude. I need a bit of help, if that's OK.'

She raises an eyebrow. 'And a drink, I hope. Nothing around here is for free, lassie.'

'Right.' I glance over the laminated menu again. 'Just a coffee then.'

Her eyes pinch with annoyance.

'Won't be a minute.' Iona takes the menu from me and heads back behind the bar. She laughs along with the men, chatting in French while stabbing her thumb on the automatic coffee machine. The gurgle and spitting noise pushes through the din.

As I watch her, I find myself wondering who the guy was, what did he do to break her heart? I closed off my feelings years ago, nothing slips through the wall I've so carefully built up around me. I did allow myself to go on a date a few months ago, but he made excuses after the first couple of drinks – as I knew he would. Adele's never had to deal with that aching feeling – rejection. It's not just the chateau; everything comes easy to her.

My fingers stray to my coat button and I begin the comfort rub. Back and forth across the smooth surface, the sensation anchoring me in the present. That thing I've been blocking out is rearing its head again and if I keep rubbing, if I just can keep present, focused on Mum and Adele, it will go away. I think about what the girl in the bakery said instead. *Curse*. What a load of mumbo jumbo. But she was frightened of something or someone.

There's a rapturous cheer. The French team have scored.

The landlady frowns with concentration as she carries the cup and saucer over to me. She places it carefully on the table.

'Here you go, hen.' She steps back. 'You look like you've got a load on your mind. Go on, a problem shared . . .'

I stir in the sugar, avoiding her eyes. 'Everything's great, I'm holidaying in the area.' I hate myself for lying and I've never been good at it. But it might get me closer to the truth. 'Just dropping in on an old friend – Adele Davenport. Do you know her?'

She looks at me.

'She wasn't home when I stopped by, and I don't want to miss her after coming all this way. Have you seen her?'

She shakes her head. 'But it's her fella that comes in here, not her.'

'Jack?'

There. That smile. The same look all the women seem to find when they talk about Jack. Her eyes are almost iridescent, and I feel a stab of anger for my sister. Surely, he hasn't cheated with Iona too?

She places a hand to her hip. Shifting her weight across.

'Thought you were the police there for a moment, hen.' She grins. 'A plain-clothes officer trying to catch me out for something or other. I'm always getting headache from them, being blamed for customers' drink driving.' She nods to the bar. 'Everyone around here does it though, living in the middle of bleedin' nowhere.'

'So, Jack comes here a lot then?'

She laughs. 'Those types always do.'

'Those types?'

'Likes a drink or two. Addictive personality. He has that something about him. You get to know the type, working in a place like this.'

I frown.

'Doesn't know when to stop. You know? He was sat just there' – she nods to the stool nearest the TV. 'Bought the entire bar a round after he won money on the football. Didn't know when to leave it that night. Had to remind him he had a chateau to go home to.'

'And a partner,' I add.

She smiles and nods. 'That too.'

I swallow down my irritation.

'When was that then?'

'Haven't heard a peep out of him since.' She looks up, searching her memory. 'We're going back to before New Year's now. He was here with a woman I didn't recognize.

She looked like she might have been from out of town. But then I guess that's not surprising since Jack owns a chateau and hobnobs with those rich types. The woman he was with reminded me of the sort I'd see Laurent Bellay with when he used to come in here – that was before the . . . Well, you know.' She stops. There's a tightening of her expression.

Laurent Bellay? He must be linked to the chateau.

'So, do you know when that was?'

She scrunches up her face, thinking it over. 'Sorry, can't help you, lassie.'

'Was there a party at the chateau for New Year's?'

She shrugs.

'What about this woman Jack was with? Can you describe her?'

She eyes me suspiciously. 'I can pass on a message for you, when he's next in.'

'That's OK.'

'Suit yourself.' She stares at my cup. 'That'll be all then?'

I quickly drain the last of my coffee.

'Thanks again for your help.' I stand to leave.

She watches me pass, but it's not just her; I feel the eyes of the entire pub staring. A silence descends as I weave through the tightly packed furniture.

I don't realize I've been holding my breath until I return to the cold. Even the sting in the frost feels like a release.

My head is whirring with thoughts of Jack. Gambling – does Adele know? Meeting a mysterious woman, sounds about right. But it's more than that. Something felt wrong.

There was a tension about the place. The people. It feels like the town is closing ranks on me.

As if they have a secret they're hiding.

CHAPTER EIGHTEEN

NOW

Sky News

Kate, any more on the actual chateau?

Not a lot but what we can tell you is it dates back to the seventeenth century and was previously owned by the prestigious Bellay family, spanning several centuries. Originally it was a hunting retreat for the French royals and aristocrats, a holiday home away from the bustle of Paris.

It became famous for its lavish parties, in particular the New Year's Eve masked ball.

The chateau was handed down from generation to generation, remaining within the Bellay family until only recently. It went on the market in March last year, shortly after the last surviving heir was found dead.

Found dead?

Laurent Bellay was found drowned in his pool by his housekeeper. The forty-five-year-old was known as a socialite and well connected in political and celebrity circles. He was discovered face down, and toxicology reports showed that he'd consumed a large quantity of drugs and alcohol. It's understood no suspicious circumstances were involved.

How tragic for the family.

Indeed, Justine, it really is. Some of the more superstitious residents in the local area say the chateau is cursed. The mystery surrounding the disappearance of the new owners has only helped cement that feeling.

A curse, now I've heard it all! Thanks, Kate. We'll have more on the Chateau Bellay disappearances soon. Moving on to our next story tonight . . .

CHAPTER NINETEEN

ERIN

EIGHT DAYS AFTER NYE

Someone's following me.

I stop and turn but no one's there. *Jeez*, I let out a nervous laugh and carry on walking to my car. But within seconds, the noise starts up again. Footsteps in the snow, the crunch of someone marching to keep up with me, and now there's a presence, I feel it creeping up behind.

I pick up the pace, taking larger strides, past the line of shops, the hardware store. I step out suddenly, boldly, into the road. As soon as I reach the pavement on the other side I turn around and there's a clanging from the nearby side alley. A shadow disappearing along the wall and the echo of feet fading into the distance.

There *was* someone.

I clutch my heart as if it's about to shoot out of me.

Who would be following me? The man from last night? I break into a run, sprinting back to my car and as soon as I'm inside I lock all the doors, my breath, jagged and painful. I try inhaling deeply but it doesn't work.

Now would be a good time to go to the police. Something's wrong. *This doesn't feel right.*

But tell them what? That my sister's not answering her phone? That there's a funny smell in her chateau?

And with everything that's happened to me back in the UK, I can't afford to draw more attention to myself. But maybe I have no choice?

My eyes rake over the town square, moving across the buildings, between the cars, checking that whoever was following me isn't still hiding there. My body is tightly sprung like a trap.

I feel another twinge in my chest as I think about the way the chateau appeared when I arrived, with no trace of Adele or Jack. And now there's the suggestion of a New Year's party.

My job as a nurse has taught me how to read people and I've become an expert at picking up on the nuances, the slightest change in expression or tone. Both the pub landlady and the woman in the bakery couldn't look me in the eye. They're hiding something.

What the teenager said keeps turning over in my head. The secret history of Bellay. Some curse. A New Year's Eve party at my sister's chateau? It doesn't add up. She seemed frightened to be seen talking to me. But why?

Nobody wants to help. Worse – I'm being made to feel unwelcome. That I should stop asking questions and leave.

I fish out my phone and search through Adele's social

media again. The last time she posted a vlog on YouTube was a few days after Christmas. TikTok, Facebook, the same. Instagram – the day before New Year's Eve. I click on the photo, pinch-zooming on her face. The over-stretched smile, the posing by the Christmas tree. The forced happiness.

That tells me nothing – except – Adele hasn't been active on social media for nine days, which is odd for her. And if she'd thrown a party – there's no question she'd have vlogged it. Adele, missing an opportunity to show off her ball gown? No chance. So maybe there wasn't a party and I'm being dragged into small-town gossip. These locals are probably jealous of her and want me gone.

I send her another message. Something angry:

WHERE ARE YOU?! There's an emergency with Mum.
I NEED you to call me.

The inside of the car is spinning – a sure sign my sugar levels are dropping. I reach for the croissant and take several large bites. The pastry is crisp and buttery, and I chomp on it so aggressively I feel full in seconds. It does nothing to calm my mind and the whirring starts up again.

This time, it's Jack.

They could have had a fight and Adele's taken off. I remember what Iona, the pub landlady, revealed about Jack and the *way* she said it, with that lustful gaze.

But Adele would call me if she found out he did it again. She'd want me to help. Wouldn't she?

I give my head a little shake as if that will bring all the pieces into place.

It is *very Adele* to take off with no thought for anyone else. She's done it before. She could be away filming content. Somewhere glamorous and interesting to match her shiny new life. She'll be back soon.

I sink back into the seat. An uneasy feeling growing.

Nothing adds up. *Nothing.* Am I overreacting, or is something genuinely wrong? So much has changed this past year, I'm not sure what's even normal for my sister any more. Old Adele would let me know if she was going away, she would have told me about a party. She may not have invited me, but it wouldn't be a secret. And old Adele would never have stopped Mum from visiting. She might behave selfishly at times but she loves Mum to pieces. This new Adele, I don't recognize.

The car window mists, my anxiety eating what's left of the oxygen. I switch on the engine and warm air charges at my face. It feels overwhelming. I'm having a heightened sensory episode and I need to calm down. Especially after what happened at the hospital, I can't let it happen again. Ever. I see his face, lips turning blue, the screech of the alarms.

Take a step back and breathe.

Adele will be back soon.

Exhale.

We'll be home with Mum soon.

Inhale.

Within the stillness, the image of the diamond earrings reappears. Glittering in the palm of my hand, they're the ones I found by the entrance to Bellay. The sort of thing you'd wear to a ball.

I feel a bolt of adrenaline. Fear has taken root and it's impossible to shake off, not until I know for certain everything is OK.

I need to go to the police.

I pull the seat belt across. As I twist back to face the front I nearly jump out of my skin. There's an old man standing there. Stooped over, peering inside my car.

I wait for him to move on, but he continues to study me and the inside of my car.

Slipping the window down, I notice he's younger than I first thought, maybe forty-five. A thick brush of prematurely grey hair that shines like silver, and his olive skin glows brightly against the cold light. By his side is a black-and-white spaniel, tugging on its lead impatiently.

'Can I help?'

'Madame Davenport's sister?' he says in heavily accented English.

'Yeah,' I say more tightly.

'She left this behind.' Now I notice the sports bag he's holding. He hands it to me and the dog follows it with shiny eyes.

'They forgot to take it with them when they came to collect your sister's things. I found it in the wardrobe.'

'Sorry, who are you?'

'It looks expensive, not something you'd want to leave behind.'

Frowning, my eyes travel from the bag to him and back again. Taking it into my lap, I unzip it. Sequins catch the light, sparkling like a bagful of diamonds. Carefully I lift it out and the heavy material drops, unspooling into the footwell. Revealing itself. A floor-length red dress. Something you'd only wear to a ball.

I breathe in sharply.

'We run the B & B – Jeanette's.' He points up the street. 'My wife and I have been owners for more than twenty-five years.' I hear the pride in his voice.

I frown. 'Adele was staying at a B & B?' Then I laugh. 'You do realize she lives here, in Chateau Bellay?'

He smiles and lowers his voice. '*Bien sûr!* When the chateau went on the market, we were all so excited, hoping for a family, children to breathe new life into the place, especially after—' He stops and clears his throat. 'Pardon, I didn't mean that to sound like we were disappointed. It's been nice welcoming your sister into our town.'

Our town. This place is starting to sound like a cult.

'I tried returning it, but no one was home. Then when I heard Adele's sister had arrived, I realized that was the easiest solution.'

Eyes everywhere. I wonder if that's how Adele feels, living here?

And I still can't wrap my head around the news Adele spent a night in a B & B. Had she and Jack had a fight after all?

'Was she alone?' I ask.

'They were both staying with us.'

'She was with Jack?' I check.

'Oui.'

'It was definitely my sister?'

'Maybe a romantic gesture, a night away from home?' He smiles suggestively.

I run my hand through my hair anxiously. 'Let me get this right, they checked out the next day but Adele forgot her dress?'

'Non, non, the men who came to collect their things left her dress.'

WHAT?

'What men? When was this?' My head is spinning.

He gives his head a little shake as if loosening a memory. 'Seven in the morning – they woke us. *Merde*, my wife and I were still sleeping, we thought nobody would be up that early on New Year's Day.'

I turn the fabric over in my hands. The sequins pricking my skin. Why would Adele check into a B & B around the corner from her home on New Year's Eve? Why would she have packed a dress? So there must have been a party? But why wasn't she home for it? And why, WHY did someone else come to check Adele and Jack out of their room?

'Tell me more about these men.'

'City boys, wearing sunglasses indoors.' He shunts air through his nose. 'Miserable and rude – they didn't even wish us *une bonne année*!'

'So, when did you last see my sister?'

'When they checked in on the thirty-first. Maybe four in the afternoon.'

'You didn't see Adele again after that?'

'We were at the pub, celebrating.'

'So where did they go?' It comes out more aggressively than I intended.

He steps back.

RUTH KELLY

'Madame, I'm not sure I can help you further.' He turns, showing me he's about to leave.

'Please.' I stop, I take a breath. 'Is there anything else you remember? Even if it seems insignificant.'

He eyes me warily, then shakes his head. The dog whines.

'I'm glad I was able to return the dress. Pass on my regards.'

Anger surges. What's wrong with these people?

'Did she say she was going anywhere?' I bite down on my lip, holding on to my frustration.

The dog whimpers and pulls at his lead.

'Good luck with everything.' He backs away, hunching into his coat. Behaving as if he'd said too much already.

'Please!' I cry out, surprising myself at how desperate I sound. The feeling of helplessness grabs me by my throat. I glare at him, full of hate. Then, almost as if he felt it, he makes a surprise turn, looking around, eyes sweeping up and down the road.

He walks quickly back to my car and leans in, closer than I'm comfortable with. His voice right in my ear.

'Just so you know, I never believed the things they were saying about your sister.'

He nods and moves away.

My breath catches.

'What things?'

But he's too far away, already disappearing, the sound of slush crunching under his boots.

CHAPTER TWENTY

ADELE

TWO MONTHS BEFORE NYE

I scramble to my feet but the shock of what I've found has turned my legs to jelly. My phone clatters to the ground. I hear the screen crack but the torch is still working, there's still a tiny glow of light.

Lunging into the inky black, I snatch it into my hand and crawl backwards. Alarm bells clanging in my head while the raw stone lances my palms and knees. I can't get out of that hole quick enough.

HELP. The word burning in my thoughts.

Someone had been trapped inside. Desperate to get out. My breath halts as an even more terrifying thought takes hold. Was somebody locked up there? Like a prisoner?

I'm moving with such speed, such force, as I squeeze through the gap it sends me tumbling backwards into our bedroom.

As if all the energy has been sucked from me, I lie still,

flat on my back. Fighting for air as I try to calm my heart and process what I've just seen.

The writing could be centuries old. A child playing hide and seek. Some sort of prank. A joke. It could mean anything.

HELP.

Yet the distance of time passing doesn't make it any easier. Whether it was a hundred years ago or ten minutes, the feeling I got from being inside there was the same. A vibration, humming off those walls, I felt it. Something bad happened inside that room.

Fuck.

My heart is thumping so violently I don't hear his footsteps. I barely acknowledge the creaking of the floorboards or the squeak of the door. It's only when I feel the shadow over me that I snap open my eyes.

'Jack!'

My scream makes him jump.

'You scared the life out of me!' I push myself upright, my head spinning with the rush of blood. 'Jesus!' Then comes the relief, flushing out my veins. The comfort of having him back home. I didn't realize how vulnerable I felt until he arrived. For several beats, all I do is stare at him, searching for my words.

'Adele?' He looks at me with concern.

'You're never going to believe what's happened.'

'Hey, hey, slow down. Are you OK?' He rushes to my side.

'Not sure.' A shuddery breath leaves me. 'I actually don't know the answer to that.'

'OK, tell me what's happened.'

I stare back at him, wide-eyed.

He crouches, touching my face. 'What's going on with you? And what's this?' He lightly brushes my cheek. 'Have you been rolling around in the mud again?'

With a shaky hand I turn and point to the wardrobe.

'In there, go have a look.'

Jack eyes me suspiciously then rises to his feet. 'OK, seriously, what's going on?'

'I found a secret room – it was on the old plans.'

He stares at me, several beats passing. There's a flash of something in his eyes but I can't tell what it is.

'You did what?'

Quickly, he crosses the room, fishes out his phone and points the torch through the hole. He shines it around but doesn't go inside.

'It's creepy in there,' I say through clenched teeth. I'm shivering. 'What do you think it is?'

He looks back at me, eyes full of irritation. 'What were you thinking, going in there?'

'Well, I didn't plan to. I came across it,' I say, surprised by his attack. 'Why would something like that be hidden in a bedroom?'

Despite the warm October heat, I'm feeling chilled, right to my core. And now I can hear a mosquito. The predatory high-pitched whine as it circles me.

I don't believe in ghosts but I'm getting a crawling sensation that tells me we're not alone, that something has climbed out of the hole and followed me into our room.

Rubbing my goosebumps, I say: 'In the films, they hide religious people in rooms like that.'

'In the films? Priest holes, you mean.'

'O-K, so why would you hide a priest in a bedroom?'

'Not in France – that's only in England,' he corrects me again. 'In the reign of Elizabeth I when Catholics were persecuted, they'd hide the priests in the walls of castles and country houses.'

More quietly I say: 'How do you even know that?'

'You sound stupid, saying things like that.'

Wow, where's this hostility coming from?

Jack drops to one knee. Placing his phone next to him, he reaches inside the wardrobe, groaning loudly as he tugs the solid stone door towards him.

'Aren't you going to look inside?' I yell above the noise.

There's a loud thud as he seals it shut. Rising up, he dusts off his jeans.

'No need,' he says.

When he turns to face me, his eyes have narrowed. A streak of anger runs through them. His behaviour reminds me of old Jack, the one I was never sure who I'd be waking up to. Moody, unpredictable.

'I thought you'd be excited about it? We've been working on this for weeks.' Is he envious I got there first? I'm struggling to understand. 'Hey, what have I done wrong?'

'It was stupid to go inside.'

'I know that now.'

'The ceiling could have collapsed. Anything might have happened to you.'

I want him to be worried for me, yet somehow it

doesn't feel like concern. What's driving this change in mood? Weirdly, I'm getting the sense he doesn't like me looking around the chateau when he's not there. It's enough to put me off telling him the full story; what's really lurking inside the hole. He'd only make a thing out of that too.

He scratches his temple. Jack has that faraway look again.

Defensive, distracted. Another flare to the past ignites. *Mistrust.* I stand up and walk over to him because I want to be able to read his face when I ask him why he's been gone for so long.

'How did the trip to the bank go?'

He looks up. 'Oh yeah, that's what I rushed up here to tell you, but then this happened.'

Again, that tone, as if I've spoiled things.

'It wasn't a glitch, there's been another deposit: thirty thousand pounds.' His eyes are now gleaming and his whole being has shifted again. 'It's crazy – triple what they gave us last time. How is this actually happening to us? You know what,' he laughs. 'It's probably best we don't ask questions. The less we know, the better.'

'It's to help with the running costs?'

He shrugs. 'This is all we've ever wanted. We fought for this, babe, and our prayers have been answered.'

We. I hold my tongue.

'Since there's not much we're allowed to do to the place, we should start thinking how to spend the money. What about a convertible? Cruising around the countryside, wouldn't that be epic?'

Thirty thousand pounds. *Thirty thousand*, that's what

I earned in a year working for the hotel. Yet I can't get excited about it because something else is taking up my mental space. While Jack reels off his bucket list, I slip into an echo chamber in my head and the only word I can hear is LIAR. Something about his trip into town doesn't add up. What took him so long? Am I imagining it, or do I smell perfume on him? Despite my fear of coming off like I'm spying, something compels me to ask:

'Did you stop off at the pub?'

His smile drops.

'Seriously, Adele, I'm trying to celebrate with you.'

'I know, and it's great. But, did you?' I'm trying to keep my voice neutral. Dialling down the edge in my tone.

He shakes his head. 'Which pub would that be?'

'The one Iona works at.'

He shrugs. 'Iona?'

'Don't pretend you don't know who she is.'

Jack clenches his jaw.

'Well,' I pause. 'It must have been *something* that kept you away. You've been gone nearly four hours.'

He moves to the chest, pulls open the top drawer and begins rummaging.

'Jack?'

'Have you seen my polo shirt? The blue-and-white-striped one?'

'Next drawer down, Jack,' I say more loudly.

'What's it doing there?'

'I did a big tidy-up.'

He jerks around, balling the shirt into his hand. 'It's not

healthy, rattling about this place all day long without a focus. Your brain's going into overdrive.'

OK. I've never seen him like this before.

'You need to find a hobby. Go into town and get to know the locals – there'll be someone you'll connect with. The contract doesn't say anything about us making new friends.'

'If you hadn't noticed, I am busy: vlogging. Trying to earn us a living for when the money *does* run out. Because that's what will happen.'

He slams the drawer shut.

'And I enjoy it!' I add. 'You could try seeming a bit more cheerful in them, you know, make a bit of an effort.'

'You do yourself a disservice, dumbing yourself down for it.'

'Hey, I'm not trying to sound *dumb*.'

'Just a friendly observation. You know how much I care about you, I'm proud of you and I think you can do better. I want you to spend more time offline and in the real world. Start meeting *real* people. Christ, you don't even know how to talk to your sister.'

He turns to leave.

'Jack,' I cut him off. 'Were you with Iona? I'm not going to ask you again.'

Slowly he turns around, fixing me with his gaze. More slowly, more carefully, he says, 'I know where this is going and that's why I'm pissed off and I'm not answering.'

'Don't know what you mean.'

'This is about you not trusting me.'

He casts me a look. Head cocked slightly to one side.

Gently, he says, 'You can't keep punishing me for the past. We decided to move on, that was the promise.'

His words smack the room into silence.

'I've said I was sorry. I can't keep doing it, obsessing over the past. We're going around in circles.'

How could he? Forgiving Jack hasn't been easy, especially as I still don't know what really happened.

Discovering the Facebook messages was heartbreaking. There were so many of them – hundreds, toing and froing with his first serious girlfriend. They weren't incriminating, per se, it was more the way he wrote, as if I didn't exist. Flirting, a sense of building up to something.

Then came the office works trip to Suffolk, a long weekend where Jack wouldn't pick up, he only sent messages. Finally, there was the photo she posted of the spa hotel with a cryptic hashtag. Jack says it was a coincidence she was in the area at the same time as him.

He says his secretive behaviour, the keeping his phone on silent, the disappearing off to take calls was because I was making him feel policed.

He'd leave the room and come back with the very same expression he's wearing now. Like I'm a stranger. Which is funny, because sometimes I feel like I don't know him at all.

The only thing I had actual proof of was the inappropriate messages, which he apologized for. His sorry was like a full stop. There was little else I could do after that other than drop it.

I made the mistake of telling Erin, who immediately tore into our entire relationship like we were a puzzle she must work out. I needed a shoulder to cry on, not a nurse fixing me. Why couldn't she just have told me what I wanted to hear, that all couples go through this.

Jack tells me off for spying on him and somehow, that's become the issue rather than what he did to make me insecure enough to snoop.

I try to leave it in the past, really, I do. I block it all out and most days when I'm manifesting goals and dreaming up our new future, I'm very good at telling myself everything's perfect. I know he loves me. People fuck up, people fuck other people, they get bored and complacent in their relationships. We've been together eight years. *Eight years*, he's bound to want to look around. I just didn't think he'd act on it.

I can't prove it though, and that's what's eating me up. The not knowing. It's why I immediately lurch to high alert when I sense a change in his behaviour. Just a whiff of a lie and I'm like a meerkat on hind legs, smelling the wind for more untruths.

The silence stretches out. There's so much I want to say to Jack but I'm afraid of another argument. Things have got better, they *are* better. We hardly ever argue now, this is our first big fight since we arrived. Being here is our chance to start over and it's what I wanted.

I swallow down my paranoia.

He moves towards me, his features softening. 'Yes, I did stop at the pub, but no, Iona wasn't working. Even if she had been there, I'm not interested in her, OK?'

I nod slowly.

'You need to stop worrying about me.'

'OK.'

'I am worried about you though.'

'Me?'

'When I got home, there was a package waiting. That's how I figured you were upstairs: you hadn't opened the mail.'

'And?'

'It was a weird doll thing.'

'You opened it?'

'By accident. I thought it was for me.'

'What do you mean, a doll thing?'

'A creepy gift from one of your fans.'

'What did it look like?'

He shrugs. 'Creepy looking?'

I give him a look.

'You! It was made to look like you.'

'Ew!' I fold my arms. 'That is weird.'

I think of the haters and the trolls who've been leaving messages. Could one of them have sent it?

'Made of wood with twiggy hands. Red string for hair. Anyway, I binned it.'

'You threw it away? You should have showed it to me first.'

'Honestly, you wouldn't want that thing lying around. Looked like some sort of voodoo doll. Makes you think about the sort of fans you're attracting. Seriously though, you've made no secret of where we live, we could get any weirdo turning up.'

I shudder, he has a point.

Best not to tell him about my other discovery. A few

days ago, I came across half a dozen dolls planted in the flower beds near the entrance. Black and sinister looking. I wondered if might be leftovers from the previous owner, although I couldn't imagine what child would want to play with those. I threw them away and forgot all about it, until now.

It'll only give him more reason to warn me off vlogging. And it can't be anything to worry about; they were probably there years before I found them.

Anyway, I don't believe in bad omens. Well, I didn't until today.

Jack catches my eye. He smiles at me with more warmth, more feeling. 'Friends again?'

There, the switch. A different Jack. The changes are so rapid it's disorientating.

'So, tell me' – he pulls me in – 'while you were treasure hunting, were you thinking about me?'

He kisses my cheek.

Horny Jack.

'Having fantasies about getting me inside that room? It's OK' – he lowers his voice – 'I won't tell anyone.'

I think I've always known there's a darker side to Jack that I can't satisfy.

Moving his lips to my neck, he kisses me. But it all feels mechanical. For me, anyway. I can't turn everything off, just like that. I'm still simmering from our argument, and the ghost of what I've seen in the hole is still present, lurking. *HELP.* The word searing like a burn. The last thing I feel like is having sex.

There's so much I want to say.

Guiding me towards the bed, he sweeps aside the clothes, the hangers clanging as they hit the floor.

But I feel pressure, like there's something I need to make up for, so I go along with it. The next script I'm word perfect on. The careless fondling of my breasts, his hand pulling my thong to the side, talking about how much I'm going to like it. The brief attempt at foreplay. The other hand tightening around my throat. I'm not ready for him when he pushes himself inside me.

I lie on my back as we make love. My eyes open, staring up at the ornate ceiling, the intricate patterns, the flower rosette in the centre, and I feel completely detached from what I'm doing.

I'm living with a man I don't really trust in a house full of secrets.

In the most intimate of moments, I've never felt so lonely.

CHAPTER TWENTY-ONE

JAckandAdeleforver Last active nine minutes ago

I love you and no one can change my mind. Don't
listen to what the haters are saying, you're stunning
and amazing and such an inspiration. Every time I
watch your vlogs I cry. ♥ ♥ ♥ ♥

CHAPTER TWENTY-TWO

ERIN

EIGHT DAYS AFTER NYE

Nearly an hour has passed since I filed the report at the front desk. The police officer hasn't lifted his eyes from the newspaper. He sniffs and rubs his nose angrily.

I check the time. It's already 4 p.m. I swallow down my frustration.

I won't be fobbed off. Especially not after what the B & B guy told me. Return to the chateau so I can be alone with my thoughts, running through everything I've seen and heard again and again, wondering if I'm going mad? No, I'm not leaving until I've spoken to someone in charge.

It feels as if that's all I've been doing these past weeks. Thrashing out what I remember, walking over old ground until it's all in the wrong order and none of it makes sense. What I did, how I did it – it's all now a blur.

I look down and my hands have rolled into tight balls. I peel back my fingers revealing ten perfect half-moons. Deep grooves where my nails have been.

The dulcet tones from a French radio station fill the heavy silence. The waiting room is stuffy and smells of instant coffee. The long window onto the high street makes it feel more like a shopfront than a police station and now the snow's started up again. It's heavier. More persistent. My stomach clenches.

I distract myself with the pinboard opposite, where there's another missing person poster. A different girl to the one I saw in the town square but they're so similar they could be twins. Big youthful smile. Beautiful but haunted eyes. She's next to an E-fit of a man with a buzz cut and tattooed face, which is beside a neighbourhood watch poster warning homeowners how to make their property more secure.

Thinking about my own break-in brings a flush of heat to my face.

'Madame.'

I look up. An officer wearing a fleece and a baseball cap appears in the corridor. He looks me up and down. 'Would you come with me?'

I spring from my seat and follow him. He's carrying a stained mug filled with something dark and watery. In the other hand, a file.

'Coffee?' he asks, leading me into a brightly lit room with two hard chairs and a table. The walls are bare, there are no windows, just a noisy ventilator that whines as it turns. He closes the door behind us with a sharp clack.

'No, thanks,' I say, looking around anxiously.

'*Asseyez-vous.*' He points to the chair and sits down first.

It's even warmer in here and I feel the heat coil around my throat. He takes off his fleece and I notice his muscles working as he shows off a blue uniformed shirt with a white T-shirt underneath. Around his waist, a heavy utility belt with an empty gun pouch. His boots are thick-soled, steel-capped.

'I'm Lieutenant Marcel Beaumont.' He opens the file.

He fishes inside his pocket for a pen. There's a casualness to all of this and I get the impression not a lot happens around here. He clicks the end of the biro and holds it over the messy notes.

'You informed the officer when you arrived that you're concerned for your sister?'

Now he's removed his cap I can see his eyes. Green with an intense stare. It catches me off guard.

'You haven't heard from' – he checks his notes – 'Adele, for several days. She's not answering her phone and there's a report of a party which she may or may not have been to.' He frowns and looks up. 'Am I missing out anything?'

'It could be much longer than a few days.'

He rubs his hand back and forth over his scalp. He has a military-style buzz cut, and a heavy outdoor tan. I suppose he's good-looking in an action man way. Clean-shaven with that strong angular jaw, he's just Adele's type. And she'd have him in a heartbeat. For some reason my throat tightens at the thought.

'Madame, what is it you'd like to report?'

I blink quickly. Now under his interrogative gaze, my words snag.

'A disappearance.'

'A disappearance?' One eyebrow goes up.

'It's not just that she's not answering her phone, there are other things,' I say quickly.

'Other things?'

'It looks like she hasn't been home for some time.'

'At her chateau?' He makes a face.

'*Yes*, at her chateau.' I frown. 'The fridge, it's completely empty.' God, that sounds feeble when I say it out loud.

He grins, which frustrates me even more.

'Madame,' he cuts me off. Places the pen down. 'Let me check that I understand correctly: you're not sure how long she's been missing for? Or even if she is missing?'

I feel a rush of heat to my face. He's watching me closely, and all the things I planned to say are now just a queue of words, jumbled in my head.

'When was the last time you heard from her?'

'New Year's Eve.'

'And when did you last speak?'

Thinking back, it's impossible to remember exactly when we last spoke. What was said will forever be burned into my memory though. The hurtful things that were said when I told her how crushed Mum was by the news we couldn't visit.

'Maybe a month ago.'

He starts. 'That's a long time not to speak to family, non?'

'Things have been difficult.'

'How so?'

'We had a bit of disagreement.'

'What about?'

I cross my arms. 'It's not something I want to get into.'

147

He stares at me.

'It's got nothing to do with this.'

He's watching me again, studying me.

'And what's the reason for your visit now?'

'She's my sister?' I shrug angrily. Christ, this feels like an interrogation.

'And is she someone who likes travelling? Perhaps she's gone away with her husband.'

'Partner.'

'Her partner,' he repeats carefully. 'That would be the most likely answer?'

'I don't think so.'

'And what does her partner do – his job?'

I frown. 'I don't know. Is that relevant?'

'Someone must be missing for twenty-four hours before we put out a report and we don't even know if she is missing.'

'I'm telling you now,' I say coldly.

He rubs his hand back and forth across his scalp. I hear the bristle of short hairs.

'Oui . . .'

Tension slides into the room. And with it come flashbacks to the interrogation I endured before leaving for France. Had I been drinking? How else could I have made such a mistake?

The room is hot, stuffy. It feels like it's swallowing me.

'It's a big place for two people to manage.'

I blink. Returning to him.

'Chateau Bellay.'

Wow, he thinks I'm making this up. Why is he focusing

on the chateau and not Adele? I knew this would be a waste of time.

I breathe in sharply. 'I don't know.'

'How could your sister afford such a place?'

'What has that got to do with anything?'

He looks at me strangely. Then he sits back and sighs. 'There's a lot here you don't know. It seems you weren't close; you don't know much about her life or when you last heard from her, which makes it impossible to know whether she's disappeared or simply had plans that she didn't share with you.'

I bite down on my lip.

'Are you upset?'

'I'm fine,' I say quickly.

'Perhaps this is more of a personal matter between the two of you.'

I look away.

There's a knock on the door. I look up as a man with epaulettes on his shoulders strides into the room.

'Marcel, *un moment*,' he says, taking instant command of the room.

He appears short next to the lieutenant. A thick neck, bald, except for a small amount of grey hair near his ears. He speaks quickly, like he's running out of time, and I instinctively don't like him.

Never mind, I just need him to do his job and find my sister.

I watch his stomach heave up over his waistband, his belt creaking under the strain. The sight of his gun makes me flinch.

'This is Capitaine Georges Desailly,' Marcel breaks from their conversation. 'He's in charge of the Bourgogne-Franche-Comté region and is normally based at our head office in Chalon-sur-Saône.'

The capitaine, who looks close to fifty, nods a vague greeting in my direction. His eyes are creased and small. Piggy eyes.

'You're the sister of the châtelaine.' His French accent is much more pronounced than Marcel's. 'Lieutenant Beaumont says you've been staying at Chateau Bellay while she's away. Do you have a key to the property?'

My hands immediately find each other, clasping underneath the table.

'I found one.' I hesitate. 'By the back door.'

He nods in a way that suggests he doesn't believe me, his mouth turning downward.

'Have you tried locating your sister's mobile? If she has an iPhone you can trace her last location from the cloud, although you'll need her password.'

A password. Adele has so many secrets, I wouldn't know where to begin.

'I could try, I guess.'

'You should try,' he stresses, making me feel stupid. 'Does she have her bag with her, her wallet, her keys?'

'She must do, I haven't seen it.'

'And what about a laptop?'

I think back to what the B & B owner said. That *they* came to collect Adele's things. My throat tightens.

'There's nothing of hers at the chateau.'

'Have you checked the hospital? Maybe she had an accident.'

Now I feel really dumb. The possibility Adele might be injured didn't occur to me.

'We can check.' He carries on: 'Do you have a photo?'

I nod, pulling my phone from my bag. I show him a picture from her Instagram. Grinning, hand lifted to the chateau behind her.

His eyes work over her. Studying Adele for a beat too long. He nods and hands it back.

'For now, I think we wait and see what happens.'

'But what about the party?' I say quickly.

The men trade looks.

'Party?' the capitaine asks.

'New Year's Eve. That's what the girl in town told me.'

'Delphine Ramousse,' Marcel reads from the file and the officers exchange knowing glances.

Capitaine Desailly scratches his chin. 'I wouldn't believe what Delphine tells you. She has a vivid imagination. She likes to smoke.'

'Cannabis,' Marcel adds.

'Oui. A fantasist, always dreaming that one day she'll be famous, one day she will blah blah . . .' He snickers. 'You should know that Delphine Ramousse has a criminal record – she assaulted the partner of her ex. It's the same old story: mother was an addict; child grows up in care and ends up in trouble.' He shakes his head. 'It's a problem in a small town where there are no jobs. Delphine is lucky to work in the boulangerie.' He shrugs. 'It'll be a miracle if she keeps her job if she continues to upset customers.'

'I'm not upset with her.'

'Better not waste time with people like her.'

People like her. I frown. She's just a teenager, her whole life ahead. I see girls like Delphine all the time in ICU, girls who've had a rough start in life. They're crying out for a bit of love and support, and in my experience the hard-line approach never works.

'Madame, I can assure you, if there was a party at the chateau, we would have known about it. We are the police.' He gives Marcel a look. 'Don't worry, I'm sure you'll hear from your sister soon.'

I wait until he's gone, then, worried for Delphine's sake, I ask Marcel: 'I haven't got her in trouble, have I? Delphine?'

'Ah non, that girl invites trouble.'

'You don't approve of her?'

'It's a small town. When someone doesn't follow the rules, it stands out.'

Rules. It sounds so sinister.

He gets up, indicating the end of the interview, and I feel relieved it's over.

'We'll call if we hear anything.' He leads me back to the waiting room. 'In the meantime, be careful on the roads – the ice can be deadly. Do you need someone to fix the broken window?'

My gaze jerks back to him.

'Nothing much happens without us knowing.' He gives me a sharp nod.

I feel my pulse quicken. The image of that man in the snow returning. The feeling I'm being followed.

'I can manage,' I say tightly.

He holds the door open for me and I smell his aftershave. Oudy, like a jazz bar.

Cold bursts onto my face and as I pass, he says, 'Could it be possible your sister is doing something she doesn't want you to know about?'

I feel a twinge in my chest again. I don't have an answer for him.

He smiles politely but small lines gather around his eyes, and I feel him watching as I leave. The heavy station door closes on my heels.

As soon as I'm outside, a ball of dread drops into my stomach and it's not the thought of another night alone in a creepy old building that prompts it. It's the implication the chateau is under surveillance.

I came for help, but now I'm even more on edge. Worse, I'm feeling strangely wrong-footed, as if *I've* done something wrong. *I'm* the one who's being investigated.

It's happening again.

CHAPTER TWENTY-THREE

TheREALAdele003 Last active thirty minutes ago

I can't stop. I keep replaying your vlog, over and over. I want your life so bad. I'm scaring myself how much I want to be you.

CHAPTER TWENTY-FOUR

ERIN

EIGHT DAYS AFTER NYE

Mum's birthday.
Password incorrect.
Adele's birthday. My fingers are working hard, striking my phone keys faster than I can think. I wait anxiously as the rainbow wheel turns, the screen buffers.
Password incorrect.
How many goes do I get before I'm locked out? I'll never be able to guess what Adele has chosen.

My gaze sprints back to the window where I've been keeping a lookout since I returned from the police station. Lieutenant Beaumont's words are doing loops around my head. He knows about the break-in. *Someone is watching. Someone is spying on the chateau.*

For a place so vast, it feels like there's nowhere to hide.

I shrug several times, trying to ease the tension that's worked its way into my shoulders and across my back. My entire body feels tight and knotted. It's now the evening and I'm exhausted, my eyes dry and gritty. I haven't slept in weeks, not properly, and now this, keeping me awake.

Could the man I saw last night be the lieutenant? But why?

This community feels creepy. There's a hostility. A pent-up anger towards outsiders, and I felt it in the police station too. Maybe it's to do with wealth, a sense of entitlement people assume you must have if you can afford a chateau.

Which brings me back to Adele and the secrets she's been hiding. What did the B & B owner mean when he said he didn't believe the things they were saying about my sister?

The air is thickening with the threat of more snow. The wind clatters as it swoops down the chimney, delivering another shower of soot into the fireplace.

Darkness is taking over. Like the tide, it moves in quickly and, before you know it, you're drowning in it. I feel like I'm treading water in this hostile foreign environment.

I can see my breath pooling and there's a sense of it being colder inside the thick stone walls than outside, but it's an illusion. Another trick this chateau is playing on me. My sister's disappearing act – still the show stealer.

Where are you, Adele?

Maybe she's doing this on purpose? Some attention-grabbing social media stunt? It's the kind of thing Adele would do when we were kids, running away from home, faking being sick to get Mum and Dad to notice. It's an awful thing to have to consider but she has previous.

I shake my head. It's Marcel's fault. He's the one who planted the seed that my sister might be hiding a secret. Adele's a good person, I've never known anyone not to like her. I have to stop listening to these people. Stop letting them get in my head.

My eyes track back outside, sweeping over the courtyard, the snow, now an iridescent blue in the pale moonlight. Drifts have collected in the windowsills. Pressing up to the glass, they're shaped like a mountain range. The woods beyond, already a wall of black. A thick impenetrable mass encircling me.

New noises creep out. Creaking. Crawling. I keep imagining things moving and the walls whispering. Like they're sharing an in-joke. Mocking me.

What am I missing? What am I not seeing? It feels like it's staring me in the face.

I shift the pieces of what I know around again. But with each new position, I become more lost. It's my heartbreak over Mum, the pressure to keep a promise. My urgency to find Adele in time is clouding all reasoning.

The dankness burrows beneath my layers, seeking a way in. I need more clothes or I'll freeze to death tonight.

The smell on entering Adele's bedroom assaults my senses.

The bleach has lifted from the rest of the house, but here, it still lingers, cloying. Wrapping itself around where my sister's things should be.

I cross the room, flinging the wardrobe doors wide, one final desperate hunt to find something of Adele's. If not hers, anything that might keep me warm.

I turn to the chest of drawers.

Open. shut.

One empty drawer after another.

I don't know why I'm bothering – it's not like her clothes would fit me anyway. Adele's at least two sizes smaller than me. A stab of jealousy as I remember that feeling of being invisible, growing up next to someone so strikingly beautiful.

As I slam another drawer open and shut, I hear a sudden clunk. The sound of something hitting the sides. I quickly pull it back and there, rolling to a stop, is the first real thing of Adele's.

Her perfume.

The one she's been wearing since she was a teenager. It feels out of place, as if someone left it there by mistake.

I spray my wrists, the familiar scent taking hold and instantly making me sad. It's the closest I've felt to my sister since I arrived. The smoky rose notes evoking happier times, I'm transported back to my first flatshare, to my twenties. Make-up spilled across the bathroom surfaces, shoulder to shoulder in front of the mirror as we got ready for Adele's first big night out. Me, supposedly older and wiser, leading my baby sister a little bit astray. Way back when she looked up to me.

At one point we were best friends. When Dad left us to begin a new family with another woman, when Mum was overcome with grief, we leaned on each other, we were inseparable.

My eyes sting with the surprise arrival of tears. Blinking them away, I turn back to face the room. Looking around at the impressive but unfriendly sight, I ask myself, is she happy? In this huge space for two people? Here, with Jack, who I know she doesn't trust.

Our last conversation – an entire month ago – ended with her telling me how bitter I've become. I'm certain it's *her* that's bitter because she's lonely. Out here in this closed-off community. Convincing herself that Jack loves her. That she should have a child with him. Obsessively reading self-help books, practising daily affirmations, manifesting, continuously striving to become a better version of herself as if she's not good enough already. You shouldn't have to work that hard to be happy.

And then there's the vlogging, an exaggerated form of talking yourself into happiness, because if you say it out loud, and you share it with thousands of people, it must be true.

My life is far from perfect, but I'd rather be alone than trapped in a relationship that robs your confidence. I wish Adele could see she *is* enough. If only she would listen. If only she'd let me in.

I wipe away the tears that have escaped.

In the same drawer, stuffed right to the back, I find something else of Adele's.

A thin floral scarf. I knot it around my neck, tucking my chin inside the fabric. It also smells of my sister and I feel guilty for how everything ended between us.

I look over the room again. Maybe I'm searching in the wrong place? Could the answer lie here, within these walls? My thoughts step back to what the girl from the bakery said. That the chateau has a past nobody wants to talk about.

But don't all historic buildings have a story to tell? Why would Chateau Bellay be any different?

There's only one place I can think of that might give me some answers. I just hope my French is up to it.

After forty minutes of poring over book spines, I find a shelf in the library with a cluster of hardbacks on the period the chateau was built. Thick, densely worded literature explaining the history of the area, the topography. Overwhelming amounts of information – and the French is beyond me. It's an uphill struggle to comb through it, especially when I don't even know what I'm looking for.

My eyes return to the shelf, tracking up to the hard-to-reach places.

I'm not sure if I've ever felt so tired yet so unable to sleep. I pull another book free. Flipping through the pages, the tiny print burns my eyes.

I have no idea what this one is about.

There's a section on architecture and the only reason I know that is because I recognize the drawing of the crest above the tower door. The chateau must have once belonged to a noble French family, passed from generation to generation. Did that all stop with Adele and Jack?

Turning the page, my eye catches on the word feu. *Fire*. There's something about the inferno of 1652, I follow my finger as I move it across the text. By all accounts the chateau was burned down and parts had to be rebuilt. That would explain the mismatch of styles, but it doesn't tally with what Delphine said.

People here don't like to talk about the chateau.

Unless – something terrible happened in the fire. Was someone killed?

It seems so long ago though. Would a grievance be carried on for centuries? Perhaps in a small community, but even this feels unlikely.

That can't be it, there has to be something else.

I return to the books and their secret histories. It doesn't help there's only a single bulb in this corner of the library, pushing out a dim circle of light. It feels like the forgotten corner of the chateau and the air seems thicker here. Rich with the past. But in a cloying way.

Tracking over the shelves, running my fingers across the spines of muted greens, blues and reds, like a magpie, I'm drawn to the bright shiny object. A much skinnier book bound in gold. Pulling it free, I'm immediately attracted to the flamboyant cover.

Rococo fashion.

That's mid eighteenth century, I think. The gilded cover creaks as I open it. Handwritten in the inside page is a note to someone called Fabian.

Forever yours, Cici.

A love note from the past. I trace my finger over the calligraphy. *How romantic.*

As I flick through the book, the thick pages release the smell of old paper. It begins with a ball. Detailed black ink illustrations of a high-ceilinged room and what the guests wore.

The fabric looks expensive. Back then, the fashion was

to wear wide hoops beneath dresses contrasted with a tightly corseted waist. The room is filled with plunging necklines and heaving chests.

Oversized ribbons graze the floor. Flared lace peeps out from under sleeves, a slit up the front reveals a petticoat.

The men fill out the corners of the room, admiring the women like ornaments. Dressed in long coats, lavishly embroidered waistcoats and breeches. Laughing, swigging champagne.

All the guests are wearing elaborate wigs. The women have theirs stacked high, a tower of tightly pinned curls with a single tendril falling into their eyes. Feathers and flowers spearing their updos.

The page makes a noise as I turn it. More drawings of the party. A banquet table. I recognize that room, the fire-place, it's Chateau Bellay.

Next page.

I'm excited to glimpse what life here must have been like then. But as my gaze settles on the room, I notice something is different. It takes a moment to see past the lavishness of costumes. The women, they're much younger than before.

Their features are soft, rounded, not fully developed. Their expressions are innocent and apprehensive. The men, on the other hand, are considerably older.

That was the era, I suppose. Introductions were made at parties like these and girls were married off young. I'd be a spinster by this value system.

But as I near the centrefold, the girls appear even younger. Teenagers. And the look in the men's eyes is more disturbing. There's a hunger there.

My skin prickles.

I turn the page.

The illustrations here depict a very different kind of party. Teenage girls in corsets and frilly knickers. Men, unbuttoning their breeches, manoeuvring the girls into position while the others stand around and watch.

I know where this is leading. I can barely bring myself to look at what comes next. A sickening feeling, growing.

It's worse than I thought, far worse.

Even though the illustrations are static, there's a sense of movement within each drawing, as the naked girls are passed around between the men. Their fear is palpable.

I want to slam the book shut, lock away the past, but I can't. I'm mesmerized by the grotesque images. Like a rubbernecker watching a car crash, I need to see how this ends.

The extravagant ballroom is swapped for a dark tomb-like cell made of stone. It looks medieval, it feels like it's somewhere in this chateau, and a girl has been singled out.

Naked, her real hair hangs loose, spilling across her face. She's chained to the wall – her arms strung up above her head, a thick metal brace clamped around her throat. She's crying.

Nearby, a bare-chested man in a black hood clutches a whip. It's some sort of sick S & M game.

Or is it? In the dim light of the library, it appears even more sinister. More violent.

It's not real, they're just illustrations. It's the artist's twisted imagination. But my attempts to soothe myself aren't working.

I slam the book shut.

Something slips out and falls to the floor.

My fingers tremble as I reach to pick it up. A Polaroid photo. It's faded and grainy and hasn't aged as well as the book but it's still possible to make out the image.

A party in the ballroom. The costumes are different, gold, glitter, platform shoes and hot pants, but the theme is identical.

Within the sun-bleached image is the outline of an orgy. In the centre of the room, a thick mass of people. Writhing. Climbing over each other. Moving inside one another. Piled high like a termite's nest of knotted limbs.

It's grotesque.

But this picture feels like the tip of an iceberg. I turn it over. It reads:

Bellay. NYE 1974

My heart clatters against my ribcage.

What have Adele and Jack got involved in? The lieutenant's words resurface: *Could it be possible your sister is doing something she doesn't want you to know about?*

I look up, my eyes widening with the realization. I have no idea who Adele is.

CHAPTER TWENTY-FIVE

ADELE

ONE MONTH BEFORE NYE

YouTube
870,000 subscribers

Secret in the Tower

Hey, lovelies, sorry I've been a little bit quiet but we are back discovering our chateau and you're going to love love LOVE what I've found. This has been by far the most requested video so it would be cruel to leave you in suspense any longer.

(walks across courtyard, passing Jack)

'Hey baby, you're on camera, wave to our fans!'

(Jack moves out of shot)

Guys, Jack's super busy working on his secret project which he can't wait to share with you soon. You're going to love it, it's a discovery we made while cleaning out the old cellar.

But first (comes to a stop outside wooden door) I'm going to show you this.

Welcome, to the tower!

(pushes open creaking door)

Come on in!

So, this is *the* original part of the chateau and dates back to the seventeenth century, unlike the rest of the building which is more modern. Wow, it spins me out thinking how old it is in here.

Hello?

(echoes)

The first thing you'll notice is the stone crest above the door which Jack tells me belongs to the Bellay family and the door is STUNNING. Solid oak with bronzed rivets, it has to be three inches thick. **(zooms in)** Really feels medieval, doesn't it?

As you can see, there's a spiral staircase leading all the way up to the turret. For all of you who will ask, that's sixty-five steps. I KNOW, Stairmaster, hello?

What makes this tower unique, apart from the fact there's only one and most chateaus have several, is that the floor **(pans camera down)** is wood, whereas the walls **(tracks camera slowly up)** are made of stone. I'm no historian **(giggles)** but clearly the stairs were reconstructed later on and that's HUGELY important for what I'm about to reveal.

Guys, you're going to go nuts when you see what I've discovered. It's epic. **(starts climbing)**

Side note – how cute are these alcoves! **(points)** Look, they even have a shelf to perch on and look out, Rapunzel style. There are six alcoves leading to the top and each one has a different view of the gardens.

(stops and zooms out through alcove) Look how green

everything is. It's November and the trees are only just turning. Have I mentioned how much I love this place? (**giggles**)

(**puffing**) It's worth the wait, guys, bear with me. I made this discovery by fluke. If I hadn't dropped my phone, I'd never have found it.

(**zooms in on the third step from the top**)

Are you seeing what I'm seeing yet?

(**whispers**) Look, it's the cutest miniature handle that you wouldn't know was there unless you were looking for it and when you do this . . .

(**pulls out drawer beneath step**)

Look, a secret drawer in the princess tower! I cannot deal with how cool this is. Like, seriously, what sort of stuff would they have hidden in here? Because I'm a massive romantic, I'm thinking love letters. Or would it have been scrolls? I don't know, but I'm envisaging a romance story right here in this magical fairy-tale tower.

Help me out, guys, if any of you history buffs out there might know, leave a message in the comment box below.

Speaking of love stories, for all of you who've been asking how Jack and I are doing, I just want to say, we are SO HAPPY. Honestly, I can't tell you how life-changing moving out here has been – it's like we're falling in love all over again. You know when you first meet someone and you discover all their cute little quirks and it makes you love them more – well, I feel like that's what's happening here. I'm learning new things about Jack every day, it's like we're on some journey of self-discovery. It's magical.

Make sure you tune in to my next vlog where I'll be

showing you more of our enchanting castle. And don't forget to like and subscribe. Love you all, darlings, bye for now.

(blows camera a kiss)

CHAPTER TWENTY-SIX

Billybob_uncle9 Active 30 seconds ago

Stupid tart. Why do you have to act like a brain-dead moron in every video. Why's it all about you rather than the chateau? You don't belong there. Someone needs to reclaim Bellay. Expose the real secret of how you landed yourself a chateau.

CHAPTER TWENTY-SEVEN

ERIN

NINE DAYS AFTER NYE

Clawing at my throat, I pull at the binds. I'm choking. Christ, I can't breathe. My heart is pounding. A thud, thrumming right through me.

I snap open my eyes and suck in the air. It was a dream. That's all it was.

I blink back into the living room, taking in the heirlooms, the ornate ceiling. The bright morning light unapologetically pushing its way in. Staining the walls butter yellow.

For a moment, the air is still, but then I remember the book. The graphic, violent drawings returning. One grotesque image after the other image, forcing their way inside my thoughts. The horror of what I found; the chateau's dark past. It's a miracle I slept at all.

I'm still fully clothed and when I see my panicked breath mist in front of me, I'm grateful I never took them off. It feels even colder than before. The thick stone walls making the room seem more like a tomb. A grave.

The girl in the drawing. Who was she? What happened to her? She was more than an illustration. I know what they did to her was real.

A sickness swells and there's that noise again. The one I heard in my sleep. A thudding. Only it's now more of a hollow-sounding knock. It takes a moment to realize – it's coming from outside. Someone's at the door.

As I swing my legs off the sofa the blood rushes to my head. I'm dizzy and awkward on my feet as I move through the rooms, hurrying to see who it is. The shadow of the library looms behind me. A creature lurking.

The heavy front door sticks, the wood has warped with the damp. It shudders free, snapping back at me.

The icy air sweeps in.

All I can see is a silhouette. Haloed in the doorway, it's the outline of a woman.

'Good morning.'

I squint into the sunshine.

'I was in the neighbourhood and thought I'd stop by,' she says cheerfully. A British accent. Educated.

'You must be Adele's sister?'

'Yes,' I say warily. Moving so I can see her properly. She's tall with short warm brown hair, wearing a fixed smile.

'Did I wake you up?'

'And who are you, exactly?'

'A neighbour, if you can call it that in this remote part of the world.' She laughs. 'Goodness knows why we moved out here.' She points into the distance. Her long coat swishing as she turns. 'We live in the other direction from town. Five miles as the crow flies.'

My eyes follow her finger but it's impossible to see past the tangle of trees. I move my gaze back to her, taking in her black gloves, a scarf tidily knotted around her neck. Her diamond stud earrings catch in the light.

She's someone you'd expect to see lounging around in a member's club, not out here.

My eyes slip past her into the expanse of white and I shiver. The heavy clouds have broken up, the sky is clear. It looks peaceful but I don't trust anything about this place any more.

'Is there something I can help you with? I'm quite busy,' I say tightly.

There's a look of expectation.

I straighten; I'm not having some stranger come inside. Especially as it's not even my home to invite them into.

'I heard you're looking for your sister.'

I frown.

She laughs. 'It's a small town, dear.'

'Yeah, I worked that one out.'

'I've also been trying to get hold of Adele.' She clears her throat. 'I don't want to alarm you, but I'm worried about her.'

Panic hits me. Followed by relief, because finally I have the confirmation I've been searching for. I'm not going mad. Something *is* wrong.

'What do you know?' I ask, urgency in my voice.

'Well, I haven't heard from Adele since our last little get-together. We had a cheese and wine night – my husband, Phil, and Jack get on like a house on fire. He's a contractor, so they enjoy chatting about their projects, they both love tinkering.' Her eyebrows go up. 'Boys and their toys, hey. Phil's been called away on a construction assignment so it's just me out here. I haven't known your sister or Jack long, but it's been nice having a pair of friendly faces nearby.'

Adele and this woman seem worlds apart. There's a smoothness, a practised way about her which I'm having difficulty warming to. I can't imagine them getting on.

'Sorry, I didn't catch your name?'

'How rude of me not to introduce myself. Rebecca.' Her smile drops into something more serious. 'As I said, Adele hasn't been answering her phone or my messages.' She looks at me pointedly. 'You arrived on Thursday?'

'Yes,' I say hesitantly. 'How did you—'

Another knowing smile. 'Small town, remember.'

I nod slowly. I cross my arms, holding myself tightly while a shiver works its way down. 'The place was deserted when I arrived,' I say. 'Did Adele mention anything about going away?'

'No.' Rebecca looks surprised. 'I suppose she might have taken a trip to Paris, but what business would she have there? It's expensive and a hassle this time of year. It's all rather odd, if you ask me.'

'A party on New Year's Eve, do you know anything about that?'

'Party?' She frowns. 'She didn't mention it during our get-together, and that was only a couple of days before New Year's.' More confidently she adds: 'She would have said if they were having a party. Besides, it seems out of character; they barely had visitors – sometimes I wondered if I was

Adele's only friend. So, to throw a party—' She stops. 'Does that sound like something your sister would do?'

The sickening images of last night's discovery return. The secrecy shrouding the chateau. 'I don't know,' I tell her.

She looks at me pointedly.

'Are the two of you close?'

I think about our falling-out and it forces me to look away.

'Oh. Have I overstepped the mark again? I am sorry.'

'It's nothing. I'm fine.'

'The truth is, I've been worried for some time about, you know,' she lowers her voice, 'Adele's mental health.'

'Really?'

The Adele I know could be self-absorbed. But not depressed. Then again, I'm learning there's a lot about my sister I don't know.

'How did she seem to you when you last saw her?' I say.

'Quiet. Distracted. Jumpy even. Like she was frightened of something. I thought she might be struggling to cope out here, that perhaps it's too isolated. Sorry,' she puts a hand on my arm and I startle. 'I don't mean to worry you, it's just, I think it's imperative that we find her. Have you tried locating Adele's phone to see where she is?'

'Of course.' I frown.

'And how did that go?'

'No luck.'

She rubs above her eye, considering this for a moment. 'Do you think she could have turned it off? Lost it, even?'

'Impossible for me to say.' I try to keep the irritation out of my voice.

'Try again?'

'Yeah, that's what the police said. But I don't have her passwords.'

'You've spoken to the police?' Something creeps into her voice.

'Fat lot of good it did.'

'I don't think there's any need for involving them yet. Let's concentrate on her phone,' she says more sharply. 'Even if it's turned off or out of battery, you'll still be able to see where Adele last had signal.'

'I know that,' I match her tone. 'But without her passwords, there's not a lot I can do.'

I feel my legs weaken. The dizzy feeling is back.

'How about we give it another go now, while we're together?'

Nausea swelling, I feel myself grimace.

'Oh, I am sorry – I've upset you.'

'It's fine.' Although I feel more drained than ever.

'Oh darling, you look tired. Is there anything I can do?'

I push the hair from my eyes. After days of going unwashed, I can only imagine how knotted and greasy it must look. Next to her polished appearance, I must appear a train wreck.

Between Mum, Adele's disappearance and the trouble I'm in, I can't see or think straight.

'What else can we do?' She moves towards me and I instinctively withdraw. 'Perhaps there's something else I can help with?'

'Look, I really need to get on—'

'I can fetch you some food, do you have anything in the fridge? Don't be shy to ask.'

'I can manage—'

'There's a casserole in my freezer. I'll come back with that.'

I shake my head and then stop. Catching her eye. 'I think you should leave.'

The wind snaps, whistling through the trees and the chimney stacks, striking the weather vane, it chimes as it spins. A haunting *ting ting*.

She turns up her collar, bunching into her scarf. There's something new about the way she's looking at me now. Cold and with intent.

I move to close the door, and for a moment, I think she's about to wedge her foot in, but at the sound of my phone ringing, she pulls back.

Caller unknown.

'I have to take this.' I turn my head away, sensing her eagerness to listen in.

'Yes, hello,' I say urgently.

'Erin Davenport?' The woman's tone is sombre and I immediately react.

'What's happened?'

'It's Fiona, I'm one of the nurses at St Margaret's Hospice. It's . . .' she pauses. 'It's about your mother.'

'I'm afraid there's some bad news. Mary's condition took a turn in the night. Her blood pressure dropped suddenly and we weren't able to stabilize it with medication.'

'But she's OK?'

'Fortunately, the doctors were able to restart her heart with defibrillation, which returned her pulse to something more regular, but the shock was a little too much—'

'But she is going to be OK?' Tears spring to my eyes.

'Mary's in an induced coma. But she's stable.'

I start to tremble. My eyes reach into the gloom, into the dark recesses of the chateau. I think I see a shadow but it must be my imagination playing tricks. Everything has gone wrong since I arrived in this evil place with the secrets it keeps. I shouldn't be here, WHAT am I doing here?

'We'll be in touch if anything changes.' The nurse hangs up.

'Is everything all right?' Rebecca says. Her voice sounds small and distant because my head is swimming.

If Mum dies, I'll never forgive myself for leaving her side.

Slowly, I turn to the stranger at my door. Full of anger and regret. But whatever I imagined before has gone. She looks at me kindly.

'What's happened?' Her eyes soften, her voice is gentle.

The smallest show of kindness tips me over the edge. I'm no longer worrying who she is and what she wants. All of a sudden I'm filled with a massive sense of relief that I'm not alone. The first vaguely friendly face in what feels like weeks. Tears crowd my eyes.

'Bad news?'

I nod. Wiping them away.

'You look like you could do with a hug – come here, darling.'

She steps inside, pulling me into her arms, her expensive

perfume wrapping itself around us. She smells like an English summer garden. *Home.*

The nostalgia tips me over the edge and I break down. The sadness, the confusion and extreme tiredness of the past few days finally surfacing. Sobbing into her shoulder, I can barely control myself.

She holds me close, speaking softly into my hair. 'It's OK, it's going to be all right.'

She rubs my back like you would soothe a baby.

'My mother's health took a turn last year – it came as a shock to us all, so I understand what you're going through.'

I feel her tense beneath her layers. Stiff and awkward, I can tell she's not used to giving out hugs. But I'm grateful for the comfort. The kindness. I didn't realize how alone I felt until now.

I shouldn't have been so rude and mistrusting. It's *me*, I'm not in the right state of mind.

My breathing steadies and when my heart finally slows, I peel myself away. But my hands remain shaky and I'm unable to loosen the grip on my phone. My skin is pulled tight, white across my knuckles.

She takes me by both shoulders and her eyes lock on to mine.

'Listen now, I'm only down the road. I'm here if you need anything, us girls need to stick together. OK, darling?'

Then she pulls a pen and notepad from her handbag. She hands me her number with an assertive nod. 'Call me anytime. And I mean that. Don't overthink it, just pick up the phone if you need to talk.'

'Sorry for crying on you like this, I feel deeply embarrassed.'

'Don't be silly.'

'And sorry if I came across as rude, there's a lot going on.' She gives me a tender squeeze.

My fingers find their way back to my button, rubbing the smooth plastic, the way they always do when I feel exposed.

'Normally I'm the one comforting people.'

'And I bet you do a good job of it,' she says. 'But sometimes even strong people need looking after. Are you going to be OK?'

I nod.

'Don't feel embarrassed. And please call me if there's any news from Adele.' She turns and makes her way down the steps, rooting around in her bag while she does so. She pulls out a key fob and the sound of the car unlocking breaks the eerie silence.

It's a top-of-the-range Mercedes, midnight blue with British number plates.

That's strange. But then, I didn't catch her last name – perhaps her husband is British. I'm too consumed with Mum to think more of it. My mind's sprinting through worst-case scenarios. What happens if the arrhythmia returns? What if Mum doesn't wake from the coma? I have no choice – I'll have to abandon the search for Adele and return home.

The engine roars into life, the heat from the exhaust launches into the cold, sending billowing clouds in its wake as Rebecca takes off down the long drive.

Turning to close out the draught, I falter. I look back at her car, a speck fading into the distance.

A thought suddenly strikes.

I never told her Mum was sick.

CHAPTER TWENTY-EIGHT

MammaSass_sass Active one minute ago

Is everything OK? Why haven't you posted? I set my alarm to watch you this Friday and you weren't there. When I didn't see you, I cried. Please post soon, I'm missing you. I'm feeling really panicky without you. Please let me know you're OK.

CHAPTER TWENTY-NINE

ADELE

THREE DAYS BEFORE NYE

Christmas passed in a blur. Mostly because it's the first year I haven't spent it with Mum. Jack insisted we didn't go home. That we stick it out here and celebrate our first chateau Christmas together.

He's really getting into the spirit of life in rural France – much more than me, if I'm honest. I barely see him. He's always disappearing, tinkering on something or other. Or if it's not that, he's watching some DIY tutorial on his laptop And he's become secretive with it. Evasive when I ask. Like he's holding his new life close to his chest.

I'm feeling a bit left out. Jack seems to be thriving while I'm shrinking. Not really how I'd planned things to be. But at least he's happy. He's not moping around or getting drunk with the boys.

I decorated the main rooms with holly and mistletoe I picked from the garden, but when Christmas Day arrived it didn't feel quite right and at times the silence was deafening. Luckily that's passed and I can look forward to New Year.

New Year, new goals. I've made a promise to box away any negativity and I'm going to start a daily gratitude journal to remind myself how much good there is in my life.

The vlog is growing and I can't quite get my head around how popular the channel has become. I'm being asked to ambassador lifestyle brands, and I've had someone approach me to be my agent, how mad is that? I've fans from all over the world but mostly Americans, I suppose they're not used to old crumbling buildings and view Bellay as charming and romantic. Just like I once did.

Speaking to my subscribers does take the edge off the loneliness and recently I've been doing more YouTube live chats to make friends. They're always eager to ask questions about our relationship and I've become expert at telling them what they want to hear.

The heating has packed in again; that's the thing about old places – they're unpredictable. Sometimes I get this ghostly feeling about the chateau. There are things I can't explain and I find myself imagining it has a mind of its own. There's a life force here, all-seeing, all-powerful. It controls us rather than the other way around.

I shiver. The boiler man is coming to fix it tomorrow. For now, we have the fire.

I've been watching the flames for what feels like hours, mesmerized by the autumn colours, gold and red, waltzing across the bark. It's hypnotic. I'm tired, so very tired. The cold has an ability to do that to you.

But I have Jack, and that's all that matters. I cuddle into

him, snaking my arm across and resting my head on his chest. We're curled up on the leather sofa, a thick blanket over us, listening to the crackle and hiss of the fire. Our Christmas tree is twinkling in the corner, the smell of warmed pine filling up the room.

A cheeseboard lies half-eaten on the table nearby. Grapes spilling over and a torn-off chunk of baguette. Jack's little surprise for me. He went to the market especially and somehow managed to source a jar of Branston's pickle to help with my homesickness. He's been making up for things ever since our big fight over the secret room.

Everything feels calm again. It's the perfect moment to share with him what's been on my mind. I have a burning question and I make sure I'm holding him tightly, that way he can feel close to me when I ask.

'Jack . . .' I look up from his chest, lowering my voice to something gentle. 'We've settled in, haven't we?'

He turns his head from the window.

'What were you looking at?'

'Oh, nothing much.'

'Come on, what? It's dark, what can you see?'

'I was thinking about Pierre. Haven't seen him today.'

I swallow down my irritation, but not well enough because I feel Jack sigh. I should probably leave what I have to say unsaid, but it's there now, rooted, and I can't let it go. Quickly, abruptly, I pull the words out.

'Have you thought more about us having kids?'

I feel him tense. His muscles contract beneath my arm.

'You know this would be the perfect place for us to raise a family,' I continue. 'All this fresh air and green around us. And it's too big a place for the two of us.' I squeeze his hand. 'What do you say, hey?'

He looks at me closely, fixing me with that same serious look he had when he asked me to move in all those years ago. For a moment I think everything is about to fall into place.

Then a frown develops and his gaze runs back to the window.

'Jack?'

I squeeze him again, but it feels like I've lost him.

He pulls away, shaking his head. 'Why? Whenever things are going well, you always have to move the goalposts. I just don't understand.'

'It's not like that.'

'It feels like nothing's ever enough for you. *I'm* not good enough.'

'We've been together eight years; surely it's OK for us to talk about having children.'

'I'm not stopping you talking about it,' he says sharply.

'Feels like it.'

'Don't make out like I'm some controlling partner. What I'm saying is, why do you have to ruin things when it's all good between us? We've worked hard to get here.'

For a moment I think he's going to reach out, touch me, but something makes him pull back. I swallow down the disappointment.

'I don't think it's *ruining* things.' I react in anger. 'It's taking things to an even better place.'

'I can see this turning into a thing and, honestly, I can't deal with it right now.'

'But it's never the right time, is it?'

'I want to enjoy Christmas with you.'

'I'm trying to tell you how I feel. I want to have a family.'

'You're more like your sister than you realize.'

'What's that supposed to mean?'

'Always some crisis.'

'Can't believe you said that.'

He scratches at his jaw; a harsh grating noise fills the gap that's widening between us.

'Look,' he says, 'I'm not sure I want kids. I like my life, our life, how it is. I don't want to have to give stuff up.'

I stare at him.

'This isn't all about you, Adele; it's my happiness too. And I'm not sure a couple of kids fits into my vision – and it's OK for me to say that.'

I've never seen him like this.

I can feel my expression darken.

'You promised, though.'

He rubs his eye aggressively. 'I never *promised*.'

'But what has this all been about then?'

'There's more to a relationship than children.'

'Not if that's what we agreed.'

'There's *us*. Stop dismissing what we have.'

'I thought we were heading in the same direction. All these years, that's what I've believed.'

'I'm sorry if you feel misled.'

'Misled!' Anger catches in my throat.

I stare at the fire. Although I can't see the flames any more for the red mist that's descended. Why is Jack not saying anything to fix it? I can feel the imaginary wall building between us. He's laying one brick after another, boxing himself in.

I don't know whether to feel relieved or stressed when there's a knock at the door. I'm so lost in our argument, it takes me a moment to realize we have an actual visitor.

'I'll go.' Jack stands up quickly, letting me fall back into the folds of the sofa.

He can't get away from me quick enough.

Except for the postman and Pierre, we never get visitors.

I can hear voices, low murmurs, it sounds like they're speaking in urgent whispers.

'Who is it?' I call out. My voice is swallowed by the lofty room. When Jack's not here, everything instantly seems more intimidating. Unfriendly. It's only 7 p.m. but the dark winter nights make it feel so much later.

He's been gone for ages, so I get up to investigate. Jack hasn't bothered with the hall light, he's talking in the dark, one of two shadowy figures in the doorway, heads bowed close together, their outline backlit by the moon.

He flinches at the sound of my footsteps. Moving aside, he reveals the visitor's face.

In the pale glow her features seem hard and lined. As I inch closer, I notice that her cheeks are pink from the cold. She's mostly hidden behind a fur hat and a bulging scarf, but there's no mistaking who it is.

When she sees me approach, her expression brightens and her smile instantly changes her face into something warm.

'Hello, Adele.'

We stare at each other. Several beats pass as I adjust to the surprise.

'Lovely to see you again, how've you been settling in?'

My eyes move to Jack, who's looking as uncomfortable as I feel. I never thought I'd see her again. *Marissa White*. It's been nine months.

'Hi,' I say more warily.

Her eyes run over me. 'You look well – healthy, the country air suits you.' She turns to Jack. 'Handsome as ever, Jack. How are you finding life here? Nice to be the king of a castle, isn't it?'

'Guess so,' he says sheepishly.

It seems even stranger seeing her out here. Threatening. Somehow, I'd boxed her away with my England things, never to be looked at again.

'I've arrived just in time,' she says.

We stare at her blankly.

'Before the snow arrives. Have you not been following the news? There's an arctic blast on its way, hope you're prepared.'

'Doubt it will affect us, we don't go out much,' says Jack.

'I so love it when it snows, it makes everything appear clean.'

I feel anger building, but I can't put my finger on why.

'Speaking of the cold,' she looks beyond us, peering inside our home.

'Oh,' Jack pulls the door open wide. 'Do you want to come in?'

I bristle. We're not used to visitors and I've become like a territorial guard dog. Or maybe it's her, she puts me on edge.

Her heels clack on the marble. Tilting her head back, she admires the decorative ceiling.

'This is spectacular! And the craftmanship is sublime. To think how old this place is, I bet these wall have seen a thing or two. You can really feel the energy, can't you?' She makes another slow turn. 'I wonder how many people have danced within these walls, how many secrets this house is hiding. Oh, my client is going to fall in love with it.'

I look to Jack and he seems as confused as I am.

She walks around slowly, with an air of authority, a letting agent inspecting a house. Nodding and smiling and making some appreciative noises. But I can sense something running behind her eyes. A checklist, as if she's calculating, totting up numbers, admiring more than the chateau.

'My client is delighted with all the work you've put in, Jack. You're a wonder with those hands of yours.'

I prickle. What work? How does she know what he's been up to?

Stopping abruptly, she turns on a point. 'It's perfect!'

I move towards Jack and take his hand, smiling hesitantly. I'm almost afraid to ask.

'Incredible!' She peers inside our living room. 'The photos don't do it justice, it's even grander than I imagined. Once we move the furniture around, we'll soon have it looking stately again.'

Hang on.

'What do you mean, *move the furniture around*?' I say nervously, my voice sounding small and throaty.

'We can't have clutter in here. We're throwing a party, for heaven's sake!'

I look to Jack and he dodges my gaze. My anger flares. 'A party? Here?' I say sharply.

'My client will be hosting a New Year's Eve ball.' She turns back to the sweeping staircase, lifting a hand and moving it around like brushstrokes in time with her words. 'I'm picturing candles here and fairy lights running along there, a blazing fire in the ballroom, champagne, canapés when the guests arrive – and I want balloons strung up to the ceiling, released at midnight. Oh, and there'll be fire-works, lots and lots of fireworks. This will be truly spectacular, the party to end all parties.'

I'm stunned into silence. And still not a sound out of Jack.

'We haven't got long to make the magic happen, a couple of days and it will be New Year's Eve.' She smiles at us. 'Where does the time go?'

I'm shocked, I'm angry, but there's also a part of me coming alive. A little kernel of excitement growing. Think of the viewers, the content will be vlogging gold: *what the guests wore*. I'm now fantasizing about my ball gown. I could either go dramatic with a Disney princess dress, or wear something sexy, figure-hugging. Something tailored that would complement Jack's sharply cut tuxedo. If he wears the red waistcoat, I could even go matching. Lady in Red.

'Is there a theme?' I ask.

'You don't need to help us with any of that, I'll be hiring a team. Put your feet up and enjoy the time out. We've found you a stunning hotel in Paris. Something really romantic for the weekend. You'll be back before you know it.'

'Sorry?' Looking to Jack. 'Are we not invited?'

'It's for friends only, I'm afraid. A celebration of sorts, I'm sure you understand.' There's an edge to her tone now. Brisk, dismissive. She's shutting down the conversation.

I want to kick Jack into life I'm so mad. Who does this woman think she is? Turning up at our home, sending us away like we're staff.

My skin prickles with anger.

Throwing a party at *our* home when we've been banned from having any guests of our own. How is this fair? Who is she? Who the hell does she think she is?

I cross my arms. 'I'm not sure I'm happy about this.'

Finally, Jack moves to speak. I hold my breath, waiting for him to defend us.

'Adele, her client does own this place—'

I blink. What?

'But *we* live here. This is our home. Our names are on the deeds.'

'And we signed a contract that says Marissa's client has the right to return when they like, remember?'

'Yeah, a stopover on the way to their yacht maybe, that was my understanding of the agreement. Not a party.'

The lawyer watches us closely. When she catches me looking, she smiles awkwardly.

'Let's chat about this later.' Jack lowers his voice.

'No.'

'Adele,' he hisses.

My jaw clenches.

The lawyer steps towards us. 'You'll have kittens when you see the hotel room. Five-star, Michelin dining. It's so romantic. See it as a mini break, one that's been paid for.' She gives me a sharp look.

Checking the time, she moves to leave. 'I have people arriving tomorrow to set things up. Pierre will be helping with the security.' She stops. 'How've you been getting on with him, by the way?'

Jack takes my arm.

'Great,' he says.

'I knew he'd be a darling. Nice to know you have someone always on hand. He's got a sharp eye, that boy, doesn't miss a thing.'

Her words feel weighted.

'Well, I better be off, I have a couple more visits I need to still make. Get some rest you two and I'll see you tomorrow. Bright and early.'

She squeezes my arm as she passes but her touch remains long after she leaves.

I can feel myself doing it – eyes sliding back, looking anxiously at the door, as if she's going to reappear with more bad news.

Her announcement has derailed me. I have no idea where we stand – is the chateau hers or ours? What rights do we really have? My head aches, a dull throb pulsing between my temples.

Even though our names are on the deeds the rules make

it so we're little more than guardians. Everything we worked towards, snatched away. This can't be right, can it? I start frantically searching for where I put the contract.

Meanwhile, Jack's opened another bottle of Chardonnay and has filled his glass to the brim.

'You haven't thought this through – what this means for us.' I riffle through another drawer. I'm talking at him and I know I sound naggy, but he has to see this isn't right. 'Strangers in our home, using our bathroom, sleeping in our rooms. Having sex in our beds. Touching all our things, *your* things, red wine stains, cocaine on the surfaces. All the soft furnishing are going to be trashed.' I feel grubby just thinking about it.

'We've had parties.' He looks at me knowingly. 'Back in the day, you wouldn't say no to a line or two.'

'But these are *outsiders*, we know nothing about them.'

'Don't stress, they're probably boring, middle-aged entrepreneurs who'll go to bed as soon as it's midnight,' Jack reasons. 'And they'll have professional cleaners to sort out the mess, so we won't be coming home to broken bottles.'

'Why are you so calm about this?'

'You know I'm not precious about these kinds of things.'

'I'll have to hide my jewellery, I'll have to pack everything away, it's not just the practicalities, it's the sentiment behind it, like we're guests in a hotel.'

'It can't come as a surprise; we signed up for it.'

'What? How?'

'You didn't want to see because you were so wrapped up in your chateau dream.'

'She didn't warn us this could happen. We've been blind-sided.'

He shakes his head. 'Stop kidding yourself. You dragged us out here, so now we have to deal with it. And I'm saying *we*, this is something we have to accept.'

Where is this coming from? I know where – typical Jack, giving up at the earliest opportunity.

'Look,' he says more gently, 'I get the feeling this client of hers is flighty, this will be the last we hear of them. It's probably some rich tosser with more money than sense. Let them have their party, we have the chateau the rest of the time.'

He doesn't get it; why can't he see? *Keep calm*, I tell myself. But all I can think about is chaos, images of unpleasant characters invading our home. I feel colder than I've ever been, tingling all over because a frightening thought has taken hold, the dawning realization – our lives are in the hands of someone else.

It was never a gift.

Our home is not our home. It never has been.

And it never will be.

CHAPTER THIRTY

NOW

Sky News

Kate, we understand there's been a development in the search for missing YouTuber Adele Davenport and her partner Jack Reed.

That's right, we're just waiting for the official announcement from the police who've been searching the chateau grounds since 3 p.m. this afternoon.

A specialist team from Paris arrived with cadaver dogs trained to detect the smell of decomposition – that's tissue blood and bones – from as deep as fifteen feet underground.

The ground is frozen but the dogs should be able to pick up a scent as long as there isn't heavy fresh snow.

Kate, can you hear me?

I'm still here, Justine. The wind's really picked up and it's difficult to hear, but I'm going to carry on talking. While we wait for the police, we have a bit more on the sister who raised the alarm, Erin Davenport.

Thirty-two-year-old Erin is a triage nurse at Bournemouth General Hospital ICU where she's been practising for ten years. We were surprised to learn she hasn't been seen at work for some time.

Due to illness?

The hospital won't confirm or deny. There seems to be a level of secrecy surrounding her absence from the ward.

I can see something happening behind you. What's going on there?
    Kate?
    Kate, have you got a statement for us?

Justine, there's been a tragic development in the disappearance of this young British couple who moved to the Burgundy countryside full of hope and promise. The police have just issued an official statement, we can now confirm – a body has been found.

CHAPTER THIRTY-ONE

ERIN

NINE DAYS AFTER NYE

Mum needs me.

She could die at any moment. She's too ill to know whether I've brought Adele home with me. I must go, now, before it's too late.

But what about Adele? This so-called neighbour confirmed my worst fears. I can't abandon her. What if she's in serious trouble?

There's no point going back to the police. It hasn't been twenty-four hours yet and it's clear they don't want to help. They'll dismiss me again and I'll have wasted more time.

What then?

Paralyzed by indecision, I've slid into a trance-like state. Numbly gazing out of the window at the oddly shaped figurines planted in the wrought-iron flower box. Little people, stretched out in a line, facing the chateau.

Partially buried under snow, they're almost impossible to see unless you're looking carefully. I frown. How do they fit in with the rest of the chateau aesthetic? I park my dilemma in the drawing room and head outside to investigate.

The morning air is fresh with pine and there's only a few clouds scudding across the sky. The bright sun and mountain scents remind me of skiing. The singles trip I went on, way back when I bothered trying to meet new people. It looks crisp and clean but it feels like something is stirring. Brewing. The calm before the storm.

I walk across the courtyard to the plant trough directly below the window. There are more of them than I thought. A dozen. I pick one up and turn it over in my palm, examining the intricate work. Dark reed. Muslin cloth. Black thread holding the limbs together.

When we were children, Adele had a little pouch of worry dolls. Miniature people you could tell your fears to and then pack them away. The idea being they would deal with your problems and you could stop worrying.

These remind me of them, only there's something sinister about the craftsmanship. The way they're positioned. Faceless people dressed in black and they're watching the chateau. A prickle works itself beneath my skin. *Bit sinister to be collecting these, Adele.* But what's even more strange is – why haven't I noticed them until now?

I look up. The creeping sensation returning.

Someone is watching me.

My skin turns cold; it feels as if something's crawling around beneath my clothes. I squint, peering into the woods but it's too dense to make out anything. I eye the chateau grounds nervously, searching for any movement.

There's no sound. Nothing stirs, not even a breeze.

My laugh breaks into the silence. Come on, Erin, there's no such thing as ghosts. Yet I can't shake the haunting feeling something is out here with me. Something tortured and angry.

Letting the doll fall into the snow, I quickly retreat inside.

I've gone through all the number combinations I can think of so I've moved onto significant words.

The Find My iPhone app is now asking me to re-enter Adele's email address. I strike the keys, biting down on my frustration. Why, WHY does nothing work? And now the poor reception out here is slowing everything down.

Last try and then I'll have to leave. There's no time left. *Password incorrect.*

I slump into the chair. Taking a final moment for myself because every part of my body is aching, I haven't properly slept for over forty-eight hours, I've barely eaten anything. My stomach is burning. My insides feel raw and achy. The thought of a long road trip fills me with dread.

I'll come back for Adele when it's all over with Mum. *All Over* – what am I saying? The uncertainty of everything I'm facing is crushing me.

Adele is resilient and the police will keep me informed – it's not like there's anything more I can do. But with every lie I tell myself, I feel a jolt. Like a small electric shock.

OK – there's one last thing I can try. I'm laughing as I type the four letters into the white box and press return. The wheel spins and I stand up, getting my things ready to leave while I wait for it to buffer.

Shoving all my bits into my rucksack, lastly, I reach down for my phone.

The shock of it makes me stumble.

My mobile screen has changed – it's expanding into something new. There's a stark white background with a compass in the centre spinning around.

THAT – that was the code?

And now it's my laugh that's swelled into something high-pitched and hysterical because I can't quite believe it. I feel a rush of energy, then guilt as the significance of what Adele chose as her password makes impact.

My name. She chose *me*.

Adele cares more than I knew. All along, she cared. I swallow the knot of pain in my throat. We should never have let things break down like they did.

My eyes are pulled back to the screen. To the choice I've been given – make her phone sound an alarm or to see its whereabouts. It won't be here, in the chateau, it can't be, so I go straight to the map.

The spinning wheel starts up again and it seems to go on endlessly.

Stop. Buffer. Loading.

Lifting the phone in the air, I swing it around, trying to catch a stronger signal. It does the trick – the image unfreezes and the screen fills up with a grid, then a map – which instantly tells me – she's in France.

But she's not in a city or even a town, there's too much green for that. The app is showing me Adele's phone is in the countryside somewhere.

200

Pinch-zooming the screen, I stretch out the image, homing in on the blue dot.

I can feel my heart accelerating. I can't get there quick enough.

It's in the area, it's not far.

Pinch-zoom. And again. Fields, outbuildings, farm tracks – then forest. I keep zooming in until I can't go any deeper into the French countryside and my fingers start to tremble with the realization.

No, that can't be right. I blink. *Impossible.*

But the blue dot continues to pulse. Like a heartbeat. While a feeling of dread lodges in my stomach.

Because, now I can see the last time Adele used her phone was – I breathe out sharply – nine days ago. At 2.43 a.m. on New Year's Day.

And the last place she used her phone was – here.

Adele doesn't go anywhere without her phone. It's as good as surgically attached to her hand.

I look up.

My sister has been here all along?

CHAPTER THIRTY-TWO

ERIN

She must have left her phone behind.

No – Adele wouldn't do that.

Then why hasn't she used it since New Year's? Did she lose it?

She would have got a new phone by now. She would have contacted me or Mum.

There can only be one answer. Something's happened to her. She's hurt or— I swallow hard. Worse.

My eyes return to the screen studying the map for answers. I can see her phone was last used in the east wing of the chateau but it's impossible to pinpoint where; it's not accurate enough to know whether it's upstairs, downstairs or which room. The bad reception isn't helping, it's making the map reload every few seconds.

I tear along the corridor, through the bedrooms, leaving a trail of loud echoing footsteps. A clack-clacking. Eyes glued to the map, hoping by some miracle a pin will drop and X will mark the spot.

It's impossible to keep my worst fears from entering my head. Not after everything I've seen and heard. This feels like the missing piece of the jigsaw I've been searching for and something, *something* is warning me to prepare myself.

As I sprint from room to room, I can hear the noises again. The tick-ticking. The creaking. The faint whistling. It's a chorus of whispers coming from behind the walls and it feels like whatever spirits are lurking here have come out to play, excited by my distress. They feel untethered, dangerous and out to harm.

Christ – I think I might be going mad.

And now I'm just upset, desperate. I can't stop myself from crying as I take in the hopelessness of my situation. How vast this place is and how small her phone is. I'm searching for a needle in a haystack, and I don't know where to begin.

Adele can't be here because I would have seen her.

She's not here, it's impossible.

Even if she was injured, if she'd fallen and hurt herself – I would have found her. That is unless— I stop dead as an even more terrifying thought takes hold. Unless she's hidden away in some secret room.

A room like the one I saw in the drawing.

My fingers tremble as I return to the only place that might give me some answers.

Adele's Chateau Life.

The one place left I can think to look. I didn't bother with her vlog until now because I couldn't see how they'd be much help. A heavily edited, curated portrait of her life? But, maybe there is something, some clue, that can help me find her phone.

I open her YouTube page and start scrolling through the videos, searching for a thumbnail that hints at something. Anything. I have no idea what I'm looking for.

I wipe the tears away but more arrive in their place. My eyes feel gritty and swollen, it's not helping that the images are difficult to read on my mobile.

'Secret in the Tower.'

The word *secret* is enough to make me click on it.

The thumbnail expands, showing me Adele in a strappy sundress, one hand on the tower door, teasing her viewers to follow her inside. She looks tanned, healthy and beautiful. A smattering of freckles and mild sunburn across her nose.

I press play and follow her into the oldest part of the chateau.

Hey, lovelies! Sorry I've been a little quiet but we are back discovering our chateau and you're going to love love LOVE what I've found.

Seeing Adele, hearing her voice, immediately brings more tears to my eyes. Even though her performance is forced, it's still my sister. The one person who knows me better than anyone.

The chateau looks entirely different in the sunshine. The sandstone walls are a light buttercup colour. Warm and inviting. I wish I could climb into her video – we'd grab the sun loungers and park ourselves by the pool. I can almost hear the sound of the ice cubes clinking in our wine spritzers. I can see why she fell in love with the place.

So, this is the original part of the chateau and dates

back to the seventeenth century, unlike the rest of the building which is more modern. Wow, it spins me out thinking how old it is in here.

I follow her up the corkscrew stairs to the top. Taking in the historic details, the crumbling stone, the alcoves. I'm itching to fast-forward but I don't want to miss anything.

Are you seeing what I'm seeing yet? Look, it's the cutest miniature handle that you wouldn't know was there unless you were looking for it . . .

My heart quickens as I watch her crouch to the floor, her tan-lined feet, the small tattoo of a half-moon on her inner arm, her sun-bleached hair falling in front of her eyes as she pulls open the hidden drawer, revealing the secret compartment.

I hit pause.

It's in the east wing of the chateau. It's as good as any place to look.

The tower in January couldn't be more different from the place Adele took me to. I hear the wind lashing the stones and I can almost feel the tower shiver with me. I put out my hand to the wall to steady myself. It feels ice-cold beneath my fingers. As painful as a burn.

I snap it back into my body and lower myself down. Crouching low, until my knees make contact with the hard wood, I angle my head, tilting until it's almost parallel with the step.

There, just like she showed us, is the secret drawer.

As I pull it free, a smell of damp lifts up. Musty and ancient, like I imagine an old crypt to be and it's sharp enough to make me cough. And there, pushed right to the back – is my sister's phone.

I'd recognize that glitter Mickey Mouse case anywhere.

I don't know whether to feel relieved or afraid. I snatch it up as if the drawer might swallow it back.

The battery is completely dead. I carry it back inside, carefully cradling it in my palm like an injured animal that needs saving.

As I walk-run between the high-ceilinged rooms I shiver. That sense of being watched coiling around me again. I stop and stand completely still, listening out for footsteps.

But for the first time, there's nothing, not even the ticking. Everything is eerily silent and it feels like I'm not the only one holding my breath – the chateau is doing the same; watching, waiting for my reaction to what I'm about to find on Adele's phone.

I give my head a shake, flushing away the thoughts. It's my imagination playing tricks on me again. There's nobody here. *No one.*

But the uneasy feeling travels with me. A force, pressing down as I cross the hall into the drawing room.

I plug Adele's phone into my charger and the red icon appears, warning me I have a while to wait. A few minutes for the battery to come to life. It's torturous. Never has time felt so drawn out.

The questions start up again. Why did she hide her phone? Who was she hiding it from? Was it even her who hid it?

More frightening thoughts, I push away. I'm not ready, not yet.

The phone boots up with a bluish-white glow and then her screen saver arrives. It's a family portrait taken at our first house. Our last home together as a family. Adele is in the centre with Mum's arms clutched around her. My awkward pinched expression next to Dad, who always hated getting his photo taken. It's not the best photo of us but never mind. We're family and that evidently matters to Adele. Much more than I ever realized.

Weirdly – there's no lock on the phone. I swipe it open and her app icons load. All the usual, plus dozens of vlog editing tools. Now the signal's returned, the missed messages and notifications start arriving. One after the other, a continuous stream of WhatsApp messages and too many fan posts to count.

This will take forever. Jesus – where do I start?

I sit down heavily in the chair by the window, the one that looks out over the courtyard, stealing several deep breaths before I plunge into her world. A social media planet that's foreign and by the looks of some of the viewer posts – hostile.

First, the messages. I open WhatsApp and notice I'm the last person to contact her. Countless angry ranty messages still waiting to be read. Below that, similar impatient prompts from friends wondering where she is. Becky, Caroline, many more names I don't recognize.

There are belated Happy New Year's wishes. Then much further down the list, *Jack*. I click on what he has to say. They're chatting about getting a takeaway, but I'm more interested in the time stamp. He hasn't been online since New Year's Eve.

Another ball of dread drops right through me.

I flick quickly through her other messages – Facebook and texts – but there's nothing there, at least, nothing I can tell of any significance. More friends chasing after her with similar pleas to mine. There are also fan posts still arriving that sound borderline obsessive.

I click out of mail and move to videos and photos.

Hundreds of selfies taken in her bedroom, her bathroom, on the balcony. The same pose, identical pout and head tilt on repeat. The last thing she captured were a series of videos shot on the thirty-first of December. Four of them, not yet edited.

I open up the first one in order.

My chest feels like it's seizing up and it's only then I realize I've been holding my breath the entire time.

The frozen image is almost entirely black. An inky pool of shadows, except for, I squint, reaching into the dark. In the top right-hand corner there's a faint outline and it takes only a moment to register what the shape is.

I swallow hard. I know exactly where Adele is.

CHAPTER THIRTY-THREE

ADELE

NEW YEAR'S EVE

The bed and breakfast is worse than I imagined. There's not even Wi-Fi here. I snap my laptop shut and move to the window. I'm not sure if that's what's pissing me off or the fact it's not home.

Jack's on the bed, propped up with a stack of pillows, scrolling through his phone. There's not been a word out of him for the past hour. I'm getting the silent treatment for cancelling our five-star mini break in Paris.

I told Marissa White I have stomach flu and not up to travelling. I lied because I need to be close to home so I can keep an eye on things. She's put us up in the B & B in town instead.

Our room looks down on Fredy Brasserie. Amber glows through the misty windows, there's Christmas lights looped around the awning. Flickering then pulsating. The C of Merry Christmas is missing.

There's something deeply depressing about this town.

When we first arrived, I loved coming in to pick up bread and croissants, but now, it's something I dread. The locals are cliquey and hostile and make us feel like we're outsiders who aren't welcome in their community.

Even the owner of the B & B gave us a strange look when we checked in, as if he knew something we didn't. They're all weird around here, except for Delphine, she's lovely, but even she can't wait to leave this town and then I'll be all alone.

I feel a surge of gratitude towards my only friend here, who's showed me kindness, a listening ear when I've been at my lowest about Jack.

Two burly men in heavy jackets and beanie hats are stooped outside the pub smoking. They remind me of Pierre, which immediately makes me angry.

My mood's deteriorating. I'm feeling derailed by not having my routines and my things around me and the atmosphere between Jack and me feels toxic. The lawyer's arrival has left a stain.

I can't stop ruminating about the reason we've been left off the guest list. I stop dead and turn to Jack.

'You know they're snobs, right? They think they're better than us, that's why we're not invited.'

Jack nods half-heartedly.

'Why else would we be off the guest list. We lower the tone.'

'Just leave it, will you.'

'The fact you're not bothered is winding me up.' I shouldn't have said that. I swallow hard. But his lack of assertiveness is driving me crazy. I'm a caged bull ready to tear down anything in my path.

I start pacing, driving my feet into the threadbare carpet, I'm not sure I've ever felt this angry. Months of pent-up frustration has boiled over and I can't calm down. I won't, not until I get it all out.

'Can you stop doing that, it's really distracting.'

Narrowing my eyes, I drill holes into him until he finally looks up.

I stare back, biting my lip.

'Seriously,' his face softens. 'What's going on with you?'

'Can you do something?' I plead.

'What do you want me to do?'

'I don't know, go speak to her.'

'The party's already underway, the guests will be arriving.'

My head fills with images of beautiful people being chauffeured to our front door. The glitzy party I've always dreamed of triggers another episode. I roll my hands into balls.

That was *my* dream. Sending out gold invitation cards, trying on dresses, choosing a gown so big I can hardly walk. Wearing killer heels with glitter and sipping champagne and espresso martinis. Fireworks fizzing at midnight. Talking bollocks to guests who are hanging on my every word, all trying to suck up to me and Jack and be invited to the next party. THAT was my dream.

And then there's my vlog. A chateau party video would generate the most viewers I've ever achieved.

New Year's Eve, a time when we should be celebrating, spent cooped up in here. It's not fair.

Jack looks at me. 'You've got to calm down. Getting

mad isn't helping in any way. Try to relax, it's out of our hands.'

Another trigger. *Out of our hands*. That's the problem: all control has been taken from us. It's not just the snobbery and the entitlement and the disrespect, it's the helplessness of the situation, something I'm not good at accepting.

If the room was poky before it seems claustrophobic now. The walls are pressing in on me, just as they did in England. I'm fighting to get air into my lungs.

Nothing matches – the curtains are too blue; the bedding is a sickly grey. The wardrobe is a tacky bright pine. A cheap plug-in air freshener masks the smell of cigarettes and I feel itchy just looking at the throw covering the bed.

'I know what the problem is,' Jack sneers. 'You're too used to living in a mansion, you've forgotten how normal people live.' He laughs but the condescending edge only fires me up more.

'That's got nothing to do with it.' But I feel a jolt as the words leave me.

He sighs, sliding off the bed. 'I need a drink.'

The thought of him boozing again, of his mood turning, pulls me together.

'Hang on, wait.' I rush towards him.

'I'm not spending my New Year's Eve like this.' He picks his coat off the chair.

I grab his arm, my voice sounds strangled as I plead, 'Don't go.'

'Why? What's there to stay for?' He looks hurt now.

'You're hell-bent on ruining tonight.' His eyes rake over the room. 'It's not the Ritz, but it's *only one night*.'

'It's not about the room, can't you see? This has to do with how we're being treated.' But I can tell he's already not listening. I try to catch his eye but he's checking his phone. *Again*. Looking intently. His expression reminds me of those times when he was unreachable. Worrying about who he might be with.

A final trigger.

I'm now running through a list of suspects for his infidelity, the way I would back in England. The Scottish pub landlady? She's really sexy. No, he promised me, not her. The girl in the pharmacy. Christ – I don't know, perhaps. Delphine? No, she wouldn't, she's my friend. The only person who seems to give a damn around here.

I crush my paranoia. I can't keep doing this, it's hurting me more than Jack.

Trust. Have faith. He moved to France to be with me.

My gaze returns to the grotty bar across the road. There can't be another woman, not out here in the middle of nowhere.

The men are still there, smoking, nursing the beers, they look bored out of their minds. And who can blame them?

When Jack looks up his expression has changed, his mood has cleared but there's now a look of determination.

'How about I head out for one and bring us back some food since we're not getting anything here.'

'So, you are going to the pub?' I can't hide the tension

in my voice. My thoughts swing to Iona and how she'll be tarted up for New Year's. 'Iona will be working tonight.'

He sighs loudly. 'I'll head to the *other* pub then, OK? That make my princess happy?'

I blink quickly. Stuck between annoyed he's drinking and relieved he won't be seeing Iona.

'Food will cheer you up. Come on, I'll bring back a burger,' he says more brightly.

Forcing a smile, I concede. 'I do like burgers.'

'Find something on Netflix to watch while I'm gone.'

'I would if there was Wi-Fi.'

'OK, well, stick something on the TV why don't you.' He moves away from me. 'And try to relax.'

Wrapping his scarf twice around his neck, he tucks it into his coat. He checks his phone a final time and slips it into his pocket. I imagined the flash of something in his eyes, didn't I?

'How long will you be?' I say more tightly.

'Just going for one.'

'Be careful out there, it's cold and *that woman* said snow's on the way.'

He laughs and pulls on his hat. 'It's only up the road.' He hands me the TV controller. 'Stop worrying. And stop thinking about that bloody party.'

Party. The word echoes as he closes the door softly behind him.

It only takes seconds for my unease to return. I cross back to the window to watch him leave.

It's bitterly cold out there. Skinny trees flanking the street bow over in the wind. I imagine the wind striking his face; poor Jack, he's so susceptible to getting colds.

My Jack, making his way up the deserted street with that shuffle walk of his. He sneezes and pulls out a tissue, scrunching his nose in that cute way he does.

It's the last thing I see as I watch him disappear from view and I suddenly feel horribly guilty for starting a fight, for mistrusting him. For forcing him to walk further in this weather to reassure me.

A burst of movement pulls my gaze back to the bar opposite. One of the men that had been smoking outside, puts down his pint. There's a hurriedness to his actions. His glass still full, his beer spilling. The angry tug on his zipper. Barely acknowledging his friend as he takes off.

I'm watching him more closely now.

Shoving his hands deep into his pockets, shoulders hunched into the wind, he takes off at speed up the road in the direction of Jack. The man left behind at the pub makes a call on his mobile.

My eyes narrow. Something doesn't feel right.

Is it my imagination or are we being watched?

My gut tightens.

Is he following Jack?

CHAPTER THIRTY-FOUR

ADELE

Without his friend, the guy left behind seems to shrink in confidence. He shifts from foot to foot, blowing into his gloves, trying hard to keep warm. Why doesn't he go inside?

He checks his phone, he looks the street up and down, he returns to his mobile, types something and then he moves his gaze upwards. Our eyes meet at the window.

He quickly looks away, but I'm certain he was checking me out. I watch as he lights another cigarette and begins smoking aggressively, like a man with a lot on his mind.

My phone buzzes:

They're serving food. 🙏

Jack's WhatsApp is immediately replaced with another.

My princess won't go hungry.

Followed by *all* the food emojis. Jack hasn't lost his humour then, he's OK.

I return to the man opposite as he's crushing his cigarette beneath his boot. He necks the last of his beer, pulls open the door, returning to the pub's warmth. The noise of rowdy drinkers swells, lingering in the crisp evening long after he's gone.

Jesus, Adele, Jack's not being followed. You're not being spied on. I was imagining it. My paranoia about Jack cheating has woven its way into every thread of my life. This place is turning me into a lunatic.

Picking up the TV controller, I force myself to think about something other than Jack or our chateau or a party I should be at and flick to the music channel. Although, my body continues to hug the street view for a while longer.

There's more movement opposite but this time from inside the bar. A shadow – the outline of someone taking a seat in the window. Broad, stocky, he removes his hat. He rubs a hole in the steamed-up glass and I duck just as he looks up. It's *him*.

He *is* watching me.

Squatting beneath the window with my back pressed against the wall, my heart rate starts to spike. I search around me, as if the answer is somewhere hidden in the hotel room. What should I do?

Are they that desperate to keep us from the party they put bouncers on our door? Who are these clowns? To my surprise, adrenaline is replaced by rage.

How DARE they?

That Marissa bitch.

I'm no longer afraid, I'm seriously pissed off.

Are we so embarrassing to them? Do we bring down the tone that much? That's why Marissa wanted us in Paris, far away so we wouldn't cause any problems. Or are they worried I might vlog their little soirée?

I laugh out loud.

Well, that's exactly what I'm going to do. I stand up. Nobody makes me feel like a prisoner. Jack might be a people pleaser, going along with their rules, but I won't. I'm an established YouTuber with over a million followers. I'm an influencer. I earned the right to vlog this party. And I will go to the ball!

I open the wardrobe where I've hung my dress. I don't know why I packed it; stupid really, I guess there was a part of me that clung to the hope Marissa might change her mind last minute and invite us. If Jack knew, he'd laugh.

I gaze at the ball gown for a long moment, *My dream dress*. Long, slinky, the red sequins glittering. Then I think about how cold it is outside and shiver.

Thinking better of it, I stick with my grey hoodie and jogger bottoms. I tie up my trainers and put on my thick puffer coat. I'm going to turn up at the party looking like the Michelin Man – not exactly how I'd planned it, but hey. At least I'll be warm.

Downstairs, the B & B is deserted. The night light is on, pushing a soft glow around the dining room. Tables have already been laid for breakfast and there's a sideboard with cylinders of cereals and muesli. A crochet doily covers the milk jug. A clock ticking breaks the eerie silence and I wonder if Jack and I are the only guests. The old boards creak and moan as I weave through the tables to the back room.

I pass through the utility room, a kitchenette humming with the noise of fridges. I unlock the back door; it creaks as it opens.

Icy air storms in, seizing my lungs. So bitterly cold it snatches my breath away.

This is a really bad idea, I think, staring into the pit of black. But – it wouldn't be the first time I've done something stupid.

As my eyes adjust to the darkness, I can make out the outline of a small backyard with a pond, a picnic bench and a low wire fence separating their garden from the fields beyond.

I know where I am.

On the horizon is a wall of black. Thick and impenetrable, it's the forest that wraps around Bellay. All I need to do is take the shortcut across the fields and I'll be home. A fifteen-minute walk at most.

I feel the rush of energy and a childhood memory finds its way back to me. Those nights I'd wait for Mum and Dad to go to bed and then climb out of our bedroom window, lowering myself from the veranda roof into our garden. Always at full moon, my little adventure into the marsh behind our house. When I looked back, there'd be Erin, watching from the window, her face as pale as a ghost.

There's nothing holding me back now.

Pulling up my hood, I step into the night.

Cheering and celebrations follow me into the shadows. The further I wade into the field; the more the noise of town is replaced with nature. The sound of the wind whistling through the long grass, the rustling of small animals. The grass reaches my waist, stirring in the breeze.

The air is thick with the threat of snow, a dry cold, but

the sky is clear and the moon is three-quarters out, big and bold. Guiding me home.

Cobwebs as delicate as silk shimmer in the silver light, breaking apart as I push through. I huddle into my coat, my breath warming my face. Every now and then I check over my shoulder to make sure I'm not being followed.

I never understood why Erin was afraid of the night. I've always felt energized by it – it's when nature relaxes, you can almost hear her sigh as she unfolds her dark sky and unpacks the stars.

If she took a few more risks, if Erin would bring down that wall and let herself go a bit, she'd be much happier.

My phone vibrates and my sister's *Happy New Year* message lights up. Her ears must be burning.

She's off to bed early then. I feel bad for her, not sharing tonight with someone. But she brings it on herself, it's not like she never gets asked out. She can look drop-dead gorgeous when she makes an effort. Erin always finds fault in the men she dates. She seeks out problems, another thing I've never understood about her.

She once opened up to me, saying she had low self-esteem because Mum and Dad don't love her. Erin's convinced there must be something wrong with her. I could never wrap my head around where she was getting that from. Before the divorce, when Mum and Dad were fighting, they didn't have much time for Erin, but they loved her.

I tap out a quick reply, then stop. I should make an effort. I think about Mum and all Erin does for her. I send a heart emoji instead. I'll write more when I'm in the right headspace, as soon as I find out what this party is all about.

A tall hedge marks the end of the farmer's field. I thread through a hole that's already been made, emerging onto a deserted country road. The final divide between me and Chateau Bellay.

Hugging the stone wall that protects our home, I follow its line as it swings around until I arrive at the wrought-iron gate and the two stone eagles on columns that mark the chateau entrance. There are voices and lights up ahead. Torches drawing circles in the dark. I shrink back, crouching into the undergrowth where no one will find me.

There are a dozen shadowy figures shouting over each other in French. It's Pierre, he's manning the gates, leaning into his earpiece, and, for the first time he looks at ease. Dressed in black, the wide collar of his coat turned up with an air of arrogance, he fits the part of a bouncer perfectly. Minding the doors to the hottest party in town.

Headlights of an oncoming car shine into my eyes, washing all black from the night. It steers away and it's not until it makes the turn into our drive that I notice the calibre of what's arriving. A Range Rover – shiny and sleek with blacked-out windows – it's everything I imagined.

A sense of urgency – FOMO – ramps up. I need to get inside.

I stalk the shadows back to where there's a dip in the wall, adrenaline coursing as I draw up images of who's on the guest list. The sort of people that get chauffeured in Range Rovers and Bentleys. My kind of party.

I check my phone: 29 per cent battery left. That won't

be enough to film everything I need. I switch it to energy saver and slip it back inside my pocket so I can use both hands to scale the wall.

I land on the other side with a crunch. Twigs snapping beneath me as I begin moving through the forest. It smells musty, of pine, bark and damp earth.

There's no clear path to take me home but deer have left tracks, making it easier to pass.

Brambles claw at my legs. The soil is waterlogged and treacherous. Leaves left over from autumn have turned to mulch, leaving a boggy, slippery top coat and water quickly finds its way inside my trainers.

It's damp and cold but, despite nature's obstacles, I'm quicker than I think. I bounce over branches; I push off trees, anger and trepidation driving me on. Strangely, this is the most alive I've felt since I arrived in France.

I'm so lost in my mission he's barely crossed my mind since I left the B & B. *Jack!* I check my phone and there's a message waiting for me.

Burger taking a while. Sorry. x

Perfect. It's bought me some time. Plus, it's probably an excuse to hang around for another pint. I quickly reply with a thumbs up and tuck my mobile away along with thoughts of him.

Staring ahead. Obsessing. There's only one place I want to be right now.

It feels like I've reached the heart of the forest, somewhere I've never been before. I'm ringed in by a dense mass of woodland. An owl loops around a tree, coming to rest in the canopy, and I feel it watching me, a guardian of the chateau. I carry on under its protective gaze pushing deeper into the knot of trees, pulling apart the tangle of branches. Deeper and deeper, until I start to panic, I might be lost.

Then, without warning, the trees thin and the forest opens out into a small clearing.

A neat, flattened circle where the soil is well trodden-in and there's a pyramid of silver ash and charred bark ringed in with stones, the leftovers of a fire. There's a log positioned alongside it and, scattered nearby, cola bottles, a sandwich carton, an empty can of sausage cassoulet.

Someone's been here.

I think I can smell smoke, but that's impossible. Unless – they've been here recently?

I feel the first real shiver of the night. I look up, my gaze pulled in an easterly direction. Through the gaps in the trees I can make out the silhouette of the chateau. Close by, but not too close for anyone here to be seen. If I hadn't stumbled across it, I'd never have known this was here.

Placing the leftovers into a neat pile to collect later, that's when I notice it, next to the log – a pile of cigarette butts.

Pierre.

It has to be. I knew it! But why has he been camped out here?

I spot a beer can wedged under another fallen trunk and the dots start to join up. This is where he's been hiding when slacking off work.

I walk around, seeing what else he might have left behind.

The fact he's left his rubbish, that he couldn't even be arsed to tidy it away, angers me more.

As I'm leaving, something else catches my eye. Past the edge of the clearing, tangled in the tall weeds. Dark and waterlogged.

I cross the hard earth to where it's boggy again and reach into the undergrowth, pulling the fabric free. In the dark, the material ravished by the elements, it takes me a moment to recognize it.

My mouth falls open.

It's my silk and lace camisole. The one I bought years ago to impress Jack. That I now keep tucked away at the back of my lingerie drawer.

The movement of it in my hands releases a smell. It's infused with the damp and the earth but the smoky rose notes are unmistakable. *My perfume.* And, it's been sprayed recently or it wouldn't still smell.

I look up in horror. My eyes reconnecting with the chateau.

He's been in my room. Pierre's been going through my things.

My other clothes that went mysteriously missing suddenly come back to haunt me. My silk shirt. My nightie.

The thought of Pierre touching my underwear makes me nauseous. A memory resurfaces, him spying on me that day by the pool. I feel violated, sullied.

I drop the camisole, letting it fall back into the mud, vigorously wiping my hands clean on my joggers.

I knew there was something off about him and now Jack better listen up because I've got actual proof he's a pervert. After tonight, Pierre's history. I don't care what Marissa's client says, I couldn't give a fuck, I want him as far away from our home as possible.

I knew he was a predator.

CHAPTER THIRTY-FIVE

AdELEandJACk13 Active 10 seconds ago

Where are you? We love you, Adele. We miss you.
Come back! 💔 💔 💔 💔

CHAPTER THIRTY-SIX

ADELE

NEW YEAR'S EVE

The lights push through the gaps in the trees. A honey yellow, warm and inviting, a life raft pulling me in.

The sound of classical music floats towards me. I can pick out violins, the cello, flutes. An actual orchestra performing in my home.

As I walk the final hundred metres, the trees become more spread apart, loosening their bind with one another. Releasing me from their grip.

Pushing through into the clearing, I let out a little gasp.

It's unrecognizable.

The normally overgrown drive up to the chateau has been clipped back and illuminated like a landing strip. Brazier fires speared into the ground throw flames and plumes of smoke into the night. There are fairy lights looped around branches and an LED installation in the fountain changing the water from purple to blue then green.

It sparkles beneath the statue. They've added something to the water to make it a well of glittering precious stones. Snowflakes have been projected onto the side of the building, twirling across the old brick.

This must have cost a fortune.

The curtains are open and all the lights are on – a show home wanting to be admired.

Watching from on the edge of the forest, I suddenly feel like a leftover. The last person to be chosen for the sports team. Alone, in my ugly coat.

What am I doing here? I can't just walk in, can I? All my earlier bravado dissolves. Jack's right, what was I thinking? I should have let it go.

There's a noise, I crouch down. Hiding from view, like a good-for-nothing burglar about to break into my own home.

A couple emerges from a path through the trees. She's leaning into him, wearing a white fur coat, her arms locked around his waist. Laughing, flirting, they seem like a couple in love.

I'm hit with a pang of jealousy.

The ache of missing out propels me forward again. I start the recording on my phone and follow at a distance. Sprinting across the lawn, from bush to urn to manicured hedge. Pathetic, but I don't care, I need to see what's inside, what I'm missing out on.

The courtyard is crowded with sports cars. Lamborghinis, Ferraris, Jaguars. Lined up side by side like a showroom. I've never seen anything like it. There's another bouncer dressed all in black, a woman this time; she's taking keys from one of the guests. Valet service – I should have guessed.

A sudden burst of laughter pulls my gaze back to the main entrance as four guests spill out onto the steps. I pick out a mix of European accents.

Three men and a woman wearing elaborate masks of gold and lace with feathers. The men are dressed in black tie and one of them has on a golden beak. In the half-light its pointed nose appears sinister, more like a claw.

She's in red. *My colour*, the dress I'd planned to wear. The silky material glides over her tiny frame, catching on her hips and her breasts, accentuating her model figure. She leans back against the wall, thrusting her hips forward in a suggestive way.

She says something and they all throw back their heads in laughter. She's funny too. *I hate her.*

The tallest of the group shrugs off his dinner jacket and drapes it over her shoulders. She gives him a lingering sensual kiss. They must be a couple.

But no sooner have her lips left his than her hand moves across to the arm of the man next to her. The way she holds him implies some kind of intimacy.

Something about their gaze, how they now look at her, makes me uncomfortable.

Finishing off her champagne, she whispers into the ear of the man she kissed and he places his hand to the small of her back, guiding her inside. The others follow. All but one, who stays in the cold finishing his cigarette. He stares into the middle distance and I falter because, for a moment,

I think he's seen me. But then he too turns his back on me, returning to the music and the party.

Now the coast is clear, like a thief in the night, I creep closer. Feeling both envy and excitement.

Crossing the lawn, I approach the window furthest from the main entrance, somewhere I can lurk in the shadows. I check I'm still recording and I step up to the window.

Cinderella may not be invited to the ball but she'll do the next best thing. The viewers will go mental when they see this footage.

My insides are rattling with adrenaline and nervous energy.

As I press my nose up to the glass and peer inside, I feel my eyes enlarge and my heart – it almost stops beating.

CHAPTER THIRTY-SEVEN

ERIN

NINE DAYS AFTER NYE

I know where Adele was.

Standing right outside the window I'm sitting beside now.

Right before midnight, Adele was here.

Every muscle in my body is strung so tightly it's painful and there's a weird sensation moving around in my stomach, like butterflies before a first date. I don't think I've ever felt this nervous.

It's a tension I always get in the emergency room when something terrible is about to show itself. When I'm doubting whether we can save a life. Everything will change when I watch the recording and I'm frightened I'm not ready and I haven't got what it takes. I move a finger over the screen, then hesitate. I blink, willing myself to go on. *Adele needs you. You can't back out now like you always do.* Adrenaline spiking, I press the button marked with a white triangle, <PLAY>

There's music, I hear laughter ringing out – I see shadows crossing a foggy room.

So, there was a party.

The heat coming from inside is so intense it's steamed up the entire window. Adele swears under her breath then there's a high-pitched squeaking as she uses her coat sleeve to rub at the glass. A small hole appears. A portal through into the room where I am.

A corridor in time.

I hear the clack of her phone as it makes contact with the glass, the noise arriving the same time Adele lets out a horrified gasp.

There are a hundred or so hazy outlines, rounded shapes shifting through a thick fog of heat.

I squint, peering into the past. I can make out a string quartet, pushed back into the corner of the room, the fire is roaring and there are clusters of tall candles in glass jars and tea lights and— I swallow, because stretched out across the dining table, painted gold, there's a naked woman.

The crusted gold leaf is cracking as it follows the curvature of her breasts. She's spread across the table like a slab of meat at a medieval feast. It looks like one of those arty events in London Adele would try to get me to go to. All faux alternative in some underground bar. Yuk.

Blurry figures begin to move into focus and a young woman in a floor-length sequin dress with a slit to her hip approaches. She folds over, inserting something tube-like into her nose.

The naked model smiles as a line of cocaine is snorted off her breast.

There's a sudden flurry of excitement, gasps and clapping as a surge of topless waitresses in frilly knickers, white ankle socks and heels enter the room in a neat line. Balancing polished silver trays with canapés, they disperse between the guests.

Not the sort of canapés you'll find at the office party. This looks Michelin star, artfully arranged. Towering stacks of chargrilled vegetables, sushi, sashimi – the guests pick them off one by one.

More leggy girls and silver trays appear, diverging like a stream around the guests. This time they're carrying transparent bowls filled with gold foil packets. It takes me a moment to work out what's been served up.

Condoms.

The camera suddenly jerks sideways, Adele swishes the phone left to right, roaming between the dark corners of the room.

I hear the change in her breathing. It's more rapid, urgent.

She stops dead and zooms in.

Lounging on the leather upholstered chair is a silver-haired man with his bow tie undone. His shirt neck is wide open, the crisp white fabric bunching around his muscular arms. A sheen of sweat across his forehead. On the armrests either side of him sit two women in string-thin underwear. They lean in, taking turns to kiss him, their tongues slipping between each other while he plays with their breasts. Tugging their waists to meet him, he brings them close.

I catch the flash of a wedding ring as his hand moves up the inside of the blonde woman's thigh. The woman on his right lowers herself to the floor, knees to the ground, both hands sliding, parting his legs, she reaches for his zip.

I clutch my mouth.

There was a party, just not the sort I'd imagined. And my sister was there, just not in the way I thought she'd be.

The camera moves in a full circle, sliding to the right, fixing on a couple less than a metre away from where I am now.

They stand with their backs to the room; her cheek is pressed so tightly against the wall her lips are forced open. I can see the profile of her face, her sculpted cheekbone, eyes half-closed in a lazy, aroused way, her head bobbing while the man behind thrusts.

It's a sex party, just like the one in the book.

Finally, I hear my sister.

'*Fucking hell!*' It's more of a gasp than anything.

The drawing of the girl strung up in the stone-walled room comes crashing back into my thoughts.

A hard ball of fear drops into my stomach.

I can barely bring myself to watch – because – I've seen it before. I know how this party ends.

CHAPTER THIRTY-EIGHT

ADELE

NEW YEAR'S EVE

Fucking, on *my* sofa.

The room swims in and out of focus, as many as a hundred guests appearing as a blur of flesh and then in HD razor-sharp definition. The spectacle still not fully registering. Then, finally, I come to my senses.

There's an orgy in MY HOUSE.

I should look away but somehow I'm transfixed by the grotesque spectacle. I'm drinking it in with a mixture of revulsion and fascination.

And all the while, my thoughts on repeat: *That's my home, my lovely beautiful home. My* chair where I catch the sunshine in the mornings editing my vlogs, that's *my* sofa where I cuddle Jack. How will I ever be able to wash away the stain of this night?

The woman in red I saw earlier moves into view, taking centre stage. She turns, catching her audience with a mysterious smile, and once she knows she has their undivided attention she begins peeling off her dress, one strap at a time, letting it glide down her body, letting it fall to the floor, revealing a red suspender belt and thong. A slit where the fabric should be.

Her breasts are perfectly shaped, a fine leather strap criss-crossing around them. The gold studs catch under the lights. There's a small tattoo of a dove on her ribcage; it feels like it has a hidden meaning.

The guests, the ones who aren't busy with each other, move closer, forming a cage around her. It's impossible to read the mood with their masks hiding their expressions.

That's when I notice her. Stalking in the background. I don't need to see her face to know it's her. The way she glides with that same air of authority and administration, as if she's overseeing the party rather than taking part. She slips between the spectators, whispering in an ear, laughing, making sure everyone's having a good time. It's her, all right. Playing hostess, lady of the manor – the bitch that had us banned from the party.

Marissa pushes her way into the circle, smiling with approval as she observes the lady in red spread her legs. A small nod of appreciation as her guest offers herself up like a main course.

I feel like I'm in a nature documentary. Out on the Serengeti watching a lone leggy spring buck circled by a pride of lions. One moves in for the kill, the rest follow.

Three men and two women, pawing her, at first courteously, they take it in turns exploring but as they grow more excited, it becomes grabbier. Aggressive licking, more fingers than there should be. Competing for a piece of her until one of the men finally takes charge. Unzipping, he slips himself inside, thrusting from behind while a woman in a white mask and a sequin dress holds her steady, grabs a fistful of her long hair, kissing her while she's fucked.

In the background, the orchestra plays Mozart's fifth symphony.

It feels otherworldly, it could be a peepshow in Amsterdam's red-light district. Somewhere tucked out of the way, hidden in a basement.

Only, it's not, it's in a grand chateau. It's in *my home*. I can't tear my eyes away.

And as I continue to stare a new sensation moves in, catching me off guard. Next thing, all my skin is prickling. Electrified.

It's crept up on me, that feeling I haven't experienced in a very long time. Arousal. And, I'm not certain I've ever felt like this.

Even though a glass pane separates us, I can almost feel what she's experiencing. I can almost smell the sex. And now I'm wondering, what must it be like, to be watched like that?

I wouldn't want to be her; God no, I couldn't have sex with random men, that's revolting, can you imagine?

I falter.

A hot mist is rising, clouding my thoughts. I can't think clearly, not when I'm turned on like this. But what I do know for certain is – I've never felt this way about Jack. Not even when we first got together, when everything was fun and the sex was often and carefree. No, not even then.

Watching the party guests experiment and let go of

inhibitions has made me see what's missing in my life. Passion, surprise, excitement; and no amount of positive happy manifesting is going to change that.

It's the strangest of moments to have an epiphany, yet, as I stand with my nose pressed to the window, I know there's no going back. The realization is so intense it forces me to look away.

Returning to the darkness, I've never felt so confused. My heart's beating so violently it feels like it could leap out of my chest. All of me is prickling.

For all this time I've been blaming myself, believing I'm the broken one and there's something about me that needed fixing, when really, it's Jack. Maybe it's as simple as I don't love him any more? I've been blinded by the truth because I want a child so badly? After this weekend is over, we should talk.

The attraction we once felt for each other has waned. But it's more than that, there's something else that's come between us. Something much darker which I can't quite put my finger on.

A loud clashing noise breaks into my thoughts. I jump and spin around. Returning to my peephole, my portal into this new world.

The room has filled out and new guests keep appearing, beautiful thin, toned bodies pressing up against each other. A small clearing has been left in the centre of the room.

The woman in red has disappeared into the corner with the man I saw her kissing earlier, but the foreplay has ended. All eyes are trained ahead and there's a collective look of expectation.

Something is about to happen.

A short muscular man bound in fetish straps and wearing a black executioner's mask smashes a gong and the crowd obediently hushes. The room falls quiet. So eerily silent you could hear a pin drop.

There's a ritualistic feel about the whole thing that sends a shiver down my spine.

The wall of bodies breaks apart, making room for someone to enter the circle. Reaching onto my tiptoes, straining, I can just about see who's taking centre stage.

Marissa White.

'Welcome.' Her voice rings out. 'And may I say, you're all fabulous!'

She turns slowly in a circle. A leader blessing her followers.

'It's with the greatest pleasure we invite you all here tonight, our most valuable and respected members. Without you, none of this would be possible. Your loyalty to us and the programme means everything.'

The programme?

'And can I just say,' she casts around. 'Wow. What a beautiful crowd we make, I can't keep my eyes off you.'

There's a low rumble of laughter.

'Most of you will know why we've gathered here tonight, why we've chosen this extraordinary chateau as our venue, but for those of you yet to be surprised, I can assure you, there's a treat in store.'

She turns and this time I notice her jewels: she's dripping in diamonds.

'You must be bored of my voice already.' She laughs.

'So, without further ado, let me hand you over to the person who can explain tonight's theme, someone you've all been waiting for . . .' She takes a step back and the room explodes with clapping, a thunderous drumming, like a tribal beat, as a tall man disguised in a simple gold mask moves inside the circle.

Dread washes over me. I'm not sure why, but I have a terrible feeling about what's coming.

His voice is deep and buttery and immediately commands attention.

'Welcome friends . . . lovers.' He sounds even more posh than the lawyer.

He's wearing a tailored tuxedo with a precisely folded handkerchief showing from his top pocket. His face is almost entirely concealed behind his mask, but I can make out the strong jawline. Clean-shaven. Well groomed. I can tell he's handsome and from the way he confidently holds himself, he's someone used to being admired.

'It's with great pleasure I can celebrate the New Year with you all in this extraordinary building steeped in history.'

It's *him*. Our investor, it has to be.

'For centuries Chateau Bellay has been the home of some of the greatest, the most memorable parties. Dangerous, exotic' – he lowers his voice – 'experimental.'

The word sizzles in the silence. It's not just the guests, it feels like the entire building is holding its breath. Waiting on his command. A general addressing his troops.

'Who is he?' I think back to Marissa's words: *a well-known public figure*. I feel myself being drawn to him in that way people of power have.

And what does he mean? *Experimental?*

'The Bellay family were renowned for their extravagance and excess,' he continues. 'To those not in the know, they appeared a devoted family, but behind closed doors they liked to indulge forbidden appetites. Mixing with the upper echelons of society they became known for pandering to the rich, the nobility, royals. Satisfying their needs while maintaining the highest order of discretion.' He takes a breath. 'Hosting parties just like ours tonight.'

A sickening feeling grows inside of me.

Smiling, he adds: 'These walls have seen things you never knew were possible. Experiments not even you could imagine. They hold secrets, dark and dangerous. Desires forbidden in *normal* society.'

My home, my fairy tale. What's he getting at? Is there some sordid history to Bellay I never knew about? What was vaguely sexy is now turning sinister.

'What is normal anyway?' He turns to the crowd. 'We don't do *normal*, do we?'

A collaborative cheer moves around the room.

'We don't follow rules. We break them!'

A general, rallying his troops.

There's more cheering. More toasting. I feel I'm witnessing a cult gathering.

'Which is why we have this safe space to play and create and to do things we shouldn't be allowed to do.'

The guests reach out to each other, hands exploring. There's a sense of a build-up. An unspooling. Something terrible is about to be revealed.

'Tonight, nothing is off limits.'

He locks eyes with his lawyer and they share a smile.

'Ladies and gentlemen, midnight is approaching and it's time this party got underway. Our bedrooms are now open for play.'

Play? The knot tightens in my throat.

'Each room features a different theme, there's something to satisfy all tastes and needs . . .'

There's an edge to his tone now. It's dark and disturbing.

Some of the guests are celebrating prematurely. He hushes with a raise of his hand.

'We have only one rule, and that is: you must be asked to enter . . .'

He shrugs his shoulders back, straightening. His eyes roam the room, skating over his guests towards the window.

I freeze. I think he's seen me, but he turns back to his audience.

'Ladies and gentlemen, welcome to Chateau Bellay, our new party house.'

Our party house? *Christ.*

'Let the games begin!'

The gong clashes and there's a roar of celebration.

I inhale sharply, a deep shuddering breath.

Jack, I must find Jack.

CHAPTER THIRTY-NINE

ADELE

'Pick up!'

Where is he? Come on, Jack, answer your phone.

The air frosts my insides. My breathing, short and shallow as I sprint for help, putting as much distance between me and the chateau as possible. Anger, panic, confusion, all duelling for space in my head. Five minutes ago, I was feeling the most turned on I've ever been and now – now I'm shit scared.

Dark, ominous thoughts crowd my head. The secret history. The parties. *The programme*, what did Marissa mean by that?

The hidden room I discovered elbows its way into view. HELP ME, scratched into the floor. Had that been a sex dungeon? I should have guessed. Within seconds of crawling inside that dark, dank chamber, I knew something terrible had taken place. The way the chill grabbed me. Tortured souls were doing laps inside of there.

Someone, please explain to me, how is torture erotic? Who are these freaks? My thoughts circling back to our investor. Who is he really?

And then an even more frightening thought swoops in. What do they want with us?

Jack, come on. I punch redial.

'Hello . . . Hello . . . Hello? . . . Just kidding, leave me a message.'

His stupid childish voicemail, I've never hated it so much.

'Where are you? I need you – urgently, call me back *now*.' I hang up.

Oh God. I stop dead. What if Jack can't pick up?

The guy I saw following him to the pub – I should have taken it more seriously. Have they hurt my Jack?

I'll have to go back for him. Although, how do I know where he is? He could be anywhere by now.

I turn in the direction of the town and immediately the woods feel darker and more threatening. Under the pale light of the moon, everything seems bent out of shape and hostile. And the temperature has dropped. It's bitterly cold, the air whispering that snow is on the way.

Out of the corner of my eye, I see a flash of colour. It's not coming from the chateau or the light display, it's further off, sitting on the horizon. Squinting into the gloom, I can just about make out a glow. A halo of light arching over a building. It's coming from the outhouse, the one that's been locked up.

Should I go look?

The logical part of my brain is screaming *Turn back. Go find Jack.*

But I need to know what's really going on.

Paralyzed by indecision, I stare at the light. Before I've thought it through, I'm striding towards the barn. *This is a really stupid idea. The worst of all your ideas.* A small hysterical laugh escapes me as I realize crowdfunding a chateau and signing a contract with a sadist might steal that crown.

It's much further out than I remember, on the edge of the forest, where the weeds tangle, the area of garden where nobody goes. There's a strange smell in the air but what it is, I can't quite place. As I draw nearer. A feeling of dread lodges.

I should let Jack deal with this, but I won't because I've lost all faith in him. If it wasn't for me, nothing would get done. It's the pressure of responsibility that's driving me on now. That, and a dangerous curiosity; I need to know how bad this really is. How much trouble we're in.

As I draw nearer, I hear voices. No, it's something else, something much more primal. *Moaning.*

Another orgy?

I stalk through the long grass until I'm only metres away. The barn door's open a crack, a strip of light spilling across the mud.

The noise grows louder, rising to a cacophony, a loud, angry discord. There's shouting, screaming, a cry for help. I'm almost too frightened to look. But I'm drawn in, a moth to the flame.

Peering through the opening, I can barely breathe.

I gasp.

The building is deserted.

Inside the lofty open space, below the beams and the yellow strip lights are three large desks and half a dozen monitors. Each screen is divided into four and within those quadrants is a moving image. Something far worse than what I saw at the party.

I slip through the gap, creeping towards the noise, to where I can see more clearly.

My eyes stretch wide.

It's porn. Disturbing, fetish sex. The violent kind.

A woman being throttled. A thick rope, wrapped tightly around her neck. One man fastening her down while the other forces himself on her. My eyes move along to the next screen where there's an blond-haired man on his knees, hands clasped in a prayer, begging for mercy as his sides are whipped raw. The sound of the whip cuts right through me. There's more. I swallow back bile as I watch someone being hoisted up by hooks.

Perhaps the most shocking video of all is of a young woman, who can't even be twenty, strung up on a medieval rack. A bucket filled with something next to her.

It's like nothing I've seen before, yet it's terrifyingly familiar. The rings, the coarse brickwork. The dark cave-like chamber. As I take in the detail of the other rooms it takes a moment longer to register. It's our house. Those are our bedrooms. Cameras – in *our home*.

My God, have they been there the whole time?

Only now do I notice the chair positioned in front of the screens.

I'm not alone.

There's a flushing noise. The heavy sound of boots. A door swings wide open and before I have time to run, a shadowy figure steps out and into the room. The outline of a man in a heavy coat.

A rabbit in headlights, I'm fixed to the spot.

I can't see who it is, but I know it's Pierre. It must be.

He steps under the light; our eyes lock and my heart almost stops.

'Jack?'

CHAPTER FORTY

ADELE

We stare at one another. Two people who've spent the best part of a decade together, studying one another as if they were complete strangers.

As the silence stretches, I'm praying I'll wake from this nightmare. This can't be real.

Why is he not saying anything? Why is he not telling me this isn't what it looks like?

'Jack?' Finally, I whisper.

I move towards him but the noise, the wailing and the screaming bring me to a hard stop. The light from the flashing images casting eerie shadows across Jack's face.

'You're scaring me, say something.'

He stands still, statue-like. A glaze over his eyes.

'Jack?'

This place I'd tried so hard to call home suddenly feels anything but. I feel cornered – trapped in a foreign country with a man hiding secrets. There's more than a wall of silence between us. We're back to the way things were in England. The waking up and never knowing which Jack I was going to get. Who is he now? I don't recognize this person.

'What the fuck, Jack! Say something.'

I can't read him. I don't know whether he's going to reach out or lash out.

'What is this?' I search around me. 'Why are you here?' It's impossible to keep the fear out of my voice.

His eyes move, his gaze slipping past me, like I've become invisible.

'Jack, what is this?' I scream. 'Tell me now or I'm going to the police!'

I see a slow change in him, his eyes refocusing, his brow furrowing. Then he lurches forward, grabbing me by both wrists, so tightly I think they might snap.

His voice, low and threatening. 'Listen to me, Adele.'

I try pulling free but I'm no match for him. A hidden strength is showing itself.

'You're hurting me!'

He shakes me hard. 'I need you to listen.'

He holds me tighter than he ever has before and a whimper leaves my mouth.

'You weren't meant to see this,' he hisses.

'What have you done?'

He lowers his eyes, he shifts from one foot to the other. His lost boy routine. I won't let him do this, not this time.

'Why are you here?' I go at him again. 'Jack? Why are there cameras in our house?'

The trigger word.

'*Our* house?' he explodes. 'It's not our house, that's not what's going on here, Adele.' There's an intensity I've never seen before. Fire in his eyes. 'What did you think would happen?' He lets go of my wrists and starts pacing. Back and forth. 'What did you expect? There's always a price to pay.'

'Come again? The price is you getting involved in sex parties?'

'I tried to warn you off. I told you there's no such thing as a free ride.'

'Don't you dare!' I scream back. How does he get to be angry? He should be the one apologizing. 'Don't tell me you didn't want this? You love our life out here, doing absolutely nothing. Living off other people's money.'

Jack laughs. 'You're deluded.' He shakes his head. 'You're so obsessed with yourself and your vlog that you don't know what's real any more. Asking people to pay for your dream life, what were you thinking?'

'But you happily went along with it, didn't you?'

'Did I?' He points to the screens. 'I'm doing this for you. It's all for you, princess, to keep you happy.'

I laugh hysterically. 'Exactly which of the clauses in the contract mentioned installing cameras for a sex party? Because I don't remember it being there.'

'How else did you think you'd get to keep your chateau? After all the papers were signed, after we'd settled in, Marissa got in touch saying I either install the cameras or we'd lose Bellay.'

'She couldn't do that; the deeds are in our name.'

'And we signed a counter contract agreeing we can be evicted at any time if we break their rules, remember?' Jack hisses. 'It wouldn't take much to prove we'd gone against their wishes. Hell, even that junk you kept bringing back from the market would count against us.'

'Oh, so this is my fault?'

Our eyes meet with fire.

'I wouldn't be in this mess if you'd accepted the hotel in Paris.'

What? I look at him in disbelief.

'There was a problem with the live stream – they called me in to fix it. If we'd been in Paris, like we were supposed to be, I wouldn't be here now, having to watch over them.'

Something in his voice makes me falter. My eyes narrow as I study him more closely.

'You think I'm enjoying this? You think I want to be here?'

I search his eyes for the truth. There's something hiding behind them, but I can't see what.

'The whole time I thought you were beavering away on projects, you were installing cameras in our home. How could you?'

'I told you: Marissa threatened we'd lose the chateau.'

'Have they been watching us this entire time?'

'I don't think so.'

'Well, that's reassuring, isn it?'

He looks away.

'Why you? You haven't got a clue about this kind of thing – you worked in the council planning office.'

He looks offended. 'Always first to put me down, aren't you.' He rubs at his eye. 'They knew I had a technical background and told me to get up to speed.'

'*That's* what all those online tutorials were about.'

He lowers his gaze.

'You sneaky—' I swallow back more anger. 'What are they doing with the recordings? Blackmailing people?'

'Nobody has told me anything.'

'What *do* you know?'

'There's a syndicate.'

'A syndicate?'

'Some sort of member's club.'

Marissa's words return to me: *the programme.*

'The steaming is for members who can't make it to the party. VIPs get special access to what goes on in the rooms.'

'Do the people in the rooms know they're being filmed?'

Jack blinks.

I'm thrown. It takes a moment to register.

'Wait,' I gasp. 'They don't know they're being filmed?'

'Look, it's only what I've overheard when setting up.'

I lock eyes with Jack.

'What the hell have you got us into?'

I turn on my camera, pointing it at the screens.

'What are you doing?'

'Collateral.'

'What? No.' Jack lunges, trying to snatch my phone away. 'Don't be crazy.'

'We need protection. Our names are on the paperwork, there's nothing linking our house and what's really going on here, to them.'

'You've been watching too many films. Nothing's going to happen to us – come on, give it here.'

'These people could be dangerous. We don't know what criminal organizations they're mixed up in. Why's our investor so rich? Where did he get his money, huh?'

He laughs. '*Now* you're asking.'

'Fuck you, Jack.'

'Have you asked yourself, why us?' he says.

I stare at him.

'Your vlogging.' He laughs. 'It's the perfect front, making the chateau appear wholesome. Meanwhile they run sex parties and God knows what else from here. We swallowed their line hook line and sinker.'

'*Christ*,' I exhale. Although, something's still niggling. I can't help feeling there's even more to this. What's Jack hiding?

We're so busy arguing, we don't notice screen seven. The grey-haired man with a beard, the one with a noose tightened around his throat: he's not moving.

The young girl straddling him drops the belt she's been using to throttle him and shakes him repeatedly, but he's not responding. She can't be older than sixteen. Rake-thin. Her features, still rounded, innocent looking.

I point. 'It's our room, Jack. That's our bed!'

The girl in the blue corset drags herself off him and searches around. Panic sets into her features. She rakes her fingers through her long hair, turns in a small circle and then, then she starts screaming.

'Oh my God.' I turn to Jack. 'I think he's dead. I think she killed him.'

Jack stares back at me.

We watch her pace back and forth, crying, trembling. A sex game gone horribly wrong. Then the door swings open and two men enter our bedroom. It's the darkness that catches my eye, how they're dressed head to toe in black. Pierre – this time it really is our gardener.

In the distance, the crowd cheers. 'Five. Four . . .' The countdown to New Year begins.

We're transfixed. Watching helplessly from the barn as Pierre's friend locks our bedroom door.

Three . . .

The girl rushes towards them, her mask falling away. The real her, the one behind the coarse make-up and the cheap underwear, showing itself. Lost. Vulnerable. She appears desperate and confused.

Two . . .

Pierre grabs her.

One . . .

It feels like we're in a cinema, watching one of those noir films. Only *it's real*. This is really happening. There's no trace of emotion. Not a hint of compassion in Pierre's sun-worn features. He stares coldly, two pools of black for eyes.

The clock strikes midnight and the party explodes into celebration. Shouting, cheering, the noise shaking the night. Then come the fireworks, masking the screams from our bedroom. The second man walks over and turns off the camera.

The screen falls dark and shock seizes me. I don't realize I'm still holding my arm up, my hand frozen in the same position with my phone fixed at the screens.

Jack grabs me. 'We've got to go.' He pulls me along by my wrist. 'Fuck. Fuck. Fuck,' he exhales.

'What was that? Jack, tell me he's not dead.'

'He's dead, all right.'

'What did they do with the girl?'

'I don't know, but we've seen more than we should have.' Jack slows to a stop. 'Shhh.'

There's the sound of voices – people moving around outside.

We wait by the door for several beats, standing perfectly still, neither knowing what to do.

My eyes leap around the barn, searching for somewhere we can hide. Apart from the toilet cubicle, there's no cover. Jack takes me by both shoulders and we lock eyes. I see my fear reflected and it's terrifying.

'Listen to me and don't argue, you're going to have to run for it.'

'No, no way, I'm not going anywhere without you.'

'For once, do as I say. These people,' he takes a breath. 'These people don't mess around. We're witnesses to what happened tonight and now we've become a problem for them.'

He doesn't need to explain. I know what this means for us.

I can feel Jack's hands on me, trembling.

All that resentment, that bitterness I've built up, falls away. The thought that something terrible could happen to him takes over. I don't care what happens to me, I don't want them to hurt Jack.

'Go!' he says.

'No!'

He shoves me away. 'Go now before it's too late.' He's cold, unfeeling, I know he doesn't mean it.

'I can pretend I'm doing my job but they mustn't see you're here.'

The sound of voices intensifies, louder, closer.
Jack looks at me with pleading eyes.
'I'll find you.'
I let out a whimper.
He mouths: 'I love you.'
Instinct finally kicks in, propelled by his promise, and I pitch, sprinting for the door.

CHAPTER FORTY-ONE

SunnyElvira47 Active ten minutes ago

It's obvious Jack doesn't love you. He's been playing you this whole time. Nobody loves you bitch!

CHAPTER FORTY-TWO

ADELE

A thick arm hooks my neck, crowbarring me into a head-lock. I elbow him in the gut – there's a grunt, a wheeze of air, the surprise blow is enough to loosen his grip and I shoot for the night.

Then a sharp tug rattles my insides, I turn and our eyes meet. The hulking shape of the man in the beanie hat from outside our B & B: he's got hold of my coat.

'Run, RUN!' Jack yells.

With gloved hands he snatches at the material, pulling me in, his expression hardening, preparing for something.

I hear a gurgling noise but it's not me. I look over. *Jack!* There's blood around his mouth and nose. He takes another hit to the stomach, so hard I hear ribs crack. Crashing to his knees, he manages to cry out my name before another fist meets his temple.

'Jack!' I scream. 'Jaaaaack!'

I feel something tighten around my throat as beanie man squeezes my neck.

'Give me the phone!' He reeks of cigarettes, beer and fusty breath and that's all I can take in as fear and adrenaline take over. I lift my leg, stabbing my heel into his shin.

His grip slips. Jerking forward, I'm able to release myself and leg it to the door.

'*Merde*,' he curses as I dive into the thicket of brambles outside.

I fall down. I get up. I scramble through the under-growth and I don't look back. Jack's words echo. Run. Run. Run.

I have no clue where I'm going or what I'm supposed to do now. Music fills the night. The beat drumming like a marching band.

I hear shouting and a strangled cry from behind me and I know it's Jack.

Tears blister. Every inch of me screaming. *Go back*.

But I can't do this alone, I'm outnumbered, the only chance of saving Jack is to get help. If I can make it into town, if I can just get to the police station.

A few stragglers, too pissed to care about the cold, stumble around the grounds in bare legs, high heels and borrowed tuxedo jackets, clutching champagne bottles.

More shadows shift up ahead. They're clutching flash-lights, searching the night, searching for me, and they're headed my way.

With nowhere to hide, I double back, sprinting for cover. Each stride feels slow, heavy, laden with guilt for leaving Jack behind.

My mind lurches to the dead man. The girl trapped in our room. Who is he? What did they do to her?

Up ahead is the abandoned chicken coop. Dropping to

my knees, I crawl through the hole in the wire, the sharp edges catching my skin, I wince, inching my way through the hutch door.

The tiny wooden space smells of old hay and dead animals. The wooden floor is damp, slippery and coated in feathers and droppings. I bite down, trying to stop the urge to sneeze. My eyes water as I hear footsteps.

'*Obtenir son téléphone!*' someone hisses. 'She has it on film. Bring me her phone now.'

A torch beam teases the hatch opening. I pull my knees into my chest and hug them tightly, suffocating me. *Make this all go away. Jack's injured, but he'll be OK. I'll wake up soon and this will have all been a very bad dream.*

I suck in the air and hold my breath, counting down the seconds until I'm caught. My last moments on earth spent knee-deep in chicken shit.

I hear the snapping of twigs, the rattle of wire and then, then there's nothing. It falls eerily quiet.

They're listening. Hunting.

A cough tickles my throat. I force down a swallow, and another, trying to push the urge away.

The footsteps grow softer, the voices fade. *They're leaving.* I edge towards the opening. Peering out, I see they're headed for the barn. For Jack.

I need to get help. The police. GO!

I crawl on elbows and knees through the mud and clamber back on to my feet. I could soon be in the forest, if I take the shortcut, it's a fifteen-minute sprint into town. I can do this, go, RUN.

Taking long strides, pumping my arms, I don't notice

the tree roots rising out of the earth, hooked and knobbly like an old person's knuckles. My foot catches and, before I know it, I'm flying through the air with the ground rushing up at me. I land on my front with a thud, a mouthful of earth and a loud snap accompanied by a sharp, intense pain shooting from my ankle.

Then shock takes over. I lie completely still, face-planted in a cold bed of decomposing leaves. The only sound is coming from my chest – little wheezy sobs and gasps.

Gently, I ease onto my side. My hands and knees are burning. Luckily my phone didn't fall far; I snatch it up and shine the beam where it hurts.

Tiny red capillaries are filling up across the heels of my hand. The blood appears black in the moonlight.

Hauling myself back up onto my feet instantly sends my ankle into spasm, small electrical shocks sparking up and down.

Is it broken?

Reaching down I can feel my ankle has swelled up. My trainer is tight and the numbing pain is now just pain. A throbbing.

Using a branch as a crutch, I carefully try shifting my weight. It doesn't buckle this time. It hurts like anything, but I can stand. I can walk-hobble.

There's no way I'll make it out of here now.

I look ahead to the tower. Backlit by the moon it appears especially creepy. Long shadows straddle the lawn. It's a dead end, but there's nowhere else left to hide.

I push down the pain and limp towards the oldest part

of the chateau. The Rapunzel tower that started my stupid obsession. Where the dream began – who'd have thought it would end here too.

I hear voices in the distance and I know they're coming for me. Terror mounting, I yank open the thick oak door. It judders but then gives easily, welcoming me inside. It's almost an invitation to die.

I drag myself up the steps, one at a time. The pain is excruciating. Round and around the spiral staircase until I reach the top where I can slump to the ground. Sweat drips, across my shoulders and runs down my back.

I check my phone. It's still recording, although my battery's almost dead. I dial emergency services but the call doesn't connect. I try again and then notice – there's no service at all.

The party. The network must have gone down with the volume of guests using their phones for New Year's. I sink back, shoulder blades pressing into the wall. A hollow sensation opens up inside me.

My phone battery has 4 per cent left. I stare at the screen with a strange feeling of acceptance. I'll leave a message anyway; I'll tell everything I know and what I've seen. My last vlog. And I'll pray it falls into the right hands.

I take a deep shaky breath and hold the camera to my face, the moonlight peering in through turret windows giving me an eerie glow. I'm as white as a ghost, I could be dead already.

With no way out, it's just a matter of time. With un-wavering certainty, I know this really is the end.

Moving it close so there can be no mistaking what I'm about to say. I clear my throat, preparing to leave my final words . . .

CHAPTER FORTY-THREE

ERIN

NINE DAYS AFTER NYE

My sister stares into the camera as if she's looking right at me.

'Someone's dead. They've got Jack, oh God, Jaaaack. If you're watching this, send for help. Tell them about the party at the chateau, what's really been going on. It's all recorded, it's all on here.'

She looks behind her.

There's a noise. A creaking, the moan of a door swinging open.

'They're coming for me,' she swallows. 'I can hear them, they're close.'

Her eyes are glistening with tears. Her voice lowers to an urgent whisper.

'Mum, Erin, I'm sorry I let you down, I'm so so sorry, I love you both more than you know. Please forgive me.'

Then with a crackle, the video cuts out. The silence that follows is deafening.

I'm going to be sick.

I *knew* it was too good to be true. I *knew* someone must have bought them the chateau, there was no way they could have afforded it. The words of the masked man in her video, ringing in my ears: *Welcome to our new party house.*

'Adele, honey, what have you done?'

All I want to do is climb into the video and rescue her. But she's gone. My heart contracts with pain. I'm too late, I'm always too late.

Jack and Adele made a deal with the devil and now the devil's taken them.

Tears crowd my eyes and at first, I don't see the darkness arrive. Like a spirit that's come to collect the dead, the shadow moves up the wall. Out of the corner of my eye I notice the darkness swell but by then it's too late. A blow strikes the back of my skull.

CHAPTER FORTY-FOUR

ERIN

First comes the throbbing, arriving in waves, followed by high-pitch ringing in my ears.

My eyelids feel swollen and heavy, it's an effort just opening them. A stream of light moves in, blinding me, but I can hear him. *Them.*

They talk loudly over each other in French. I'm too woozy to understand but I hear my name and then Adele's, which immediately triggers the memory of the video. Her frightened final words in the tower. My sister, what have they done to her?

I jerk upright, sending a whoosh of blood to my head. Then, two hands plant on my shoulders. I start and the grip tightens.

'Easy there, slow down,' he says with a strong French accent.

'Adele?' I call out, but even that hurts. 'Adele! She's in danger!' It feels like shards of glass are tearing at my throat.

I lurch sideways but there's more searing pain. I look

266

down: my body's at a funny angle, twisted and bent out of shape.

'Erin?' His voice is deep and authoritative.

There's blood in my mouth, thick and sour.

'Are you hurt?'

Slowly, I turn to him. Our eyes meet and his face comes into focus. It's the handsome police officer. Marcel.

'What happened?' I reach for the back of my head. When I pull away, my fingers are glazed red and the sight of blood makes me panic.

'You must have fallen and hit your head. *Please*, stop moving or you could make it worse.' He maintains eye contact.

I blink slowly and try to remember what happened, but a hole opens up. I can't think for the ringing in my ears. Everything is ten times louder than it should be, and the light, it's so bright it's burning. I shade my eyes with my hand, but it does little to help.

'You might have concussion, let's get you to the hospital.'

'I'm not going anywhere; not until I've found my sister.' I try moving again but I'm thrown off balance as I'm hit with a rush of light. Flashbacks. The glamorous guests arriving at a masked ball. Couples flirting. An orchestra playing, the glow of candlelight pushing through the windows. One image after another, rapid like gunfire and then suddenly, nothing. A pit of black.

'There was a party, *here*, on New Year's Eve, and Adele was watching from outside.' I scrunch up my face, trying to remember more from her video.

'I think you're confused.' Marcel leans down towards me. 'It looks like you'll need stitches.'

My memory of the night picks up again with Jack. His strangled cry ripping through the air. His face, the blood between his teeth. The phone shaking in Adele's hand, the vivid white of her sneakers as she sprints across the lawn. But who was she running from? As I strain to find the answer, pain surges and the information recedes, like sand slipping between my fingers.

It all feels out of sequence and nothing makes sense and then, from out of the gloom, Adele appears. Her face a ghostly white as she turns the camera on herself.

I rock, trying to lift up onto my feet. 'She's in danger!'

'Hey, take it easy.' He forces me back down.

'It's all on her phone.' I lock eyes with Marcel. Suddenly remembering where I last had it. I squeeze my hand around her mobile but my fingers collapse into my palm.

It's gone.

'Where is it?' I search around me. My eyes fix on Marcel. 'You took it!' I sound hysterical. 'Give it back!'

I try freeing myself from him but I'm no match for his strength. His grip tightens as he casts a glance over his shoulder and the shadow that's been looming steps into view. It's the capitaine and he's eyeing me mistrustfully.

'There's no phone here,' the capitaine says coldly.

'I had it, here.' I look to my hand in disbelief.

'The capitaine arrived first and found you like this, unconscious by the window,' Marcel explains.

My gaze jogs between them, slowly processing the infor-mation, then comes a jolt of panic.

'Why are you here?'

They swap looks.

'How did you get in?' My words slur, my speech is slowing.

'We were passing by and thought to drop in and see if you'd heard from your sister,' Marcel says calmly, but the grip on my shoulders feels like something else.

'The door was open when we arrived,' the capitaine adds.

I eye them cautiously.

'How did you get those injuries?' The capitaine's voice now has an edge to it.

The shadow creeping up the wall, the creak of floorboards, a fragment falls into place as I try walking back through those final moments before I blanked out.

Picking up mid-train of thought, I say: 'I found Adele's phone hidden in the tower, I came back inside and,' I hesitate, the hole opening up again, 'and then someone must have attacked me.'

The capitaine looks puzzled. 'Who attacked you?'

I falter as another thick fog descends. An immense pressure building. I try to retrieve the images of New Year's Eve but everything feels jumbled and blurred.

'Listen to me, there was a party and Adele was here and they were after her and Jack,' my voice breaks.

'And you've been assaulted?' Marcel confirms. 'Or your sister?'

'I was . . . she's,' I take a breath. My words sounding clumsy. 'It sounds crazy, I know but . . .'

'Take your time,' Marcel says.

'I'm sorry, I can't remember.'

Marcel and the capitaine exchange looks.

'Where's the phone now?' Marcel asks.

'I don't know. The people who've kidnapped Adele must have it.' But my voice has shrunk to nothing. My conviction disappearing with my memory.

The capitaine sounds incredulous. 'So, you think your sister has been abducted? Or she's been . . .' He takes a breath, but the hesitation is enough. The suggestion she could be dead hits like a blunt force and I burst into tears.

I should have come earlier. All along I've known something was wrong. I'm her big sister, I'm supposed to protect her.

I look up, glaring. 'Do something! Why won't you help? She's been missing for days, why aren't you searching for her?'

'Calm down, madame,' the capitaine says, raising his voice.

Pressing the heels of my hands into my eyes, I try diving deeper into lost memories but it's all just out of reach. Faces blurred, images distorted, but I can feel her fear. Adele's adrenaline is now pumping through me, it's so intense my skin prickles.

She's trying to tell me something. We've always had an unexplainable connection, even when we haven't been close. Adele's trying to lead me somewhere now.

'She filmed the party and then she hid her phone because they were coming for her.'

The capitaine looks almost amused. 'They?'

Why is he forcing me back around in circles?

'Why would someone abduct her?'

I shake my head. Trying to loosen the memory.

'Why would they want to harm her partner, Jack?'

'I don't know.'

'What *do* you know?'

I can't breathe.

'Is there anything you can tell us?'

Guilt, fear, crushing my chest. I've let her down.

'Maybe she saw something she shouldn't have,' I whisper.

'Such as?' He keeps up the attack.

Why can't I remember? Why won't it show itself?

'I don't know, I DON'T KNOW!' Tears stream down my face.

The capitaine heaves a sigh.

Marcel speaks, more gently: 'Where in the tower did you find her phone?'

'In a drawer,' I sob. 'She hid it in a drawer.'

The capitaine snorts a laugh. He crosses the room to my side, peering down at me. 'To be clear: you found your sister's phone in a secret hiding place which holds video evidence of an assault and her possible abduction, and it's now mysteriously disappeared.'

He's making me sound crazy.

'Someone broke in, assaulted you and took your sister's phone.' He's slipping Marcel more looks. He shakes his head as he laughs. 'What would you like us to do?'

I want to scream. *Your job! Do your fucking job!* My skin prickles with anger.

The capitaine walks around, studying the pictures on the wall, the antiques. He picks up a porcelain figurine from the sideboard, frowns and puts it down. Casting around with a look of disapproval.

'Doesn't appear anything was taken.'

He nods to Marcel, then returns his gaze to me. Narrowing his eyes into slits, he looks at me too closely. Stony-faced.

'We've spoken to the people from your hospital.'

'The people?'

'Your superiors. It appears you're on leave pending disciplinary action. There's an investigation into your negligence.'

The air's been punched out of me. How did they find out?

'Several staff reported you'd been behaving strangely.'

I shake my head. 'It's not like that.'

'Acting irrationally, out of character.' He sounds triumphant.

'It was an accident, what happened was a mistake, they would have told you that. What about the party? What about what they did to Jack?'

'So you *do* remember what you saw.'

'I remember the ball . . . Adele . . . saying someone is after her.'

'But you don't have the phone?'

'I told you, someone took it.'

'Your story keeps changing.'

'No. NO.' I'm shaking my head.

'You gave the wrong drug to a patient who went on to have a seizure. It's clear – your mind is unbalanced.'

I look between them. Taking in their accusatory tone.
'Wait, you think I have something to do with Adele's
disappearance?'

CHAPTER FORTY-FIVE

ERIN.

My life slowly slid from my control after I took Mum in. When she started relying on me for everything – to feed her, to wash her, to take her to the toilet – I struggled to cope. The constant worry whether she was going to make it through the chemotherapy while keeping up with my shifts at the hospital became impossible to manage.

And the one person I needed most – my sister – wasn't there for me. I should have reached out for professional help, I should have told my boss what was going on, but that's me all over, trying to fix problems alone.

It had been a routine when my body was barely functioning due to exhaustion, and I couldn't keep my eyes open. I dropped the ball, I didn't check the charts carefully enough. I failed to notice the nurse whose shift I was taking over from gave my heart patient his medicine right before he clocked off at 7 p.m.

Carelessly, I doubled the patient's dose and he had a seizure as a result. An awful, terrifying reaction to the drug I gave him. The sound of the alarm, the panicked cries from the doctors, rip through my thoughts as Capitaine Desailly drags me back into the emergency room.

It was touch and go due to the patient's already weakened condition, but the doctors managed to save his life. *Human error. We all make mistakes*, some of the kinder nurses tried to reassure me, but I can't forgive myself.

Since then, I've lost all confidence in my judgement and reasoning. I've become a nervous wreck, jittery, second-guessing absolutely everything. The anxiety has worsened since I've been suspended. Now my future is uncertain.

My confidence in what I've seen, what I think I saw on the video, is slipping away.

My face, I can feel it getting hot under the intensity of their interrogation. It's like being back in that boardroom, under pressure to explain.

'There was a lot going on, I was struggling to cope . . . I made a terrible mistake—'

'Sounds like you're excusing it.'

'I deserve whatever punishment they hand out, but it was a mistake. If I could take it back . . .'

The capitaine stares at me coldly.

'We're going to need your passport until we can verify your statement.'

He walks over to where my packed rucksack is waiting on the chair. Rooting around inside, he pulls out my passport triumphantly.

'You can have it back as soon as everything checks out.'

'Wait!' Panic seizes me. 'I have to get home, my mum's in a coma, she's critically ill.'

He slides it into his pocket.

'Please.'

Marcel passes me a worried glance.

'Maybe that's not necessary, sir.' Marcel turns to his boss, swapping to French.

'Does your sister know the trouble you're in?' the capitaine cuts him off, sliding my only ticket out of here into his pocket.

I blink at him.

'Thought not!'

I shake my head.

'You've been keeping secrets from her too then. Maybe she knew she couldn't trust you. Perhaps you had an argument, something that got out of hand . . .'

My pulse accelerates and the room sways with the pain from my head injury. The high-pitched ringing in my ears is now so intense I can't think. I feel nauseous, I'm going to be sick.

I twist to the side, retching. Marcel holds me steady while the capitaine moves away to the window. When I look back, he's watching the snow. The profile of his face backlit like a shadow puppet.

He's not interested in finding my sister. He's too busy turning over stones to find dirt on me.

'Here.' Marcel takes off his fleece and rolls it into a pillow. He pushes me down and at first I resist, but the struggle has become too much. He seems much warmer and more gentle than when we met in the police station. It's hard to think this is the same person.

Tears fill my eyes. 'I told you Adele was missing and you did nothing, *nothing*,' I whisper to him. I feel weaker by the second.

He puts a hand on my arm. 'I'm looking into it.' But his words don't marry up with the shift in mood. It feels like I'm the one they're investigating. I'm under suspicion.

The realization is sudden. A desperate need to explain myself. 'They've been following me since I got here!'

They've been waiting for me to lead them to Adele's phone, to retrieve and destroy the incriminating evidence. They would never have guessed Adele's love of sneaky hiding places, they needed me to lead them to the tower and, like the fool I am, that's exactly what I did.

The creepy man in the snow. The shadowy figure following me to my car. Saying it out loud – it seems to make sense.

The captain laughs. 'Ah, the mysterious "they" again.' There's an impatient sigh. 'I don't know what you expect us to do, madame.' He does a slow full turn of the room. 'There's no phone, no sign of a party or a struggle or evidence of any violence.' He casts around again and shrugs. 'The most likely explanation: your sister has gone on holiday, she'll walk through the door and that will be the end of the crisis. You've had an argument. You've not been invited to spend Christmas – whatever it is, this is a family matter.'

His expression hardens. 'Either that or there's been an argument that got out of hand—'

'And I suppose I knocked myself out?' I try fighting back but my words are small, lacking all conviction.

'You could have fallen and don't remember, tripped on that expensive rug of your sister's.' He shrugs. 'I can't see any sign of forced entry or a burglary.'

Marcel frowns; I can tell he's conflicted. Tentatively, he says: 'We could get a search team to look around?'

'A waste of resources,' the capitaine says impatiently.

'I don't mind taking a look, sir.'

'We're overstretched as it is, running eight investigations, we don't have the resources to deal with a wild-goose chase.'

The capitaine switches to French. I don't need a translator to know he's angry. From what I can pick out, he wants to get back to head office instead of being stuck here. After getting his speech off his chest, he says under his breath: 'Too much money, too much time on their hands.' He's a word away from spitting 'rich foreigners'.

Marcel stiffens, uneasy.

'It's better we make sure, sir.'

The inspector dismisses him with a brush of the hand. 'Later.'

'She needs medical attention.'

He nods. 'I'll take her to the hospital.'

Panic.

'I'm not leaving!'

Marcel squeezes my arm. 'That head needs looking at, it could be concussion.' He talks over me. 'I'll call for an ambulance.'

'It'll take too long with the snow; it's easier if I drive her.' The capitaine crosses the room.

'I'm not going anywhere!' I break into their plans. If they won't help find Adele, I'll do it alone.

'We can't leave you here, injured.' The capitaine towers over me. Roughly, he takes my arm, pulling me to my feet. I catch the acrid tang of stale coffee on his breath.

I wince in pain and Marcel looks troubled at how aggressive his boss is being. It's clear they don't get along but there's little he can do when the capitaine pulls rank.

Struggling worsens the pain and my knees give out.

'Hey, easy does it!' Marcel reaches out and takes me by my other arm.

Together they carry me towards the car. I'm like a rag doll, limp and broken. My head rolls to one side.

Outside the light is low, a copper wash across the snow. Hours must have passed, how long have I been out of it?

Out of the corner of my eye I notice another one of those small dolls, planted by the entrance.

A blackbird on the porch caws and flaps up into the sky. The alpine scents rush at me, the smell of pine needles, and all of a sudden, I'm overcome with a sense of déjà vu. Something about the way the elements have come together tells me I've been here before. But when I turn to look back at the chateau, the feeling is gone.

I'm doubting my sanity – what I'm feeling, what I saw. Marcel opens the rear door and gently eases me into the back of the car – where the people who are arrested go. He helps me with the belt buckle and as he leans across, our eyes meet. I didn't notice how pale green his eyes were until now and all of a sudden, the air feels charged. The heat of his body covers me and for a fleeting moment, it's the most protected I've felt since I arrived in France.

'Help me find her, please.' My voice is not even a whisper.

Capitaine Desailly calls out to him and our moment is lost. I'm left wondering – did I imagine it? The frisson between us. All my senses are smudging into one, it's impossible to tell where one ends and the next begins.

The nausea is worsening. The back of my head is throbbing, just keeping upright is an effort. It's not only the head injury – it's lack of sleep, I've never felt so drained of energy.

The car sinks as the capitaine climbs behind the wheel. The rancid smell follows him and I wish it was Marcel taking me to the hospital.

He twists around to face me. Through the glass wall, I finally catch a glimmer of empathy.

'You'll feel better soon,' he says, starting up the engine. The automatic locking system activates.

I look back at Marcel and see a flash of something. Almost as if he's passing me a message with his eyes. There's an intensity about his gaze as he watches us drive off. Only this time it leaves me chilled, colder than I am already.

As we wind our way up the drive the overarching trees feel like they're clawing us. Trying to stop us leaving.

It's then that it decides to return. An image from Adele's video. Rapid and aggressive, forcing itself inside my thoughts.

The silver Volvo. The capitaine's car – it was parked in the courtyard on the night of the party.

CHAPTER FORTY-SIX

ERIN

I can see it now, clear as day. Sticking out like a sore thumb among the sports cars. I remember wondering who the Volvo saloon must belong to, right before I saw what the party was about.

It's all coming back to me. Like a pressure cooker released – vivid sexual images race through my thoughts.

The underage girls. The performance sex, drugs, the S & M. The syndicate and their pledge to take over from where the Bellays left off.

And then, finally, the grey-haired man, killed in a sex game gone wrong. The flashback so powerful I clutch my mouth to stop myself being sick.

The engine revs and the car picks up speed. Terror washes over me as I realize I'm trapped and I'm with *one of them.*

Capitaine Desailly was at the party and he's been lying from the moment I walked into the police station: covering up evidence, planting doubt in my head. He knows about Adele. He knows what's happened to her.

It was him who attacked me. He arrived earlier than

Marcel, giving him enough time to knock me out and take Adele's phone. He's probably got it stashed away in his pocket.

My hand lifts to my throat. What have they done with my sister? And what's he going to do to me now I know his secret?

The capitaine hasn't said a word, but there's a loaded silence, stretching out like the barren white landscape ahead.

I hear him breathing. Throaty, congested from years of smoking. I can feel his mind working, processing.

Every now and again we meet in the rear-view mirror. His small, pinched eyes studying me. I'm fighting to keep the emotion out so he won't guess.

I've remembered. I know who you really are.

I take a breath and make an effort to smile. As long as I can convince him I have amnesia, that my memory is hazy and patchy and not worth anything, I might stand a chance.

But as we travel deeper into the countryside, any glimmer of hope fades. We've been driving for what feels like hours through narrow lanes that wind and bend. There's nothing out here but farmland and abandoned outhouses and barns. I haven't seen another house for miles.

The sky is dark and moody, pressing down like a tombstone, and I'm struggling to get air in. I hear it rattle through my lungs like the storm wind outside. With every laboured breath I become more light-headed.

This can't be the way to the hospital but I'm too frightened to say anything. Instead, I rub at the button on my jacket and hold on to the silence, because, as long as nothing's said, I can carry on believing.

Believing Adele's still alive. Trusting he won't kill me for knowing the truth.

We slow for crossroads. Turning right, we head even further into countryside and my adrenaline spikes. With it, comes dizziness and there's now a dull ache behind my eyes from the strain of watching the road.

My brain feels swollen, like a giant lollipop head, lolling side to side with every jerk of the brake. There's a constant whooshing – the sound of the sea – filling up my ears.

A memory of Adele when we were children finds its way back to me. Playing in the sand dunes on holiday in Devon, squabbling over who was getting first go with the kite, and I'm hit with a wave of nostalgia so strong, it brings me to tears.

My baby sister. She's alive, I know it. *I'm coming for you, sweetie, hang on, I'm nearly there.*

This is the mantra I play on a loop to keep me calm. A hope I'll bring her home to Mum, still rooted.

Everything will be OK.

Then we turn off into a farm track that takes us up a steep hill towards woodland and my stomach drops.

The car wrestles with the snow. We slide backwards and there's a roar of the engine as he stamps on the accelerator. '*Merde*,' he swears, changing gear. His rage swallows the space between us. He erupts into a fit of coughing, a dry hacking wheeze.

How could I have not seen it? When the capitaine was pretending to search Bellay for signs of a robbery, I assumed his contempt was for the wealthy and entitled. But no, Capitaine Desailly longs to be part of the rich crowd, partying in chateaus like Bellay. He despises the ordinariness of his life – overlooked, tasked with overseeing a small rural community. Bitter, hateful, he'll go to any lengths to get the life he's after.

The syndicate must have invited him to the party in exchange for his silence. Having police sniffing around would have brought an abrupt end to their masked ball. Did Desailly know the Bellays? I bet he kept their secrets too. Burying evidence, making sure nobody asked questions about the missing girls. He made them disappear. And now he's going to do the same with me.

We lurch forward and I'm thrown into the back of his seat. Grabbing the headrest, I cling on as we climb towards what looks like a nature reserve. A forest even denser than the one guarding the chateau. A mass of fir trees buried under snow.

Nature's cemetery. Dark and threatening, it's somewhere you'd be lost and forgotten.

The road ahead is uneven and the snow squeaks like a small creature caught beneath the tyres. We pass into the tunnel of trees and the last of the light is snuffed out.

He turns on the headlights and the glare bleaches out the night. It feels like a theme park ride. The tension building, the drop approaching. A rapid pounding taking over my chest.

Then he clears his throat, finally breaking his silence.

'I'll never forget that day we found the body. Out here, in the middle of nowhere,' he says calmly while watching for my reaction. 'François was devoted to his farm and his family and then one day he vanished. As if he'd never existed. Some said he had debts. Many said there was another woman, but I knew him: he wouldn't leave his wife and the boys.'

Another silence drags out.

'It took a month to find his body, once the ice had thawed.' He reaches into the past with a strange smile. 'He'd been perfectly preserved, buried under four foot of snow. Can you imagine? Although by the time we found him, the foxes had got at the body. He was missing half a face and there were no hands left.'

He quietens, letting the horrific image take hold.

'His poor wife, she had to identify what was left. I don't think she ever got over that. You wouldn't though, would you?' He catches my eye.

I look away, the sick feeling growing.

'The snowstorm of 2010, I remember it well. Days passed without being able to leave home. We were living off canned food and beer.' A small laugh. 'Eventually a post-mortem told us François died from a fall, he must have slipped on the ice.' He makes certain he has my attention. 'Alone out here, you could easily come to harm.'

It's worked. My stomach heaves.

'This isn't the way to the hospital.'

His sniffs, gaze fixed on the road ahead. Studying it with dangerous intensity.

'Where are you taking me?' I'm trying to keep the fear out of my voice but failing. All the blood has drained from my face. I catch my ashen reflection in his rear-view mirror. I look like a ghost. Dead already.

'The roads are blocked. We're going another way.'

'To the hospital?'

I look behind me. The way back has eclipsed into a pit of black.

'Where are we?'

His hands find a new grip on the steering wheel.

'We need to turn around; the snow's worse here.'

'It's not far now. This is a shortcut.'

'Turn around!' My voice sounds strangled.

'You need to relax,' he says coldly. 'Try to rest. How is your head?'

'It's bad, I'm in a lot of pain, I need to see a doctor.'

'Have you remembered more about the party?'

Play dumb, Erin. Pretend you don't know.

'It's all hazy.'

'Nothing?'

'Nothing,' I echo.

He works his eyes over me in the mirror. He knows I'm lying.

We fall back into silence. His mood feels more subdued, as if there's a quiet acceptance of what needs to be done now the end is near.

Up ahead, a wrought-iron gate seals off the road with a sign marking the land as private property. Somewhere dark and tucked out of the way.

The car rolls to a stop. Leaving the engine running, he gets out, turning up his collar to the wind. My heart punches my ribcage as I watch him reach into his pocket and pull out a key on a rope. He unlocks the padlock and forces the gate, throwing all his weight against it.

It whines loudly like it hasn't moved in years and my heart jumps up into my throat. I don't want to die, not out here.

It's now or never.

I try the door but nothing happens.

Again.

I pull the handle so far back it might snap off. COME ON! Pain sears as I throw my entire body against the door. Bashing it with all I've got.

It's useless. He's locked me in. There's no way out.

Helplessly, I watch him return to the car. His eyes briefly drift to meet mine, his mouth set in a hard line. There's no feeling there at all.

CHAPTER FORTY-SEVEN

ERIN

He stands stock-still, his brow creasing as he fumbles inside his pocket for his phone.

The capitaine takes the call. With the howling wind, it's impossible to hear what's being said but something in his features has loosened. His mouth slackens.

He ends the call with a grunt, wipes his nose and finds his way back to me. A fresh determination filling up his eyes.

The car shudders as he slams the door. The capitaine takes a moment, sighing heavily before crunching the gears into reverse.

'There's been a change of plan,' he says.

Relief washes over me when I see the lights of the town blinking on the horizon.

I'm safe.

My amnesia performance must have worked. Whoever the capitaine spoke to would have realized it's too big a risk if I were to disappear. I draw in a long, steadying breath. My body sighs into the seat and the pain in my head loosens for a moment.

As soon as I'm safely at the hospital I'll call the police in England, I'll contact the British Embassy. I'll inform everyone I know where I am and that my sister's life is in danger. Stay calm, Erin, hang in there.

The road ahead is deserted. It feels apocalyptic; deathly still with a big open sky the colour of bruised purple. The last of the light fading into the horizon. As we near the town, we turn off into somewhere much darker. An industrial estate crammed with warehouses and chrome storage units.

'Where are we?' I try to keep my tone light.

He keeps his gaze fixed on the road ahead.

'Is this the way to the hospital?'

We snake through more darkened roads, travelling deeper into the industrial rabbit warren. Passing vast corrugated buildings housing agricultural equipment, curling around and around until we eventually reach a dead end. Up ahead there's a modern brick building, one storey high with no distinguishing features other than a sign with a pharmacy logo.

'What is this place?'

'The medical centre,' he says, pulling up to the kerb.

'I thought you were taking me to the hospital?'

'This is closer. Try not to worry.'

Outside, a young man is shifting from foot to foot, blowing into his hands. He looks like he's been expecting us.

The engine cuts dead and the capitaine locks the doors behind him. The men greet each other with a friendly handshake then slip into something more intense, throwing me the occasional glance. The man nods submissively, as if he's being given instructions.

The capitaine passes him a piece of paper, they look at one another conspiratorially, before walking quickly towards the car.

Something feels wrong.

The lock releases and my door swings open.

'Time to go,' Capitaine Desailly says briskly.

The young man stoops and smiles. 'Salut, madame, I'm Doctor Albertine, I hear you've had an accident.'

'Accident?' I blink at him.

'Let's get you inside and cleaned up.'

I try moving but the concussion has worsened. As soon as my legs make contact with the tarmac, they give way. The men catch me before I fall and carry me towards the building. The sliding doors open for us and then, like jaws, snap shut.

It smells like a hospital – it has the same sharp notes of antiseptic, the rush of warm stuffy air – but there are no nurses, no doctors rushing around. The building is deserted.

Bare walls, no furniture, it's a shell of a building. It feels like no one's been here for months. This can't be right.

'What's going on? Where am I?' I search around me.

The capitaine passes the doctor a look. Their eyes skate over my head.

'Try to stop worrying, I know about your fall. We have something inside that can help,' says the doctor.

'What? No, I didn't fall, I was attacked.'

'We're concerned you might try harming yourself again, that's why we want to keep you under observation.'

'Harm myself?'

'You've been having hallucinations and vivid dreams,' he tells me.

'What, no!' I look sharply at the capitaine. 'He's lying. I'm a medical professional, I'm an ICU nurse with ten years' experience, there's nothing wrong with my mental state.'

'*Was* a nurse,' the capitaine corrects me.

'Better we check – to be sure,' says the doctor.

'Listen to me – I'm not crazy,' I try pulling free but I'm too weak.

The doctor's brows knit together as he talks over me: 'You were right about her condition.'

'Hey!' I cry out. 'Hey!'

'I did warn you,' the capitaine says triumphantly.

They switch to French and I pick out a mention of a 'treatment plan'. The hopelessness of the situation dawns on me. No passport. Nobody knows I'm here. I left England in such a hurry I didn't tell anyone where I was going, not even Mum. I didn't want to worry her. My throat tightens. Why didn't I tell someone?

'You need to calm down.' I feel the pinch of the capitaine's grip.

'I'm not hallucinating. I'm not making this up,' I plead as they steer me down a long corridor into the bowels of the building.

It's much colder here and it smells of mould. I'm led into a windowless room with a noisy ventilator and shelves overcrowded with medicine, blister packs, bottles, sachets, towering to the ceiling.

What is this place? A dispensary of some sort?

At the far end there's a bed and a drip bag swinging from a hook and – my heart stops. Attached to the bedframe are restraints.

'Wait!' I dig in my heels, but the floor is slippery and I fall down. They pull me along on my knees and the capitaine gives the doctor a hurried nod. An OK to proceed.

'We'll give you that sedative now to help you relax,' the doctor explains.

'Get off! GET OFF!' I try to fight them.

'To take the edge off—'

'I don't want to RELAX. I want to find my sister.'

A shadow appears in the doorway. The outline of a woman. She moves into view and I instantly recognize her. Her helmet of hair shining like a show pony under the lights. The party host, the bitch who pretended to be Adele's neighbour and friend.

'Hello, Erin,' she says coldly, then gives the men a decisive nod.

They pull me onto the bed and hold me down. The restraints are ice-cold, the touch of metal clamping around my wrists strikes like an electric shock.

'Time to rest,' the doctor says.

He turns his back to me, stooping over the metal trolley and there's a ripping sound – the hurried noise of plastic being torn apart.

Helplessly I watch him fill his syringe with a clear liquid, tapping away the air bubble with a confident flick of the finger.

'You'll feel better soon.'

Terror takes over. I thrash around, pulling at the

restraints, my hands snatching at air, while the woman watches from a distance.

'We should never have let this happen,' she says tersely. 'Thirteen got carried away, as usual, and now I have to clean up his mess. When are the others arriving?'

'They're on their way,' says the capitaine.

'Good. There's been a lot of interest in tonight's performance. You can take over when I'm gone.' She turns to the doctor. 'Hurry up, we need to get on with this. I'm leaving in five minutes.'

The capitaine pins me down by my shoulders, pushing my jumper to my elbow and exposing my skin. It gleams, milk-bottle white. In the height of panic, I'm thinking about how translucent my arms are, how vivid blue my veins appear.

The doctor squirts a small amount of liquid into the air and lowers the point.

'Adele! What have they done to her?' I scream at him.

Her name plays over and over in my head as the needle breaks my skin. As the cold liquid forces its way in. My last lucid thought:

Adele . . .

CHAPTER FORTY-EIGHT

ERIN

TEN DAYS AFTER NYE

There's a clicking noise then a harsh white light hits my eyes. So bright, it's impossible to see. I try lifting my hand to shield them from the glare but it won't move.

I look to my wrists, they've been fastened down by cable ties.

My last memory slowly returns. The medicine room, the injection, but I'm not tied to a bed any more. I'm strapped upright in a chair.

My legs have been pulled apart and all I have on is my underwear and a vest.

I'm so frightened, I don't feel the cold at first, not until I look down and see my fingers are white and my toes have turned blue. I start trembling but I'm certain that's fear rather than cold.

There's a blur of movement. The glare is blinding but I sense I'm not alone. There are figures treading softly around me.

Circles of light hang in the air, glowing through the dark like cat's eyes. It takes me a moment to realize – they're holding torches. A light for every person crowding around.

Finally, my eyes adjust enough to see the camera. Raised on a tripod, the lens is fixed on me. A red light pulsing like a heartbeat through the gloom.

I'm being filmed.

Someone takes a step towards me. Their movement makes an odd noise: scratchy, like plastic. I look down again and that's when I notice – there's a transparent sheet beneath me.

My stomach loosens with dread.

His face is hidden behind a bronzed mask in the shape of a beak. I say *he* but it's impossible to say for certain.

'Welcome, Erin.' He speaks through a voice distorter. A robotic voice that sends a chill down my spine.

I yank at the binds and my head jerks backwards. Something wrapped around my neck just got tighter. It's cutting into my throat, I can barely get the words out.

'Where's Adele?' I choke.

'The more you fight it, the more this will hurt.'

Laughter rumbles from the darkness. It's more of a snigger.

He moves closer still.

'Show me happy. Come on, smile.' He turns and waves at the camera.

Someone else steps into the circumference of light. The man in the executioner costume. Bald. Short, his thighs thick like trunks and they're glistening with oil. A black leather mask hides his face – a hole where his mouth should be and tarnished metal prongs for teeth. He's clutching a second camera and presses it inches from my face. I feel his wet breath, hot and excited as he films my body.

'Don't be shy.' The other masked man laughs. 'How can two sisters be so different? One loves the camera while the other wants to disappear.'

'Where is she?' I say through gritted teeth. I look around, from one shadow to the next. The wall of bodies is closing in.

'Our VIP members are with us.' He waves and smiles to the camera again. 'I was warned you might put up a fight, which is why some members travelled to be here in person.'

I glance around, from one shadow to the next. The wall of bodies creeps closer and I can smell money. Their expensive aftershaves. Syndicate members, it has to be.

The hand he's been concealing behind his back appears – revealing a long-curved knife. The handle is gold and jewelled. It looks old, something ceremonial. He holds the flat edge to my cheek. The cold touch of the blade makes me flinch.

'This could be fun.' He leans in. The whites of his eyes gleam through the holes in his mask. 'Some of us here think you'll put up a fight.'

There's more cackling. A feminine laugh rings out.

'WHERE IS SHE?' I lurch forward, forgetting the restraints. 'What have you done with her?' I cough.

He lifts the knife, the hooked end looks like a claw.

'You've one chance. Make this less painful and tell me: where is Adele's phone?'

What?

He lowers his voice to something even more creepy. 'Since we've strip-searched you, we know you haven't got it.'

A shiver crawls along my spine.

'Come on, stop playing hide and seek.'

He readjusts his grip on the knife, slowly lowering it to my face. I feel the cool tip touch the corner of my eye.

'Where have you hidden it?'

The capitaine has Adele's phone. He took it when he knocked me unconscious.

'Tick tock, Erin.'

Is this a game? My mind is scrambling, trying to work out what they're really after.

He lowers the knife, past my jugular, towards my breasts. 'Time is running out.' He teases my top. Slipping the blade beneath the fabric.

This is what they do, isn't it? Play games. I bite down, clenching my jaw. And for the briefest of moments, I feel like my sister. Brave. Defiant. Against all odds.

'GO TO HELL!'

Tilting his head, he studies me like an animal in a zoo, considering something. Then he lurches, wrapping a gloved hand around my throat and squeezing.

'Fuck you!' I wheeze. Pushing out a little smile.

His grip tightens, throttling me so hard my neck feels like it could snap off. I gasp in my fight for air but I still manage a glimpse of what's underneath his mask. The shape of his mouth. His dark stubble.

'GIVE ME her phone.'

I laugh hysterically.

'I don't have her phone.' It's barely a whisper.

He lifts the knife and strikes. I hear the tear and instinctively shut my eyes. I wait for the pain to arrive.

The room falls eerily quiet, as if the shadowy figures that make up my audience are holding their breath in the final act. Silence fills their theatre.

I feel completely numb. I peel open my eyes and tilt my head forward, holding my breath.

He's slashed my top in two. The fabric hangs loosely off my shoulders. My bra and knickers are still there but something tells me not for long.

I glare back at all of them. The sadists in the room and the ones watching from their superyachts, their mansions; their sprawling estates.

I'm nothing like the models at their sex parties. I'm not thin, I'm not beautiful. I'm sitting here in my least attractive bra. Why are they even filming me?

Something is now building within the stillness, a predatory excitement.

Think, Erin. THINK.

I have nothing to bargain with. *Nothing*.

They have my sister; they've taken care of the evidence – almost all of it. What can I do except play along?

'OK, I'll give you the phone – if you let Adele go.' I enter their game. It's impossible to hide the terror from my voice.

I sense their arousal. There's an excited murmuring as the watchers step forward. Their masks catch the light. Incandescent. A wall of gold.

My gaze jerks between them and the knife, while thoughts of the party play on repeat.

I know that what's planned for me will be far worse than what I saw being done in those rooms.

The man with the knife laughs. 'You're in no position to bargain. Tell me and I'll spare you from everyone having a turn.'

I shut my eyes and I imagine Adele is with me. Sisters together. Memories of when we were children return. Peering down from my bedroom window at Adele's face, glowing under the pale light of the full moon. She holds out her hand, smiling, willing me to find the courage.

I want to take it. I want to go with her.

'Your last chance. After this, I won't be able to stop them. The things they do will be . . . irreversible.'

He pauses, waiting for my answer.

He sighs. 'You're a fool. Don't say I didn't warn you.' The scratchy noise of their feet shuffling closer drowns his final word.

Shutting my eyes, I think of Adele. This time, I reach out, I grab hold of her hand.

CHAPTER FORTY-NINE

ERIN

TEN DAYS AFTER NYE

Gunfire rings out.

There's the drumming of boots. Heavy thuds and yelling. Officers wearing stab vests burst through the door and in comes the light, pouring into the room.

Within seconds the space is crowded with police armed with guns and flashlights, criss-crossing the gloom like lightsabres.

It's all so surreal I feel like I'm still floating, transfixed by the bright white outline of the door ahead. This must be it, the famously documented walk towards the light in your final moments on earth.

Am I dead?

A rush of cold air follows them inside and small specks of white pick up and swirl. Backlit by the light, the snow-flakes sparkle like diamonds. It's mesmerizingly beautiful pitted against the chaos unfolding around me.

The syndicate are brought to their knees. Maybe half a

dozen of them, I'm too dazed to count. With a gun to their temple, they place their hands behind their heads. Their identities remain hidden by their masks.

More snow blows in, twirling, dancing for me. I feel the snap of cold as it breaks against my skin. Delicate as porcelain.

'You OK?' A voice comes from my left. The words arrive slow and distorted like my head is held underwater. I drag my gaze across and see Marcel standing by my side holding a knife, just like the one *he* had. He crouches, cuts through the restraints, first releasing my hands and then my ankles.

'Erin?' Marcel tries to connect with me.

I can't move. It's as if the binds are still there. More snow kisses my skin. If I were dead, I wouldn't be able to feel anything?

'Come on, we need to get you out of here.' He pulls me out of my trance, lifting me from the chair.

My bare feet leave the ground as he hauls me up, right into his arms. He's damp with sweat but I'm enjoying the feeling of his warmth, of his muscles working beneath me. There's that fizz again, little sparks between us. Something's there.

More police arrive, the pulsating blue and red lights from their vans reaching inside the room, strobing along the walls and the ceiling. The shelves of medicine come into view. I've been held in the same room all along.

Five. I count five masked syndicate members on their knees as we pass through. Their heads bowed, their hands cuffed behind their back.

'On the ground!' An eager officer shoves one of them

in the back with his boot. *'Tout le monde à terre!'* He swings his gun around, forcing them all onto their stomachs. They plant their faces to the floor and squirm.

From the shape of their bodies I can tell, they're not all men.

Instinctively I bury my face deeper into Marcel's neck. Chasing the feeling of his skin on mine. I have this over-whelming need to feel something real. Anchored.

The light outside is calling to us. It's sunrise. It's actually the next day, which means I've been locked up for fourteen hours – or, I shudder, even longer. I'm still woozy from the sedative they gave me.

'Almost there,' Marcel reassures me.

There's a fleet of police cars outside, officers following us with their rifles. More marked vans arrive but they don't look like local police. Marcel warns them we're coming out.

'Ne tirez pas! Don't shoot!'

As we're reaching the door there's a sudden burst of movement. A streak of gold as the man who held the knife to my throat jumps to his feet and makes a run for a side door.

'ARRÊTE!' Someone chases after him.

Marcel turns on a point, he shoves me away and places himself between us.

A shot rings out, so loud it's deafening. Blood reaches my face – wet and warm across my cheeks.

Marcel!

For a terrifying moment I think it's him that's been hit, and I feel the scream rise up in my throat. But when I open my mouth, nothing comes out.

Not even a sound as I watch the man with the knife drop to the ground with a thud. Landing at a funny angle. Left arm caught beneath his body. The gold beak skewed to one side.

'*MERDE!*' the officer who shot him curses, rushing over.

More police file in, one after the other, and someone's radioing for an ambulance but it's too late. He looks dead.

Death has scared the remaining syndicate members into silence. They lie perfectly still, statue-like except for the tremble. A new smell enters the air – the tang of urine. One of the officers also notices and laughs at the one who's wet himself with fear.

Marcel pulls out his gun and crosses the room, finger grazing the trigger. He reaches the body and crouches beside him, feeling for a pulse. He looks back, shaking his head.

My shoulders drop, I feel an immense wave of relief.

Marcel then returns his gaze to the ringmaster. I notice him take a breath, then he pulls off the mask.

CHAPTER FIFTY

NOW

Sky News

We have breaking news from our team in Rémy-Vienne in Burgundy, France, where we've been reporting on the disappearance of YouTuber Adele Davenport.

Kate, what have you got for us?

'Evening, Justine, as you know, earlier today there was a tragic development in the disappearance of the young British couple who moved into Chateau Bellay just over four months ago.

Less than thirty minutes ago the body of a young man was pulled from the ground on the fifteen-acre estate. We can now confirm the deceased is Jack Reed, the thirty-one-year-old partner of Adele Davenport.

Have the police released any details about the cause of death?

The death is being treated as suspicious and the investigation has now become a murder inquiry. Mr Reed's body was found to the east of the chateau. The ground is frozen but the shallow nature of the grave made it possible for the dogs to pick up a scent.

The news has come as a shock to the local community and, as you can see from the crowd growing behind me, there's a sense of fear and unrest.

Is there any news on Adele Davenport?

Not as yet, but the grim discovery earlier today has heightened concerns this case could become a double murder investigation.

CHAPTER FIFTY-ONE

ERIN

TEN DAYS AFTER NYE

She's photographing them from every angle. My wrists. My ankles. Taking pictures of my red skin and the purple bruises around my throat.

It will be used as evidence to prove I was held against my will.

'Can I put my clothes back on?' I ask.

Although they're not my clothes. My underwear has been taken away for forensic testing.

I ease myself into the blue hospital gown. The starched fabric feels stiff and unyielding. Then I crawl back up onto the raised bed. My gaze slips past the photographer into the brightly lit corridor outside where doctors and nurses hurry past. I'm in the hospital he should have taken me to. The capitaine – who's been arrested and charged.

I've been given a private room and, for the briefest of moments, I forget there's an armed officer guarding my door, that my life is in danger now I'm a witness.

Marcel hasn't left my side since the rescue. I study him now, the set of his shoulders, gently lifting and falling as he watches the snow. Still wearing his stab vest, his gun strapped to his waist, he appears more action hero than small-town officer.

There's that strange tension between us again.

'All done,' I say, and he turns back to face me.

Those minutes he was looking the other way have left me anxious and I suddenly start hyperventilating. My throat, it's burning from where the binds were tied around my neck. Every breath, still painful.

Marcel quickly comes to my side. He pulls up a chair, right up close, and takes my hand in his. His face is pinched with worry.

'You're cold,' he says, rubbing me lightly.

'Not sure I can feel anything,' I wheeze.

'I'm sorry.' He takes a breath. 'I wish I could have told you.'

There's a loaded silence. He's waiting for forgiveness, but I can't give it to him. Not yet. I'm furious. The police used me as bait.

It turns out, Marcel suspected his boss of criminal activity as soon as he was transferred to his new post in the town. The sports car he'd recently bought. The luxury holidays he was taking his family on. They were the first clues of bribery. Initially, Marcel thought Capitaine Desailly might be stealing confiscated money and drugs, but then they put a tracker on his phone and hacked into his calls.

On reporting his concerns to head office, Marcel was taken into the sting operation known as Club Maison, a five-year Interpol investigation into an organized crime syndicate known as Twelve Homes, led by renowned Parisian prosecutor Raphaël DeMellier.

Interpol initially suspected Adele might be involved. And me, when I showed up out of the blue. Which explains Marcel's hostility and mistrust when I arrived at the police station looking for help.

Marcel had known about the New Year's Eve party all along and he'd been keeping tabs on me from the moment I arrived, although I now know it wasn't him watching me in the snow that night but the man the police shot: Pierre Moreau.

It took me a moment to work out where I'd seen him before as I watched him lie in a pool of his own blood. Then, it hit me like a punch. Pierre was the thug in Adele's video, the one who was sent to clean up after the sex game got out of hand. Apparently, he'd been moonlighting as Adele and Jack's gardener, keeping close tabs on my sister while reporting back to the syndicate. He'd also been keeping tabs on me, which would explain that constant sense of being followed.

The news of the old man dying at the party was a breakthrough in the case. The police started searching Chateau Bellay for a body the moment I left with the capitaine.

Interpol used me as bait to draw out members of the syndicate. After months of studying their behaviour, they knew the spectacle of me being tortured would be something they couldn't resist.

What the squad running the sting operation overlooked,

however, was Georges Desailly knowing the region like the back of his hand and shaking off the vehicle sent to tail him. Hence the delay in rescuing me. That's why Marcel won't stop apologizing; it could easily have ended with me dead.

Eyebrows drawn together, he passes me another apologetic look then hands me back my passport. Our fingers graze and I'm caught between hating him and savouring the fizz his touch leaves on my skin.

I sit quietly, overwhelmed with emotion and information, as Marcel reveals more about the people who kidnapped me.

'They go by the name of Twelve Homes after the twelve mansions they own across the world,' he says.

Marcel explains that the syndicate operates as an organized crime gang, offering exclusive club membership to their most valued customers. A thank-you to like-minded individuals who enjoy group sex, S & M and torture.

The list of their criminal activities is exhaustive: trafficking, prostitution, drug dealing, underage sex. As well as money laundering through the properties.

Each one of their twelve *homes* has a sordid history. The more tortured the better. Helps get them aroused, apparently.

'Not all the buildings are as grand as Chateau Bellay. It's the history that excites them.' Marcel's tone darkens. 'And often these homes aren't for sale. The syndicate is known for going to extreme lengths to get their hands on a property, offering owners a deal they can't refuse.'

I think about the offer they must have made Adele.

Gifting her and Jack a chateau. Fulfilling her childhood dream – who wouldn't say no to that?

Marcel suspects it was Adele's initial crowdfunding vlog going viral that put Chateau Bellay on their radar. When their research uncovered the chateau's dark history of sex parties, they couldn't resist.

Marcel runs his hands over his face. He looks as exhausted as I feel.

'It's been a game of cat and mouse for years,' he sighs. 'They've been buying properties with offshore accounts, shell companies based in Cyprus and the British Virgin Islands, making them impossible to trace. I've joined the search late in the game.'

'But at least you're helping now.'

'Chateau Bellay would have been more of a challenge for them though.'

I blink, not understanding.

'It's easy buying anonymously in countries like the UK, but not here in France. Our government is determined to crack down on tax avoidance, so courts intervene when a buyer tries to conceal their identity. I think this is why they used your sister.'

I nod slowly, trying to take it all in. 'They must have really wanted Bellay.'

He looks back at me sombrely.

'To avoid detection by the authorities, the syndicate make a point of never returning to the same party house twice. That's why they've been so hard to catch.'

I frown. 'But that's not true – they were planning to use Chateau Bellay as a permanent base for their parties,

I heard them on Adele's video, they announced it at the ball.'

'That doesn't add up.' Marcel shakes his head. 'Why change the pattern now? It only puts them at risk. Unless—' His eyes widen. 'Unless your sister made it possible for them to change the rules. *Oui*,' he nods, '*c'est ça!* Adele's vlog would have been the perfect cover for them. British influencer moves to rural France. Nobody would guess the dark secret hiding behind the walls.'

'Adele . . .' my voice wavers, 'do you think she's—' I stop, the words catching in my throat.

Marcel places his hand on mine, giving me the courage to go on.

'Is she still alive?'

He looks away. Afraid his eyes will say too much. '*Oui*. I think so.' More gently he says, 'We haven't found a body.'

I start at the word. *Body*. I know the police have been searching the chateau grounds since I left him, but nothing's really sunk in until now.

'She's been trafficked then?' I ask, my voice cracking.

He doesn't answer this time.

'That's it, isn't it? They've taken her to be used at another party.'

'We think we know where they might be going next,' he says quickly. 'A property in Spain has just come off the market. Somewhere that fits their criteria. An old hospital where *alternative* treatments were carried out.'

'What sort of treatments?'

He hesitates. 'Experiments. Shock treatments for patients who'd nowadays be diagnosed with clinical depression.

Back in the sixties, they were using pain therapy to redirect the "hurt inside their heads". Eventually Dr Perez was found out, but by then hundreds had been experimented on.'

I feel sick. I try deep breathing, but it does nothing to calm the horror film now playing in my head. I'm imagining what they'll do to Adele. What ceremonies they'll perform to summon up the past.

Oh God.

'It should've been me.' My eyes sting with tears. 'I was meant to protect her.' I wipe them away but fresh ones keep appearing and my heart is now reaching for Mum. How will I tell her? I can't, it'll break her. It'll be her last thought as she dies – and I won't be the one to do that. I'm not brave enough.

I've made a career from observing grief. Watching families crowd around the hospital beds of loved ones. Comforting them, while relieved it's not me. This is what it feels like – losing my entire family.

I can hear Adele's voice, her playful, cheeky tone ringing out, and it immediately brings more tears to my eyes. Suddenly I'm crying. Deep, heavy sobs. My chest is heaving and, for the first time, I'm reaching out for help.

Marcel leans across the bed and pulls me close, wrapping my bruised, aching body into his. He smells of the same fresh scent as when we first met. Clean, like hotel sheets, and I never want him to let me go.

It's been a lifetime since anyone's shown me affection.

The tiredness, the hopelessness of it all – it's too much. My sister could be anywhere in the world. Frightened, in pain. I cling to Marcel, burying my head in his shoulder.

There's a clang then the door swings open. An officer strides into the room and I feel Marcel tense up. He pulls away, a flush of pink marking his cheeks. I suppose this doesn't look very professional.

The officer gives Marcel an awkward nod and hands him a transparent bag.

'I'm sorry I have to ask you this now, but there are some things we need to know.' Marcel clears his throat, sounding officious. 'It's about Jack.'

Jack. I'm not sorry he's dead. When Marcel told me they'd found his body in a shallow grave in the woods, I felt a small fizz of relief. The news of how he'd died left me cold; he'd been shot in the head, but there were also injuries consistent with torture.

Marcel hands me the sealed evidence bag marked with a number.

'We found this on Jack.' He studies my face as I turn it over in my hands.

It looks like a credit card but it's much heavier. Entirely black except for four tiny cubes outlined in embossed gold. Barely noticeable, but as I hand it back, I falter. Held at an angle, they take on a new form. The cubes are shaped like a house.

'Have you seen it before?'

I shake my head. 'What is it?'

'We think it's a membership card.' There's a flash of excitement in Marcel's eyes. 'The first real proof the club exists. We think that must be their official logo.'

'Was Jack involved?'

'Marcel looks at me sombrely. 'I think so, *oui.*'

313

'Jesus.' I let out a long breath. I knew he was a rat.

'We think he was getting money from the syndicate in return for doing various jobs for them. We discovered the joint bank account where your sister and Jack were receiving contributions from Twelves Homes, but he had a second account where large sums of money were being deposited from abroad. This month he opened two more accounts and records show he's been moving money around. Was he planning something? Do you think he intended to leave your sister?'

'Wish he'd left much earlier,' I say bitterly.

I try to remember what Jack said to Adele on the video. That he'd been forced to plant the cameras. What if that was another lie and he had been paid to do it? It would sit better with my impression of Jack – always on the take.

The parties would have appealed to his sexual appetite. The cheating. The addictive personality – he'd have begged to be part of their twisted club.

'Is there any significance in the number twelve?' I study the card one last time before handing it back.

Marcel shrugs. 'We can't be certain. But we think it could be a play on the twelve disciples with Judas being the twelfth, betraying Jesus in the garden of Gethsemane. According to some reports, their leader is known as Thirteen – the fallen angel, Lucifer.'

'The man who bought Bellay for Adele and Jack?'

'Only a select few know his real identity.'

'Do you know anything about him?'

He nods. 'We think he's British, worked in finance and now lives off favours. Blackmail. It's rumoured he's worth as much as six billion pounds. But nobody knows who he really is or how he made his fortune. When there have been sightings, he's never alone, always with a tall woman who we think must be handling his affairs. A lawyer of some kind.'

I let out a small laugh. 'So that's who she is.'

'You've met her?'

'She turned up at the chateau pretending to be Adele's friend, but I knew my sister wouldn't get along with someone like her.' I take a breath. 'She was there when they kidnapped me.'

He squeezes my hand. 'I'm sorry we weren't able to catch her. She knew better than to stick around.'

I feel the softness of his skin on mine. I push out a smile.

'But the five syndicate members that our sting operation managed to draw out have been arrested and charged with kidnapping, assault, trafficking. Mostly rich land owners from around here, due to the narrow window of time they had to reach the clinic they were keeping you captive. But still, wealthy, important people who will be crushed when their faces make the news. I shouldn't tell you this, but one of them was a local politician, Bertrand Verve, who was hoping to run for leader of the National Rally.' His shoulders lift. 'His political ambitions are in ruins now.'

'At least it was all for something.' I let out a sigh.

'There are hundreds more to arrest but this was a big win for us.'

'And the people in charge?'

'Still searching,' he says sombrely. 'If we can find your sister's phone it will strengthen our case.'

'That's the weird thing about all this: they were asking *me* where it was.'

He frowns. 'That doesn't make sense.'

'I think it's why they kidnapped me – to frighten me into handing it over.'

'But if Twelve Homes don't have Adele's phone, who does?'

'Someone in the syndicate must have it, surely?'

Marcel frowns.

His phone buzzes. He gets up, hurriedly crossing the room to the corner by the window. He keeps his voice low, like he's trying to hide something from me. A scowl forms, deepening as he listens.

He looks back and my stomach drops.

'What?' I try to read his eyes. 'Oh God no . . .'

He looks at me gravely.

'What's happened?' But I know what he's going to say.

Marcel clears his throat, his expression darkening. 'We've found another body. It's a woman.'

CHAPTER FIFTY-TWO

TheREALAdele003 Active two minutes ago

I had to see this for myself. I never appreciated how famous you were until now. I mean, I've always known you were special, something to be treasured and admired, but this recognition, it makes me tingle – and in all the right places.

Don't worry, they can't see me, I'm clinging to the shadows – watching through the trees. You know me, always careful. Forever your guardian angel, dearest Adele.

CHAPTER FIFTY-THREE

ERIN

TEN DAYS AFTER NYE

The sound of dogs barking carries on the wind. I swallow back my grief as we make the turn into Chateau Bellay.

I've talked Marcel into letting me come. The doctors strongly advised I stay in for observation, but how could I lie in a hospital bed when my sister could be out here?

Ripping off the price tag, I ease my arms into the ski jacket I picked up from a charity shop in town. Boots, gloves, thick socks; finally I have something warm to wear.

It's only 4.30 p.m. but the sky, heavy with cloud, is almost black. Night is drawing in, cancelling what's left of today.

My eyes rake through the forest. The wind howls and I imagine it twisting around the trees. Its pervasive force pushes through anything in its path.

I feel a lurch in my stomach. The horror of what went on here, returning. We lean into the final bend and my breath catches.

Reporters, photographers, news vans weighed down with satellite dishes tailing right back up the lane. Large areas of the woods have been marked off with police tape. There's noise everywhere. How did they get here so quickly?

Up ahead a group of die-hard fans have gathered, T-shirts printed with Adele's face showing beneath their jackets. They travelled all this way in the snow? I don't think I've really appreciated how famous she is until now. On seeing us approach, they hold up their iPhones. Filming my grief.

'Head down, now,' Marcel says quickly as we slow for the cordon.

Like swarming ants, press photographers race towards us, the hard clack of their lenses on my window sounding like gunfire. Light forces its way into our car as their cameras flash.

'What do they want from me?' I sink lower into my seat.

'A chateau murder – news reporting doesn't get juicier than this. Don't give them the satisfaction of seeing you.'

I hide behind my hands but it's through the gaps in my fingers I notice her.

Hoodie pulled up around her face. She's standing perfectly still while the others elbow around, shove their way to the front. I feel a stir of recognition.

Adele?

I blink and she's gone. Almost as if I imagined it.

Officers up ahead pin back the crowd, their arms straining to contain them. We pass through the police cordon and drive round to the back of the building.

Police four-by-fours churn up the snow. Equipment is

being unloaded from Interpol surveillance vans. Cadaver dogs weave back and forth, noses to the ground. A spaniel sprints off ahead, leading its handler into the woods.

More unmarked cars arrive and Marcel informs me it's the SWAT team from Paris. Even though it's bustling with activity, it seems eerily quiet back here. Like the chateau is holding its breath. Waiting for my reaction.

We find a space and Marcel turns to me with a warning: 'Wait in the car.' He points a finger. 'Remember, you're not supposed to be here. If they catch you, I could lose my job.'

He then remembers what he's come to do. Placing a hand on mine, he adds: 'I'll be back as soon as I have news.'

The touch feels electrified and I keep my hand there, feeding off the warmth and comfort it brings.

'Agreed?' He makes sure his message has impact.

I give a small nod.

He sighs as he gets out, as apprehensive as I am of what's to come.

As I watch Marcel leave, I notice a new confidence. A solid silhouette of a man striding purposefully into the distance. My eyes leap ahead – into the woods. Through the trees to where there's a smudge of white on the horizon. Forensics. *The crime scene.*

I wait for him to disappear from view and then open the door.

Up ahead there's the old hunter's lodge. A rickety hut made of wood with a corrugated-iron roof that's half missing. Forensic officers are searching nearby. Dressed in opaque white overalls, they remind me of spacemen with their slow, exaggerated steps. Taking care where they plant their feet so as not to not disturb the evidence.

My footsteps are light and quick in comparison. I weave between the trees, trying not to draw attention. I find a wide trunk to hide behind and shrink back, my shoulder blades pressing up against the cold bark. I hold on to my breath so it doesn't give me away, but my heart won't stop hammering.

There's a sudden barking. A high-pitch yapping. I freeze. But then comes the cry.

'Here! Over here!'

There's more yelling: 'We've found another one!'

Another one? Another what?

I peer around and my throat tightens.

Between the knot of trees, half a dozen mounds of earth and piled-up snow. Forensic pathologists, folded over with an intense look of concentration. Brushing earth away from what looks like bones. Human remains.

What is this? A cemetery? But where are the gravestones?

All of a sudden, the forest gloom is lit up by the crime scene photographer. The white light bleaching out all colour. There's someone filming the grim discovery and an officer planting numbers by the graves. Marking the dead.

Marcel didn't say anything about this.

Adele? Is she buried here? My stomach heaves.

I need to get closer; I need to know.

I creep through the undergrowth, branches snapping beneath me. The dog starts up again, its bark grows more insistent, louder, as if it's right behind me.

Shit.

I freeze, shrinking back, tucking myself in behind a tree in an attempt to make myself as small as possible.

The noise fades, the bark quietens, until I'm alone again and all I can hear is my breathing. Hot air frosting around me.

Carefully, I edge back around.

An officer with a slender face wearing a blue cap startles. Only metres apart, we lock eyes.

'Hey!' He raises his gun in surprise. '*Que fais-tu ici?*'

Slowly I get up, I back away.

'ARRÊTE!' His yell scares the birds into the sky, their wings expanding across the cold light.

I panic. He's going to get between me and Adele, and so I do the most stupid, irrational thing.

I turn and run. Pumping my legs, I plough through the snow towards the crime scene. The cold air, rushing at my skin.

Heads are whipping around, drawn by the commotion. Officers in stab vests with guns form a line: a smudge of blue through the trees as they sprint towards me.

The snow is slowing me down. Thick and clotted, it feels like I'm wading through treacle, while sweat pools beneath my new thermals. Everything is getting hotter, tighter, stopping me from breathing.

Up ahead, I see Marcel, crouched over a grave. His head snaps up, his expression darkening as he sees me heading right for him.

'Wait!' Marcel stands up, holding up both hands. 'Keep her away!'

Just try stopping me.

I feel a surge of adrenaline and the momentum of my feet takes over. I launch myself at him like a torpedo.

'*ARRÊTE!*' Several officers break off, spreading out in all directions while the rest form a tight wall. Advancing.

The cold seizes my lungs. I'm wheezing as I search for a way through. The thought of my sister being in the grave is making me sick and light-headed. I'm not thinking clearly. With nowhere to go, I charge straight for them, leaning in and shouldering my way through.

My head crunches and there's a sharp pain as my arm's wrenched behind my back, so tightly it feels like it's about to snap off. It brings tears to my eyes and I scream out. I twist, I'm kicking. I don't care who I'm hitting.

'SHE'S MY SISTER!'

A shooting pain seizes my shoulder.

'Get off! Get off me!'

Out the corner of my eye I see Marcel approach. Hands waving, signalling for them to stand down.

'*Arrêtez! Arrêtez, elle est avec moi!*' he tells them, his voice thick with irritation. Disappointment written across his face.

Reluctantly they release their grip and I stumble forwards, my face planting into Marcel's chest. There's a moment, then it's gone. He frowns, fixing me with angry eyes.

'I told you to wait in the car!' he hisses. '*Merde!*'

'How could I, when she's here!'

'Calm down, OK.' He gives me a little shake. 'I know you're upset and a lot's happened, but these officers are armed. You could have been shot.'

'Why won't they let me see her?' Tears spring to my eyes. If there's a ledge, I've stepped right off it. I break down, heavy sobs filling up my chest. My lungs drowning under the weight of grief. 'Please,' I beg. 'I'm the only person who can tell you if it's her. You need me. Please.'

He stares back, eyes softening. Marcel nods slowly.

'OK, OK.' He places a hand on my shoulder.

'I can't go on like this – the not knowing.' My voice a hoarse whisper.

His hand slides across my back and then, to my surprise, he draws me towards him. His embrace feels tender and it seems his team notice this. I feel their eyes on us and I sense confusion and irritation. Relaxing into his chest, I finally let myself be vulnerable.

'Listen, I'll take you to see her, but I need you to stay calm, OK? It'll be distressing, so prepare yourself.' He looks at me steadily.

'Tell me – how bad is it?'

IT. I can't even bring myself to say her name. The fact Marcel won't meet my eyes is all I need to know.

'Does she' – I take a breath – 'look like her?'

He looks closely at me. 'If you don't think you're up to this . . .'

I bite my lip and give him a small nod.

'All right, let's go.' He stiffens, bracing for the both of us.

He updates his team and they watch us closely as we leave together. To my surprise, Marcel leads me away from the hut and the bodies and further into the wood.

CHAPTER FIFTY-FOUR

ERIN

As we head deeper into the forest, I turn back to look at the mass grave.

'Who are they?' I say softly.

'We think they could be victims of the old way.'

'The old way?'

Marcel looks at me gravely. 'The reason Twelve Homes chose Bellay.'

I nod. 'I found a book in the chateau's library. It had' – I swallow hard – 'illustrations of what went on here. There's a room where they did terrible things.'

Anger moves across Marcel's features. His eyes harden. The faint lines around his eyes deepen.

We walk in silence for a few more minutes, then I hear Marcel take a breath.

'The Bellay family have a lot to answer for. We think Capitaine Desailly must have been covering up for them, allowing their crimes to go undetected for so many years.' He clenches his jaw. 'If only I'd been posted here sooner.'

'It's not your fault.'

'This never should have been allowed to go on for so

long. Everyone from around here knew what went on, but they didn't have the power to stop it.'

I recall the hostility of the villagers when I told them I was Adele's sister. When the community heard about the party, they must have assumed she was involved, that she was taking over from where the Bellays left off. Continuing the legacy. *The curse*. It makes sense now.

'How long have they been buried?' I swallow, there's a lump in my throat.

'Hard to tell. Some bones are more than a hundred years old. Others, more recent. The soil is very alkaline, which prevented decomposition. But Forensics say what's left are mostly between 1945 and 1985.

'Christ, this has been going on that long?'

'With power and money, you can make any problem go away. I suspect the Bellays had been paying people off for centuries.'

'Hush money,' I echo. 'How old would the victims have been?'

'Young. Forensics can tell by the bone formation. One has an obvious fracture to her skull, a blunt trauma to the head.' He stops, I hear him swallow. 'All girls. Barely teenagers. What went on here' – his jaw clenches – 'it hurts more than you could know.'

The forest seems to respond with a shudder. A sheet of snow rains down from the canopy above and that feeling of being watched returns.

As we move further into the woods, silence comes to meet us. It's eerily quiet in the forest and I imagine what it must have been like to be a hunter back in the day. Alone in the creaky wooden hut with only your thoughts for company. Stalking nature.

We pass pockets of silver, a thin shiny film where the snow has turned to ice. The cold swirls around our ankles like mist, whispering secrets we'll never understand.

Up ahead, two officers come into view. Stooped, shoulders heavy, they're keeping watch over what I've come to identify.

I stop dead.

Marcel looks at me sideways. 'You OK?'

'Yup. Fine.'

'You don't have to do this. You can identify her at the hospital when she's been cleaned up.'

Cleaned up. Oh God.

'Erin.' He steps in front of me, shielding me from what's ahead.

I tighten my jaw and the taste of blood bursts into my mouth from where I've bitten down too hard.

'I'm a nurse, I can do this.' I grit my teeth.

He sighs and moves aside.

Marcel gives the officers a nod and they make room for us. We pass a shallow grave which must have been where they found Jack. A hurried job by the looks of things. The knot in my stomach tightens.

Ahead, a second grave. Cocooned in a black body bag, waiting to be taken away, she rests on the snow. A bed of ice.

The zip's been pulled down to her waist and I immediately notice the red on her fingers. Bright crimson nail polish – Adele's favourite.

I resist the urge to be sick.

WHY? Why didn't I do more? As I approach the body, I run through all the things I should have said and done. The angry voice in my head is growing louder and louder.

I step heavily onto the ground sheet that's there to preserve evidence. Swallowing hard, I lower my eyes.

Skin as pale as snow, her lips are grey with a smudge of red lipstick. Purple bruises ring her eyes and across her throat – a gash so deep you can see arteries and veins and chipped bone. Cut almost through to the other side.

Marcel touches my arm. His eyes crease with worry and he leaves his hand on me while I take in the grisly sight.

There's not nearly enough blood for the injury is the first thing that comes to mind as I stare at the gaping wound. Shock will do that to you, make you have absurd thoughts.

But then again, I already know she wasn't killed here. She's wearing the same corset as when I last saw her. Cornflower blue.

It's the girl from the party. The one from the sex game gone wrong.

My shoulders sag in relief.

Tragic. It's horrific. But – it's not Adele.

CHAPTER FIFTY-FIVE

ERIN

'Who do you think she is?' I say softly, now noticing the needle punctures on her arm, too many to count. My heart aches for her.

'We'll begin running checks on missing girls in the area,' says Marcel. 'She could be from a neighbouring town, or even Paris. Someone the syndicate picked off the street, possibly a sex worker they brought in for the party. To them, who she is doesn't matter. People like them prey on girls like her.'

'I suppose when you're desperate you'll do anything for money.' I let out a painful breath. My heart breaking some more.

'Vulnerable. Frightened, alone, suffering from drug addictions, these girls will do even the things you described in Adele's video. The men at these parties don't care what happens to them. They use them and throw them away.' There's sorrow in his eyes. 'They must have killed her when the sex got out of hand. She was a liability, she knew too much.'

My gaze finds its way through the trees to the mass

grave, to the blurred shape of the forensic team, picking at the frozen earth. The cordoned-off area is being extended. It's now twice the size it was when I arrived.

Were they from villages around here? Teenagers brought in to entertain wealthy aristocrats?

I think about the missing girls in the posters, then I think about Adele, beautiful and fresh-faced, just like them, and I feel the swell of terror.

'Adele's not here, is she?'

He tenses. 'It's impossible to know.'

'But she'd be here. You'd have found her with Jack?'

His brow creases, Marcel's torn between the facts and what I want to hear.

I look back at the dead girl. The words leave me before I've thought them through: 'Maybe Adele is better off dead.'

'Don't say that! We'll keep searching, this isn't over.'

But it feels over as I stare out across the vast estate. All I can think about is what Twelve Homes is doing to my sister. I've watched documentaries on trafficking, when organized crime gangs use drugs to control young girls and they become helpless to fight their way back.

'I'll do everything in my power to find her,' Marcel promises.

He's about to say something else but stops, noticing that the snow has started up again.

'We should get back. There could be news from the team.'

As we pick up speed, a sense of déjà vu returns. A flashback from the party, slipping past so quickly I can't hold on. Like a train leaving a station.

I stop and turn, searching around me. I'm met with stillness. A deathly silence. I feel a prickling across my skin that makes my hair stands on end.

I make another slow full turn, peering through the trees, but there's no one there. Just the looming outline of the chateau. In the fading light the large windows look like eyes. The shutters blink at me.

What am I missing? What am I not seeing?

Marcel tenses, as if he's felt it too. 'Come on, let's go.'

The track's been swallowed up by freshly fallen snow, so we follow a new path that bends and stutters around fallen cedars and broken-off branches. We pass through a clearing that has the leftovers of a fire, picking through the trees until the forest decides it's had enough of us, eventually spitting us out on the opposite side to where we started.

We emerge into the courtyard, just as Adele would have that night. Her home, unrecognizable with lights blazing and a party unravelling. The view that greets us in the last of the light is dark and unfriendly.

'*Merde*,' Marcel says under his breath as he clocks a group of fans milling around, chatting, reading their phones. 'Quick, before they see us, let's get back to the car.' He points to a track hugging the side of the woods.

But before we can get away, a voice rings out.

'THAT'S HER!'

'We need to go,' Marcel says quickly.

'Adele's sister! She's over there!' The excitement grows.

The fans pivot and pitch, racing towards us. Eyes widening in recognition.

'Come on, we don't have long.' Marcel warns.

The group has tripled in size since we arrived. Around thirty fans, clutching their posters and their smartphones, shoving each other out of the way, they're thirstier than the press pack. Chasing after anything that brings them closer to their obsession – Adele.

But – maybe they can help? Maybe one of them knows something? They could put out a message to her vlog community?

I slow to a walk.

'Erin!' Marcel looks back at me. 'Hurry! We don't have time!'

I feel my resolve weakening as desperation takes over. I stop dead, allowing the scrum to catch up.

They scramble, pushing and elbowing in a race to be first to speak to me. Women and men, a mix of ages and accents but with one thing in common – their unwavering devotion to my sister. I feel the intensity of their emotion as they form a tight wall around me.

'Have you heard from Adele?'

I turn and a phone is pointed right in my face.

'Help me?' I say. 'Has anyone seen or heard from her?'

They push their phones under my nose. I see my sister staring back at me from their T-shirts and pictures. Her pixelated eyes, grainy and haunted like the posters in town.

'Erin. Come on!' Marcel yells. 'They won't help you.'

'Please.' I make a slow turn. 'If anyone knows anything.' I can hear the desperation in my voice, but someone must know something. Maybe one of them lives around here and saw Adele in the days leading up to her disappearance?

They gaze back at me. Eyes wide and enthralled. Excited by my distress.

'We love Adele, tell us about her.'

'I need information—' I look between them.

'What's her favourite food?'

'Did Jack cheat on her?'

'WE LOVE YOU, ADELE!' the brunette screams from the back.

'Can you help me?' I beg. The high-pitched voices ring in my ears, flaring.

'Where does she buy her dresses from?' A slim woman plants herself in my path.

A much taller lady talks over her: 'Can we see her clothes? Bring us something of hers.'

There's a communal squeal. A thrum of anticipation.

The ground feels like it's moving and I'm swaying. The doctors were right, I shouldn't be out here with a concussion.

I feel a burst of pain. A memory of New Year's Eve dislodges, although I can't quite see it.

This was a terrible mistake.

'Erin! *Merde!*' I look over and see Marcel trying to force a path through the crowd.

'ADELE! FREE ADELE.' They close the wall around me.

The dizziness returns. My vision fades and then comes back.

A woman with piercings, wearing a skull-print bandana, muscles her way to the front. There's a jolt of recognition, so strong I feel winded.

I'm sure I've seen her before. No not her, but someone else. Someone at the party.

She pulls out her phone and presses record.

'How does it feel to be the sister no one cares about?' she grins.

I'm stunned into silence. We stare at one another and I notice her enjoyment – the little laugh – as she films my reaction.

'Your sister's an entitled bitch,' she crows.

The words land like a punch. I feel the rush of tears and I look away. I can't let them see I've been hurt.

'A stuck-up bitch who deserves to be dead!'

Her parting shot.

The hysteria around her grows. Outrage, anger – how dare she attack their beloved Adele. There's a lynch mob feel to the group now and it's frightening.

I feel the heat of them pressing against me. The ringing in my ears, so loud I can't think. The ground rushes up, then a hand lands on my arm, gripping me tightly. I'm wrenched backwards before I pass out.

'What are you doing? Don't speak to them.' Marcel elbows us free from the scrum. 'Why are you always running off? *Merde!* You're so wilful and stubborn.'

We break into the open and I suck in the air like it's running out. But the stillness is quickly replaced with fresh panic. More shouting and the clunk of boots. I look over Marcel's shoulder to see reporters sprinting our way.

'Erin!'

'Erin, over here – Mark from the *Telegraph*. Have they found your sister's body?'

'Over here, Ms Davenport!'

Everywhere I look there are people. Swarming.

'Erin, did you kill your sister?'

'MOVE BACK, give her room,' Marcel barks. 'MOVE.'

A business card is thrust into my hand. 'If you want to tell your side of the story . . .' a strongly accented voice says.

The sensation of being knocked and shoved loosens a memory again. Just like the fans and the media scrum, it forces itself to the front of my mind.

Adele? No. It can't be her; she was watching the party from outside. But who is it? Who else do I know who was there that night?

I need to get away from here. I have to think. I yank myself free from Marcel's grip and hurry towards my car, still standing where I left it in the main courtyard.

'Where are you going?' Marcel calls after me. 'It's not safe, come with me.' He swears under his breath.

'There's something I need to do,' I yell back. Closing the door just in time, I hear the *thunk* as the reporters slam into my car. The harsh flashlight reaching inside as I start the engine. I imagine how my face will look in tomorrow's papers. Bleached-out, bloodshot eyes.

As I nudge the car through the crowd, she pushes her way back inside my head.

Willowy. Slight build, she slips through the crowd with ease. So thin her collar and hip bones are jutting out.

The image fades and then tiptoes back into view. An intense pressure swelling between my temples. I feel a swoop of nausea and grip the steering wheel more tightly, trying to retrieve what I saw on Adele's phone.

Cameras strobe as I reach the police cordon. A fist pounds on my bonnet and the noise of the party creeps back in. Naked bodies pressing up against each other. She's wearing strappy heels and bright red lipstick, and she carries a polished silver tray loaded with champagne. Smiling, accommodating, she's the kind of beauty that could silence a room.

It's Delphine. She was waitressing at the party that night. *Christ.*

I can picture her now, clear as day. I didn't make the connection because she looked unrecognizable in that context. Now it all makes sense – why she seemed so frightened to talk to me. She tried to warn me. She knew about the syndicate and what they would do to me if I asked too many questions.

A link to Adele, finally. Delphine might have seen something, she might be the only one who can help me find my sister.

There's a hard wedge in my throat and I'm suddenly painfully aware of how little time I have left. Because, if I'm right, the syndicate will want to cover their tracks and they'll stop at nothing to erase all loose ends.

I feel a chill as my eyes fix on the road ahead. The windscreen wipers battle the snow with an aggressive swish swish. I can barely see more than a few metres ahead but I stamp my foot down on the accelerator. With a burst of courage I throw caution to the wind.

CHAPTER FIFTY-SIX

ERIN

'Hello?' I knock.

The door falls away under my touch and light from the street spills into the hallway. There's a pile of shoes and unopened mail pushed up against the wall.

Iona gave me Delphine's address. Apparently, I'm not the only one worried. She hasn't been seen around town for days. The entrance to her apartment is near the pub, just off the high street.

Delphine?

I push the door wide open. Overheated air and the tang of ripe fruit hurries towards me. Voices drift from inside.

'Delphine? Hello?'

I make my way along a narrow corridor painted black. The place is suddenly sweet with the smell of marijuana and the voices grow louder, speaking over each other in French.

'Hi? Hello?'

The darkness unfolds into a dimly lit room, a kitchen-cum-living area. The blinds are pulled down and slivers of light creep through slats. I suck in my breath as I take in the mess.

Broken glass on the countertops. The high stools have been kicked over and a fruit bowl turned upside down, shrivelled mouldy fruit spilling across the table. It looks like she hasn't been here in a while.

In the living room, drawers have been rifled through and their contents turfed out. Papers cover the floor.

On the opposite wall a TV blasts French news on full volume. Aerial footage reporting from Bellay. I recognize the crime scene tents; from above, they appear as harsh white tiles.

I turn it off, throwing the apartment into silence except for the steady dripping of the kitchen tap.

Slowly I make a full turn, trying to make sense of it. The place looks ransacked. What were they searching for? Adele's phone?

I set my bag down and go over the room more carefully. There's a pinboard with Polaroid photos. Several beach shots of Delphine wearing a big smile and a sun dress, but mostly nights out with friends holding up plastic cups with florescent straws. She reminds me a little of Adele: the posing, the need to be the centre of attention.

I check over a bookshelf crowded with trinkets and dust, then the low coffee table, where there's a battered silver tin. I look inside, releasing a smell of marijuana. It's brimming with weed and loose cigarette papers.

Moving back to the kitchen, I check over the surfaces again. Beneath the sink, where you'd normally expect cleaning products, a cupboard full of wine bottles and spirits. Wow, that's a lot of alcohol. Could Delphine have a drinking problem?

I'm about to stand up when something else catches my eye. I lower onto all fours to get a better look.

I run my finger lightly over it.

Oh my God.

Dried into the floor tiles – a fine spray of blood.

The shock discovery makes me lose my footing. I stumble, smacking into my back. I slide up the cabinet until I'm standing, my heart thundering.

I'm too late.

I look around with fresh eyes, seeing the room for what it is – a crime scene. There was a struggle and someone was injured, or—

'Delphine?' I yell.

An echo for a reply. I know the only link to my sister is gone.

A sense of hopelessness returns and I'm hit with a wave of grief so powerful I can barely keep my legs working as I step over the broken glass towards the back of the flat where there's a short corridor and three more rooms behind closed doors.

I'm almost too frightened to look.

Breathing in sharply, I turn the handle.

But it's only a small wet room with a shower and a filthy toilet. I quickly move on.

The next door moans on its hinges, an invitation into more darkness. I step inside. The ceiling is much lower and the curtains are drawn. I can hear the faint whirring of a helicopter in the distance, the muted *whomping* as it hovers over Bellay, telling me how close I am to my sister's chateau. A painful reminder how far we're apart.

I snap on the light, revealing a storage room painted black, full of bin bags spilling over with clothes. Strappy dresses, jeans, shoes with killer heels are strewn across the floor. The smell of cigarettes clings to the fabrics. Slung over the back of a chair is a heavy shearling jacket – the same one I saw Delphine wearing outside the bakery.

My eyes rake over the mess, searching for a clue, although what I'm looking for, I don't know.

I feel a sudden chill, as if someone is watching me. Skin prickling, I turn around and startle.

In the corner of the room, behind the door, is a camera on a tripod, a ring light and a white bed sheet strung up along the wall.

Dread lodges in my stomach.

It's an expensive-looking camera. A Nikon. Totally at odds with the run-down feel of the rest of the apartment. Something like that would cost at least £5,000. Not the sort of thing you'd leave behind.

The darkened room, the cameras, the terror of what the syndicate had planned for me – the memory of that night replays like a horror film and this bears all the same hallmarks.

Warily I step towards the camera, certain that whatever I'm about to find will be more terrifying than anything I've discovered here.

Delphine, what have they done to you? I feel sick at the thought.

Sleek and black, the camera is a complex series of dials and knobs. My hands lightly run over it, as if it were a bomb that could go off at any second.

I find the playback option. A red button, just like a trigger.

Swallowing hard, I press <PLAY>

CHAPTER FIFTY-SEVEN

DELPHINE

AFTER

YouTube

Hello, my lovelies. It's Delphine here and guess where I am? Oui, I'm in Chateau Bellay.

Adele isn't feeling well so I'm taking over her channel until she's better. But she says hi and she misses you and loves you all so so much.

I'm her best friend. (**waves**) Salut! Don't say you don't recognize me? You met me on Adele's episode MEET MY NEW BEST FRIEND, I'll leave the link below if you haven't seen it.

Ahh, bon, so today I have a petite surprise for you all, I'm taking you somewhere very special, to une chambre Adele hasn't shown you . . .

(**walks past pool, crosses lawn**)

It's one of the oldest rooms in the chateau.

(**crouches to pull loose brick from wall, removes hidden key**)

See, I know all of Bellay's secrets.

(opens back door)

Follow me inside, and, bienvenue, welcome to my new home. (flips camera around and smiles)

(cuts out)

'Allo! (giggles) I'm back and I'm in my favourite room. Can you guess? (crosses to dressing table, sees reflection in mirror, waves)

What do you think? (spins around) It's Adele's dress, the yellow one with the daisy flowers which you all commented on and liked. It looks good on me, non?

She makes everything pretty. Adele, ma chérie, I've watched you so many times from my special place in the forest, looking through the trees, sometimes wearing your clothes to be close to you. This feels like the start of my fairy tale and soon, finally, we'll be living it together.

(picks up perfume, spritzes it across body)

I imagine her sitting in front of this mirror (inhales scent) styling her hair, putting on lipstick, making herself ready for the day. I wish I could be more like her. I wonder – what must it be like to be perfect? To have that special something that makes everyone stop and turn to look at you, just like a famous actress.

Not long to wait. (smiles) And now Jack won't be around, I'll be helping, looking after Adele in ways he never could.

I can't wait to show you all our new vlog. Our fairy tale together.

(cuts out)

Say hi, Adele.

(zooms in)

Don't be shy, it's OK, you can tell them our secret. I told them all about us.

Adele?

(scowls)

She's not chatty today but that's because she's sick, poor thing, Adele had a fever in the night, but it's OK, don't worry, my lovelies, I'm taking good care of her and she's getting better. Aren't you, ma chérie?

Adele? Did you miss me? I wasn't gone long and I brought you some of your favourite treats. You need to tell them what a good person I am, how much I've done for you.

(approaches bed)

Adele? Stop being that way, you need to tell them.

Hey, I'm speaking to you!

(smashes glass of water on floor)

Don't make me not feed you again! That'll be the fourth meal you'll have missed because you're being ungrateful, you stupid girl.

(starts crying)

I'm sorry baby, I didn't mean to lose my temper. *Je suis vraiment désolée!* (kisses Adele's hand repeatedly) You need your strength to get better. You need to tell them about what we have planned. That I care about you, more than anyone else.

Merde! (cuts out)

CHAPTER FIFTY-EIGHT

ERIN

I rewind and watch it again. My heart threatening to jump out of my chest.

Harsh white tiles for a floor and walls give a hospital feel. A filthy single mattress. A green sleeping bag. There are no other identifying features. My finger punches the button, anger rising as I run over Delphine's vlog again and again, searching for clues. Trying to make sense of what I've found.

Is there anything I recognize? Anything at all about where she's keeping Adele prisoner?

Adele appears critically injured; she could be losing blood; she's either been given a sedative or the blood loss is what's causing her to lose consciousness.

I replay the vlog. Forcing myself to remain calm, to be that person I am in the emergency room when faced with the pressure of saving someone's life.

I scrunch up my eyes and snap them open. How can I not freak out – it's my sister! What's she done to her?
Rewind.

Tiles, low lighting, low ceiling, no windows. *Rewind.*
No windows. None at all. I look up.

Christ, it's a basement. Adele is trapped underground.

I search around me, seeing the room with fresh eyes. The entire apartment has taken on a new meaning.

'Adele?' I scream. 'Can you hear me, Adele?'

Racing from the room my foot snags on something. I look down, grimacing as I kick away the filthy jumper. She actually lives like this? As I step over the heap, I do a double take of recognition. I notice something else. Something familiar. I reach down, seizing the pink hoodie into my hands.

It's Adele's. I'd recognize it anywhere.

Rifling through the bin bag I pull out more of my sister's things. Her silk shirt, the black one she wears on evenings out. Her beloved Mickey Mouse nightshirt Dad got her on our family Holiday to Florida.

I look up. 'ADELE!'

I rip down the hall towards the final room.

'Adele, where are you?' I charge into Delphine's bedroom. The reek of BO and cigarettes cling together like a filthy couple, so sharp, it makes me gag. I can't see the floor for the heaped clothes and used underwear. There's a black lace thong tangled into the sheets.

On the side table is a glass of water that's gathered a skin and a blister pack of pills. *Diazepam*, a potent anti-anxiety drug. Taken at a high enough dosage, it would cause drowsiness. Could she have drugged Adele with it?

I check under the bed. More unwashed clothes and balls of dust.

Standing up too quickly makes the blood rush and the floor tilts. I can feel my body creaking, my head is thumping

– warning me to slow down. I bite down on the pain and cross the room.

I pull open the wardrobe and I suck in a breath. My hand instinctively reaching for my throat.

The inside doors are wallpapered top to bottom with photos of Adele.

Hundreds of printed-out images of my sister. Grainy and pixelated, they look like stills grabbed from her vlog. There's head shots and close-ups of her eyes, her lips, even her breasts. It feels as sexual as it is obsessional.

There's more – a study into what Adele wears, what she likes to eat, her day-to-day life. My baby sister, thrust under a microscope. Delphine has picked apart every last piece of her. A dangerous infatuation. My stomach lurches.

And there's more. Pasted onto the opposite door are surveillance-style photos of Adele.

Watching her walk down the high street, chatting to people, in the supermarket. Then my mouth falls open as my eyes find *the chateau collection*.

Adele in her bikini by the pool. Adele rubbing sun cream into her skin. Adele undressing. The silhouette of her body in her bedroom window. Delphine must have been spying on her from the woods. The thought of her creeping around, stalking my sister, brings an instant shudder.

Hang on, has Delphine been stalking me? Was that *her* following me in town? And the girl wearing the hoodie in the crowd of fangirls I mistook for Adele. Was that her?

I drop to my knees and begin rooting around the back of the wardrobe. Is there something here that can lead me to my sister? I pull free several rolled-up pieces of paper.

Smoothing them out across the floor I notice my hands are trembling.

They're sketches of Adele's face. Hard black lines drawn in biro. Her lips, swollen, in an eroticized way. Delphine's interpretation of my sister stares back at me.

With adrenaline surging I dive back into the wardrobe, ripping open the shoe boxes. Dozens of tiny black dolls tip out onto my feet, identical to the ones I found at the chateau. Faceless with two white stitches for eyes. Evil-looking things. I can't bring myself to think what they could mean.

I tip out what's left in the box and hear the clunk of something hard hitting the wood. Snatching it up into my hands, I can't quite believe what I'm holding.

Bright, glittery, it's Adele's phone.

My God – It was Delphine who attacked me.

All the missing pieces of the puzzle rush together at an explosive speed.

I know why the syndicate tortured me. They've been as in the dark as I have. We've been searching for the same things.

It all makes sense now.

Almost all – except, where is my sister? And what does Delphine want with her?

CHAPTER FIFTY-NINE

ERIN

I rip between rooms screaming out her name.

'ADELE! Can you hear me? ADELE!'

There's no door, no obvious way into a basement or a cellar. The apartment can't be much older than fifty years, would it even have a lower ground floor?

Back in the living room, I search through the mess for some sort of clue. My eyes going over the photos, the books. I burrow through the drawers, I tip out the marijuana box, where is it? If she's locked Adele in somewhere, there must be a key.

Nothing.

I straighten and make a slow full turn, raking over old ground. Who lives like this anyway? What sort of person is Delphine? I think about the wine bottles, the drugs by her bed. I remind myself of Capitaine Desailly's description of her: a fantasist with a history of violence. Terrifyingly, it's probably the one truth in all his lies.

Think, come on, think.

If I was a psychotic, obsessive fangirl, where would I hide the key to my secret room?

The room holds its breath. A suffocating silence except for the drip-dripping of the tap, as rhythmical as a ticking clock.

Time draining away. If Adele's losing blood, she won't have long left.

Maybe she's not even here but in some outhouse somewhere. With such a vast area to cover it'll be like searching for a needle in a haystack. I feel weak at the thought, my knees give out and I drop down heavily into the lumpy armchair.

I'll never find her.

How did I not see? It was all a performance. The frightened little girl act to throw me off, to scare me into leaving town. Delphine did tell me she wanted to be an actress.

I think about Delphine's vlog, that charged-up face full of determination. What is she planning for my sister?

Pain throbs between my temples, I slump into the chair, surrendering to the worn-out fabric. My head feels swollen and heavy and gravity pulls it to one side. All I want is to shut out the world and make it go away. Defeat washes over me and I start to close my eyes.

Hang on.

I blink quickly. What's that?

I tilt my gaze to the right. Just a smidgen.

OK, that's weird.

I lower myself onto my knees. Planting my face to the floor, I study the rug more closely. I run my fingers over it, just to be sure.

Barely visible, there's four – blink and you'd miss it –

grooves in the fabric. As soon as I stand up, the divots disappear. The sofa – I think it's been moved.

I heave it out of the way and snatch up the corner of the rug, pulling it back in one. Dust motes swim around me and the place now stinks of fusty old carpet but at my feet – there's a hatch door. *A secret room.*

Cut into the wooden floorboards there's a sawn-out hole with just enough room for a finger.

I pull the hatch towards me, releasing a smell so rancid I have to cover my nose and turn away.

It's a smell I know well from the hospital. It's the stench of death.

CHAPTER SIXTY

ERIN

Peering inside, my heart sinks. How could anyone be alive in there?

'Adele?'

There's no reply except my echo.

A steel staircase leads down, the steps disappearing into a pit of black. There's no light switch and I'm terrified of the dark.

I can't do it.

A thick soup of nothingness. My throat tightens as I imagine it reaching over my head and pulling me under. My legs turn to jelly. *I just can't.*

Flashbacks of Adele disappearing into the marshland resurface. How I'd watch from the window as the night would swallow her whole. *I don't have the courage. I'm not like her. I'll never be as brave as her.*

I take a breath.

What if Adele's not dead? How will you forgive yourself for not trying? Come on, Erin, she needs you.

You can't keep running, you have to face your fears

head on. Adele's words. The ones she'd whisper, soothing me back to sleep.

Stop running, Erin.

Trembling, I clamber onto all fours and gingerly lower myself through the trapdoor onto the top step.

It rattles under my weight and feels like it could snap apart at any moment. I take a deep breath, I grit my teeth and I begin my descent into gloom, the metal clanging violently with each step.

The deeper I go, the sharper the smell, wrapping around me so tightly I can't breathe. The cold isn't helping, it feels as chilled as a freezer compartment.

'Adele? Are you in here?'

Nothing.

I step off the staircase onto something slippery. Sweeping my phone torch across the surface I catch something glistening. It looks like water but it's impossible to tell.

There's now a strong smell of excrement in the room and a deathly silence. It seems like I'm in a bunker buried deep underground. My footsteps are muted, the walls feel insulated. Somewhere you'd never be heard. What is this place?

I aim the torch in front, a pathetic arc of light.

'Adele?' My voice splinters. 'Are you in here?'

I move through more darkness and silence. My body prickling.

'If you're here, make a noise.'

Swishing the torch from left to right, the beam catches on something. The end of the mattress. Then, a pair of bruised swollen feet. I lurch forwards.

'Adele?'

Relief surging, I rush to her side.

'Adele. It's Erin!'

There's no movement.

'Adele?'

She's lying on her back on top of the sleeping bag. Eyes closed; arms rigid by her side like a dead person.

Please God, no.

Her cheeks have hallowed out. Her arms look painfully thin. She's still wearing the grey hoodie and joggers from the night she went missing.

'Adele, wake up!' I shake her.

She feels ice-cold. Her skin a mottled blue under the pale light.

I'm too late.

I can't feel a pulse. I place my ear over her mouth, listening carefully. There's a faint whistling, a wheezing noise. A fight for air.

She's alive. *Oh, thank God.*

My eyes travel across her body, taking in her injuries. Her right foot is badly swollen, her ankle looks broken and there's a gash crusted in blood. Ten days without moving has led to significant muscle atrophy in her legs. She's going to struggle to walk.

There's a groan followed by a hand twitch.

'Adele!'

She blinks open her eyes, closing them seconds later.

'Delphine?' she says weakly.

'Oh God, what has she done to you?' I stroke her arm. I check her vitals. She's dehydrated but the drowsiness is something else – I examine her wrists and ankles for signs of restraints but I can see no obvious marks or bruising. Her lack of consciousness tells me she's been given some sort of sedative, an opiate maybe. Something much stronger than the pills I found upstairs. I check for needle marks and the inside of her arms are riddled with punctures.

'Adele, can you hear me?' I lightly pat her face. 'Come on, wake up,' I urge, my tone more firm. A voice I use on patients to keep them conscious. 'Adele, are you with me, honey?'

I check her pulse again. It's faint, weakening. Hypothermia is setting in.

'Adele, honey, blink, just blink if you can hear me.'

'Erin?' She smiles faintly.

'Listen, I'm going to get you out of here.'

'I'm tired.'

'I know you are, sweetie, but we need to go.'

'My leg . . .' She winces. 'It hurts so bad.'

'We'll fix it, don't worry. Where's Delphine?'

Adele makes a strange gurgling noise. 'Liar!'

'Come on, try putting your arm around me.'

'She's a LIAR! She promised she'd help me . . . protect me from them . . . she promised.' She coughs. 'Where's Jack?'

Adele winces as I try moving her. 'Ooww, my leg, I can't, stop, stop, it hurts!'

I try hooking her arm around my neck, but it slips off and she slides back onto the bed.

'Come on, TRY.' I glance back at the stairs, the steep climb out of here.

Despite the cold, my skin is burning. Prickling with urgency. I shine the torch around, searching for something that could help me lever her off the bed. The light catches on a pile of used needles. Syringes, wrappings. Broken-open vials with leftovers of a bright orange liquid. *Morphine.*

There's also a half-empty bottle of water and a plate with shrivelled bread crusts. In the corner of the room is a toilet bucket. Delphine must have carried her over. That's something, at least.

'Where's Jack?' she groans.

My head whips back to her. 'ADELE. LISTEN. You've got to try to hold on.'

'O-K.' Her eyes shut on me again. Her arm slides off. She makes a *thunk* noise as she falls back onto the mattress.

It's no use. I can't do this alone. I need help. I need Marcel. I reach for my phone and find twenty missed calls from him. The signal's flickering in and out of service. One bar, then no bars.

I arc the mobile through the air, trying to catch some signal. It's no good, it's not picking up on anything now.

I turn to Adele. 'I'll be back, promise.'

She attempts to push herself upright and then cries out.

'My leg, owwww, Jesus it hurts. Don't go,' she wails. 'Don't leave me with that crazy bitch!'

'It's OK, I'll be at the top of the stairs, I'll be right here.'

THUD.

My head snaps up. 'What's that?

'Don't you dare leave me.'

'Shhhhh!' I turn off my torch. Holding my breath to listen.

Another thud and then footsteps. Heavy clomping from above, moving along the hallway. The noise growing louder. Closer.

'It's *her* . . .'

'SHHHH, shut up.'

'She's not who she says she—'

I clamp my hand over Adele's mouth. 'She'll hear us.'

THUD. THUD. THUD. Then nothing.

I can feel Adele's breath, hot on my hand while I hold on to my own.

She's seen the hatch door open. She knows.

The noise starts up again, but much more muted this time, as if she's taking careful steps, treading lightly around the hatch door.

The noise picks up, it's more like a pacing now. An agitated back and forth. And then.

THUNK.

The tile of light in the ceiling is extinguished.

CHAPTER SIXTY-ONE

ERIN

There's a loud scratchy noise. Like furniture being dragged across the floor. The sound of being buried alive.

Why – WHY – didn't I tell Marcel where I was going? No one will ever know we're down here. I turn to Adele, her face strained with pain. I grab hold of her hand, holding it tightly in mine.

'I'm sorry. I'm so sorry I didn't find you sooner.'

'It's her, she's here, isn't she?' Adele slurs.

I drop my head, pressing it into her hand. Searching for her warmth. 'I'm so sorry.'

She strokes the back of my head lightly. 'Stop saying sorry.' She manages a smile.

'I came out here to bring you home. There's something I needed to tell you about Mum.'

'Oh God, no.'

'She's sick and—'

Adele shuts her eyes. 'Stop, don't saying anything. Please stop.' She swallows loudly. Her voice cracking. 'It's my fault, I should've been honest . . . about everything. It's me who's to blame.'

Tears swell. A knot of emotions tightening as I cradle my sister.

'We're screwed, aren't we?' She manages a small laugh.

I can't bring myself to answer.

We fall into silence, comforting one another, just as we'd do when we were children. Despite how bleak our future looks, I feel calmer knowing however this ends, we'll be together.

Time seems to slow to a standstill. Minutes dragging by as we listen to the muted noises from above, the sound of our captor. Her footsteps, the hiss of water running then muffled voices as she turns the news back on. I call up an image of Delphine, watching news reports on the search for Adele on the big screen, smiling at her best-kept secret.

Anger rises into my throat and I have to fight the urge to scream, kick, lash out. *Me?* The one who's always calm and controlled. I want to break something.

'I'm going to try the police again,' I whisper.

'*Erin*, no, stay here.'

'I have to do something.' I get up abruptly.

'Don't be crazy.' She starts coughing. 'Erin, no.'

With slow careful steps I creep back up the stairs, every muscle in my body tensed, trying not to make a sound.

The noise of the TV drifts through the floor and I'm close enough to hear what's being said. The news reporter is talking about Adele.

'*Elle est présumée morte.*'

Come again? I angle my ear, straining to hear.

'*Oui, cette histoire a une fin tragique.*'

Presumed dead? A tragic end to this story? Wait. I glance

back at my injured sister. They're giving up? No! Why? That means they'll be calling off the search. Our last hope of being found, snuffed out.

'Erin, come back,' Adele says, an urgent whisper.

I reach out my phone – one bar. No bars. One bar. Come on! ONE BAR. I call Marcel, adrenaline spiking as I listen to the broken dial tone.

'Come on, pick up, pick up.'

'Erin?'

Relief grabs me and shakes me so violently I can't speak.

'Hi, Erin?'

'Marcel,' I wheeze. 'Listen, I'm in trouble.'

'Say that again . . .'

'I've found Adele. It's Delphine. She's been keeping her—'

'Erin? The line's really bad.'

'Marcel?' I say more loudly.

'*Merde! Je ne peux pas t'entendre.*'

There's a loud thud and I freeze. The dragging noise starts up again. Louder, quicker than before.

She's heard me.

'Erin, hurry,' Adele croaks.

I can't get down from the stairs fast enough. My foot misses a step and I stumble, drop, smacking onto the hard tiles.

The hatch springs open and a face appears – a silhouetted oval swimming in light.

'Coooeee.' Her voice echoes. 'You OK down there?'

I scramble backwards to Adele. My right hip throbbing from the fall.

A click and the room's suddenly bright. Lit up by a

single hanging bulb on a bare thread wire which won't stop flickering. It strobes every few seconds like a disco ball, lighting up our prison. A tiny space with just enough room for standing. I wonder if once upon a time it was used to store food.

And now – us.

The noise of her biker boots clanging on the staircase fills the tense silence. A metallic rattle. She jumps the final steps and straightens, sweeping her long hair over her shoulders. She's much taller than I remembered and breathtakingly beautiful. In a fragile bird way.

Her long skinny legs are accentuated by tight leather trousers. Her tiny frame is drowning in an oversized black jumper. She's wearing thick-soled DM boots and heavy black eye make-up. Goth-cum-biker chick. Her long unbrushed hair swings across her back like a pendulum.

She's smiling at us, an excited, electrified grin.

'Ooh la la, when I saw the hatch open, I panicked, I thought I'd lost you, Adele.' She whispers, tightening her grip on the straps of her backpack. 'But then I saw your sister's bag and I knew both of you were here and everything was OK again.' There's a giggle. She looks us up and down, 'Mon Dieu, you look nothing alike!'

Her eyes linger on my face with disappointment. 'Nothing alike at all.' Her gaze drops to where I'm holding my side. 'You OK?' She speaks before I can answer. 'Don't worry, I'll take care of you. Sisters together now, OK.'

'Let us go!' Adele shrieks from behind me.

Delphine shakes her head. 'That's not a good idea, it's not safe for you to leave.'

'I want to see Jack, where's Jack?'

Delphine throws me a look. 'You want to tell her, or shall I?'

'Tell me what?'

'Shhhh. It's OK.' I reach for Adele's arm and stroke it.

'Tell me what?'

'Jack's dead.' Delphine says coldly. 'I was waiting until you were better to tell you, but you've forced my hand. They killed him.' She shrugs.

Adele rolls her head to me and with a small hysterical laugh she says: 'She's lying?'

The lump rises in my throat.

'Erin?'

'Tell me she's lying.'

I shake my head.

'Jack's dead?' Adele whispers. I see her working hard to swallow. 'I did this, didn't I? It's my fault, because I left him. If I stayed and tried to help . . .' Blotches of red spread across her cheeks. Her eyes grow big and watery as she dissolves into tears. 'I should have stayed and protected him . . .'

'Don't cry.' Delphine's face crumples. 'Please don't be sad. I hate seeing you unhappy.' She jerks towards my sister, but I scramble up onto the bed, placing myself between them.

She flashes me a look. A warning.

'I saw the way he looked at other women, he had *les yeux baladeurs* – wandering eyes, yes. You're better off.' Another wide smile. 'You have me now!'

'What are you on about, you crazy bitch, I want Jack!'

The sudden sharpness in Adele's tone – the rejection – startles Delphine and her expression darkens. She tucks her hair behind her ear and takes a breath.

'I know you didn't mean that.' She forces a smile. 'You're not well.'

I rest a hand on my sister and hiss, 'Shhh. Don't say anything.'

'I want to see him; I need to see Jack,' Adele says to me.

A low humming breaks out as Delphine murmurs the words to a French song. Shifting from one foot to another.

With the same calm voice, she repeats, 'You're not feeling well.' The rocking motion is becoming more pronounced.

Adele's sobbing only sets Delphine off more.

'*Do something*!' Adele snaps at me.

'I know what' – Delphine swings around, her eyes flicking between us, wide and eager – 'we'll make a vlog! *Oui, oui, c'est bòn*, it'll be *magnifique*! We'll get dressed up and I'll do our hair and our make-up. Make us pretty for the big announcement.'

The big announcement? Dread coils inside me.

She starts pacing the room, an excited skip to her step. I feel Adele tense under my hand.

'Hey, lovelies, this is Delphine and Adele.' She mimics my sister in her heavily accented voice. Clearing her throat, she starts again. 'Welcome to our new vlog. Adele and Delphine's chateau life.' She beams at us. 'How do I sound? I've been practising.'

Adele laughs.

'You like it?' Delphine grins. 'I knew you would.'

In disbelief, Adele says: '*Why* would I do a vlog with you?'

'Because we're sisters,' she says matter-of-factly.

Adele's mouth falls open.

Delphine pushes her sleeve to her elbow, revealing a tattoo, a black inked half-moon, identical to Adele's. 'See, sisters!'

Adele breaks down into a fit of giggles. Hysterical, pain-induced laughter. Her shoulders shudder into the mattress.

Delphine watches her carefully. The air becomes charged and I feel frightened. Adele's laughter rings out like a clown in a horror film. A mad, endless echo that brings a deranged smile to Delphine's face.

Seconds later, it arrives: The switch. Delphine leans in. 'That's all you can say after EVERYTHING I'VE DONE? I save your life and this is how you thank me?'

It must be the morphine because Adele won't stop laughing and it's triggering Delphine into a deeper psychosis.

Delphine shuts her eyes and begins some breathing exercise, her breath whistling as she calms herself. She blinks back into the room and there's a sense of her having pulled back. A hesitation before she speaks again.

'It's OK, I don't hate you, Adele. You should rest now.' Then she turns on me. '*I* saved her. Not you, ME.'

Quickly, I hold up my hands in a gesture of surrender.

'And I'm so grateful and indebted,' I assure her. 'You're a kind, generous person.'

She eyes me suspiciously.

'Adele's lucky to have you.'

She nods and seems satisfied with the appreciation.

'It's a miracle. How did you save her?' I try to keep Delphine engaged.

The pacing starts up again. She wants to talk, to be heard.

'In the tower.' She shakes her head in disbelief. 'Of all the places where *ma chérie* could be hiding,' she says, alluding to Adele's fixation with princess towers.

I smile at her encouragingly.

'I was waitressing at New Year's and I needed a smoke, a break from those rude, idiotic people. I'd been given so many rules – do this, don't do this.' She pulls a face. 'Stupid control freaks. Anyway, I'm told I mustn't be seen smoking, so I snuck off.' She looks up. '"*Snuck*", that's how you say it, yes?'

I nod warily. It's hard to believe she's nineteen; she comes across as so much older.

She smiles.

'There were lots of guests outside watching the fireworks, so I went into the tower and that's where I found Adele. Mon Dieu!' She shakes her head. 'She was in a bad way and so very frightened. I couldn't leave her like that. *Non*. It was my chance to show Adele how much I love her. How she needs me.'

'How did you manage to get away?'

'Those gorillas who had Jack didn't think to look in the tower. I waited for them to head off in the other direction and then took Adele into the forest. I know that wood like the back of my hand. I brought her home to where I could look after her.' She looks back at Adele, shaking her head.

'It wasn't easy, carrying her, but I managed.' She smiles adoringly at my sister, like a lovesick puppy. 'For you, I'd do anything.'

'Make her stop,' Adele groans.

Delphine pretends not to hear.

'And I've been caring for her ever since. Keeping her safe.' I swallow.

'Adele told me about the old man in her bedroom. Puffing out his last breath while getting fucked.' She laughs. 'Meh, I couldn't care less what these people do at parties as long as I'm paid. And all this fuss over the past and what the Bellay family did. I'd have been crazy to say no to their money. Especially when I'm offered the chance to spend an evening inside the chateau, where I can feel close to Adele and her life and all the things I love about her. I couldn't stop smiling every time I recognized something from her vlog.' Delphine giggles.

Sensing a shift in mood, I try to keep her talking. 'Who asked you to work that night?'

Delphine's eyebrows lift as she reaches into her pocket for a cigarette. She dips her head as she lights it.

'Some stuck-up British woman pulled over in her flashy car while I was walking home from work. In her posh accent she pretended to be important, offering the experience of a lifetime – a night in a real French chateau. Ooh la la. But I could see through her: a cheap madame, organizing prostitutes for her pimp.'

Delphine inhales, drawing the nicotine into her lungs.

'But I played along. Why not?' She blows smoke out of the corner of her mouth. 'What do I care?'

As I study her – the show of defiance, the defensive posture – I wonder about her bruises. What happened to turn her so hard? Who treated her so badly?

'Is there anyone you can call family?' I ask gently.

She laughs.

'Someone you can lean on for support?'

'You didn't meet my sisters then?'

I blink quickly.

'My dolls. My sisters. They've been my family since they put me into care. And I made sure they were never far from Adele, keeping her safe.'

Christ.

Behind the disillusionment is a sadness though. No qualifications. Growing up in a backwater town dreaming of one day escaping. It suddenly dawns on me that Delphine and Adele might not be that dissimilar after all. Both wanting to escape their life. Both lost in the dream of a fairy-tale ending.

I can see it now – Delphine scrolling through social media feeds of girls her age who have it all. Girls who wear designer clothes, live a life of luxury, holidaying in exotic locations. Who can blame her for wondering – why them and not me?

She watched Adele being bankrolled into a glamorous life a stone's throw away from her miserable room and she thought – why *her* and not me? I get it.

I think she truly believes Adele and her are friends. That they have a future together. It's tragic, part of me feels sorry for her. Delphine needs help.

But first – I look back at my sister – I must help Adele. We need to get out of here.

'What would you like?' I eke out the conversation. If I can just calm her down, reassure her I'm no threat, she might let us go.

'What would I like?' Delphine shakes her head as if it's the silliest thing she's ever heard. She gives up on her cigarette, crushing it under her boot and the mood shifts again. 'Everything was going perfectly. Adele was healing. I'd managed to get her phone back – our insurance if they threatened us. We had a plan. Once everything had settled down, I'd move in. And then' – she glares at me – 'you arrived.'

My stomach tightens.

'Pretending to care.' A finger emerges from her long sleeve. Long and spidery with chipped black polish. She stabs the air. 'Never once did Adele mention *you*. On vlog forty-five, sixteen minutes in, there's a reference to her family, but not *you*. That's how little she cared,' Delphine says triumphantly. 'You didn't exist to her. I'm her sister. I CARE.'

I have no idea what to say to her now. When someone is behaving in a delusional manner – a temporary psychosis – the priority is to keep them calm.

Drawing on my medical experience, I approach the patient with a steady careful manner.

'We can work this out, everything will be fine, but first, let's get Adele some medical assistance, hey? She's not well, and,' my voice wavers, 'she'd want you to let me help her.'

Delphine shrugs the rucksack from her shoulders and places it on the ground. Keeping her eyes fixed on me, she unzips it.

'Let's get Adele to hospital and then we can talk about the future.'

She reaches a hand inside the bag. Nodding to herself, she pulls out a knife. It's long and serrated, like something that belongs in a slaughterhouse.

CHAPTER SIXTY-TWO

ERIN

The singing has resumed. Delphine hums along to a French song. That deranged smile. It's me she wants to hurt. I'm standing in the way of her future.

Twisting back to my sister, I whisper: 'On the count of three, we're leaving. I'll pull you off the bed and we're getting out of here, OK.'

Delphine shoots me a look. Taking a step towards us, she's more agitated than ever.

'We're leaving now,' I tell her, forcing myself to sound overly confident. 'And you won't get in our way.'

Delphine moves closer still, smacking the flat of the blade into her palm. A theatrical whap-whap. She stares me down through a wall of hair. Her eyes appear as slits and there's a fresh mania about them, like a child about to have their toy taken away.

Keeping my attention fixed on Delphine, I thread my head under Adele's arm. Breathing in and bracing to take her weight.

'OK ready, one two . . .' I groan. 'Three.'

Adele howls with pain as I haul her to her feet.

'You're hurting her!' Delphine panics. She swipes the knife sideways, hacking at the air. 'Put her down!' She lunges. I twist, shielding my sister from the blade.

There's a sharp scratch, a feeling of skin separating and then the heat of warm liquid. The shock of the knife cutting my side makes me lose my grip on Adele. I feel her slip from my shoulder, helplessly watching her sink to the floor. She looks up at me, eyes glistening with tears.

'You're bleeding!' she sobs.

Under the dim glow the blood looks ink black, gluing my jumper to my side. No pain yet. For now, the adrenaline is numbing me.

Delphine holds the knife outstretched. 'You can't have her.' She waves it around and I notice the tremble in her hand.

My hands are shaking too as I fish out my phone.

'What are you doing?' she says.

Fingers trembling so violently I can't press the buttons easily.

'Put the phone down,' Delphine hisses.

I move my hand up to my ear.

'Put. Down. That. Phone,' she says through gritted teeth.

Defiantly, I hold it to my ear and press dial.

She lunges. I show her my back and she shunts into me, arms snapping around my body like a vice while I struggle to keep the handset out of reach.

She's far stronger than she looks and her nails tear at my skin while we twist and spin in a perverse kind of dance. I stretch out my arm so far, I think it might tear from its socket, holding the phone away so Marcel can hear my screams.

'HELP. It's Delphine. HELP US.'

I have no idea if the call's even gone through but I keep on yelling because that's all I have left.

Adele's on her front, pulling herself across the floor.

Delphine smacks the iPhone from my grip and it hits the wall with a sharp crack. She throws me to the ground effortlessly, knocking the wind out of my lungs. Then she walks over to the phone and stamps on it with her boot until it breaks apart.

She turns to Adele.

'Where do you think you're going? The only way you're leaving here is with me. Just like you promised.'

'I didn't promise you anything,' Adele cries.

'You said we'd be sisters.'

'You're insane.'

'You invited us into your life. You took us on your journey, your highs, your lows, you invited *me* in and now I'm staying.'

Adele shakes her head. 'It's a vlog, it's not REAL.'

Delphine blinks. Startled. An angry silence joins the room and I can feel something unfurling. Adele's pushed her too far.

Her brow draws together. 'IT IS REAL.' Her lips draw back, baring her gums.

With fire behind her eyes, she strides purposefully towards my baby sister. I launch myself at her. Grabbing her legs, I knock her off balance and pull her to the ground. We land with a *thunk* and the knife clatters into the corner.

The tiles are cold and I can taste blood as it fills my mouth. Behind me, I can hear the *squeak squeak* of

Delphine's leather trousers sliding across the floor as she crawls towards me. I raise my hands to defend myself.

There's a flash of silver. I look up and Adele has managed to pull herself to her feet and raise the knife above her head. Teeth gritted; eyebrows pulled back like a cartoon character. I recognize that look. The same determination as when we were kids.

'You mad bitch!' Her voice breaks through. The knife arcs through the air, spearing Delphine's hand.

There's a sickening snap of bone, a ting as the blade meets the stone floor.

Delphine studies her wound, eyes wide and unblinking. Then comes a whimpering, an animalistic high-pitched wail. She rounds her shoulders, cradling her arm like you would a baby. The knife is sticking out of her hand and a tide of crimson spreads beneath her.

So much blood it turns my stomach.

For several beats nobody moves, no one says a word. We're all transfixed by the gore.

Delphine starts to rock on her haunches, a steady rhythmical back and forth.

I look to Adele. 'Go!' I can hear the hysteria in my voice.

Delphine's head snaps up. Eyes glassy and emotionless. Robotically, she gets to her feet, straightens and, in one snap movement, she pulls the knife out, releasing a spray of blood.

Adele staggers to the ladder, dragging her leg behind while Delphine comes after me.

'Adele, HURRY!'

I can't hold Delphine off for much longer, she's too

quick, too strong. She closes the space between us, making light work of the distance. Small quick steps, jabbing like a boxer. Pow. Pow.

Adele pulls herself up the stairs. One step at a time.

The blade makes a whipping noise as Delphine hacks the air in front of me.

'ADELE, HURRY.'

There's nowhere left to go, Delphine has me backed into the corner.

Two more steps and Adele's out.

'Shut the door!' I scream at her.

'I'm not leaving you.'

'LOCK US IN.'

'NO!'

I swerve and the blade whistles past my ear.

'GO! GET HELP NOW.'

The steel strikes the wall and it chimes like a percussion triangle. Delphine adjusts her grip on the knife and I can smell the blood – her blood, my blood – and it makes me want to vomit. The ground moves, everything is swaying, I'm light-headed and overcome with a sense of duty to protect my baby sister.

This is it. I stare at the blade. This has to be it.

She comes at me again, the serrated point hurtling my way.

'ERIN!' Adele snaps me out of my daze. 'RUN!'

Delphine springs forward and I swerve, but this time, the knife plunges into the grouting between the tiles. The tug to pull it out throws her off balance, just enough for me to kick her away and sprint for the light.

I slip on the wet tiles, I get back up. The staircase clangs and rattles and threatens to fall apart but I'm up and out the hatch before Delphine has time to get up.

I look down at her – Delphine's wild eyes blazing are the last thing I see before slamming the hatch shut.

Adele spreads her weight over the trapdoor while, with the last of my energy, I haul the sofa across.

Delphine fights back, punching at the door, shrieking like a wild dog.

'YOU OWE ME, Adele.'

A caged animal.

'Don't leave me,' she screams. 'Don't leave me in here!'

I scrunch up my eyes, trying to block her out.

We slump against the sofa, hearts pounding, catching our breath. Adele's nursing her ankle. It's a miracle she managed to get up the steps at all. That's the thing about my sister – she can do anything if she puts her mind to it.

The bleat of police sirens sounds in the distance, filling me with relief. I blow out a long breath. Unable to process the violence of the past few days, my body shivering uncontrollably. One thing's for sure, life will never be the same. I'll never look at the world in the same way. But maybe that's not such a bad thing.

We sit side by side in silence while noise breaks around us. Screaming from below. Sirens screeching outside. Within seconds there'll be the drum of boots and more yelling as Marcel and his team charge in. But for now, it's just us.

Erin and Adele.

My sister rolls her head onto my shoulder and looks at

me, really looks at me for the first time in – so long I can't remember.

'Take me home.' Her voice is barely a whisper.

I manage a small nod. 'OK.'

Adele snaps her hand around my wrist. Fixing me with her gaze, she says: 'No, Erin, take me *home*.'

CHAPTER SIXTY-THREE

NOW

Sky News

We are live from Rémy-Vienne where there's been an astonishing development in the Chateau Bellay case. We can confirm missing YouTuber Adele Davenport has been found and taken to hospital with serious but not life-threatening injuries.

We're outside the apartment at 5 Rue Moulin where Adele was held captive for ten days after she was kidnapped by her stalker Delphine Ramousse, who'd become obsessed with Adele and wanted her life.

Police have just recovered Ramousse's mobile phone, which shows evidence of online stalking. Ramousse was going by the name of TheREALAdele003, an avatar she hid behind in her relentless pursuit of the YouTuber.

The nineteen-year-old has been arrested and is facing charges of abduction, kidnapping and false imprisonment. Very serious offences that, if convicted, could lead to life imprisonment.

Kate, what do we know about Delphine Ramousse? Is there anything linking her to the bodies that have been discovered in the chateau grounds?

At the moment there doesn't appear to be any connection, but Delphine's story is a tragic one. The teenager has been in and out of care homes since she was six years old and has suffered a troubled upbringing surrounded by violence and abuse. She has a criminal record, including drug-related offences, and it's thought she suffers from what's becoming widely known as Celebrity Worship Syndrome.

Can you explain what that is?

Celebrity Worship Syndrome is when the curated life of a celebrity provides someone with an escape from what might be a gruelling reality. For example, turning to your favourite YouTuber when feeling lonely. The comfort influencers like Adele Davenport provide can lead to extreme dependence, where the person suffering from the syndrome starts living their life in a distorted reality.

The danger often comes when the admirer starts to feel the relationship is not being reciprocated. They believe it was them that put their idol in a position of power and feel entitled to their time, to their life, because they believe they are where they are because of them.

Extraordinary Kate and anyone wanting to know more can tune in to our special hour-long investigative report next Tuesday when we will be examining the syndrome in more detail. More on the grim discovery at Chateau Bellay coming up.

CHAPTER SIXTY-FOUR

ERIN

ELEVEN DAYS AFTER NYE

'You don't have to do this,' I remind Adele.

'I want to. It's OK,' she reassures me.

We emerge from the gloom of the hall into the outside, blinking away the morning light.

With a crowd building and police officers flanking either side of us, it smacks of some royal occasion, the queen waving from her stone balcony or some disgraced MP emerging from their country pile to make a press statement. A grand televised event at any rate and I'm here to give my sister moral support.

I push her wheelchair to the top of the chateau steps while a semicircle of thirsty reporters waits below. A sea of heads and outstretched recording devices, eager to get every word down.

In the distance, behind the TV crews and the police cordon is Adele's faithful army of fans, waiting till she gets around to seeing them. She gives them a smile and a quick wave and that's enough to make them squeal with delight.

'Adele! We LOVE you, Adele!'

It feels weird, being in her world – and I'll be glad to leave it.

We arrived at Bellay early this morning. Most of last night was spent giving statements to the police and at the hospital. An X-ray revealed Adele's ankle to be fractured and it's been reset and cast. We eventually went to sleep in a guest house nearby. Even if the police had allowed us to return to the chateau, I would have refused. The thought of spending another night in that graveyard with the ghosts of tortured girls makes my skin crawl. I feel the shadow of the hallway behind, looming, the door – an open mouth, waiting to swallow us back inside.

Quickly I look sideways to something safe. I catch Marcel's eye and he gives me a reassuring nod. A half-smile. It feels like it was just for me and I get a rush of heat which forces me to look away. I'm embarrassed because I'm sure he can tell. Or maybe he noticed the moment he saw I was wearing make-up. I've never had a reason to get ready for someone before and it feels foreign and strange but surprisingly nice.

I look back but Marcel's eyes have moved on, his gaze now fixed ahead, focused on what he needs to do: keeping the crowd under control and managing obnoxious reporters. *Protecting us.* I've come to think of him as my guardian angel. Ask me a week ago if I'd be attracted to a macho French police officer and I would have laughed you off stage. But now – I can't stop thinking about the rescue, him picking me up into his arms. Stupid really.

The memory of how he nearly took a bullet for me makes me think about him more. I feel a twinge. My skin prickling. I wonder if we'll see each other again.

Adele clears her throat. She lifts a bony arm, the hospital band still wrapped around her wrist, she waves the crowd to silence.

'Thank you for being here,' she says. Her voice is weak and hoarse. 'I don't have much I want to go into right now but I think it's important I say a few words. Firstly, I want to thank my sister, because if it wasn't for her, I wouldn't be alive.' She takes my hand and squeezes it. The cameras flash mercilessly and for several beats, I can't see anything except Adele. We're cocooned together in a protective circle of light. She keeps hold of my hand.

Her face becomes more strained.

'Nothing I say can undo what went on here and I'm not even going to pretend I know what those affected have been through. I promise neither I nor my family have any involvement with the crimes that have taken place here.'

'Was your husband involved?' a reporter shouts.

'I hope that you will honour our privacy and give us the space we need to grieve and to come to terms with what's happened,' Adele continues, trying to make herself heard over the raised voices.

'Who's the dead girl? Is she a prostitute?'

Adele looks up at me with pleading eyes.

'We have nothing further to add,' I say quickly, taking the handles of her wheelchair.

A reporter wearing a cap forces his way to the front.

'What? Adele's camera shy all of a sudden? What about the dead girls? Are the Bellay family responsible?'

'How can you not have known?' a loud voice demands. 'You must have known what's been going on here?'

Marcel moves in front of us and holds up his hands.

'I can assure you the police investigation will overlook nothing. We are now in possession of incriminating video footage that we will use to bring those responsible to justice. The process of identifying the deceased victims found on the property is underway but will take some time. We will have more information for you soon—'

'How will you make the Bellays pay for their crimes? It's too late!' someone screams, their voice choked with emotion.

'Erin, get me out of here,' Adele whispers. 'You were right, this was a terrible idea.'

Marcel shields us from the violence of their words. We retreat inside the chateau, our hearts heavy with grief – and for the first time, it offers us sanctuary.

Desperate to leave, less than half an hour later Adele has everything she needs for our journey home packed into the back of my car. We're tucked around the rear of the chateau, away from prying eyes, which is just as well because I don't want anyone to see me, to read my face when I say goodbye to Marcel.

He holds the door open for me and our eyes meet – for several beats longer than they were meant to. I'm not imagining it; I know he felt it too. Marcel doesn't say anything though, not a word, only a slight nod of the head to indicate it's time to leave.

'I'll contact you soon about the trial,' he says matter-of-factly as I climb behind the wheel. I get the feeling he's keeping his emotions tightly under control. I know this case has been emotionally draining for him.

'OK, speak then.' I smile shyly.

Adele is in the passenger seat. I can feel her watching, studying Marcel and me in that nosy, inquisitive way of hers.

'It will probably begin within the next few months, so you'll have a bit of time to prepare.'

I'm the key witness in the case against Capitaine Georges Desailly and four other members of Twelve Homes they were able to catch that day. They've been charged with kidnapping and a string of other offences.

'Speak soon then,' I say more quietly.

'*Mais oui.*'

There's another awkward silence and I feel my cheeks heating up.

'Safe journey.' He closes my door.

I can't bring myself to look at him for the pink that's bloomed across my cheeks. I can feel Adele holding on to her words. When we're out of earshot, she chimes: 'He likes you.'

I give her a 'don't meddle' sigh, the sound of the snow crackling beneath our tyres drowning out her mischief.

As we swing around to the front of the building where the press and fans are still waiting, I notice something has changed and I slip my window down, just to be sure.

Yes, I am right. It's as if a weight has been suddenly lifted. The air seems different. Less thick and doughy – that feeling of it having to be kneaded out has gone.

The wind has dropped, the clouds are separating and the sun is breaking through.

I glance into the rear-view mirror and notice there's now a top coat, a slick of golden light over the chateau. Its stone walls are glowing like a holiday tan and, for the first time, it doesn't seem threatening.

The snow appears a liquid silver, melting under the heat of the sun. Soon it will be gone and everything that was once hidden will be exposed.

CHAPTER SIXTY-FIVE

ERIN

TWELVE HOURS LATER

We each take a hand, both of us holding on to her fading warmth as we sit either side of her bed in the hospice.

It's much calmer here than in a hospital. There isn't the intrusive bleeping of heart monitors, the noisy rush of feet, the swooshing of curtains being pulled across rails. It's quiet here by the window that looks across the city park.

I glance up and say something about the weather brightening. Something to break the terrible enduring silence and Mum smiles and nods and pretends to listen.

Mum was too weak to question Adele when she arrived on crutches. But her face lit up and that was the end of it. Her baby had come home, that was all that mattered.

Even though it was painful to watch and sparked feelings of inadequacy and jealousy, it also brought me relief knowing I'd fulfilled her dying wish and she could finally be at peace.

My nursing experience has taught me it's hard for people

to let go, to accept it's the end until they know everything will be OK. I can see the look of contentment in Mum's eyes now. The acceptance. It makes the ache in my heart a little less sore.

She squeezes my hand and I think she's trying to tell me something. I might have been right about how much she loves Adele, but maybe – perhaps – I didn't see how much she loves me too. Tears form and I bite down on my lip to keep them there. I don't want Mum seeing me upset, I must be brave for her. We don't know how long she has left but I want to make certain every moment together counts. That I don't live to regret a second of it.

Adele catches my eye and mouths, 'Are you OK?'

I nod. A warmth spreads through me.

It should be me asking if she's OK because poor Adele's also suffering with the grief of losing Jack. She knows everything about him now, she's learned who the real Jack was – his siphoning off of the money, his much deeper involvement with Twelve Homes, his plans to leave her, the twisted fantasies he kept secret from her – but that doesn't stop her feeling the loss. They were together almost nine years. Adele misses the Jack she knew, and now she must learn how to live without him. But as I study her, it's clear she's less strained, more natural, more like the Adele I remember. Something tells me it won't take too long for her to adjust.

Adele's facing some big decisions. She's still officially the owner of Chateau Bellay and she needs to decide what to do with it. There's no denying it's a stunning work of architecture and she believes it can be beautiful again, but she knows she can never live there, not after all that went on within those walls. Instead, she wants to donate it to the community, and work alongside the locals to restore it – she's determined to win their confidence and trust, and to prove she had nothing to do with what went on there. With their help, she'll scrub away the sins of the past. She's hoping to feature the renovation on her vlog, just as she'd originally planned to do.

The YouTube money will allow her to buy herself a little cottage somewhere nearby. Something small and manageable. In true Adele style, she's likened letting go of her fairy-tale chateau to releasing an animal back into the wild to be happy again and run free.

Nothing is beyond saving, she told me in her determined voice.

Nothing.

The memory of her words makes my thoughts turn to Delphine. I wonder what will happen to her when she comes out of prison. Her lawyer's plea of diminished responsibility should ensure that her sentence will be nowhere near as long as those handed down to the capitaine and the syndicate. The court case is months away but the French media are already turning into a show trial.

She'll be released and will return to obscurity and then what? Social media platforms capitalize on the human need for connectivity and community. I hope someone *real* offers her help, love and a chance to turn her life around. *Nobody is beyond saving.*

I'm suddenly feeling exhausted, I haven't slept properly for so long I've lost count of the days. I stand up and ask

Adele if she'd like a coffee. She nods and I take off down the corridor to the family room with its archaic vending machine.

I have some big decisions to make of my own as I await my disciplinary hearing. I've been told that I'm likely to get off with a warning and, due to staff shortages, I'll be asked to return to work almost immediately, albeit in a more junior role, until I've passed various competency tests. The question keeps haunting me though. Is this what I want?

I criticized my sister for running away, but is muddling through life, complaining, feeling unfulfilled any better? I'll be thirty-three next month, and then what? Like Adele, I want more. I just need to figure out what.

The coffee machine is so old it doesn't take contactless. I drop the fifty- and twenty-pence pieces into the slot. The coins chink as they land and then there's a gurgling noise as the machine spits out caramel-coloured liquid into a paper cup.

I take a seat on one of the hard hospital chairs, stealing a moment to myself. On the low coffee table is still yesterday's *Telegraph*. Creased and ringed with coffee stains, I pick it up out of curiosity and begin browsing the pages.

Nothing really grabs me, my head's filled with Mum and all the chores I need to do when I finally get home. I turn the page and the next, until I'm in the weeds of the paper, the stories at the back nobody cares about. I'm about to give up when I feel a sudden jolt of recognition. Enough to make me do a double take.

Adrenaline kicking in, I flatten the paper across the table. Nausea swells within me as I stare at the photograph.

Heavily wrinkled with a bush of grey hair, he's buried with the obituaries but it's unmistakably him, the old man from the party. The syndicate member. The one who was choked to death.

> Julian Clarence Foster died peacefully aged sixty-one at his home in Surrey last Friday with his family around him. A judge and respected member of the community, he leaves behind his wife Jennifer and two children, Rebecca and Saffron. He will be dearly missed.

He was a husband and a father? *A respected member of the community?* And all the while leading a double life. The horror of his death replays in my head and I'm immediately transported back to Bellay with its dark, gloomy rooms, and all my hairs stand on end.

Julian's poor family, not knowing what he was really like. The lies, the duplicity. It reminds me of Jack and a life my sister has narrowly escaped. Who knows what Jack would have gone on to do? Maybe he wouldn't have left Adele but continued leading a double life.

The syndicate has to be behind this cover-up of Foster's death. It shows the lengths they'll go to in order to protect their members, the privileged people who matter in their world – unlike the girls they use and discard.

My anxiety rapidly turns to anger. I take a picture of what I've found and send the photo to Marcel with a brief explanation.

He immediately responds:

> There's been a breakthrough in the case. We can now
> confirm Twelve Homes have bought the old hospital in
> Spain. Interpol are moving the investigation there next.

The intensity of his passion for the job leaps off the screen. I've missed him.

> That's great news!

I surprise myself with the speed of my reply.

Three dots pulse on my screen as if he's thinking of what to say next. Then they stop and my heart sinks. I'm about to tuck my phone away when a new message appears.

> Come over before the trial and help me look into Julian
> Foster? My English is rusty and I could use a translator.

His English is significantly better than my French. He can't be serious? I hold my breath as the dots appear again. Then:

> X

Kiss? He sent a kiss this time. I feel a fizz of excitement, which is quickly followed by dread. I didn't think I'd have to face anything to do with the syndicate so soon. Not until the trial.

Or is it more than that? Is it the fear that someone might actually like me?

In the past I'd instantly have replied *no*. Stepping away from the safety net of my routines – are you insane? But now, as I study the message, as I think about Julian Foster's family, I'm feeling something unfamiliar.

I sit back heavily in the chair, drawing air into my lungs. What if I could make a difference?

A burst of courage blooms inside me. Growing, spreading in my chest and across my entire body. Electric pulses awakening parts of me that have been dead for years.

I breathe out.

It's not like I have much of a life here any more. If Adele decides to relocate permanently to France, it could make sense to be there too. And, maybe there is something I can do to help, however small.

What is there to be afraid of, Erin? What could possibly be worse than what I've been through with my sister? The horror of the past week has shown me I'm not the hesitant frightened person I thought I was. Perhaps I never was. I just couldn't see it until now.

I've grown in strength and confidence and if any good has come out of this evil, it was discovering I'm more resilient than I thought. I don't have to tiptoe through life any more.

This won't be an escape. I won't be running away from my life. I'll be making a conscious decision to be more.

I want to make sure parties like the ones held by the Bellays never happen again. I can work with Marcel to try to get Twelve Homes shut. In doing so, I'll give myself purpose. And then, just maybe, I'll lower the wall and allow myself to explore the possibility Marcel could be someone I like.

For now though, I must be here with Mum and Adele, but there's no reason why I can't start helping at a distance.

As I strike the keys, a smile builds.

I can't think of anything I'd rather do.

I pause. Then add:

X

EPILOGUE

MARISSA WHITE

The last of the evening light pours through the stained-glass windows. A wash of brilliant blue is projected across the building, creating an underwater effect. It dapples the exposed brickwork; it ripples across our guests. It's as if the church was built for tonight.

The fifteenth-century building stands alone, jutting out from the cliff edge. There's nothing else around for miles but that's not what caught my attention. It was the steeple silhouetted against the sunset – the sharply pointed spire reminding me of a knife point.

The church has been left untouched for centuries because nobody has wanted to face the memory of what happened here. *The curse.*

Beyond the sudden drop there's the azure blue Adriatic Sea below. The crystal-clear waters that Montenegro has become famous for.

There's only one way up, via a narrow dirt track bending and stretching its way to the top. Not a problem for my guests though – most of them have been chauffeured in four-by-fours, climbing the mountainside with ease.

I can overhear their conversations now. The comparison of their journey time. The ever-present one-upmanship. But that's how I like these events – with a hint of competitiveness – because that's what really gets them going and what it all comes down to. Who will be the better fuck.

The smell of traditional incense spikes the air. Candles in large glass cylinders, hundreds of tea lights crowding every surface. Ringing the pulpit. When the darkness moves in, which it will do soon, there will be only candlelight. The perfect mood enhancer.

The faint sound of music drifts up into the dome ceiling, slipping between the knot of rafters. I've instructed the orchestra to keep it down, just for the awakening part of the ceremony.

Members wander around clutching champagne glasses, wearing crimson robes with hoods, tied in a bow at the throat. Their faces hidden within the shadows. Beneath the fabric is their chosen creation, something carefully tailored for tonight's theme.

It's hard to imagine this was once the location of one of the worst church massacres in history. Where we chat and laugh and mingle, there was once a heap of bodies. Old scriptures say the corpses were piled so high they almost reached the ceiling.

I like to view tonight's club party as a cleanse. Purging the past with the raw intensity of our carnal desires. This location has really tickled our members, all the more so since it wasn't easy to find.

The crowd is much smaller than usual because we've had to tighten the circle while we wait for the media attention to die down, the police to give up on tracking our scent. Those who have made it are the most high-ranking: our gold members. There won't be any rooms to disappear into tonight, everything has been stripped back to create a communal platform. A stage where no rules apply.

The sound of a helicopter breaks into our celebration. The noisy *whapping* brings the hall to a hush as the significance takes hold. It's the arrival of our final guest.

There's the sudden rush of activity as the girls start preparing the room. The clack-clack of their high heels across the mosaic floor. A line of girls pretty enough to be models, hand-selected by me, walk the length of the room theatrically swinging thuribles, perfuming the air with incense.

It's time.

I step up into the pulpit and, when the crowd is silent, I remove my hood. There's a collective gasp as I reveal my identity. I'm looking forward to explaining this departure from our usual procedure.

'Welcome,' I say, opening my arms. 'Welcome, ladies and gentlemen, to our Spring Equinox party.'

There's a celebratory cheer. Nothing too raucous, that will come later.

'As you've been made aware, tonight's theme is all about cleansing. With the turn of the seasons, the shifting into spring – for one night only we step out of the shadows. Instead of continuing our tradition of wearing masks, *tonight* we'll reveal who we really are and what are our deepest, *darkest* desires.'

I feel the arousal building. The air has become charged.

'You're aware of the sudden and tragic passing of Thirteen.' I take a breath. 'I'd like to take a moment to celebrate his final triumph. Look around you, be in awe. A tribute to our old leader, it was him that spotted this jewel in the crown.'

The room falls eerily silent. Some of the guests even bowing their heads to pay their respects.

I almost feel bad for what I did. But I had no choice, I must protect the club and its members. It would have been over in seconds, the men I hired are the best. And he was in his happy place, on his yacht in the south of France. Thirteen was getting sloppy, he was taking too many risks. We should never have considered using the chateau as a recurring venue. *Never.* I'll have to keep a careful eye on the Davenports from here on.'

I breathe out heavily to relax the tension that's worked into my shoulders.

'Ladies and gentlemen,' I raise my voice, 'tonight is a very special occasion as we welcome into TWELVE HOMES a new visionary.'

Before I've finished, the solid church doors swing open, the moan of the ancient wood shaking the old walls. Icy March air follows closely at her heels, rushing to be by her side.

There's another collective gasp, a sharp intake of air. Now I can feel it, the vibration. Just as I could with Chateau Bellay. The building is holding its breath for our guest.

The crowd parts to make room for her. Our new Thirteen.

She's dressed in a silk tuxedo jacket. Oversized, skimming the tops of her thighs with nothing underneath. She walks confidently down the aisle, shoulders back, statuesque, just like in the films. A diamond-studded dog collar buckled around her neck with a silver chain slipping beneath the fabric. It's attached to her nipple ring. I know because I saw it earlier, when she sent me the private photos.

The only thing to break the long line of her legs is a diamond ankle chain. Simple and understated.

I step off the pulpit to make room. I've briefed her on what she needs to say. So far, she's doing well at taking advice.

'Thank you, Marissa.' I feel her heat as she brushes past me.

She clears her throat and I can sense the intensity of their gaze. Watching, waiting. She knows how to hold a room with that blockbuster charisma. Her face brightens as she unleashes her famous smile, the one that's made her a household name in Hollywood.

'It's an honour.' The actress dazzles.

Quietly I smile to myself, relishing my achievement. My best work yet.

I'm still getting acquainted with the cultural differences – some of our American starlet's mannerisms are not quite as refined as the previous Thirteen, who was cut from the same silk as me. But with a little fine-tuning, I'll get there. With the contracts now signed and safely stored in the vault, there's nothing left to do but *enjoy*.

'Thank you for your trust, thank you for your confidence in me,' she continues. 'I'm here to help protect and to serve all of us. But above all . . .' Her smile unspools, her eyes glitter as she raises her glass in a toast. 'I'm here to make sure we have the most unforgettable night EVER.'

The sound of heavy fabric falling to the floor fills the hall. The guests release their robes, revealing how they've decided to interpret the equinox.

Tonight's party will be smaller than usual but promises to be a great deal more intimate.

ACKNOWLEDGEMENTS

Writing is normally a fairly torturous process for me but, for some unknown reason, I flew through this book and enjoyed every moment of it. I loved imagining I was in France, in a big old house steeped in mystery, that creaked and groaned. A place you couldn't quite trust.

Crossing the finishing line, however, was something I couldn't have done alone and there are some very special people I'd like to thank for their help.

Firstly, my talented editor Alex Saunders, who has the most meticulous eye for detail and story development. Thank you for showing me how to make a scene work harder and giving me confidence to bring out the best in my writing. I'm truly grateful.

The whole team at Pan Macmillan – you are phenomenal. Your passion for books shines through and I feel so lucky to have a home with you. A special mention goes to Chloe Davies, who is a PR wizard, and brilliant fun to work with.

My agent, Jordan Lees, who backed my idea for *The Escape* from the get-go and has encouraged me every step of the way – always offering reassurance when I need it most, calming me down when I have mini panics.

The entire team at The Blair Partnership – you are

amazing. It really does feel like I have a team behind me, rooting for me to do well.

Thank you, Michael, for being my sounding board. Always ready to help me break through my writer's block, to work through plots and characters and give me a boost of encouragement when I need it most. And thank you for all those trips to France, helping feed my imagination.

To my friends, I'm very lucky to have such special people in my life. An extra big hug goes to Marija for being awesome.

Thank you, Dad and Basil and my close family, who are always there, championing me every step of the way.

To Mum, who I would brainstorm all my books with. *The Escape* was the last plotline we chatted through together and that's why this book will always have a special place in my heart.

THE VILLA

A Villa in Paradise

It's destined to be the ultimate reality TV show. Ten contestants. A luxurious villa on a private island. Every moment streamed live to a global audience who have total control over those competing for the cash prize.

A Journalist Undercover

Reporter Laura is told to get the inside scoop on her fellow contestants. But once the games begin, she soon finds herself at the mercy of a ruthless producer willing to do anything to increase viewer numbers.

A Reality Show to Die For

There is more to every contestant than meets the eye, including Laura. They all have secrets they'd like to keep buried, and the pressure in paradise quickly reaches boiling point. How far will the contestants go to secure audience votes? And would somebody really kill to win?

If you enjoyed *The Escape*, then you will love *The Villa*. Read on for an extract and order today.

THE PRODUCER

Aruna, Balearic Islands

NOW

Broken glass crunches beneath my trainers as we move towards the pool. The sun is setting over the villa, the golden light that once bathed it in glory now a dull tarnished amber.

Detective Inspector Jose Carlos Sanchez lifts the blue and white police cordon and bows underneath. He raises it for me and I notice the forensic gloves he's wearing. Milky white – signposting me to what lies ahead. He stops and makes a visual sweep of the area.

'Tell me where all the cameras are located, señora.'

Despite the sea breeze, the heat is cloying. It's attacking me and I'm sweating in places I didn't know were possible.

'Señora?'

The locations. Every single one I know by heart. Months of meticulous planning had gone into designing and hiding the cameras. Positioning them in such a way we'd capture even the slightest nuance in the contestants' expressions.

There were no secrets on my show. I surrendered all of myself to create perfection – constructing the greatest entertainment show of all time.

I point to the magenta plant beside the sunlounger. 'Have a look in there.' The leaves are now dry and shrivelled – how quickly things die when they're not being nourished.

We walk in step towards it. He peers inside the terracotta pot and nods. Then he signals to one of the many officers guarding the crime scene from press and rubberneckers. Since the news broke, the villa's location is no longer my best-kept secret. I notice the camera's red 'recording' light has stopped flashing.

'Where else?' asks Sanchez.

'Over there.' I point up, into the palm tree shading the jacuzzi. 'There and there.' I reel off ten more locations.

'And the one closest to the pool?' he says. Drawing me towards her.

My stomach contracts. It's coming. We're almost there. I want to look away, but a morbid curiosity is pulling me in.

There she is. Face-planted on the hot stones. Her platinum blonde hair fanned around her head like a halo. Blood still leaks from her skull, seeping into the pool. Streaks of crimson run through the turquoise water, diluting into nothing, like a watercolour painting. If it wasn't so disturbing it would be beautiful.

'It's over.' I whisper the words as I stare at her.

Sanchez looks at me. 'What did you say?'

My gaze lifts and meets his. 'This wasn't how it was supposed to end.'

I shut my eyes, imagining how it should have played out. The fireworks exploding across the sky, perfectly timed to music. Their colours reflected by the ocean. Millions of viewers cheering from their living rooms. The pantomime handing over of the cheque.

I don't know what shock is but I'm certain that's what I've slipped into. My fingers and wrists tingle. The corners of my mouth prickle and I still can't tear my eyes from her.

'Miss Jessop, I need to know the location of the camera closest to the body.'

Body. Dead. No longer spoken of as a person with a name. She's become a thing to be processed. I swallow back the bile that's crept into my throat.

'It's in there.'

I point into the water, to the camera embedded in the side of the pool. Finally I divert my eyes away from the grisly scene.

Two men and a woman in white forensic overalls arrive. I watch as they put on shoe covers, as she tucks her hair into her hood. They approach the body like spirits who have come to collect the dead. They carry what resembles a cool box, but I know there isn't any finger food and chilled wine inside. They are the crime scene examiners and they have come to collect evidence.

Evidence. Crime. The words sink like rocks to the pit of my stomach.

A second white gazebo is being erected over where more blood was spilled. Now rust-coloured, peeling in the heat.

Two more officers arrive holding a stretcher and a black body bag.

'They're taking her away?' I turn to Sanchez. Of course they are, Michelle. Shut up. Use your fucking brain. *She's dead.*

She'll be the last contestant to leave the villa. That really will mark the end. The thought panics me more than anything. I don't want to let go.

'We'll need to perform an autopsy after the examination is complete.'

'Have her family been told?' I ask.

'They're on their way to Madrid.'

I feel sick at the thought of their grief.

'Anything else you need me for? I've so much to do, there's a lot I need to take care of.'

Catastrophe management. Reputation salvaging. I have an entire production team waiting for me to explain what's going to happen next. A press statement to prepare. I check my watch. Lost time fires up my adrenaline. Nerves prickle. *Move out of my way, Sanchez.* I turn to make my retreat.

The detective inspector holds up his hand. 'I'm afraid we need you to come with us to the police station.'

'What? Why?' I snap my head around, my veneer of patience and cooperativeness falling away. 'I've helped you with all I can.'

'You are the producer of the show.'

'Yeah, I'm the producer, but no, this isn't my fault.'

His eyes narrow. 'I'm afraid some might see that differently, señora.'

He turns, makes another hand gesture and two officers approach. 'You need to leave with us.'

He points me in the direction of the black and gold door. The same door that sealed in our contestants.

'Can't I answer your questions here?' Panic seizes control of my voice.

'I'm afraid not. This way.' The officers move either side of me, their posture stiffening in case I resist.

'Our boat is waiting,' Sanchez says again, his voice now thick with irritation. He isn't used to a strong personality like me. Someone who thinks what they do is equally important.

Our stand-off is broken by a thunderous whirring from above. We all look up at the same time and see a cavalier news channel breaking the airspace restrictions. The helicopter's flying much lower than it should.

This is a no-fly zone. I should know, it's why I chose it.

Their cameras are trained on me. Now I'm the one being filmed.

'We need to leave *now*, Señora Jessop.'

I relent. Sanchez steers me back underneath the tape, towards the next cordon that wraps around the entire villa. Shards of champagne bottles lie in our path. More smashed glass – on the bar and tables. Pool towels, strewn across the decking. Flies swarm around decaying food. The silver strands of a party wig flap in the breeze. A sudden gust of wind lifts the wig from its resting place, sending it cartwheeling into our path. What was once dazzling, now reminiscent of a Wild West film set.

My baby. My beautiful creation, decomposing before my eyes.

I turn to face Sanchez. 'It wasn't supposed to be like

this.' Tears rise. I stop dead. Rooting my heels into the ground. 'I'm not leaving.'

'Señora, the boat is waiting.' All pleasantries have gone.

'I'm staying!' This is where I belong. Here, in the world I curated, that I directed. I can't bring myself to face the reality. The judgement that's waiting for me.

Sanchez has had enough. There's no reasoning with me. He signals his officers to grab my arms.

CHAPTER ONE

THE REPORTER

The Record newsroom, London

EIGHT WEEKS AGO

Bingeing on coffee and sugary snacks had created the perfect storm in my stomach. The burn had risen to attack my throat. I swallowed hard but the pressure of meeting the deadline, and the guilt of knowing the harm my story would cause, was firmly lodged in my mind.

Mike Baron, retired England football captain and national treasure. As famous for his game off the pitch as his goalscoring. Back in the day, he was known for his partying, drinking, and womanizing.

But that was then. The 'real' Mike couldn't be more different from the headlines, from his 'lad' reputation. Loyal, kind, a father of two and a devoted husband. This Saturday would mark his twentieth wedding anniversary and he'd just found out his wife was dying of cancer. He didn't mean to tell me, it slipped out in our interview because he was grief-stricken. Because I had a way of getting people to talk. That was my gift. Although it didn't feel like a superpower now.

Having his heartbreak splashed across the front page of a tabloid newspaper would destroy him. I knew that – but the pressure to deliver was crushing my ability to reason.

My phone rang.

'Where is it, Peters?' He always used my surname when we were on deadline. 'I'm holding the page for you.'

My eyes were pulled across the newsroom, through the glass panel walls and into his office. Slouching behind his desk – my features editor, Ben Foster. Our eyes met and a tremor ran through me.

Holding my gaze, he said: 'Well send it the fuck over, then. What are you waiting for?'

He slammed the phone down. It wasn't meant as a question.

I stared at the screen, at my exclusive. The cursor blinking impatiently.

The interview with Mike had taken place on his sprawling estate outside London. Instead of showing off his trophies he'd talked about what really mattered to him. He couldn't keep the tears from his eyes as he reminisced over the day he first met his wife. As I'd got up to leave, Mike had pulled me into a hug and held me for a long moment. Seeking comfort after baring his soul.

His agent had stopped me on the way out. Aware Mike had opened up to me, wary I'd got more than I should have from the interview. He insisted on reading the story before it went to print. I couldn't look him in the eye when I promised I'd see what I could do. That was not something we ever did at *The Record*.

Destroying lives wasn't what I signed up for when I joined

the paper. They'd promised me investigative reports, stories that make a difference. Campaigns that raise awareness. Yet somehow, I'd been sidelined into writing celebrity exposés. Who's shagging who. Grubby journalism. It had become about tearing things apart rather than making a difference.

Every time I plucked up the courage to tell my boss I was fed up, he'd remind me I was still learning: 'You need to prove yourself.' He said the kind of stories I was after come later.

Five years on and I was still trying to show I was worth something.

Whenever I questioned why I didn't just leave, I came up against the same dilemma: what else was there for me?

I'd lost everything.

The job helped me to forget. If I kept running, if I kept chasing exclusives and deadlines, I wouldn't have room to think about *him* and how my life was supposed to turn out.

There was also that other teeny-tiny issue of *money*. I'd been struggling since I'd broken up with my ex, so quitting was not an option. In my most delusional moments, I'd daydream about how it would feel to win the lottery. The chance to turn the page and start all over again. What would I do for that?

You always have a choice. Listen to me, Laura, you can say no, the voice in my head told me. It didn't feel like something I could turn away from, though. None of it did.

The phone rang again. Unable to face another earbashing, I pressed *send*, my eyes shutting involuntarily as I did so.

*

By 9.30 p.m. we'd filled out the basement bar in London's Soho. My team – clustered beneath the arches of the vaulted ceiling. Colonel's was a dive. Wine stains soaked into the tables. The dirty floor hidden under a layer of sawdust. A patch-up job. Something we were very familiar with on the paper.

Jamie, one of the news reporters, appeared with another bottle of cheap Rioja, topping up my glass before I could say no. I wouldn't have turned it down anyway; I'd been gasping for repeat hits ever since I'd finished my exclusive. Relishing alcohol's divine ability to help me forget.

'Hey – and me!' Sarah from the celeb desk emerged from the gloom with an empty glass. We filled her up, clinked and said 'cheers' to the end of another fraught day.

'Do you reckon we can put this through on expenses?' Jamie ran his eyes across the receipt. 'I'm planning on getting monumentally wasted.'

This was how it always played out in Colonel's. As Sarah began to bitch about one of the other reporters, my thoughts drifted. Their conversation was drowned out by the drum of feet from above, by the bar's crappy nineties playlist, but mostly by my jealous thoughts.

I'd been watching him intently all evening as he worked his way through the group. Noticing the beer slosh over his glass because she made him laugh so hard. Kate, the new features writer, had caught his attention. I tried on several occasions to meet his eye, but he was too busy holding court, regaling her with stories of when he was a junior reporter.

In the low light, after four or so glasses of wine, there

was a small resemblance to George Clooney. Grey hair, greying stubble. Angular jaw. Seventeen years older than me, he wasn't my usual type but for some reason I was drawn to him. Perhaps it was his wealth of experience and knowledge. A mentor of sorts. That old cliché. I snorted to myself. The wine was really kicking in.

I was tired of feeling invisible. I stepped away from the group, ignoring the tuts and pinched looks as I pushed through the throng of city workers. With every step I took away from them, I felt lighter. That said it all really, yet still I persisted in ignoring what my body was telling me. I'd stopped trusting my intuition long ago.

Then I felt his touch on the small of my back.

'Where you off to?' he asked in that low tone he reserved only for me.

Or so I'd thought, until I saw the way he was chatting up Kate tonight.

'Toilet!' I said indignantly, the alcohol giving away my jealousy.

'Without me?'

A wry smile moved up his face, igniting the memory of the archive room. Last week in his lunch break – with the smell of old newspaper and the electrics humming as he took me up against the door. Despite my anger, I couldn't control the prickle that had spread across my skin.

Next thing I knew, his hand was around my waist and I was being guided into the disabled toilet.

There was nothing sexy about the small airless cubicle. The tang of excrement and vomit hung around us. The unforgiving bright light strobed overhead. I grabbed hold of the disabled rail to steady myself as he tugged at my tights from behind.

Every time I tried to part my legs they sprang back together. I kicked off my right shoe, stumbling as I slipped one leg out of my tights. His hand caught my waist, pulling me back upright.

It was all so urgent, pressurized, just like life in the newsroom. His breath, warm in my ear. He was rough but the pain made me feel alive. Noise from the bar drifted through the door while my temperature rose with every thrust. My knuckles turned white as I gripped the rail.

It was over in minutes. He'd zipped himself up before I'd turned around. I rushed to keep up – a quick wipe with toilet tissue before pulling up my pants. I twisted my tights into place and tugged my skirt down to my knees. Then I met his gaze.

He hooked his finger under my chin, lifting it to reach his mouth.

'You still turn me on.'

Said like a congratulations between boozy kisses. I was still dizzy with the abruptness of it all.

'See you out there.' He unlocked the door, checked the coast was clear and left.

I felt high, but at the same time utterly empty. It didn't help that I hadn't eaten for hours. I'd been doing the usual, putting self-care on the back burner. I fell against the wall, pressing into it as I slipped my shoe back on.

I couldn't bring myself to look in the mirror, fearful of the shame and guilt that would meet me in the reflection. Instead, I stepped back into the fray, returning to the group like a homing bird. Thankful for the alcohol numbing the rawness between my legs.

'Where've you been?' Jamie asked, handing me a shot of something dark and sickly-sweet smelling. I took it and knocked it back. 'You look—' He stopped short of the insult. Instead, he mimed a brushing action. Heat rushed to my cheeks as I smoothed my sex hair down.

No one in the newsroom had any idea what was really going on. It was our little secret.

'Laura,' his voice carried across the din. His tone much firmer than it had been minutes earlier. I turned to face my boss. 'Over here.'

Ben was in a booth, sitting opposite Mark Cush, the editor of the newspaper, who only graced us with his presence on very special occasions.

All of a sudden, I was hit with a rush of importance. I was being singled out. *Me*. I imagined all the other reporters had noticed and were glowering with envy.

I shrugged back my shoulders, lifted my head and catwalked towards them.

'Good work today, Laura,' Mark congratulated.

I pushed my hair from my eyes, trying to appear sober as I slid into the empty seat.

'You've made a sparkling addition to the team.'

'Oh, I don't know about that, but thanks.' I felt more like tarnished silver.

Ben and Mark locked eyes. 'We think you've got talent, but . . .' he paused, 'there's potential for more.'

If by potential he meant fucking people over, I didn't want it. I turned to Ben, willing him to give me one of his looks that showed me he cared. Nothing in his expression told of the intimacy we'd just shared. He lifted his pint to meet his mouth. The wedding ring catching in the booth's spotlight.

'Got a job that you're going to love,' he said instead.

I braced myself. 'OK.'

'You've got an audition for *The Villa*.'

'*The Villa*?'

'A new reality dating show.'

He waited for me.

'Haven't you heard the buzz?'

I shrugged.

'Where've you been, Peters? Gold tiles on Instagram ring any bells? With a silhouette of a palm tree? Midnight last Tuesday, thousands of influencers posting at the same time. It's grown some sort of cult following already. Models, celebs, they're all getting in on it.'

He fished his mobile off the table and began scrolling. 'Click on the tile and you get this' – he turned his phone around.

A glossy sun-drenched image filled his screen. A crowd of beautiful people on a beach, drinking champagne, dancing, having the time of their lives.

I looked away.

'The whole thing's been shrouded in secrecy. There's no official press release. It's all word of mouth and a slick social media campaign.' Ben returned to his phone and cleared his throat. 'But this is what people have been saying:

'*For one week only, a group of sexy singletons will be living it up in a luxurious villa in paradise, hoping to meet*

*their ideal type, couple up and convince the public they've
met their match in order to win the cash prize of £50,000.'*

He smiled as he read out the next bit. '*With time against
our contestants, what lengths will they go to in order to
win?*

'But the juicy bit is what they're promising: a unique
VIP experience for the viewers.' His eyes were sparkling as
he returned them to me. 'Wonder what that could be?'

What was Ben getting so excited about? *The Villa*
sounded boring. Another trashy dating show featuring
vacuous twenty-year-olds peacocking around in bikinis.
Mind-numbing chat by the pool. I couldn't think of anything
duller. And the prize wasn't even that much. As for the
chances of finding love on a show like that – ha! All relationships were a waste of time anyway. I'd never allow
myself to get hurt again.

Somewhere in the thrum of the pub I could hear my
mum's voice ring out. 'It was *just* a break-up, it's not like
someone died!' So why had it left such a deep stain on my
life?

'Pegged as the entertainment of the summer,' continued
Ben. 'Filmed in a top-secret location . . .'

It had ended so abruptly I'd been left questioning
everything. Why? How? Was there someone else? My
thoughts had spiralled so far from reason that at one
point I thought I'd actually lost my mind. Instead of
moving on, I'd spent the past three years blaming myself,
trying to fix the things that were wrong with me, the flaws
that made him leave. Maybe that was also why I'd stayed
in this job. To prove to him *I am capable*. I'm not

worthless. But why can't I hear the words? They still refuse to sink in.

'Laura, are you listening?' Ben's brow crumpled. 'Anyway, that's all we know for now.'

Tired format. Dwindling viewer ratings, did anyone actually watch this kind of show any more?

As for 'luxury villa', it was more like a zoo enclosure. The sort of place where secrets were prised out of you. Perfect tabloid fodder. The Rioja had blunted my senses but finally I caught up with what they'd done.

'Wait, an audition? You entered me for this show?' I looked between them. 'Without asking me first?'

'We plan to make history; be the first paper to get a journalist on the inside. Find out what really goes on in these shows. Are they fake? Are they scripted? Are the contestants really single? Unearth the lies. Let's expose the sham.'

The rapid fire of questions was making me dizzy. When I didn't reply, he sighed again.

'Do you realize how hard it was to get you an in?' He looked sideways at Cush. 'Our picture and graphics teams spent hours editing your photos.'

I blinked.

He handed me back his mobile.

'We sent these ones in, aren't they brilliant?'

He had my Facebook photos on his phone, only they now showed a heavily photoshopped version of me. Thinner, with flawless tanned skin and platinum blonde hair. They'd even superimposed me onto a beach in the Caribbean.

My head was spinning. They couldn't be serious?

'We'll also set you up on Instagram and TikTok. Under your new name, of course. We can't have them knowing you work for us.'

'New name?'

'Thought you'd be happy. You're always whingeing how I don't send you out on the good stories.'

I bristled, suddenly aware of how he was making me appear in front of the editor.

'I don't complain.' But my voice had shrunk to something small.

'Yeah, you do.' He exchanged looks with Cush. 'Far more than you should.'

Fuck you.

'This is your big break, Peters, we need this story,' said Ben, more forcefully. 'I'm trusting you with it, show us what you've got. I'm confident you'll win them over at the audition.'

The audition. My heart quickened at the thought of it. The idea of taking my clothes off for some beauty pageant parade filled me with dread. My body wasn't what they'd promised in the photos. I'm not who they think I am. If they knew what I was really like they'd never have entered me.

'Why me?'

Cush finally chipped in. 'Because you're the only one in the office who stands a chance of getting in. You're young-ish, slim, pretty.' He glanced to Ben. 'Can I say that?' They both laughed.

'You'll have to change your appearance to match our pictures,' said Ben. 'And you'll need a new ID.'

I let out a little gasp. Was that even legal?

'Like, a fake passport?'

'Just leave that to us. You focus on your disguise.'

'But, I . . .' My words fell away. 'How long have I got?'

'Audition is Monday.'

Monday! That gave me just the weekend to prepare. There must have been a way to say no, but with Mark Cush looking directly at me, with an assumption that I wouldn't let the team down, I lacked the strength to find it.

Ben's eyes softened for the first time since our conversation began.

'Blonde.' He grinned.

'What?' I frowned at him.

A hint of lust returned to his eyes. 'You're going to look cracking as a blonde.'

BOOK CLUB

EXCLUSIVE TO

WHSmith

EST·1792

Exclusive Additional Content

Including author interviews,
eviews and much, much more!

RICHARD AND JUDY ASK RUTH KELLY

Adele is almost shockingly trusting of her and Jack's mystery benefactor, isn't she? Jack's more suspicious but allows himself to be persuaded. Was simple greed at the bottom of their catastrophic decision to accept this 'free' chateau?

Greed was certainly involved because there was no way Adele and Jack would be able to upgrade their lives to chateau status without a handout of some form or another. But the decision to overlook the dangers of entering into such an agreement was also down to Adele's obsession. Her fixation with living the life she'd dreamt of ever since she was a child. She had become so tunnel-visioned by her plan of becoming a princess in her castle, of escaping abroad and rebooting her relationship with Jack, that she jumped at the offer without thinking it through. The parallels between Adele's level of obsession and Delphine's are uncanny.

Adele's initial appeal for crowdfunding to help her and Jack buy the chateau blows up in her face. Do you think she is 'an entitled (expletive deleted)' as one online troll describes her, or just incredibly naive?

Definitely naive. There was a mild sense of entitlement in terms of *all the other influencers are doing it, so why can't I?* But I don't think Adele reached as far as thinking how the public might perceive her and Jack for asking for handouts. All she could envisage was the end goal, *I must have Chateau Bellay*, and the wine and whisky didn't help matters!

We loved your description of the claustrophobic secrecy shrouding the nearby French market town. Is it based on an actual place? Have you been there?

The market town is based on a real place in central France which I've passed through a number of times during my travels. As described in the book, it has a small cobbled square with a bakery, a butcher's, a pharmacy and a bar owned by an expat. The place has a run-down, claustrophobic feel about it. Paint peeling off shutters. Plaster chipping off the walls. All muted greys and creams. But it's the trees that I remember most vividly. They'd been pruned so crudely – with their branches sawn right down to the stump. In the dusk light, their amputated silhouettes looked very sinister and gave me the chills. The town is so off the beaten track I could imagine tourists like me would stick out like a sore thumb. The question of whether the locals would be welcoming is where my imagination took over.

There's a touch of Great Expectations *about this story – a mysterious benefactor; unseen consequences. Was Dickens part of the inspiration behind it?*

Dickens wasn't my initial inspiration behind *The Escape*, but bringing a more old-fashioned approach into the plot was entirely deliberate. My aim was to blend the old with the new and make the contrast speak for itself. I love featuring shady, just-out-of-reach characters for villains. I did the same with my previous book, *The Villa*, about an island-set reality TV show that goes murderously wrong. The overarching villain was also a secret benefactor who was funding the show. Mysterious, louche; he, just like Thirteen, was someone we never get close to or know too much about. It's an old-fashioned notion that still applies today – how the 'baddies' at the very top of the food chain mostly get away with their crimes, because they have money, because they have status and contacts. They have the power to make themselves disappear if they so wish.

To find out more visit our website –
www.whsmith.co.uk/richardandjudy

RICHARD AND JUDY BOOK CLUB – QUESTIONS FOR DISCUSSION

The Richard and Judy Book Club, exclusively with WHSmith, is all about you getting involved and sharing our passion for reading. Here are some questions to help you or your Book Group get started. Go to our website to discuss these questions, post your own and share your views with the rest of the Book Club.

1. How big a role do weather and seasons play in your enjoyment of a book? Are you naturally drawn to stories set in summer or winter?

2. Adele and Jack launch into an agreement with a mystery benefactor without thinking it through. Is there something in your life you want so badly you'd be willing to overlook the danger if someone offered to buy it for you outright?

3. The masterminds behind Twelve Homes escape justice. How does a book where the overarching

RUTH KELLY

'villain' seemingly gets away with it leave you feeling?

4. If you were to make a YouTube video about your life, what would it be about? What would you show to your fans and what would you keep hidden?

To find out more visit our website –
www.whsmith.co.uk/richardandjudy

THE BUZZWORDS BEHIND THE WRITING: WHAT INSPIRED *THE ESCAPE*

DESTINATION

I always begin a book by setting the stage – location, location, location – and I knew, before anything else, the stage for *The Escape* would be rural France in the dead of winter.

I love nothing more than immersing myself in vivid descriptions that evoke all the senses and I want the location to drive the narrative, almost becoming a character in its own right – setting the mood, the tone. This was very much my intention when I wrote *The Escape*. I wished for Chateau Bellay and its dark, menacing forest to have a heartbeat, to be a living, breathing creature that comes alive in the dead of night. An entity that throws obstacle after obstacle in Erin's path. Creepy, spine-tingly and Gothic-scary.

ISOLATION

France is one of my favourite countries and I've explored all four corners over the past ten years, but it's the countryside that draws me back time and again. It feels vastly different to the rolling hills, fields, farm tracks and villages of where I grew up in Somerset. Somehow it appears more isolated, more spread out and disconnected from everywhere else, and in the peak of mid-winter, rural France can seem downright spooky and sinister. What if there was an emergency – would help reach you in time? That state of anxiety, that heart-pounding fear of being cut off from the world, is what I wanted to drip-feed throughout the course of *The Escape*.

NOTHING IN LIFE IS FREE

I watch YouTube. I dip in and out of videos, mostly tuning in to what's presented in front of me via the algorithm and I often don't watch until the end. I do it to switch off from my writing.

Over time I've noticed a shift away from the traditional influencer – who documents their life, uploads the video and earns money through views and advertising revenue – to the new breed of 'GoFundMe influencer'.

People are becoming increasingly less shy about asking viewers directly for money, whether it's to support a reno-vation project, their travel adventures or even a daily cup of coffee. There seems no limit to what's being asked, which got me thinking about the *real* cost. Is there ever such a thing as a free lunch? What's the catch? And, to the mind of a thriller writer, could these hidden costs turn deadly?

Unsurprisingly, there has been a huge backlash to the GoFundMe movement. People are angry and resent the ease in which these influencers slide into their new life, whereas they've had to struggle, save up, live cautiously. Some say they are begging. *Scroungers*. But if they're also providing videos/content (i.e. entertainment) is that not a fair exchange? The argument intrigued me and I was desperate to explore it more in *The Escape* through Adele and Jack's appeal: *Buy me a chateau*.

DANGER

I couldn't explore the world of youtubing/influencing without touching upon the dangers that come with showcasing your life on the internet to complete strangers.

Adele films her chateau world, allowing people she's never met access into her home and her innermost thoughts. In her most lonely moments, she even turns to these strangers for comfort. It wouldn't take much for a fan to find out where she lived. One quick Google search and they could be on her doorstep. That vulnerability. That sense of threat from an unknown force who could be capable of anything if triggered – *a loaded gun* – is something I really loved developing in *The Escape*.

FAMILY

I recently lost someone very close to me so describing loss and grief, what it feels like to sit helplessly by a loved one's bedside as you watch them slip away, came fairly easily to me. I thought it would be painful to write about but it was surprisingly cathartic, which proves the magical powers of writing – how putting your emotions down on paper can be enormously helpful.

I chose sisters for my dual narrative because I've always imagined what it would be like to have one. I enjoyed exploring Adele and Erin's relationship, their bond – the frustrations, the rivalry and competitiveness, but more importantly the friendship and the unconditional love that binds them so tightly together. The force propelling Erin forward in her desperate search to save Adele.

SECRET HISTORY

Describing Chateau Bellay was one of the most enjoyable elements to writing *The Escape*. I drew a little from experience, having had the wonderful opportunity of visiting several chateaux, but mostly it came from my imagination, dreaming up how Bellay would look, sound, how it would feel to spend a night in a creepy mansion with the ghosts of centuries past. As with all old buildings, I'm fascinated by the history and the story behind them. That well-trodden phrase – if only these walls could talk – was doing loops in my head while I wrote. Chateau Bellay became 'the keeper of secrets' with its hidden doors and passageways and crawl spaces that could lead you into a new world. It kept my imagination spinning and weaving new plot threads.

OBSESSION

Celebrity Worship Syndrome is something I've read a lot about recently; especially now social media allows for an almost intimate level of access to 'celebrities', which was never the case before. It's not that difficult to see how someone as vulnerable as Delphine might become fixated with Adele thanks to how familiar Adele was appearing in her YouTube stories.

This type of obsession is often fuelled by a need to disassociate from your own life. Delphine's fixation with Adele was obviously taken to the extreme, but we can probably all hold up our hands to using social media as a distraction. Scrolling, immersing ourselves in other people's lives to delay our to-do list and procrastinate some more. Me included: YouTube, case in point. And this was the wider issue I wanted to touch on in *The Escape*. Is social media fuelling an unhealthy level of escapism?

That said, if I hadn't been so easily distracted by my YouTube algorithms, I might never have come up with the idea of featuring a YouTuber as the star of my novel. So, I'm all for procrastination, if it feeds the imagination and keeps me doing what I love.

On that note, I do hope you enjoyed reading *The Escape* as much as I have writing it. Having your support means everything. And in the words of Adele, I love you all so SO much. XOX

Our latest Book Club titles

RICHARD & JUDY
BOOK CLUB
EXCLUSIVE TO
WHSmith
EST · 1792